The truth is that one never gets out of oneself. That is one of our greatest miseries. What would we not give to see, if but for a minute, the sky and the earth with the many-faceted eye of a fly, or to understand nature with the rude, simple brain of an ape? But just that is forbidden us. We cannot, like Tiresias, be men and remember having been women. We are locked into our persons as into a lasting prison. The best we can do, it seems to me, is gracefully to recognize this terrible situation and to admit that we speak of ourselves every time we have not the strength to be silent.

-- Anatole France

There are two spiritual dangers in not owning a farm. One is the danger of supposing that breakfast comes from the grocery, and the other that heat comes from the furnace.

-- Aldo Leopold

DELIVERED TO THE GROUND

MARK MURPHY HARMS

Delivered to the Ground is a work of fiction.

A ByProduct Imprint

ByProduct Publishing
2608 York Ave. N
Robbinsdale, MN 55422

ISBN 978-17340726-0-0

Book design by ByProduct

Interior drawings by Douglas Ross

thepeltast.net

For my sister, Jenny, and her indomitable spirit.
(Sorry about the pigs.)

Many thanks to all whose support and assistance was invaluable.

PART ONE

IONIA

Chapter 1 | The Music of the Spheres

NEARLY an hour into the flight his knees began to ache from being pressed against the back of the seat in front of him. The turbulence didn't help. He was already sore from days of hiking in the Canadian Rockies and a cramp was coming on in one of his calves. He rubbed it and tried to keep it relaxed. A drink might help if the flight attendant ever came by.

A sudden jolt knocked the plane hard enough that he could feel it in his spine. The mousy girl next to him squeaked, startled from whatever book she was reading and from whatever she was listening to through her earbuds. She had seemed nervous when they boarded the plane -- hadn't said a word except a shy thanks when he helped put her bag into the overhead compartment -- but now she looked frightened.

"Kind of a bumpy ride," he said, smiling reassuringly.

The girl pulled out an earbud, looking at him as if he might have said something important.

"What?" Her voice cracked a little.

"It's all right," he said. "I'm sure the pilot will find smoother air shortly."

She smiled a smile that was little more than a wince, put the earbud back in, and returned to her book. He thought about the kind of fear she must be feeling. Was it simply a fear of flying or a more general fear? He suspected the latter. Such a different experience of the world she must have. It occurred to him that he was glad to be who he was. His sinewy 44-year-old body had nagging complaints but it was fit and strong. He naturally commanded respect, even deference, wherever he went. He wasn't above feeling fear by any stretch -- he remembered an encounter with a bear on a trail in Montana that had put him in a state of exquisite, paralyzing terror -- but fear wasn't a part of his daily life. Passing young toughs on the street invoked no intimidation, only amusement, if anything at all.

Fear, however, began to tingle his solar plexus. He had been looking idly out the window at the night sky when spasms of lightning illuminated a billowing cloud. It was strangely spherical and seemed to be expanding rapidly in all directions. He felt the plane banking away. Good, he thought, let's put some distance between us and what must be a pretty intense storm.

"Wow, that's so weird," the girl exclaimed.

He turned to her. "What? What's going on?"

"The music just stopped and I'm getting these strange tones. Spooky, kind of, like nothing I've heard before."

"There's a storm nearby, probably just some interference," he said.

"I don't know. I think it's more than that. Here, you should listen." She offered him an earbud. "It's just so bizarre."

Somewhat reluctantly he leaned over and put in the earbud. At first it sounded like white noise with sporadic ringing tones. A pulse of static electricity must have put her phone on the fritz. He was about to take the earbud out when the sound expanded and resolved itself into something much more detailed.

She was right. It was bizarre, and not like anything he'd ever heard. A fevered genius musician going crazy on one of those old analogue synthesizers with a hundred knobs and sliders couldn't have produced such sounds. Deep resonant tones pulsed and droned, intertwining with each other somehow, and higher tones seemed to streak in arcs and curlicues, coming and going, sometimes distant, sometimes nearby. He was struck by the multi-dimensionality of it, like super stereo but only through one earbud.

"This is amazing," he said.

"It's beautiful," she said.

She was right again. The sounds *were* beautiful. More than that, they were sublime, invoking the same kind of awe as when he had first seen the Grand Canyon. He felt himself being immersed in them. What was it they were hearing? A window into a reality they normally couldn't perceive?

The plane was vibrating. Other passengers were getting anxious but he found himself not caring, enthralled by this other-worldly music. He was drifting into its rhythms, riding its waves. The plane jolted downward. The girl's seatbelt was unfastened and she flew out of her chair. Reflexively he grabbed her and she came down on his lap. He held her tight as the plane shook violently.

The earbud had popped out of his ear but the music remained. He drifted further into its vast, overwhelming melody and soon about the only other thing he could sense was the girl's body pressed against his. Everything else faded out -- the screaming passengers, the loose items flying around, the bright flash, the rupture that opened in the fuselage.

Chapter 2 | Grounded

HE sensed he was lying on his back. His vision returned as if coming out of a bad head rush, revealing a night sky filled with stars, the Milky Way clear and bright. The music was gone now. Where was the girl? He remembered holding her, trying to keep her from flying away, then everything went dark and silent, except for the music, which had lingered.

Sensation started to return to his hands and he could feel something between his fingers -- grass, he was lying on some kind of grass. He heard voices in the distance.

"Over here ... think she's alive."

Good, alive. Maybe it was the girl, he thought. He wanted to sit up and look but he couldn't get himself to move. He felt drowsy and sunk into a half slumber.

Voices again.

"Hey ... you awake ... you hear me?"

He opened his eyes and there kneeling over him was a very large man. The man had a beard, wore a plaid shirt and seemed like an oversized lumberjack. He moved his mouth to respond but no words came out.

Another voice, a woman's voice.

"... must be in shock ... over to the fire."

He felt arms slide under his legs and behind his shoulders. The giant lifted him as if it were no big deal. The giant carried him toward a burning light and set him down near it. His head settled on something soft. The woman, who was very large too, propped up his legs and put a blanket over him. He felt tired and slumber overtook him.

"Rest now, you'll be okay," the giant said softly.

~

He woke curled up on his side clutching an airline cushion. The sun warmed his face. A dark lock of hair was in his eyes. He brushed it aside and felt the tug of it on his scalp. That couldn't be right. He was bald. He ran his hand over his head and felt a mass of thick hair. He pushed himself upright. The hair he now had fell across his cheeks. He felt something strapped to his chest under a jacket and shirt (which weren't his). It was a bra.

"How did this ...," he said but cut himself short.

The pitch of his voice wasn't the one he knew as his own. It spooked him as much or more than the feeling coming from his groin which told him in no uncertain terms that he was no longer a man.

~

"She's awake," she heard the giant say.

She was sitting with her knees pulled to her chest, staring at the landscape. They were in a sort of valley or meadow surrounded by forested hills. Black smoke rose from a hillside. The giant walked over to her carrying a plastic cup with steam rising from it.

"Hi. I managed to make coffee. Would you like some?"

The smell hit her nose and it seemed like the most wonderful thing in the world. She reached out and took the cup. It was a cheap airline cup but it was so large now in her hands. She sipped carefully, feeling the stinging heat of it on her lips.

"You look like you've seen a ghost," the giant said. "You okay?"

She tried to smile but it wasn't working. Her eyes moistened. The sensation dumbfounded her.

"Ah, look, that was a dumb thing to say. It's been a horrible experience for us all," he said. "But, hey, we're still alive. Soon they'll find us and we'll be going home."

"Thanks ... sorry ... I'm a little confused right now." Her voice, so not who he was, or she was.

"Well, you're in good company. The coffee should help," the giant said. "My name's Hank, by the way. What's yours?"

Such a simple question. What is your name? And so easy to answer. My name is ... But it stung her like an electric shock. She struggled to answer.

"Fred," She said meekly.

"Fred? That's a funny name for a girl." A concerned frown formed under Hank's beard.

The large woman who had put the blanket over her approached and stood beside Hank. She recognized the woman as the flight attendant. The blouse of her uniform was smudged and a sleeve was torn. But the flight attendant hadn't been that tall, she remembered. The giant, Hank, only stood a little taller. It dawned on her that they weren't giants at all, but normal sized. It was she who was small.

"You doing okay?" The flight attendant asked. She had a southern accent.

"I don't know. I ..."

"Are you hurt? Are you in pain?"

"No. I'm not injured."

"That's good. You should move around a little, get the blood flowing."

"We're going to look for more survivors," Hank said. "There's some granola bars and such over there. You should try to eat something. Holler if you need anything."

~

She was glad they left her alone. She needed to think this out. Maybe it's just a vivid dream and she, or *he,* is actually unconscious in a hospital bed suffering from a brain injury. She finished her coffee. Walking seemed like a good idea so she stood up and when she did, she realized she needed to pee. She went to a copse of scrubby trees and bushes near the camp. She could smell the urine and feces of others who had been there recently.

She found a spot that was hidden from all sides and unzipped the loose-fitting jeans she was wearing, revealing the swell of her hips and orange panties. She sighed. She pulled down the panties and there it was: a tuft of pubic hair devoid of any appendage. She wasn't exactly sure what to do next but "pointer versus squatter" ran through her mind. She squatted and the rest followed naturally.

A fly landed on her knee and she could feel its legs as it walked along her skin. That sensation, so small and random, yet so present, along with the sensation of relieving her bladder, convinced her that this was not a dream.

When she finished, she realized that a bit of toilet paper would be handy. She went through the pockets of her black, hooded jacket and found a crumpled napkin. She wiped herself quickly, not ready to dwell too much on what was, or wasn't, down there. She pulled up her panties and jeans and zipped the fly. She brushed leaves over the wet spot on the ground and covered the damp napkin. The pink drawstrings of her hoodie dangled as she did so. Shit, she thought, this is what the mousy girl wore.

She walked back to the camp. The action of walking came naturally enough but it felt different -- short steps, a little extra swivel at the hips -- than the long strides *he* had had. She found several bottles of water, drank half of one, unwrapped a granola bar and started chewing. She was hungry. After that she started on a packaged Danish and sat on a nearby rock.

What had happened, she asked herself. How had Frederick Harper become the girl sitting next to him? Or had he? Could people really switch bodies? The idea was silly, like a bad sitcom episode. It occurred to her that she might be suffering a kind of delusional amnesia. But she could remember so much -- growing up in Sioux City; going to college in Mankato; playing basketball; the short, anguished marriage; his job as a software engineer; the people he worked with; his parents; his brother, his sister; his friends; his hikes; his hunting trips; the games he played; his philosophical musings; his arguments at the coffee shop.

With the warming of the day, she unzipped her jacket. Its loose fit and dark color did a fair job of hiding the swells on her chest but the gray t-shirt did not.

Still, it was just so ridiculous. Could it be that she had made up the details of Frederick Harper's life, lived them in her imagination, then, with the trauma of the crash, the male alter ego came to the forefront and the memories of who she really was were suppressed? The idea didn't feel right, but it seemed the most reasonable alternative. The mind and the body were intertwined, inseparable, different aspects of the same whole. That's what *he* believed. You couldn't just swap minds around like chips in computer.

Half way through the Danish she felt full. So quickly? She was going to discard it but decided she should eat the rest. She washed it down with the remaining water in the bottle.

She could see the other survivors in the distance moving around the grassy valley, picking up luggage scattered from the plane. The wreckage was a couple hundred yards further on. The fuselage was in two pieces and a wing had broken off. Yet it seemed more intact than it ought to have been.

She wasn't eager to deal with people right now but she decided to investigate. Maybe she could find something that could help answer the questions swirling in her mind. She set off quickly, noticing as she walked the black canvas high-top sneakers she wore. *He* had worn the same kind of shoes only *his* were dusty white. She saw the others putting the luggage and other items into a pile. A couple of folks were looking through the stuff, probably trying to find their own things. It was kind of strange, no one seemed to notice her. She saw Hank carry a large suitcase over to the pile. She continued toward the wreckage.

"There you are," Hank said, coming up beside her. "You must be feeling better."

"Yes, thanks. The coffee was good and I ate a Danish," she said.

"You ate one of those? They're horrible."

"I was hungry."

"Hey, I wouldn't go over there," he said. "It's ... pretty grim."

"Have you found any more survivors?" She asked.

"No, not yet. Just the seven of us."

"How many were on the plane? There must have been a fifty or more?"

"Seventy-three, according to Nancy. She's the flight attendant we talked to earlier."

She had been so wrapped up in her own confusions she hadn't thought about all the people who had died. She shuddered.

"Yeah, it's bad," Hank said.

"Why are we still alive?"

"Good question. What's strange is none of us is seriously hurt. It seems that everyone who survived was thrown from the plane. I remember trying to get back to my seat then I was sucked out. I don't remember anything after that. What about you? If you don't mind my asking."

"I'm not sure ..."

She remembered the music and that she as *he* was holding the girl and then, nothing. The music had continued. She had no memory of when it had stopped.

"Well, no need to dwell on it now," Hank said. "I'm going to get some water, then check out that smoke. I'm a little worried about it."

Part of her wanted to look in the plane to see if she could find *his* body. But she realized she wasn't ready yet to deal with the sight of mangled corpses.

"Wait, I'll go with you," she said.

~

Nancy, the flight attendant, was at the camp. She looked harrowed, her previously stylish blonde hair hung in strands. She was drinking a bottle of water.

"Hi," she said, managing a weary smile. "Oh, Emily, I think this is yours."

Nancy handed her a small leather backpack purse. It was scuffed but intact. Emily? Was that the girl's name?

"Um, thanks," she replied and took it.

"You don't look so sure," Nancy said.

"I'm not sure of much right now."

"Go ahead. Looking through it might jog your memory."

She sat on the ground cross-legged. She noticed her legs flexed easily and her knees were comfortable in that position. She opened the bag and examined its contents: a packet of tissues, a handkerchief, lip balm, sunscreen, fingernail clippers, a small flashlight, a little makeup kit, lipstick, a couple of pens, a notebook, a set of keys on a little panda bear keychain, a wallet, a tiny bottle of perfume, hand lotion, a whistle, a comb, a turquoise barrette, a toothbrush, toothpaste, dental floss, a stick of deodorant, a condom, and a wrapper containing a tampon.

Useful things, she thought, but she didn't feel like she had owned them. They invoked no familiarity. The wallet was decidedly unfeminine. It was made of cowboy style leather with a picture of a running horse imprinted on it. It contained $113, several coins, a bank card, a picture of a cat and a driver's license.

The face on the license stared back at her. It was the girl. Dark, straight brown hair cut at the shoulder and parted in the middle. It was a plain, squarish face with brown eyes, a small nose and a small, down-turned mouth. Was that her face now? She couldn't tell. She had no mirror. She picked up the makeup case and opened it. Her hands shook a little as she as she held its mirror next to the driver's license. Other than tousled hair, the same face stared back.

Emily Cecelia Svoboda was the name on the license. The date of birth indicated that she was 22 years old, older than *he* had thought.

"Can't you remember?" Nancy asked.

She shook her head.

"I'm sure it'll come back to you soon," Nancy said.

She doubted it. The objects were so absent of any feeling of being hers. She put the items back in the purse. Hank, who had gone off to "take a piss," returned.

"I'm going to check out that smoke," he said. "You still coming, Fred?"

"Her name's Emily, not Fred," Nancy scolded.

"She said Fred. Until she says otherwise, that's what I'm going with."

"Yes, I'm coming."

~

Hank wore hiking boots and took long, purposeful strides. She had to quicken her pace to keep up. The forest started abruptly and it was like entering a different world, cool and dark with sunlight only poking through in spots. Nearly all the trees were tall with broad trunks, creating a canopy high above. The ground was surprisingly clear of clutter or vegetation, some deadwood here and there and a few assorted plants that could make a living on meager amounts of light.

"This is old-growth forest," Hank said. "There's not much of that around anymore."

"Do you know where we are?" She asked.

"Not sure. Must be southern Canada somewhere or northern Montana. You do much camping?"

"Yes, I just spent three days hiking in the Yoho Park."

"Really? Beautiful country."

"It is."

"I wasn't far from there. I was helping out with a census of buffalo in the area."

"You're a biologist?"

"Yeah, I suppose so. I teach biology at North High in Detroit."

The grade had become steep as they climbed toward where the smoke was coming from. She was breathing heavily and starting to sweat.

Hank stopped.

"I should let you catch your breath," he said. "You really hiked for three days in the Yoho?"

She looked up at him. She figured he must be about six feet tall which would make her about five feet, maybe. The thought disheartened her.

"It's true, I did, and I didn't," she said.

Hank furrowed his brow. "You speak in riddles, little grasshopper."

She wished she could manage a smile. "My mind is filled with riddles right now."

A waft of something caught her nose.

"I smell plastic burning," she said.

"We must be getting close."

She took off her jacket and hung it on her purse pack. Her t-shirt had very short sleeves and a v-neck. She caught Hank's eyes scanning her body.

"Let's go," she said.

A few minutes later they found what they were looking for. It was a wheel from the plane's landing gear and its tire was engulfed in flames. An area around it was burnt but the damp ground had kept it from spreading. It wasn't close enough to any trees to ignite their bark.

"Lucky," Hank said. "I don't think we could put that out if we wanted to. At least the smoke should act as a signal."

They looked at the burning wheel for a while. It seemed like an alien thing that shouldn't be there. Hank fetched a water bottle from a satchel slung across his shoulders. He took a drink and passed it to her. He pulled out two bags of peanuts and handed her one.

"Lunch time," he said. "A little protein will do you good."

She didn't feel hungry but she had to agree. She nibbled a few of them and drank some water.

"Do you believe in the transmigration of souls?" She asked.

"What? You mean like reincarnation?"

"Something like that, I guess," she said. "'Soul' probably isn't the right word. More like can a mind that existed in one form later exist in another?"

"I tend to think our minds and brains are pretty much the same thing," Hank said. "I suppose, theoretically, you could do a brain transplant. I remember a show where they transplanted a human brain into a robot body."

"What about brain patterns? There are people who think that someday they'll be able to upload their minds into a computer and preserve themselves that way."

"I don't know. Doesn't seem plausible to me. But I suppose we don't know enough about what minds are to say for sure. Why do you ask? Do you think something like that happened to you?"

She nodded.

"I think you're a troubled girl," Hank said. "But, given what's happened ..."

"Troubled, yes," she said. "But my license says I'm 22, so I guess I'm not really a girl."

"Twenty-two. Oh. I didn't think you were that old," he said. "Sorry if I've been condescending."

"You haven't really. You've been kind and helpful. Thanks."

"We should get back. A search plane ought to fly over soon. I'm surprised there hasn't been one already."

~

They walked more slowly now. Hank paused occasionally to look at a plant or feel the bark of a tree. His heavy steps and big boots made considerable noise. Her steps were much quieter and, if she concentrated, she could move almost silently. *He* had liked to hunt deer in the fall. *He* had trained himself to walk as quietly as possible. But her feet were half *his* size and she weighed half as much as *he* did, and that made it so much easier.

Hank halted again and ran his fingers along a vine that wound its way up a tree.

"This is a species I haven't seen before. I wonder what it is."

She stepped over to look for herself.

"I don't recall seeing vines like that in the north woods," she said.

"Yeah, it does seem like something you'd see down south," Hank said.

"You hear that?" She asked.

"What?"

"Sounds like running water. Over that way," she said, pointing to her left.

She walked toward it and Hank followed. They came to an outcropping of rock that harbored a gurgling pool with water flowing from an eroded groove, creating a small gully as it ran down the hill.

"It's a spring," Hank said. "Good ears, Fred. This will come in handy if we need more water."

She bent over and stuck her hand in the pool. It was ice cold. She cupped a little and took a sip.

"It's clean and good," she said and straightened herself up. She realized that bending over like that would have been more of a strain for *him*.

They followed the brook a ways before turning back toward the camp. About a hundred yards on, they saw a piece of wreckage leaning against a tree. A fallen branch lay on it, its leaves still green. As they approached, she could make out the contours of a seat.

"You'd better wait here. I'll go see if anybody's alive," Hank said.

She found herself heeding his instructions. As Hank neared the debris, she could see him grimace. He pulled at the branch to get a better look. Something fell out of the branch. She moved up a little to see what it was. It was a dusty white hi-top sneaker. Her heart began to race. Bile welled up in her throat. She took deep breaths and tried to steel herself.

She walked over to the sneaker. The foot was still inside, severed at the ankle. Her stomach knotted. She had harbored a vague hope that if *he* was still alive, things might somehow return to normal. A familiar scuff on the shoe withered that hope. She had to know for sure. She ran around to the other side of the branch. The wreckage included a piece of the fuselage and two seats still bound together. They lay on top of a body, a tall man, his head pressed into the earth. She willed herself forward although her limbs were reluctant to move. She crouched beside the tall man. The orange polo shirt was *his*. The jeans were *his*. She saw the bulge in the front pocket where *he* kept *his* wallet. The seatbelt suspended the man's waist above the ground. She reached into the pocket.

"What are you doing!" Hank exclaimed.

A tear dripped down her face.

"I have to know," she croaked.

The fucking wallet didn't want to come out but she managed to wriggle it free. She opened the smooth, brown bifold and removed the license.

There *he* was with *his* rugged face, aviator glasses, blue eyes and that half smirk that always seemed to appear on these kinds of photos. The name: Frederick Harper.

Hank knelt beside her and put a hand on her shoulder.

"You knew him?" He asked.

She nodded. The license fell from her fingers.

"I'm sorry," he said.

Hank picked up the license.

"Frederick Harper. Is that where Fred comes from?"

She nodded again.

"Was he a relative?"

"He was me," she said, her voice barely audible.

~

Hank put the license back in the wallet and stuffed the wallet back into the pocket.

"We'd better leave that for the investigators," he said.

He lifted her to her feet and led her a few paces away from the body. He found a napkin in his satchel and handed it to her. She dried her eyes and wiped her nose.

"Thanks," she said.

They walked silently back to camp.

Chapter 3 | Stranded

WHEN she and Hank returned, the other survivors -- three men and a woman -- were at the camp with Nancy. No one was talking. Puffy clouds had appeared along with several ravens circling high above.

"Did you find what was burning?" Nancy asked.

"It's one of the tires from the plane's landing gear," Hank said. "Doesn't look like it's going to spread. We also found a cold spring and another body, a man. He was a friend of hers."

"Oh," Nancy said.

The others looked impassive, dwelling in their own thoughts. It occurred to her that they had likely lost loved-ones in the crash. The woman sat in a folding chair and looked as if she had been sobbing. One of the men was lying prone with a golf umbrella propped up to shade his face. Another was looking up at the sky.

"See anything, Alex?" Hank asked.

"No, nothing," Alex said. He was smaller and slimmer than Hank, had short-cropped black hair and a hawk-like nose.

"What's strange, I haven't even seen any contrails," Alex continued, his voice high-pitched for a man. It sounded gravelly and stressed.

"We must be in a pretty remote area," Hank said. "Did anybody find a working phone?"

Alex shook his head. "No, nobody's is working. Maybe the plane's locator beacon is out too."

"Those things are well protected," Nancy said. "It should be working."

Nancy had combed her hair and put it back into a ponytail.

"Well, it hasn't been that long yet. They should find us soon," Hank said.

The man lying under the umbrella sat up. He was rotund at the waist and thick-limbed. The top of his head was bald and he had a gray beard.

"I hate to bring this up," the man said. "But we may have been here longer than we thought. My watch says it's the 27th."

He wore an old-style watch with a silver wristband.

"That can't be right," Nancy said. "Today is July 26th."

"It seems to be working fine. I've never known it to jump ahead. It might fall behind, I suppose, if I forgot to wind it."

While she was concerned about the possibility of a lost day, it did suggest other weird things had happened and not just to her.

"My God, we were abducted by aliens," the woman in the folding chair said. She was heavyset and had dark curly hair. The joke induced little laughter.

She sat down in her comfortable cross-legged posture. Everyone was silent for a while. Hank paced around the camp. She wondered what would happen after they were rescued. What kind of life would she go back to? The thought of having to deal with Emily's family and friends distressed her. And what about *his* family and friends?

"Okay," Hank said. "We've got to assume that Bob's watch malfunctioned somehow and Sasha's wrong about the aliens. Rescuers should be coming soon. We just have to be patient."

"What if they don't come," asked the other man who hadn't yet spoken. He was young, thin and a little taller than Hank. He wore a baseball cap, cargo shorts and a t-shirt with the logo of a rock band emblazoned on it.

"Well, Tim, I guess we walk out of here. Eventually, we'll come to a road or something," Hank said.

She noticed how everybody's eyes looked to Hank, eager to receive reassurance and direction from him. Without even consciously realizing it, they were making him their leader. She remembered times when people had looked to *him* for direction. *He* had been a reluctant leader but took on the role when the situation demanded it. *He* could set his voice to a commanding tone and people readily obeyed. The power unnerved *him* a little and *he* hadn't cultivated it. *He* felt no thrill in telling people what to do.

But she knew that if *he* were here, *he* would be the leader. Hank would be trumped. Hank didn't have it in full measure. She saw qualities in him that she liked and she was glad he was around, but he lacked a certain hardness or edge. He did not seem the type who could effectively lead men into battle.

Then there was Nancy who stood up and straightened her blouse. The men's eyes went to her womanly figure.

"All right, we probably shouldn't just sit around," Nancy said. "Those clouds might mean rain and we don't want to spend the night getting soaked. We're lucky there was camping gear and tents on the plane. Who knows how to set up a tent?"

She raised her hand as did Hank and Tim, the thin young man.

"Oh, I almost forgot," Nancy said. "Everyone, this is Emily. Emily this is Sasha, Bob, Alex and Tim."

She smiled as best she could and the other folks nodded or said hi. They weren't looking to her for leadership. Their eyes immediately returned to Nancy or glanced over to Hank.

~

She, Nancy, Hank and Tim would bring the tents over and set them up while Bob, Alex and Sasha would gather up any food they could find and other useful items like sleeping bags, cooking pots and utensils. The work lightened the mood and folks started chatting, even occasionally laughing. Tim remained sullen, however.

"He was with a church group," Nancy told her while they were setting up a small dome-like tent. "He's the only one that lived."

"What about the others?" She asked.

"Sasha lost a friend she was traveling with. Alex and Bob were returning home from a conference. I think they lost a couple of colleagues but no one close. Hank was by himself. I didn't really know the other flight attendant or the pilots. I was filling in. I'm normally based in Atlanta."

She pounded in stakes with a rock. She was sweating and the bra was feeling sticky and uncomfortable.

"What about you, Emily?" Nancy asked. "Hank said someone you knew was killed. Is your memory returning?"

"I have plenty of memory, just not of being Emily," she said.

"What do you remember?"

"I remember being a man."

"The man you saw dead?"

"Yes."

"Oh dear, what are we going to do with you?"

"I'm wondering that myself."

~

While carrying a tent back to camp, she saw in the pile a large, red suitcase. It was an old style hard case with no wheels. It was *his* suitcase. Another thing that had gotten lost in the turmoils of her mind. She decided it was best not to open it or say anything about what was in it. Not yet.

They erected six tents. One could easily fit two people. Four were set up toward one side of the copse and two toward the other.

"Okay, this is the girls' side," Nancy had said. "Emily, you can stay with me in the big one."

Everyone seemed satisfied with the arrangement. She would have preferred her own tent but she didn't feel ready to resist Nancy's mothering. Or maybe she didn't want to.

They had found quite a bit of freeze-dried camp food, energy bars and such. Bob, the older man with a gray beard, had found a small cooler packed with trout fillets, presumably freshly caught during someone's fishing trip.

"We might as well cook these before they spoil," Bob said.

"Nice find," Hank said. "Looks like we're eating good tonight."

She had just finished setting up the large tent when Sasha came over to her holding a small canvas suitcase.

"You're Emily Svoboda, right?" Sasha asked.

That question again. The one she didn't know the answer to.

"Um, yes," she replied.

"This has got your name on it," Sasha said.

"Oh, thank you. Um, I'm glad you found it."

She put the suitcase in the tent.

Sasha also had found two collapsible five-gallon plastic jugs which Hank and Tim took to the spring and filled with water.

~

Darkness came quickly after the sun sank below the western ridge. Hank fried the fish while Sasha prepared a side dish -- rice with freeze-dried peas and carrots. Nancy passed out plates and utensils and served everybody when the food was ready. Alex stoked the campfire and they all sat around it to eat.

"I think we should say a prayer," Nancy said.

Sasha and Tim were beside Nancy. They bowed their heads and held hands.

"Our heavenly father, we give thanks for the nourishment you have provided for us. We thank you for sparing our lives. We ask that you show mercy and forgiveness to those who have died. We ask that you grant us the strength to endure our present ordeal so we may become better people for it. Thank you for all your blessings. In Jesus' name, amen."

"Amen," Sasha said.

"Amen," Tim said.

She and the others remained silent.

The food was heavenly, anyway, she thought. She ate with relish but, again, became full quickly and stopped after one piece of fish. Hank, Bob and Tim gobbled up what was left when the others had finished.

There was some idle conversation but it was subdued. Hank talked about his trip counting buffalo. He complained that he had spent most of his time riding in a small airplane. He'd rather have been on the ground hiking. Others worried about what their loved-ones were thinking back home.

"How long do you think we should stay here if no rescue party comes?" Alex asked, looking at Hank.

"I don't know. Let's see what tomorrow brings. If nobody comes, we'll make a decision then."

The air had become chilly so she put on her hoodie. Feeling a little useless, she went around and picked up the plates.

"I'll get the dishes cleaned up," she said.

"Thanks, Emily."

"Yeah, thanks."

Nancy smiled approvingly.

When she finished she sat close to the fire. Bob opened a small, flat case and removed a cigar.

"Would anybody else like one?" He asked.

Nobody accepted. *He* would have, but she thought better of it. *He* smoked only occasionally but the urge could be strong sometimes. She didn't feel the urge at all.

"Come on, Emily," Nancy said. "It's been a long day. We should get ready for bed."

~

Once inside Nancy hung a flashlight from a cord dangling from the top of the tent and started undressing. The tent wasn't high enough for her to stand erect so she removed her skirt from a bent posture. Then she stood on her knees and unbuttoned her blouse. She deftly unclasped her bra and slipped that off. Nancy had large and lovely breasts. To have this kind of front-row seat would have been a young man's dream. *He* would have been aroused, intensely so. She felt small and a little intimidated.

"You better get those clothes off and air them out," Nancy said. "You'll stink to high heaven if you don't."

Tentatively she took off her jacket, jeans and t-shirt. Imitating Nancy, she pulled down the bra's shoulder straps, spun the bra around and undid the clasp. There they were -- bulging little teacups with round nipples. She shook her head then wrapped an airline blanket around her shoulders. She unzipped Emily's suitcase.

"I wish I could find mine," Nancy said.

She opened the lid and neatly folded on top was a gray dress made from stiff cotton. She lifted it up. It had short sleeves, a collar, black buttons and a matching cotton belt. It was around knee length, she supposed, and had black lace at the hem.

"That's a nice dress," Nancy said. "You could doll up pretty good in that."

Nancy was relentless, it seemed, probably thinking she was helping to jog Emily's memory. She set the dress down and continued through the suitcase's contents: a long gray nightshirt; two pairs of panties; a bra; an orange one-piece swimsuit; two t-shirts, red and orange; a pair of black spandex leggings; three pairs of white socks; a pair of calf-length stockings, black with a subdued argyle pattern; a pair of leather flats that looked brand new; a toiletries bag; a small wooden box that contained a pair of earrings and a necklace.

The earrings were dangling pewter globes with tiny semiprecious stones embedded in them. Were her ears pierced? She reached up with her hands and felt two small studs in her earlobes. She had not noticed them before. The necklace was a string of shiny hematite spheres, alternating smaller and larger.

Tucked in the corner of the suitcase was a plastic horse. It was a nicely detailed rendition of a sorrel mare with a dark mane. Had Emily had a thing for horses?

The dress, the jewelry and the shoes seemed more formal than *he* would have expected of the mousy girl. A funeral? She didn't know. Was Emily dead now? Had her mind been lodged in *his* body which was crushed in the crash? Had Emily been the lucky one?

She suddenly felt sad for Emily. Her young life, perhaps troubled, she didn't really know, cut short because of some improbable sequence of events, the tragic outcome of a cosmic roll of the dice. But her sadness for Emily's demise, somewhat perversely or paradoxically, suggested that, no, *he* had been the lucky one. *He* was still alive and she wanted to stay that way.

Chapter 4 | Wild Things

SHE woke feeling sore from the previous day's exertions. It was a good kind of sore, the kind that let her know she would be getting stronger. Nancy was sitting up on her sleeping bag, applying makeup. Beside her was a small camp cooking pot filled with water, a damp wash cloth and a couple of towels.

"Ah, sleepy head's awake," Nancy said. "Here, you might as well wash yourself a little and get into some clean clothes."

The fact that Nancy's mothering tended to be sensible didn't make it easier to take. Nevertheless, she reached for the pot, washcloth and a towel and started wiping herself down.

"Why are you putting on makeup?" She asked Nancy.

"I don't know. Habit. Plus I bet we're rescued today. When they find us, there'll be cameras and we'll be on TV all over the world. Don't you want to look good? Maybe you should put on that cute dress, maybe go say hi to Tim and cheer him up."

More dumbfounding suggestions that felt surreal, the kinds of things *he* would never think of. But she was beginning to get an inkling of their practicality, though wearing the dress didn't seem very practical in their present situation.

She wetted down her hair, ran a comb through it, applied deodorant, put on clean panties and her jeans. She was putting on the orange t-shirt when she decided she ought to put the bra on, too.

"I'm going to the bathroom," she said.

"There's some toilet paper just outside the flap," Nancy said.

~

She ate one of the camp biscuits that Sasha had cooked up and drank a box of orange juice. Then she cleaned up the breakfast dishes. *His* habit had been to stretch in the mornings and meditate so she resumed the habit. The problem was that stretches that were painful for *him* were hardly stretches at all for her. She would have to come up with a different routine. While doing this, Hank approached.

"Hey, Fred, see that peak poking out of the trees?"

"Yes."

"I'm thinking of climbing it and seeing what we can see. I've got a pair of binoculars. Want to come?"

"Sure. That's a good idea."

"It could take a while. We'd better pack some water and granola bars."

Gathering up the provisions for their expedition, she realized her little backpack purse wouldn't do. The narrow straps dug into her shoulders with the weight of the water bottle. She found a boy's backpack with pictures of superheroes printed on it. It fit just about right.

Hank grinned.

"Shut up," she said.

"What? I didn't say anything."

"Be careful you two," Nancy said.

She stopped beside Tim who was sitting on a rock, scraping the ground with a stick.

"Would you like to come, Tim?" She asked.

"Nah, I really don't feel like it right now. Thanks, though," he said.

∼

They headed for the hill to the south. It was the tallest of the ridges that framed the little valley they were in. They found a game trail that wound its way up in the general direction they wanted to go so they followed it.

"I'm beginning to like this place," Hank said. "It's so pristine. I'd love to come here under different circumstances."

"Yeah, me too."

"Some of these trees must be hundreds of years old. I mean, look at that sucker. I've never seen an oak ..."

"Shh. I hear something," she whispered.

"What?" Hank whispered back.

"Wait here."

Slowly, quietly, she advanced up the trail. The sound was sporadic -- an intermittent clopping and crunching. She soon saw an opening where trees gave way to rocky ground. There was a deadfall to her right, behind which she might approach unseen. She crouched low and moved even more slowly. *His* back would be burning right now, she thought. She got behind the thick trunk and slowly lifted her head to look over.

She saw a kind of goat or sheep. It had large, thick, curved horns with bony ridges. Its fur was smooth and light brown, becoming almost white at its belly. It had black hooves, a black nose, and pointed ears. It wasn't a bighorn, it wasn't a pronghorn, it wasn't a mountain goat. What was it?

The animal was grazing, plucking plants growing up from between the rocks. She looked back and could see Hank watching her. She waved him up and put a finger to her lips. Hank moved as quietly as he could. The creature looked up. She motioned Hank to stop. It went back to grazing and she waved him on. They went through this routine a couple of times before Hank was able to see the creature for himself. He mouthed a silent "Wow." Hank tried to edge closer. The animal looked up, thought better of sticking around, and bounded off, moving nimbly up the rocky terrain.

"Holy shit!" Hank exclaimed.

"You know what it was?" She asked.

"I'm pretty sure it was a tur," he said.

"A tur? What's a tur?"

"A kind of mountain antelope. But they only live in Asia."

"How'd it get here?"

"I have no idea but if there's a population of them around, I mean, boy, what a find that would be. I must say, well done, Sacagawea. Any time you want to do some wildlife spotting, you've got a job."

"Thanks." She felt the stretch of a grin on her face.

~

They took a break, drank some water and moved on. The tur's route looked too treacherous so they continued up the game trail which wrapped around the rocky ground. As they neared the open peak, they encountered a prominence of sheer rock. Trees still hid any broad view.

They circled around and found a spot where the outcropping wasn't so high or steep. It was low enough that Hank was able to hoist himself up. *He* had been even taller and could have climbed the ledge easily but it was too high for her. Hank reached down and pulled her up.

The slope was gentler here and led to a flat peak above the forest canopy. They emerged into a vast blue sky, the morning sun nearing its apex. Below was a broad plain and what she saw down there overwhelmed her.

"Mary mother of Jesus," Hank muttered.

~

Before them stretched, for what must have been miles, uncountable thousands of animals grazing the grassland below. The sight was bigger than what her mind could readily take in. Her imagination struggled to grasp it. She felt the tingle of wonder and the goosebumps of horror. Just where in the hell were they? Long moments passed before either could bring themselves to speak.

"What are those? Bison?" She asked.

"Not American bison," Hank said.

He fumbled with his satchel and with shaky hands put the pair of binoculars to his eyes.

"No. I'll be goddamned if they aren't wisents, European bison."

"There's so many of them."

"Too many. They're practically extinct," he said, continuing to scan the herd. "Ah, hell. It just can't be. I see lions down there."

Hank handed her the binoculars and directed her to the spot where he had been looking. It took her a while but they finally came into view -- a pride of lions lounging around a kill. The dark mane of a large male made it clear they weren't cougars.

"Are we in Africa?" She asked.

"No, bison don't exist in Africa, that I know of."

Looking at the herd, she saw there were some antelope mixed in with the bison. She handed the binoculars back to Hank and sat down. He kept looking, making remarks about what was going on. To her right, tall mountains loomed in the distance. They didn't resemble the Rockies she was familiar with, American or Canadian. Another wave of goosebumps. She looked up at the sun.

"Hank?"

"Yes."

"That's south, right?"

Hank looked to where she was pointing. "Yeah, definitely."

"Then why are there mountains to the south? Shouldn't they be to the west?"

He looked at the horizon, looked at the sun, pulled out a compass, looked at it.

"Fuck me," he said. He plopped down beside her.

"Where are we, Hank?"

"I don't know, Fred. Not in Kansas."

~

They sat in silence looking at the wonder below. The mass of bison slowly drifted eastward. A distant line of trees in that direction suggested a river that likely flowed northward away from the mountains.

"I sometimes imagined what it would be like to see the great herds that roamed the West," Hank said. "I never dreamt I'd actually see one. I wish I weren't so scared, I could enjoy it more."

Although hardly hungry, she knew she'd better maintain her energy. She took out a granola bar and Hank did the same. They chewed on them slowly.

"I suppose we'd better get back and tell the others," Hank said. "We have some decisions to make."

"No one's coming to rescue us, are they?"

"Doesn't look like it."

~

She and hank talked little on the way down. Her mind was dazed by all she had seen and all the sensations that were so new to her. Thoughts and speculations came faster than she could keep track of. Strangely, it all worked to keep her in the moment as she drank in the experiences.

She was frightened, there was no doubt about it, but she did feel acutely alive.

Nearing the bottom of the ridge's slope, they heard screaming.

"That's Sasha," she said.

"God, what now?"

Hank took off and she ran after him, pumping her short legs as hard as she could to keep up. They emerged from the forest to see commotion near the wreckage. Nancy was hurrying toward them.

"An animal pulled one of the bodies out of the plane," Nancy said.

She and Hank kept running until they could see what was happening. Sasha, Alex and Tim were facing off against a large, dog-like creature. It was striped and had thick haunches that narrowed at its rump. Its long hackles were sticking up and stretched the length of its back. It straddled a woman's corpse and snarled viciously through its massive muzzle.

"It's got Chloe! It's trying to eat Chloe!" Sasha wailed.

Alex and Tim were trying to shoo it away from the body.

"Get back! Get away from it!" Hank shouted. "It'll tear you apart. It's a hyena."

Hank got them back to a safer distance. The animal resumed feeding.

"Oh no, Chloe, no," Sasha sobbed.

Hank was looking around, probably trying to find something he could use to drive it off. She, however, did know of something. She ran back to the luggage pile and saw the corner of *his* suitcase beneath several other bags. Nancy came up beside her.

"What are you doing?" Nancy asked.

"Help me get these bags off," she said. "I need to get to that red suitcase."

Once uncovered, she dragged the suitcase out, sat down and undid the latches. She threw aside the clothes except for a white t-shirt which she spread flat beside her.

"What on earth ..." Nancy said.

"Not now, Nancy," she said, more harshly than she intended.

From the bottom of the suitcase, she lifted up what looked like a large sock. She reached inside, removed its contents -- the parts of a disassembled rifle -- and set them on the t-shirt: a barrel, a wooden stock, a bolt, a trigger assembly and two thick, black screws. The trigger assembly had a cable lock running through it that prevented it from functioning. She turned the dials of the lock to 7-3-8-4 and released the cable. She fished around the suitcase for something else.

"Where the fuck is it?" She snapped.

Then she remembered -- the lid pouch. From that came a stainless steel multi-tool which she placed on the t-shirt. She grabbed the barrel, lined it up with the stock, and slipped the trigger assembly into place. She inserted the screws with her fingers and tightened them with the multi-tool's screwdriver. She flipped the rifle upright, clicked off the safety and slid the bolt into the receiver.

She searched the side pockets of the suitcase and removed a cartridge magazine. Empty.

"Goddammit," she said.

She searched some more and found another magazine. This one had five rounds in it. She shoved the magazine in place in front of the trigger guard, worked the bolt and chambered a round. She clicked the safety on, got up and walked toward the hyena.

"Everybody, get back!" She shouted.

Nobody seemed to listen. *His* shout would not have been ignored.

"Hey!" She shouted as loud as she could.

Alex, Hank, Tim and Sasha looked at her.

"Get behind me. Now!"

They did so.

She raised the rifle to her shoulder and clicked the safety off. It was a lightweight rifle but it felt heavier now and longer. She settled the bead into the notch, took a deep breath, exhaled, put steady pressure on the trigger ... Boom. The crack of the shot lingered in the air. Loitering ravens flew up in unison.

The bullet struck the hyena in the neck and it went down. It struggled to stand but couldn't as blood flowed from its body. It saddened her to kill it like every time *he* had shot a deer. If Sasha hadn't been so distraught, she probably would have preferred to let the hyena be. There could be worse fates for a corpse than to sustain the life of an animal like that. She chambered another round and kept the rifle pointed at the hyena.

Hank moved toward it.

"Wait," she said. "Let it die."

In her head she counted off the seconds. When she reached 100, she approached slowly with the rifle still aimed. When she got close enough she poked the animal with the barrel. It was dead. She flicked the safety on, knelt beside it and put her hand on its mane.

"Sorry, big guy," she said.

~

She walked back toward *his* suitcase. Nobody said anything but they were all watching her. Nancy was crouched by the suitcase. She had been inspecting its contents. Nancy was holding what she now wanted. She cradled the rifle in one hand and reached out with the other.

"Give me the knife, Nancy," she said. "Please."

Slowly, Nancy handed it to her. The handmade knife was in its leather sheath. Its birch handle had smooth, rounded contours. The blade was single-edged, about four inches long, and its thick spine tapered to a razor-sharp edge. *He* didn't believe in precious objects -- one shouldn't get too attached to mere things -- but this knife came close to being an exception. *He* had bought it as reward after killing *his* first deer. Called a puukko, the style was traditional to the Finns and the Sami people of northern Scandinavia.

She went back to the dead hyena. Hank, Alex and Tim were standing over it, still not saying anything. She handed Alex the rifle.

"Here, hold this," she said.

Alex took it and held it as if it were a cursed thing.

"Hank, Tim, help me get this thing away from the body and turned over."

They did and she began to field dress it. First she cut the tissue around the anus then cut away the genitals (this one was male). She made a shallow incision in the animal's stomach near the pelvis, being careful not to puncture the intestines. Using two fingers of her left hand to guide the blade, she sliced the skin up to the sternum. Straddling the beast and holding the knife with two hands, blade upward, she cut the sternum. It took multiple strokes, many more than *he* would have needed, but she got the chest cavity open. She reached into the cavity and cut the esophagus, then used the knife to saw through the pelvic bone. When she had it split apart, she proceeded to pull the organs out, slicing connecting tissue as needed. This action revealed the tenderloins under the ribs. She cut them away.

"Guys, turn it over and spread its legs out so the blood drains," she said.

She stood up, holding the knife in her right hand and the tenderloins in her left. Her shirt and jeans were splattered with blood. Her right arm was drenched with it. Some had gotten on her face.

"I have a rule," she said, "that I should eat any animal I kill."

No one ventured an objection.

"Awesome," Tim said.

~

She sheathed the knife and put it in her back pocket. She retrieved the rifle from Alex who gladly turned it over. She went to the red suitcase and found the rifle's sling, attached it to the swivels and shouldered the weapon. She went back to the camp and put the tenderloins on the makeshift grill. She fetched Emily's suitcase from the tent along with a towel and a washcloth.

"I'm going to the spring to clean up," she said.

At the spring she removed her bloodstained shirt and jeans, rinsed them and wrung them out. She took off her underwear and stepped naked into the chilly pool. Quickly she wiped herself down with the washcloth then submerged herself completely. She stepped out, shivering, and dried herself with the towel.

She didn't want to wear the wet clothes so she put on the red t-shirt and spandex leggings. The way the leggings hugged her thighs and hips felt weird. They were too revealing, she thought, but what else could she wear? There was nothing for it. She pulled the gray dress over her head. It made her feel ridiculous.

She rinsed the knife, dried it off and returned it to its sheath which she slipped onto the dress's belt. She put on her sneakers, gathered up her things, slung the rifle and headed back to camp.

Nearing the camp she heard talking. When she walked into view, they all stopped. She could feel the men's eyes taking her in. They looked at her like *he* would look at a woman who had caught *his* eye.

"Hi," she said and smiled as best she could.

"My, aren't you a sight," Nancy said.

She felt blood surge to her cheeks.

~

Hank suggested that she let her wet clothes dry over by the wreckage. Tim volunteered to take them over for her and she let him. Hank said the group needed to start following what he called "bear protocol" -- anything that might attract a predator, like fresh blood, should be kept away from camp. She agreed and started thinking that it hadn't been such a good idea to shoot the hyena but, in the excitement, she had gone into hunting mode and was following *his* routine.

She set the rifle against a rock. Sasha approached her.

"Thank you, for what you did out there," Sasha said. "I'm sorry I acted like that. I was out of my mind. I panicked."

"No problem," she said, putting a hand on Sasha's back.

Sasha took the gesture as an invitation to embrace and squeezed tightly, practically lifting her off the ground.

~

The group gathered in a circle for a pow-wow. Tim returned from the wreckage and sat next to her. Everyone sat on the ground except Bob who used the lawn chair. He was flushed and sweating and his breathing labored.

Alex: "Hank thinks we ended up somehow in Asia, but that's impossible. The plane would have to have been going in the wrong direction. And we weren't up that long before the storm hit, not long enough to cross the Rockies and the Pacific Ocean."

Hank: "I don't know how it could have happened, but it's the only thing that makes sense given the animals we've seen and the fact that the mountains are to the south."

Alex: "Could it be we're in a peculiar spot? Because of a trick of geography, we only see mountains to the south?"

Hank: "I don't know. Maybe. But that doesn't explain the animals. Hyenas and lions and turs just don't exist in North America."

Bob: "Could we be in a hidden game reserve? A billionaire's wildlife experiment perhaps?"

Hank: "It's a stretch. I don't know. It just doesn't seem plausible."

Alex: "Nothing seems plausible at the moment. What do you think, Emily?"

She noticed the men's eyes were more often looking at her now when they talked. Does a girl really have to kill and gut a hyena to get some respect?

She: "I agree with Hank. I think we're probably in Asia. I know, very personally, that weird things have happened. That storm was not normal. We got caught in something beyond our understanding."

Alex and the others nodded. Silence prevailed for time. A breeze had picked up. Fortunately, they were upwind of the wreckage and the dead bodies within. Thick clouds rolled across the sky.

Hank: "Well, it's kind of an academic point, anyway. Wherever we are, I don't think they're going to find us here. I think we have to hike out. Whether we're in Asia, Africa or some mystery spot in Idaho, if we keep going in one direction, we'll come across a road or town sooner or later."

Everyone expressed their agreement, except Bob, who didn't object, but didn't look as if he relished the prospect of a long trek.

Nancy: "I think we'd better get the fire going and cook supper. It's going to rain soon. I feel it."

$$\sim$$

Sasha, Nancy and Alex worked on the meal. She, Tim and Hank went to the wreckage and dragged the dead hyena over to the forest's edge where they hung it from a branch with a length of nylon rope.

"It won't keep for long," she said. "But it should be good for a couple of days if something else doesn't get to it."

On the way back to camp, Tim said: "That's a cool rifle, Emily. What kind is it?"

"A hunting carbine made in the Czech Republic."

"Thirty cal?"

"More or less, seven-point-six-two-by-three-nine."

"That's what the AK uses," Tim said.

"That's right," she said. "Do you shoot?"

"Yeah, my grandpa's into it. He's got a cabin in the U.P. We go shooting there a lot. I've got a .22 he gave me. I'm saving up for a 9 mil. Someday I want to get an AR."

Typical of young guys to want the military semiautomatic stuff, she thought. *He* had liked to shoot, but slowly, one shot at a time, striving for good technique and precision.

"Can I look at it?" Tim asked.

"Sure."

"Wow, it's so light," he said.

He kept his finger off the trigger and handled it like he was accustomed to guns.

"I like the striped wood grain," he said.

"So do I," she said.

"Just open sights. Can you put a scope on it?"

"Yes, but I'm not fond of scopes."

"Cool." Tim handed it back.

"Hank, do you know how to use a rifle?" She asked.

"Sure, I have a thirty-aught-six at home."

Her dress was turning out not to be such a bad garment. Its sturdy fabric and stitching should be pretty durable. The problem was the lace. It threatened to get caught on stuff as she walked. She wondered if Nancy or Sasha could cut it off and hem it up.

~

Back at camp they ate supper. They could see flashes of lightning in the western sky. She grilled the tenderloins and divided the meat up between herself, Hank, Tim, Alex and Nancy. Sasha didn't want to try it. Bob said he wasn't hungry and just ate some freeze-dried lentil soup. The meat was fairly tender but gamy with a strong iron taste. An invocation ran through her mind: May this meat bestow some of the hyena's strength for the journey ahead.

At Hank's suggestion, they decided they would spend the next couple of days gathering up everything that could be useful, taking inventory and deciding what they could carry with them. Maybe they would get lucky and rescuers would find them before they left. She knew that they wouldn't.

~

The rain started coming down and they all retreated to their tents. Inside the drops pounding the canvas sounded like bacon frying at high volume. She was glad Tim had not been idle that morning. He had scraped a set of small trenches that would channel water away from the tents.

She set the rifle and knife beside her sleeping bag then stripped to her panties. She folded the dress neatly and put it in the suitcase. She wished she had a book to read but it was too late to look for one now.

Nancy had taken off her skirt and was unbuttoning her blouse, looking at her in a curious way. *He* had seen that kind of look before. She was confused.

"It's true, isn't it?" Nancy asked. "You really are Fred Harper, or were."

She nodded.

"I didn't believe it, of course," Nancy continued. "But when I saw you undo the combination of that lock, the way you spoke to me, that look on your face when you were putting the rifle together, I knew you weren't the girl I'd seated on the plane."

Nancy moved closer.

"And then you shot the hyena, and butchered it, and you were covered in blood. It was like something out of ... It gave me chills."

Nancy removed her bra. Her splendid breasts were close enough to touch.

"I'm sorry I doubted you, but I don't know if I'm sorry about what happened. It must be a kind of miracle from God."

That made her laugh.

"More like a joke of the gods," she said. "I can see Apollo and Athena sipping cocktails on Mt. Olympus, having a good chuckle."

Nancy giggled. "I bet they are."

Nancy put her hand on her shoulder, caressing her arm until their hands met. What was she doing? She could feel her heart pumping. Nancy lifted her hand and pulled it to one of her breasts.

42

"Do you still like women?"

She did. Nancy's breast was wonderful to touch. But it was different. There wasn't that aching pressure at her groin, more of a tingling. Nor that white-hot desire, more of a warmth. And apprehension. What was happening? Should she be doing this?

Nancy put her hands to her stomach, moving them up slowly until they enveloped her little breasts. She kept pushing up, stretching them until they almost hurt.

"I kind of wish this had happened to my ex-husband. It would have taught him a lesson."

I should just push her away and stop this now, she thought. But she didn't. One of Nancy's hands moved to her backside, pulled her closer, and slid her panties down. The other hand moved down her stomach until it reached that tuft of hair.

"We're you a bad man?" Nancy asked. "Did you get your penis taken away?"

Nancy's hand went all the way down, her fingers quickly finding the right spot. She gasped.

"You poor boy," Nancy cooed. "But it's not so bad, is it?"

A hum of pleasure rose in her throat. Some part of her told her she should disengage, but that part had lost all power. It felt so good.

Nancy's lips came to hers, tongue probing. She kissed back and hugged Nancy tight. She moved her hand over Nancy's rump, around her thigh and to her genitals.

"Oh, good girl, Emily, good girl."

Chapter 5 | The Origin of Nightmares

SHE needed to pee. The rain had stopped. Nancy snored lightly in her sleeping bag. She put on the nightshirt and stepped out of the tent. Darkness was receding but the sun hadn't yet risen. The damp air smelled fresh. The grass was wet and cold to her feet. Everything was quiet. She half expected to see or hear more hyenas at the wreckage. Why hadn't more come? The question felt important but she had trouble focusing on it.

She was thinking about last night's love making. The exquisite pleasure of it, and then how she felt a little hollow when she had retreated to her sleeping bag. Humbled. Small. She knew how to use a knife and shoot a gun. She knew she retained *his* capacity to kill and *his* willingness to fight. But all that was swept aside by Nancy's loving projections. She had been overmatched. Not a fair fight at all. Nancy had put her in her place, acknowledged and consummated *his* new form. *He* was a she now and that wasn't going to change.

After peeing, she sat on a rock and shivered as she watched the sun rise over the eastern ridge. Soon everything glistened in its yellow morning light.

Emily. It had a nice sound to it, a little girly perhaps but not bad. She thought about the mousy girl, whom she knew must have been much more than what *he* had perceived, very much more. It seemed fitting to honor her passing by adopting her name. "Fred" wouldn't really do. Maybe as a nickname like the way Hank used it, but "Fred" couldn't be her real name, not anymore.

She recalled Hank asking what her name was and how she struggled to answer. She had an answer now. She would be Emily. "Hi, my name is Emily," she practiced aloud. The words spooked her, jarred something deep, but she did not renounce them.

Emily's teeth were chattering and she realized how cold she was. She ran back to the tent and into the warmth of her sleeping bag.

~

After breakfast, Nancy and Sasha agreed to help her remove the lace from her dress. Nancy found a pair of scissors and carefully cut the lace off. Sasha had a sewing kit and started working on the hem. Emily watched with interest. It seemed like a useful skill that *he* had never bothered with.

"If you show me how to do that, I'll show you how to shoot the rifle," Emily said.

"Deal," Sasha said.

Emily got the hang of it quickly, her fingers deftly handling the needle and thread.

"Why, you're a natural," Sasha said.

He had never sewed anything before except a couple of botched attempts to attach buttons. It occurred to her that she retained some of the old Emily's muscle memory. Was there anything else? It was slow work and Sasha left her to it to go help the others gather supplies for the journey.

She finished before lunch. Sasha helped her tie off the hem. She went into the tent, took off the nightshirt and put on the dress. It was shorter than she had wanted. Nancy, she thought. The woman was determined to drive her insane.

~

After lunching on ramen noodles, the group reviewed the food supply. It was surprisingly large, more than they could carry and still bring other necessary gear. Alex was writing everything down in order to figure out how much they could carry and how many days worth they would have. Hank suggested they should bury any food left behind so they had some place to retreat to if necessary.

They found a couple of framed backpacks made for serious hiking, a couple of fairly large ones with hip belts, and various others. Figuring out just what to bring and what each person could carry was turning out to be more complicated than they had thought.

"We might need another day to get ready," Bob said.

Emily thought they needed to leave sooner. She was getting the feeling that they had overstayed their welcome. She went to Hank who was adjusting one of the framed packs.

"Why haven't any more hyena's come?" She asked. "Aren't they pack animals?"

"Yeah, I thought about that," he said. "I'm guessing the one you shot was a rogue, kicked out of his pack for some reason or looking for a new one. The bison herd probably keeps the packs from coming up here. Why abandon their steady food supply? I imagine it helps that nearly all the bodies are inside the plane."

"That makes sense, I guess," she said.

"Are you worried about something?"

"Yes, but I'm not sure why."

Sasha approached. Although she carried more weight than she should, she moved easily and lightly. Emily could tell she was quite strong.

"You going to show me how to use the rifle?" Sasha asked.

"Sure."

Emily unloaded the weapon and fetched the empty magazine to use for practice. There were only four rounds left so they couldn't do any live shooting. Sasha quickly picked up how to work the safety and the bolt, how to hold it and aim. She dry fired it a few times.

"This could be fun," she said. "I wish we could shoot it for real."

Nancy, Alex and Bob came over too, wanting to know how to use it. Emily obliged. She went over the basic safety rules: Always point it in a safe direction, always check if it's loaded, don't put your finger on the trigger until you're ready to shoot, and so on.

~

Hank wanted to hike up to the peak to take another look around. Everybody wanted to go with him except Bob. He was looking better but didn't feel up to the climb. Emily volunteered to stay behind and help keep an eye on the camp.

"I'm not sure I'm up to the hike we're planning," Bob confided when the others had gone.

"We'll take it slow, you'll be okay." She tried her best to be reassuring but had her own doubts.

"So what kind of conference were you and Alex attending?" She asked.

"Materials science," Bob said. "I'm a professor. Alex is an industry engineer."

"A physicist?"

"Yes, that's correct."

"Do you know much about wormholes and such?"

Bob chuckled. "That's what the theoretical guys are interested in. Materials guys are more down to earth. Why do you ask?"

"Just thinking that storm was something more than a storm, maybe a freakish rupture that the plane got caught in."

"Can't rule it out, I suppose, but not likely," Bob said. "If it was a random wormhole and we survived going through it, we'd almost certainly end up in empty space, not back on earth."

"If it wasn't random?"

"Aliens again?"

"Yeah, I know, it's silly, but there's that lost day on your watch. How do you explain that?"

"I don't know. The magnetic field of the lightning pulled the date indicator forward," Bob said. He didn't sound convinced.

~

Emily decided to skin the hyena and cut more meat from it. They might as well eat it while they could and save the packaged stuff. She changed into her damp jeans and t-shirt. The blood stains were still visible.

She went to where the hyena hung and lowered it to where she could reach it easily. The task took nearly all her strength. She missed *his* strength and felt a wave of frustration. She longed for that easy power *he* had had to force resistant objects to *his* will.

She distracted herself from her anguish by carefully cutting and peeling the animal's hide. She had it off in about an hour and managed to keep it in one piece. She used a flat rock to scrape away the fatty tissue from underneath the hide. The hackles were still up, frozen in place after the hyena's death throes. With its striped flanks, it resembled a Native American headdress. It was beautiful in a way. She wished she could keep it.

He had only butchered a deer a couple of times. A hunting buddy had showed *him* how, but then *he* got lazy and started taking the carcasses to a processor. She cut away some meat and put it into a plastic bag.

She wanted to pull the carcass back up but doubted she had the strength. She considered calling Bob over to help but thought, no, I will do this myself. She had to jump and yank at the cord, emitting squeaky grunts as she did so. Eventually she got it up to the height it had been and tied off the cord. She hung the hide on the cord as high as she could reach.

She went back to camp, washed up and changed back into her dress and leggings.

~

Emily and Bob had the cooking fire going and she was busy sharpening her puukko when the others returned. They all had been astonished by what they had seen. Although the bison herd had moved further to the east, Hank reported, scattered carcasses were left behind with hyenas and carrion birds tending to them.

"I see you skinned the hyena," Hank said. "That would be something to hang on your wall and tell your grandkids about."

It struck her with a mixture of horror and wonder that she could get pregnant and bear children. It was too much. She tried to push the thought from her mind. It was something *he* didn't have to worry about, except in the abstract. It wasn't a real, physical thing that could happen to *him*. But it could happen to her.

~

Alex: "I figure we can carry about ten days worth of food but not that much water. We'll have to rely on finding water along the way. If we can average, say, fifteen miles a day, then we can travel 150 miles before we run out of supply. I doubt there are many places in the world where 150 miles wouldn't get us somewhere, as long as we keep going in one direction."

Hank: "I don't think we should go east toward the bison herd. Too dangerous, too many predators around. If we go south, the terrain could get difficult and we'd probably be less likely to find a road.

"That leaves north or west. North appears to be the direction the river basin flows. It looks like open country. The walking would be easier and we'd have water. A river might be the most likely place to find people. A downside is that we'd be exposed to heat and wind and possible bad weather.

"To the west there are hills and forest. That has the advantage of more shelter from the elements and the heat. Water would be iffier but trees like these don't grow without water so we'd probably be okay."

Sasha: "I say we go north. We're more likely to be spotted by someone if we're out in the open."

Emily was inclined to go west. Growing up in Sioux City, *he* had always liked the woods and the bluffs. The endless stretches of flat farmland had held little appeal. Later *he* had come to appreciate the prairie but *he* still preferred forests and gravitated to them.

Emily: "I'd feel more comfortable in the forest but that's me. I do see the logic of going north."

Hank: "I say we tentatively plan on going north. We can decide for sure after we've slept on it."

~

Tim sat next to Emily while they chewed tough hyena meat. She should have tried to tenderize it before cooking it. Sasha and Bob still weren't interested. Tim talked about his life back home, his delivery job, his classes at the community college, the heavy metal bands he liked. She hadn't heard of most of them. *He* had come to like chamber music or jazz and wasn't up on the current rock scene. She guessed the old Emily would have been, and quite possibly would have hit it off with Tim. She supposed he was a decent looking guy in a wiry cowboy sort of way. He talked to her as if she were someone close to his own age. She was, of course, and wasn't. There was something appealing about Tim's attentions but she knew it would become wearying before long.

"What gets me the most is the lions," Hank was saying to Alex. "The only population of Asiatic lions that I know of is in India. And I'm pretty sure we're not in India."

"I've read," Emily said. "That lions used to exist in the Middle East not long ago, ranging as far up as the Caucasus."

"True but they were killed off a couple centuries ago," Hank said. "That's a point, though, lions can survive in colder climates than Africa. Maybe we're in a secret Russian wildlife refuge."

"I don't relish the idea of getting eaten by one," Alex said. "I'm wondering if we shouldn't keep a watch at night."

"I think that's a good idea," Sasha said. "We've probably been pushing our luck as it is."

It did seem like a good idea, Emily thought, but maybe they would be safer staying in their tents, as long as they kept food smells away.

"I suppose we could do that," Hank said. "We could keep the fire going through the night."

"Then we'd better gather up more wood while we have some light," Nancy said.

~

They would take one-hour shifts using Bob's watch to keep time. Bob would take the first watch followed by Hank, Alex, Tim, Nancy, Emily and Sasha. The watch person would carry the rifle.

"Don't shoot unless you absolutely must," Emily said. "Otherwise wake everybody up and get the rifle to me, or Hank or Tim."

She had doubts and the look from Hank suggested he did too. The rifle was its own kind of danger but it had become a talisman of safety for the group. She checked it before handing it over to Bob for the first watch. She went to her tent and found Nancy already in her sleeping bag. The clear sky had brought a chill with it.

She took off her clothes and saw Nancy lying on her side with the sleeping bag part way open. Nancy smiled and patted the space beside her. Emily removed her panties, switched off the light and crawled in. They kissed and entangled their limbs around each other.

~

She heard Tim whisper outside the tent. She nudged Nancy to get up for her shift. It seemed like no time at all had passed when she woke again to Nancy stroking her hair.

"You're turn, my little man-girl," Nancy said.

She put on her clothes and took the rifle to the folding chair by the fire. She stoked it and walked around a bit to wake up. She sat in the chair and wrapped herself in a blanket. She kept herself awake by thinking about what gear she would bring for the journey, wondering how much she could carry on her small frame. She was getting stronger, she could feel that, but, still, nothing like *his* strength.

Before the hour was up, Sasha crawled out of her tent.

"I might as well take over now," she said. "I woke up and couldn't get back to sleep."

Emily checked the rifle, handed it to Sasha and went back to her tent. She stripped down again, put on the nightshirt and slipped into her own sleeping bag, not wanting to wake Nancy. It didn't take long before she fell back to sleep.

~

Suddenly she was awake again. She sat upright. Her heart was racing. She had heard something but wasn't sure what. She went outside. The sun was just creeping into view. She heard movement coming from the copse, a scraping sound followed by a low rumble.

"Sasha!" She shouted. "Sasha!"

She ran into the copse, saw nothing, and emerged from the other side. What she then saw stopped her as if running into a wall.

A huge beast was dragging Sasha across the grass toward the north line of trees. Her head dangled, neck broken, and her pants were bunched around her ankles. The beast's fur was velvety orange with black stripes. It moved quickly -- Sasha's body was little more than a rag doll to it. Its long tail flicked in the air. It was a tiger and it was as big as any grizzly *he* had ever seen.

Slung across Sasha's shoulders was the rifle.

"No!" Emily yelped.

She picked up a rock and ran after the monster as it moved into the trees.

"Emily! Stop!" Nancy screamed.

Emily plunged into the forest. She had to get the rifle back.

Running as fast as she could, she was closing the distance, but the tiger quickened its pace and she couldn't keep up. She threw the rock and struck the tiger's rump.

Releasing Sasha's body, the tiger turned and swiped the air, its long claws fully extended. Its eyes locked onto Emily. It roared and bounded toward her. She staggered backward and fell on her butt. This was it, she thought, the end of the short life of the new Emily.

The tiger leaped and landed just in front of her, its massive forelimbs straddling her legs. Its fiery face filled her vision, its bloodshot eyes bored into hers. The skin of its snout rose to reveal long yellow fangs. It roared. The sound vibrated her body and its hot breath blew her hair back. She could see down its throat.

The roar stopped and the tiger bounded away. It picked up Sasha and continued up the slope, disappearing into the trees along with the rifle.

"Holy shit! You okay?" Hank said as he ran up to her. He was holding a large stick like a baseball bat.

She got up and threw her arms around him, pressing her head into his chest. The feeling of his arms around her eased her terror.

"You're all right, Fred," Hank said. "It's over now."

~

Emily's legs trembled so much she could barely walk.

"You want me to carry you?" Hank asked.

"No. I'll be fine in a minute."

She stumbled. Hank caught her and picked her up.

"No reason to be ashamed," he said. "You're easily the bravest person I've ever known."

Nancy came running up.

"Oh my fucking God. Emily, you stupid, stupid girl!"

Chapter 6 | Moving On

BOB was dead, too. Apparently he died in his sleep. Alex said Bob had had heart problems and that must have been the cause. Nobody seemed surprised.

Emily sat in the lawn chair wrapped in a blanket that Nancy had put around her. The fire was still going and she stared into it. The others were talking but she wasn't paying much attention, still recovering her senses after the encounter with the tiger. Hank said she had been brave (Nancy's "stupid" was more accurate), but she knew that *he* would not have been so brave. The thought was unsettling.

"It had to have been 700 pounds at least," Hank said. "Bigger than anything I've seen in a zoo."

Hank had been recounting the event. Alex and Tim had caught only a glimpse of the tiger.

"What are we going to do now?" Alex asked. "We can't stay here with that thing around. Without the rifle, we're defenseless."

The rifle. It *had* been a talisman, she thought, for her especially. It was a tool that had protected her, given her status, compensated for her diminished size and strength. Even disassembled in the suitcase, it had been a source of security. She knew she had the means to kill. Now it was gone and she felt vulnerable.

But the way they were glancing at her -- waiting, it seemed, for her to speak -- suggested the loss of the rifle had not diminished her status. As far as defenses went, she would just have to find another means. She still had her puukko. Even a tiger might feel its bite.

"We're safe for now," she said. "The tiger won't hunt again for a while."

How was she so sure? She didn't know, but she was.

"That's right," Hank said. "And now that I think about it, it's been the tiger that's kept other predators away. We're in its territory."

"And Sasha's life was the price of our safety," Nancy said in a low tone.

"Okay, let's leave tomorrow as planned," Alex said. "Before the thing decides to take another toll."

"I'm not sure we want to go north now," Tim said. "The tiger went that way."

"I think we should go west," Emily said. "There will be peaks we can climb that will give us a good view and help us plot our course."

"That makes sense to me," Alex said.

"I'm with Emily," Tim said.

"Well, I guess that's settled," Hank said.

Nancy stood behind Emily and massaged her shoulders.

~

They spent the day finishing their preparations. Hank and Tim carried Bob's body, still in its tent and sleeping bag, over to the wreckage.

The superhero pack was too small so Emily found a largish day pack that fit pretty well. She wanted to find something that she could use as a scout bag for any side journeys to forage or explore. She spotted a small camera bag and removed the busted contents. In it she could fit a liter of water along with other odds and ends. She also found a canister of pepper spray which she slipped into a side pocket.

To conserve space, they would take three tents. Nancy and Emily would stay in one, Alex and Tim in another, and Hank would have his own. Her pack contained her clothes, most of the old Emily's possessions, food, and assorted other gear like a first-aid kit, emergency rain poncho and eating utensils. Her sleeping bag was strapped to the top of the pack. She wrapped a blanket around a leather belt which she would wear around her waist. The pack could rest on the blanket and take some weight from her shoulders.

He had liked to use a walking stick because it helped reduce the strain on *his* back and knees. She suggested they all fashion walking sticks and they agreed it was a good idea. They buried the leftover food along with some extra camping gear then foraged for suitable branches.

After supper around the fire, they sawed and whittled their sticks into shape. Emily noted that Nancy didn't say a prayer before the meal. Was she having doubts or did it just slip her mind? Nobody suggested keeping watch. What was the point? The tiger was the god here. They lived at its mercy.

Emily and Nancy zipped their sleeping bags together to give themselves more room and crawled in. No love making, they just held each other tight until they fell asleep.

~

Nancy cooked hyena-meat omelets for breakfast using powdered eggs and some greens Hank had picked. Though hardly a taste treat, it was a good meal for the start of their journey. Emily wore her dress and leggings. Nancy never found her suitcase but she had found clothes that fit reasonably well. She wore a blue, collarless shirt dress over tan leggings that had colorful Mayan patterns. Hank wore a large camp knife on his belt. Emily recognized the brand -- high quality, expensive, with a stacked leather grip. Tim wore cargo shorts, a blue t-shirt and a baseball cap. Alex wore jeans and a polo shirt with green and blue stripes.

Hank took a compass bearing before they left and Alex recorded it in a notebook. They slung their packs and trudged up the western slope. Emily took the lead followed by Hank, Nancy, Tim and Alex. They all were breathing heavily when they reached the crest. Emily could tell that her wind was better than it had been a couple of days ago. Hank took another compass bearing, shouted it to Alex. They moved down the slope. This was where the walking sticks were particularly useful, supporting their descent and helping them keep their balance and footing.

Reaching the bottom biting flies started harassing them. They stopped, applied insect spray, drank water, and moved on. The next slope was too steep so they hiked northwest along its base until it became gentler, then went up, trying to hold due west as best they could.

They stopped again at the crest. Emily's pack was already getting heavy although she probably wasn't carrying more than 30 pounds. The slope leveled off and the going got easier. The trees, if anything, were even bigger here. The air was cool and damp. It was like walking in a fantasy movie's sylvan setting. She half expected a dryad to dart between the trees.

"What's that over there?" Tim asked.

To their right, sunlight came through an opening in the canopy, illuminating a cube-like formation.

"Just some rock catching the sun," Alex said.

"I'm going to take a look quick," Tim said.

Emily didn't feel like expending energy for the side journey, nor did the others, but she was glad Tim was checking it out. They needed to stay out of the mode that happens on long hikes where you get too focused on the ground in front of your feet. They needed to stay alert for clues and signs that could help them figure out where they were and where they should go.

"Whoa, you guys got to see this," Tim said.

"What is it?" Nancy asked wearily.

"It's like a weird doghouse. It's got a tiger's face painted on it."

With renewed energy, they went to join Tim. In the middle of a grassy area was a small hut made of stone, maybe six feet by six feet. The walls were granite slabs with a thick slab as a roof. It was situated on a short rise with flat rocks leading up to it like steps. The entrance was a perfectly round hole. Only a very small person could squeeze through. Above the hole was some weathered orange and black pigment that depicted a simple, almost childlike image of a tiger's face.

"Well, I'll be damned," Hank said.

"I guess someone's been here before," Nancy said.

Emily took off her pack and so did the others. The tiger was a god, she thought, and it had worshipers, or once did. Alex was looking closely at the stones and the pigment.

"I don't know, a kind of temple perhaps," he said. "The structure is much older than the pigment."

He fetched a flashlight from his pack and shined it into the hole. Emily crouched beside him. There were bones scattered on the floor but otherwise it was empty.

"Looks like animals have taken advantage of it," she said.

Hank had followed the flat stones away from the hut and down the rise. He was peering into the trees beyond.

"That's got to be a trail," he said. "It's overgrown but I bet we can follow it."

"That's good news, isn't it?" Nancy asked.

"Yes, I think so, I hope so."

"We should celebrate with a nice energy bar lunch," Alex said.

~

"Ouch," Nancy said when she sat on the ground. She reached around behind her. "It's something metal."

She held up the object. It was a small spherical piece of bronze with part of a broken chain attached to it. It was hollow, open at the top and had triangular holes around its circumference. One side was cracked.

"It's a censer, I bet," Alex said.

"For burning incense?" Nancy asked.

"That's what it looks like. Maybe it was used in a ritual."

Nancy handed it to Alex who examined it closely.

"It's been here a while, that's certain, but I don't think it's ancient. Decades, maybe, but not centuries," he said.

"We'd better leave it here," Hank said. "If there are indigenous folks around, we don't want to upset them by taking stuff from a sacred site."

~

They put on their packs and continued walking, Hank taking the lead this time so he could try to keep them on the trail. Emily followed close behind. They headed in a northwesterly direction through a flat area between ridges. Emily's legs were burning but she was glad she wasn't feeling any blisters on her feet. It must have been three hours, she figured, since lunch when they came to a stream. Without any word, they unslung their packs and plopped to the ground.

"Well, we probably shouldn't push too hard until we've got our hiking legs," Hank said. "I say we camp here tonight."

"I second the motion," Alex said.

Emily took off her sneakers and socks and massaged her feet. She left the socks to air out on a rock and went to the stream. It gurgled around moss-covered stones clearly placed there as a means of stepping across. She soaked her feet in the cool water. It felt wonderful. She cupped some in her hand and took a sip.

"The water's nice and fresh," she said. "I don't think we need iodine tablets."

She went and fetched her walking stick and scout bag.

"I'm going to take a quick look on the other side," she said.

"I'll go with you," Tim said.

The others just nodded as they rested against their packs. Emily and Tim crossed the stream and climbed up the far bank. The trail was clearer here. It went west for several yards before curving to the right. About ten yards beyond, there was a small clearing and a circle of stones that defined the edges of a fire pit. They weren't the first people to camp here.

"Hot damn," Tim said. "Looks like we're going the right direction. I'm glad we went the way you wanted to go."

They poked around the site and found some broken pieces of pottery. Emily took care where she stepped. Just beyond the fire pit, she found an old leather sandal. It was big, sized for a man, she thought, with long straps that would tie up around the calf. One of the straps was split and the heel had a hole worn through it. The sandal looked like what a Roman solider might wear.

"That's pretty weird," Tim said.

They went back to the others and told them about the campsite. They all picked up their gear and moved across the stream.

"Who knows?" Hank said, looking at the sandal.

They lit a fire and set up the tents.

"We might as well take advantage of the stream and wash up," Nancy said. "Ladies first. No peeking, now, or I'll sic Emily on you."

"We definitely don't want that," Alex said.

"Most def," Hank said.

Standing naked in the stream with Nancy, Emily thought it was like they were living a scene from an old fable -- two nymphs bathing in an idyllic woodland realm. She wondered if Tim maybe was sneaking a peek. Let him, she thought. It would be something he'd always remember.

That night she and Nancy slipped into their doubled up sleeping bag. They were too tired for anything more than a prolonged kiss.

~

The morning brought rain and they stayed in their tents until it lightened to a drizzle. They set off after a cold breakfast of granola bars and boxed juice. Emily took the lead again, the idea being that her keen ears might warn them of anything approaching. The others made too much noise, she thought. To really play the scout, she should be 100 yards ahead, but she doubted they would go for that.

She noticed a pile of scat that looked like it had come from a large dog except it was gray with hair sticking in it. Most likely a wolf, she thought. She had seen similar scat before. She pointed it out to Hank and he nodded. It didn't worry her much. Wolves tended to be wary of humans. *He* had never seen one in the wild, despite all *his* hiking in wolf country, except once at Yellowstone from a long distance.

Around midmorning, a squall blew over and drenched them. The oaks and hackberries were giving way to larches as the trail moved onto rockier ground. By midafternoon the clouds had broken up and the sun was shining. They came to a large clearing of scrubby grass and brush.

"I think we should stop here and dry our things while we have the sun," Nancy said.

They made camp and Nancy set up a clothes line. Emily changed into her blood-stained jeans and t-shirt and draped her wet clothes on the line.

"There's a peak over there that looks like we could climb," Hank said, pointing up the eastern ridge. "We should take a look around."

Everybody wanted to go but they agreed they shouldn't leave the camp unattended, so they decided on two people -- Alex, because he had been sketching rough maps in his notebook and getting a broad view would help tie things together, and Emily, because she drew the short straw.

She took her scout bag and her hoodie in case it got chilly. Alex brought the binoculars, compass and notebook. They climbed slowly. The ground was steep and uneven but traversable. The walking sticks helped. Emily reached the top first and turned to give Alex a hand.

The peak was a rocky prominence that rose above most of the larches. To the west they saw forested hills and ridges beyond which lay a vast body of water of the deepest blue Emily had ever seen. It filled the horizon and they couldn't see across it.

"This gets more impossible all the time," Alex said. "I know that can't be the Pacific. Is it Lake Baikal? It couldn't be the Caspian Sea."

Emily looked at the mountains to the south. They extended right up to the shore of the water. She looked north and saw how the hills and forest turned to flat grassland. She tried to visualize the terrain on a map to see if it might fit anything she remembered. An idea occurred to her. A couple of years ago, *he* had read a book about Hitler's failed campaign to seize the Soviet Union's oil fields near Grozny and Baku. The book had a foldout map that showed where the major battles had been and detailed the terrain of the region.

"I think we could be in the foothills of the Caucasus Mountains and that's the Black Sea," she said.

Alex shook his head. "That's on the other side of the earth from Calgary."

"Just a guess," she said. "But the terrain fits."

Alex looked through the binoculars to the west.

"I wish I knew my geography better but, yeah, the terrain does match up from what I remember," he said. "Still, it can't be. There are cities all along the Black Sea. Where are the airplanes, the railroads, the highways, the radio towers?"

"I don't know," she said.

Alex sat down. He got out the compass and started sketching in his notebook. The top of a larch was obscuring the easterly view so Emily moved to get a better look that way. To the northeast, the hills gave way to open plains. In the distance she saw a bison herd (perhaps the same one they had seen earlier). Part of the herd was running. Were those horses and riders chasing them?

"Alex. Quick. Bring the binoculars."

He came over and handed them to her. "What is it?"

She looked through the lenses. Yes, they were riders, too distant to get much detail but she could tell there were a dozen or so. They wore colorful clothing and appeared to be carrying lances.

"There are people down there. Riders chasing bison, look." She handed the binoculars to Alex, pointing out the direction.

"I'll be damned," he said. "They're hunting buffalo with spears. They're wearing pointed hats."

Emily unshouldered her scout bag and set it on the ground near the ledge. She folded her hoodie into a wad and set it on the bag.

"Here," she said. "I want to see if I can get a steadier view."

She set the binoculars on the hoodie, lay on her stomach and peered through them. It took a few seconds to get a fix on the riders. Tapping the knob she got as good a focus as she could and strained to make out what was going on.

The riders had separated a bison from the herd and were chasing it. A smaller rider was out ahead and galloped beside the animal shooting a bow. The bison slowed. Other riders caught up and threw spears into its flanks. Soon the animal stopped, teetered on its feet, and fell over. Emily relayed what she saw to Alex.

"Incredible," he said.

It didn't look as if the riders were wearing stirrups. Some of them had their feet pulled up along their horses' flanks. The colored tunics, red being most prominent, the pointed hats, the spears, shooting a bow from horseback -- the scene was ringing a bell in her head but her memory wasn't offering up anything.

~

Back at camp, she and Alex told the others what they had seen.

Regarding the body of water, Hank said: "I'm thinking it must be Lake Baikal. It's huge, almost as big as Lake Superior, and it's pretty remote."

Could be, Emily thought, she had no notion of Lake Baikal's geography.

"What about the people?" Nancy asked. "Should we try to catch up with them?"

"How far away do you think they were, Fred?" Hank asked.

"A couple of miles, at least," Emily said. "There's a lot of rough ground between us and them."

"They'd probably be long gone before we got there," Alex said.

"And we wouldn't make it before nightfall," Hank said. "Assuming we could find a way to get to them."

"Should we try to catch up with them tomorrow?" Nancy asked.

"Seems iffy to me," Alex said. "They're on horseback and we're walking. Plus we'd have to deal with lions and hyenas."

"Yeah, I say we stick to the trail," Hank said. "We're doing good on food and we're bound to run into someone pretty soon."

A sensible course, Emily thought, but something about the riders tugged at her imagination. Was it the old Emily's fondness for horses?

"Who are they?" Tim asked.

"Reenactors, maybe," Alex said.

"They could be indigenous people practicing their old traditions," Hank said.

It occurred to Emily that they were steppe nomads, like the Huns or the Mongols who roamed the plains from China to Europe. But the Huns and the Mongols used stirrups. Were these people something older?

He had been a military history buff and *he* often attended war-gaming conventions where there were guys who focused on ancient warfare. They would create their dioramas and paint their miniatures with loving detail, putting uncounted hours into being as precise and historically accurate as possible -- Greek phalanxes, Roman legions, Egyptian charioteers, and other types of armies. She remembered when *he* had kept an eye on one of the battles where a player had managed to outflank his opponent's Persian infantry with a force of light cavalry. The horsemen were colorfully painted. They wore pointed caps and their minimal saddles had no stirrups. Then she remembered. They were Scythians, the steppe nomads who predated the Huns by a thousand years, give or take a couple of centuries.

"Maybe we've gone back in time," Emily said.

"Don't talk like that," Nancy scolded.

Chapter 7 | Rescue

THE morning brought clear skies and a steady breeze. Emily, Nancy and Alex broke camp while Hank and Tim made a quick trip up to the peak. Everything was packed and ready when they returned.

"We didn't see any riders," Hank said.

"The view is freaking awesome," Tim said.

They hoisted their packs and set off. The trail kept its northwesterly direction for most of the morning then turned due north, winding its way up and over a ridge. The descent was longer than the climb and when they reached the bottom of the slope, the trail veered to the southwest, skirting a large, reedy swamp with massive willow trees growing here and there along the edges. Myriad birds sang and flitted about. The flies were ferocious and they were glad they had insect spray, although Emily hated the smell of it. She wondered if the places they passed were ever given names. She would call this place Willow Bog. It was eerily beautiful.

The trail turned due west again and went over a lower, less steep ridge that was covered with oaks. Coming down they emerged into a grassy valley. A small river meandered through it. The trail led up to its banks where they saw the remains of a wooden footbridge.

"Camp here?" Alex asked.

"Let's," Nancy said. "I like the smell of it after that swamp."

"It's a little early yet, but what the heck," Hank said.

~

The grass was green and lush. The valley would be a good place to let horses graze, Emily thought. In her mind, she named it Sweetgrass Valley. A gap in the ridges revealed tall mountains looming over the forest. She watched Tim rummage through his pack and pull out a pocket fishing rig.

"I'm going to try to catch something," he said.

"I'll get a spade. We can dig for worms or grubs," Alex said.

Emily, Nancy and Hank walked around to find a good spot to set up the tents. The ground rose mildly from the stream and plateaued about fifty paces away. They saw a small, conical structure. It was a kind of oven made of carefully set stones. Inside was a grill made of iron rods caked with rust.

"There must have been a village here," Hank said.

"It's a beautiful spot for one," Nancy said.

Emily stepped on something sticking up from the ground. She knelt down, brushed the grass aside and saw the charred remains of a log. She traced its length and found another one set at a right angle, the remnants of a small building. She told Nancy and Hank and they found others like it. Nancy found a copper pot coated with soot.

"A wildfire must have swept through here," Hank said.

Emily doubted it. She was looking at a charred skeleton lying face down, made almost invisible by the grass growing around it. The skull had a great cut in it as if struck by a heavy, sharp blade.

"What are you looking at?" Nancy asked, kneeling down beside her. "Oh ... oh my God."

"I think the village was pillaged then burned," Emily said.

~

Tim and Alex caught three trout which they cooked in the stove along with a few wild yams Hank had dug up. He also found some chickweed which they munched on as a kind of salad. The feast would have been a happier one except for the thought that the place had been the scene of violent death many years ago.

When night fell, they could hear the distant howl of wolves. But the howling was not the source of Emily's unease. The most dangerous creatures they were likely to meet walked on two legs.

~

Emily woke to Nancy caressing her thigh. Like every morning since the crash, she realized anew that she was now a woman.

Outside a thick mist covered the valley. Waiting for the sun to burn it off, they bathed in the river and cooked instant oatmeal over a fire. Nancy took the time to apply her makeup. She had slimmed down a little and, it seemed to Emily, looked more striking than ever. Her face was ruddier, her crow's feet had perhaps deepened, but she mellowed those with touches from her brush.

"I have a feeling boys and girls this is the day we get found," Nancy said, snapping her makeup case shut.

It was midmorning when they crossed the river and continued on. The trail followed the river the length of the valley and into the forest. After a couple of hours of walking, the slow current became rapids and plunged into a steep, narrow ravine. The trail turned away, due west, up a steep slope. The crest was not far and the downslope was much gentler. They moved through stands of huge beech trees. Not far beyond the bottom of the slope, the trail merged into a larger one. It was considerably wider and had parallel ruts along its course. To the right it headed northwest, to the left southeast. They paused, set down their packs and drank from their bottles.

"Encouraging," Alex said. "This trail looks like it gets used once in a while."

"Which way do we go?" Tim asked.

"Might as well go right and keep our general heading," Hank said. "We've got to be coming to something soon."

~

About a half an hour later, they entered a meadow. Nancy started hobbling and threw down her pack.

"Ow, ow, I've got a cramp," she said, grabbing her calf.

"Sit down," Emily said. "I'll see if I can massage it out."

Emily set Nancy's leg on the pack, pushed her toes toward her knee with one hand while rubbing her calf with the other. Nancy grimaced as she did so. After a few minutes, the cramp subsided.

"Thank you, dear," Nancy said. "You're a peach."

Emily heard something. A knot formed in her stomach.

"Someone's coming," she said. "I hear galloping."

They all stood at once, except Nancy who was putting her shoe back on.

"I'm not hearing anything," Hank said.

"You will," Emily said.

Then it was obvious -- the sound of hooves pounding the ground. Three riders emerged from the forest on the other side of the meadow.

"Oh, thank God," Nancy said. She had her shoe back on and ran toward the riders waving her hand.

"No, wait!" Emily shouted. She ran to catch up with her.

"Hello! Hello!" Nancy shouted to the riders. But as they neared, she stopped and held her tongue.

The lead rider raised his hand and all three reined to a stop. The horses snorted heavily through flared nostrils. The leader's hair was a shaggy, black mane that hung to his shoulders. His beard, streaked with gray, hung to his chest. He carried what looked like a short spear or javelin. A sword and a knife hung from a broad waist belt wrapped around a tunic made of hide. The appearance of the other two was similar though their beards weren't as long. They all had eyes on Nancy.

The leader grinned widely, revealing a less-than-full set of black teeth. His eyes squinted underneath thick eyebrows. He said something. The words were unintelligible but the tone was deep, coarse and menacing. He dismounted. He was shorter than Hank but powerfully built. He moved toward Nancy who was now blanched with fear.

One of the other riders spoke, looking back the way they had come, his tone one of concern.

"Shkatzee!" Was what the word the leader shouted sounded like. He approached slowly, drinking in Nancy's form, clutching the javelin in his right hand.

Hank and the others came running up. Hank had his hands out.

"Hey, we don't want any trouble," Hank said. "Our plane crashed and we're just trying to get home."

The man ignored him. He reached out with his left hand, which was soiled and sweaty, and touched Nancy's face. He grunted low words. The stench of him was withering.

Emily got between them and tried to push the man away with her walking stick. He grabbed her and flung her aside. She went sprawling to the ground. It surprised and bewildered her that she could be manhandled so easily.

"Hey motherfucker, leave her alone!" Tim yelled and rushed the wild-haired man.

The man pivoted quickly and thrust his javelin into Tim's chest. Tim looked astonished as he sank to his knees. The man tried to pull the javelin free but it was stuck.

Hank drew his knife and came at the man, more tentatively than he should have, Emily thought. The man took the opportunity to back away and draw his sword. It was a short, broad, double-edged blade that widened toward the end before angling to a sharp point. The man was in a good fighting stance, sword cocked at his hip. Hank was not. The man spoke goading words, gesturing for Hank to attack.

Don't duel him, Hank, she thought, you don't stand a chance. *His* experience with fighting had been more academic than actual but it was enough to know they were in a bad situation. The wild-haired man could kill them all.

Hank circled, his stance too open, too flatfooted, his knife too far extended. He should have been using his walking stick. It would have been a better weapon. The wild-haired man grinned. Emily knew that he knew that he could kill Hank at any time.

When the man's back was turned to her, Emily sprung to her feet and rushed him, trying to crack his head with her stick. He heard her, wheeled around and swatted her aside with his free hand. Emily's blow missed his head but connected with his shoulder.

"Ahh!" The man shouted.

With a roar, Hank charged the man like a linebacker. They both went to the ground, wrestling and trying to stab each other with their weapons.

Emily saw one of the other riders raise his javelin to throw. She hurled her stick at him. The rider ducked just as he was throwing and the javelin sailed high and into a bush. Emily unsheathed her puukko and charged the horseman, screaming wildly. The horse reared up and the rider struggled to stay mounted, backing into the other man's horse. Alex threw rocks at them. The other man yelled something and galloped off. The rider who had thrown the javelin had just regained control of his horse when Emily jabbed him in the thigh with her knife. The man yelped and galloped away.

~

Tim lay on his back, his legs pinned awkwardly beneath him. Emily could tell he was dead. The javelin had pierced his heart. The wild-haired man was dead, too, his tunic shredded and bloody. Hank was on his back, struggling to breath. Blood pooled under his legs. He had a gash in his side from the wild-haired man's sword and it looked like somehow the man had stabbed Hank in the groin. Nancy was kneeling over him. Alex was getting the first-aid kit.

"Hang in there, Hank. Stay with us," Nancy said.

Emily went over to him and held his hand.

"I'm sorry, Hank," she said.

Hank coughed, tried to smile.

"Don't worry, Fred. I'm glad you're okay."

Alex came with the trauma pack but was too late. Hank's eyes glazed over. He was dead.

~

Emily wept convulsively. She couldn't remember that *he* had ever felt like this. *He* had cried like a baby when his dog died, but this was different. She had only known Hank for a few days. Why did she feel so much grief? It seemed like a long time had gone by when Nancy put her arm around her.

"C'mon, honey," Nancy said. "We need you back with us."

Emily stood up. Nancy handed her a tissue and a water bottle. She could see that both Nancy and Alex had cried as well.

"This is just so fucking insane. It's too much," Alex said. "Hank and Tim killed by fucking swords and spears. Where the fuck are we and what do we do now?"

Emily heard horses' hooves again. The cadence was different and there were more of them. It occurred to her that they should run and hide, but she knew there wasn't time. Alex and Nancy soon heard them, too.

"Ah fuck," Alex said. "We're fucking dead."

He walked over to the wild-haired man's body and reached for the bloody sword.

"I'm going to fight this time," he said.

Through the trees on the far side of the meadow, Emily saw something red bobbing up and down.

"Don't," she said. "I think it will be different now."

Alex left the sword on the ground and returned to stand with Emily and Nancy.

"I hope to God you're right," he said.

About twenty riders emerged from the forest. They moved at a brisk canter in orderly formation. The lead rider wore a bronze helmet with a plume of red horse hair. He wore a leather cuirass over a white tunic bordered with red. A round shield hung from a saddle that seemed little more than a thick blanket. A sword hung from a shoulder sling. The other riders had on brown tunics bordered with blue. They wore bronze helmets and carried crescent-shaped shields and a couple of long javelins each. A few had swords.

As the formation neared, the leader shouted and the man riding beside him raised a javelin which had a red flag tied near the tip. In unison, the formation came to a halt. Nancy, again, drew their eyes.

The leader surveyed the scene, taking in the corpses, the packs on the ground, Alex, Emily and Nancy. He was clean shaven, his face a deep tan.

"Poyus essay? Milot!" he said, addressing Alex.

"I'm sorry, we don't understand you," Alex said.

The leader frowned, shouted back to his men. A rider broke rank and trotted forward. The rider addressed Alex and spoke words that sounded like a different language.

Alex shook his head. "Sorry."

The leader, who looked like he was in his thirties, shouted more orders. He looked at Alex, pointed at the wild-haired man's body, then pointed down the trail, saying something in a questioning tone.

"Ah, yes, yes," Alex said. "They went that way. Two riders." He held up two fingers.

The leader nodded. One of the men had dismounted and knelt beside the wild-haired man's body, putting his hand on its chest. He said something to the leader who nodded again. He barked orders and the formation cantered off.

Three men stayed behind. They dismounted and unloaded their gear which they set next to a tree. One of the men led the horses to a grassy area and let them graze. Another went about picking up stones and setting them in a clear spot. The third took off his helmet and approached Alex, Nancy and Emily.

"Geyan," he said and smiled.

His teeth were yellow but seemed healthy otherwise. He was one of the riders who wore a sword at his belt. He smelled of sweat and horse but nothing so awful as the wild-haired man. Emily figured she probably didn't smell much better. The man had brown hair and was about the same height as Alex but more muscular. He had an image of a stag tattooed to his shoulder.

He pointed to himself.

"Byon," he said. He then pointed to Alex and offered a hand.

"Alex," Alex said and shook the man's hand.

The man, Byon, repeated the routine with Emily then Nancy. He treated Nancy with more deference. Nancy smiled at him and he seemed to blush. He then went into a pantomime act of pointing and gesturing combined with words. The message became clear enough: They would wait here until the others returned.

"You know, I think he's speaking some kind of Greek," Nancy said. "My grandmother was from Greece and used to speak it to me when I was a child. It was our secret code. I wish I could remember more of it."

"I was thinking the same thing," Alex said. "I took a course in ancient Greek. I can read a little but can't speak it."

"Now what do we do? Nancy asked.

"Wait and see what happens," Emily said. "It feels like we're safe with them, for the time being at least."

"I hope they bring us back to their town or wherever they live," Nancy said. "We should be able to find a phone or something."

"I don't think phones have been invented yet," Emily said.

Chapter 8 | Deliverance

NANCY wouldn't believe it. Alex didn't say anything. They sat in the shade of a tree, looking despondent. We're they thinking of their loved ones? Nancy's 19-year-old daughter? Alex's young son and wife? Emily knew they would never see them again. She knew she would never see *his* family again, but she had known that for a while, probably since that morning she and Hank had looked out on the vast herd of bison.

Two of the men that were with them went to gather deadwood from the forest. Byon had arranged several rocks to form a fire pit. Emily went over to him. He was sitting and whittling a point onto the end of a stick that came to a "Y" at the other end. A similar stick lay beside him. Emily picked it up, sat down and whittled the end with her puukko, its sharp edge making quick work of the task.

"Emm-ee-lee," Byon said.

"Bi-on," she said back.

He indicated that he'd like to hold her knife. She gave it to him. He handled it a bit, sliced a strip of bark off his stick.

"Arista makhayra, pol aykameero," he said and handed the knife back.

The sticks would hold a spit over the fire pit. While Byon pressed them into the ground, Emily looked over the three javelins leaning against his saddle pack. Byon came over and picked one up.

"Akantee-ah," he said.

He pointed to a tree maybe 30 yards away and threw the javelin. It struck the trunk dead center about chest high.

"Good throw," Emily said. "Um, arista?"

"Arista," Byon said with a wry smile, pointing his thumb at himself.

Emily picked up one of the javelins.

"May I?" She asked.

Byon shrugged and nodded. Emily wound up and with all her might heaved the javelin at the tree. It barely flew ten feet and flopped awkwardly on the ground. Laughter erupted behind them. The other two men had returned with bundles of sticks. Byon struggled to keep a straight face. Shit, she thought, I threw it like a girl.

Byon retrieved the javelin, showed her how to hold it and demonstrated the proper motion. The key it seemed was not wrapping her thumb around the shaft but keeping it underneath. She threw it again. This time it sailed straight but still landed well short of the tree.

"Arista," Byon said.

He slapped her on the back, the force of which made her stumble forward. Byon became red-faced.

"Sygnumo," he said. "Emm-ee-lee."

"It's okay," she said, smiling, and slapped him on the shoulder.

~

Byon and the other men played games with their javelins. Emily watched intently. Byon won most of the time but clearly all three were experts. She was amazed at how far they could throw them, sixty yards maybe, she thought. They seemed to be speaking in yet another language as they jeered each other.

"Hey, I think someone's coming," Emily said.

Byon looked at her. She pointed to her ear then to the other side of the meadow where his squadron had come from. Quickly, Byon and the other two gathered up their javelins and put on their helmets. He motioned for Nancy and Alex to come to the fire pit. The men appeared ready for action but not overly concerned.

The noise grew louder and soon a column of footmen, two abreast, marched out of the forest. About forty of them, they wore helmets and brown tunics. Each carried a shield and three or four javelins and had satchels slung across their shoulders. Behind the soldiers came three wagons pulled by mules. A dozen unarmed men and a couple of teenage boys walked beside the wagons.

One horseman was with the group. He broke off from the column and rode to Byon. Someone blew a whistle and the column halted. The rider resembled the leader of the cavalry squadron except the plume on his helmet was orange, his hair was dark and his face bearded. Byon talked to him, motioning toward the corpses and then to Alex, Nancy and Emily. The rider shouted orders and the column broke up. Soon the meadow was a flurry of activity. The rider dismounted.

"Ah-lex, Nahn-see, Emm-ee-lee," Byon said as an introduction.

The horseman indicated his name was Cosmas. His eyes kept coming back to Nancy. He smiled; Nancy smiled back.

"Omorfa," the man said. "Nymphi? Prinkpia?"

Byon shrugged. "Poyus zerai," he said.

~

Cosmas walked to where the bodies were. He shouted orders and soon a few of the unarmed men -- dressed in simple flax tunics, leather caps and sandals -- came over. Two were carrying coarse blankets and one had a broad-bladed ax. Cosmas yanked the javelin from Tim's chest, threw it aside, then picked up Hank's knife. He examined it then put it into the sheath on Hank's belt. The men with the blankets wrapped Hank and Tim's bodies in them.

Cosmas took the ax and, with a precise stroke, severed the wild-haired man's head.

"Hydakoles enay nekros," he said.

One of the unarmed men put the head in a bag and carried it to a wagon. Others hauled the headless body into the forest.

"What are they going to do with Hank and Tim?" Nancy asked.

"I don't know," Alex said. "They're being treated respectfully. I'm sure it's clear Hank killed the wild man."

"With Emily's help," Nancy said. "If it weren't for her, we'd all be dead, or worse."

Soon many tents were up and campfires built. Emily, Nancy and Alex set up their own tents in a spot Byon pointed to.

"I bet those soldiers are Thracian peltasts, a kind of light infantry," Emily said. "Mercenaries most likely."

"Who are Thracians?" Nancy asked.

"A warrior people who lived in the area we'd know as Bulgaria," Emily said.

"I still can't believe it. We can't have gone back in time," Nancy said.

"If we have gone back in time, Emily, *when* do you think it might be?" Alex asked.

"Iron age but before stirrups," she said. "That puts us somewhere between 1500 B.C. and 500 A.D."

"That's just impossible," Nancy said.

~

As the sun set, the squadron of riders returned and two of them held up the heads of the wild-haired man's companions. The men in the camp cheered. The riders dismounted and the unarmed men tended to their horses. They must be slaves, Emily thought.

Emily, Alex and Nancy sat at a campfire and Byon sat with them. The man with the red-plumed helmet approached. Byon stood and made introductions like he had before. The officer's name was Callias.

Callias felt the fabric of their clothing. He kept a stern face as he did so but his eyes kept going back to Nancy. He felt the fabric of their packs and their tents. He murmured words to Byon. He spoke a few words to Nancy, his tone soft and reassuring. He issued a command to Byon and walked away.

Emily was hungry but suggested they hold off eating their own camp food.

"I don't think we want to show them too much," Emily said. "Even a ballpoint pen would seem magical to them. We don't want to come across as a supernatural threat."

"The one officer said 'nymphi,'" Nancy said. "Did he mean 'nymph,' I wonder."

"I think so," Alex said. "A nymph is a kind of sub-goddess. They may think our appearance here is the work of the gods."

"Maybe we should play that up," Nancy said.

"No," Emily said. "We shouldn't assume these people are less intelligent than we are. They'll see through any act sooner or later. The fact that Hank and Tim are dead already shows we're not immortal."

Byon studied them intently as they talked. What was he thinking, Emily wondered. His blue eyes were intelligent and curious. He was looking at Emily primarily now. It was an evaluative look, she thought, with what seemed like respect.

Three unarmed men carried over a steaming bronze pot, a large wine skin and several wooden bowls. They ladled a kind of barley gruel into larger bowls and handed them spoons. Beside them they placed smaller bowls and filled them with wine. The barley concoction was garlicky and had a minty undertaste. The wine was watery, tart and refreshing.

Several campfires burned throughout the meadow. The men talked and laughed and sometimes sang. Emily noticed sentries were posted around the perimeter. Was it standard procedure or were there enemies around? The general mood suggested the former. A few of the men held hands. The boys tended to and ate with the officers. After the meal, one of the teenagers sat next to Callias who stroked the boy's hair.

~

Later, in their tent, Nancy said, "I noticed you flirting with Byon."

"I wasn't flirting with him," Emily said.

"You might not think so but he might. You should be careful. You're more attractive than you think."

"I don't think Byon is dangerous that way."

"He is well behaved," Nancy said. "I think the officer knew what he was doing when he chose him as our watchdog. But the best of men can turn ugly at times. I know."

~

Emily woke to commotion outside. She stuck her head out of the tent to look around. There was only the dimmest of morning twilight. The meadow was alive with men packing and getting ready to move out. She nudged Nancy.

"We'd better get up," she said. "Looks like we're going soon."

For breakfast they were served flatbread with a bowl of diluted wine. Emily noticed that others would soften the bread by dipping it into the wine. After eating, Emily, Nancy and Alex packed up their tents and awaited further instructions.

"What's going to happen to us?" Nancy asked. "I've never felt so uncertain."

"I won't deny it. I'm pretty much scared shitless," Alex said.

"I'm scared too," Emily said. "Maybe we should pretend we're anthropologists and try to learn what we can about them, especially their language. It'll keep our minds off our fear."

Byon trotted over on his horse. He motioned for them to pick up their things and follow. Nancy and Alex carried Hank and Tim's packs in their arms. They followed Byon to one of the wagons where a couple of unarmed men loaded the packs into it. Hank and Tim's corpses were in it, too. Byon indicated that Nancy should sit on the wagon beside the driver. She hesitated.

"It might be a good idea," Alex said. "If they think you're nobility, we should probably go along with it for now."

The driver said something and nodded solemnly at Nancy.

"Thank you. You're very kind," Nancy said.

~

The column moved out, following the trail west then southwest. Most of the riders were up front. The infantry was split into two groups, one in the middle of the column and one at the rear. Nancy's wagon was near the front, in sight of Callias, the red-plumed leader. Alex and Emily walked behind the wagon with Byon nearby on his horse.

Some of the footmen ranged out along the flanks. Emily was sure riders scouted ahead. The column would be difficult to ambush.

"Why did Hank call you 'Fred?'" Alex asked her.

"Because when he first asked me my name, that's what I told him," Emily said.

"Why'd you tell him that?"

"Because I was Fred Harper before the crash."

"Okay. I don't get it."

"Neither do I. Basically, before the crash, I was a man. When I woke up afterward, I was a woman. My mind or memories or thought patterns -- whatever it all is that makes you think you're still you when you wake up in the morning -- ended up in the body of the woman sitting next to me."

"That's crazy."

"I thought so, too, but I ruled that out, at least to my own satisfaction."

"How?"

"A few things. Maybe the most convincing to someone other than myself was the lock on the rifle. Fred Harper and Emily Svoboda did not know each other, only exchanged a few words on the flight, yet I knew the combination of that lock. I know it's not really proof to you. I doubt I could ever prove it so a skeptic would believe it."

"Does Nancy know?"

"Yes."

"Does she believe it?"

"Yes."

"What about Hank?"

"He knew and I think he believed it after a while."

"But it's impossible."

"So is surviving unscathed after getting sucked out of an airplane, so is ending up on the other side of the world, so is going back in time."

"Do you know how it happened?" Alex asked.

"No, but I'm guessing it had something to do with the music we listened to," Emily said.

"Music?"

Emily described as best she could what happened on the flight.

"Quite a story," Alex said. "You'll forgive me if I remain skeptical."

"You're forgiven. I would be too."

"Should I call you 'Fred?'"

"You can if you want. But in trying to come to terms with the situation, I've accepted that 'Emily' is a more fitting name. It'd be kind of a denial to continue to think of myself as 'Fred.'"

"Wow, what a mind-blower. But it does explain some things when I think about it."

~

The column moved steadily along through deep forest. Without having to carry her pack, the going was easier than previous days. Alex went up to the front of the wagon to keep Nancy company. Emily walked beside Byon's horse. It was a dark brown gelding with white stripe on its forehead and what looked like a white sock on its right rear leg. She looked up at him.

"Geyan," she said.

"Geyan."

She pointed to the horse. "What's the word for horse?"

"Elogo," Byon said.

Was it the horse's name or was it the word for horse? She wasn't sure.

She pointed at her leg, at the horse's leg and at his leg.

"Pode," he said.

She pointed at him.

"Andros."

She pointed at herself.

"Koritsa."

Did he mean girl or woman? She pointed at Alex.

"Andros."

She pointed at Nancy.

"Gynika."

She pointed at herself again.

"Koritsa."

Damn, she thought, he considers me a girl. She continued the point-and-name game. She pantomimed various actions to get the words for "walk," "run," "over," "under" and so forth. She learned words for "tree," "dirt," "leaf," and several others. When she'd had enough she pointed to the things and repeated the words back to Byon. He patiently confirmed or corrected her. She indicated she needed to stop and they walked in silence for a time.

Byon broke into a song, one with a simple melody, a child's song. She was able to catch a couple of the words but most she didn't understand.

The horse jumped over the something
The girl something something something
The man did something else

Byon's voice was pleasing but gruff. He gestured with his hands for her to sing along. She hesitated. It seemed so silly, but it would be a good way to get a feel for the language even if she didn't understand the words. Byon sang a line and pointed to her. She sang the line back. He sang another line and she repeated it. As she did this, her singing became more confident and louder.

He couldn't carry a tune if it had a handle, she thought, but she could actually sing, not a diva's voice, but clear and sandy sweet. It was exhilarating and, at the same time, disturbing. It was like announcing to the world she was female.

Some of the men joined Byon when he sang his lines then listened eagerly for her to repeat them. The song told a story that felt like maybe a Little Red Riding Hood theme. On the last line, Byon held the last note. She repeated the line and held the last note as long as she could until her voice broke into falsetto. The song was over. Everyone seemed pleased. She felt herself blushing intensely.

~

When the sun was directly overhead, the column stopped for lunch -- pickled meat, dried fruit and more watery wine. The rest period was short and they soon moved on, the trail winding upward into large hills. The oaks were replaced with larches and, when they got higher, with scrubby junipers.

At one point the trail became particularly rocky and men had to help push the wagons along. The riders dismounted and led their horses. Nancy got off to lighten the load and offered to help but they wouldn't let her. They were happy to have Alex pitch in, however.

The trail, more of a road now, turned northwest and descended into a ravine which widened into a treeless stretch of rocky ground, with grass and brush popping up in patches. Emily saw a pack of wolves that ran off when the column approached. Then she saw several dead men and dead horses. A battle had been fought here not long ago. The bodies resembled the men they had first encountered. Their clothes were crude, their hair long and unkempt. She remembered the word the orange-plumed officer, had used when he had cut off the wild-haired man's head.

"Hydakoles?" she said to Byon, who was still leading his horse.

He said something she didn't understand but the tone affirmed her question. Hydakoles, she thought, must have been a bandit leader. She guessed the point of the expedition had been to hunt his band down. It amused her to think that they couldn't have known that a group of castaways from the 21st century would end up killing Hydakoles.

Emily saw that Callias had remounted and was now riding beside the wagon Nancy sat in. They were exchanging words. Nancy was trying some of her childhood Greek on him. Emily couldn't tell how well it was going but they smiled at each other and laughed from time to time. Now who was doing the flirting?

By late afternoon the flanking ridges had spread apart to form a long valley. She saw smoke rising in the distance but it caused no alarm. They passed through fields of wheat and barley and came to a village. She guessed there were fifty or more structures -- small, circular dwellings made of stone and wood with grass roofs.

A group of men with spears assembled. Smaller and leaner than the soldiers in the column, they wore simple tunics of undyed flax, but no helmets, shields or armor. They were led by an old man wearing a leopard-skin tunic. He had a necklace of animal's teeth and wore several bracelets, some bronze, some carved of bone or horn.

The two plumed officers rode out to meet them. Callias cried out several words ("Hydakoles" among them). The men of the village cheered. Callias kept talking and pointed back to the wagon Nancy sat on. There were wide-eyed ahhs and hmms from the men.

The old man wearing the leopard skin walked quickly by the officers and horsemen to Nancy's wagon. With a furrowed brow and without any word of introduction, he felt her dress, took one of her hands, looked it over, touched her hair, sniffed it, sniffed her bosom.

"Pleased to meet you too," Nancy said.

"Ah tarra gotai om kassi so," the old man said. The language wasn't Greek.

He went back to the spearmen and spoke to them. They cheered again.

"Maybe they think she's a good omen," Emily said.

"Let's hope they're not cheering because they think she'll taste good," Alex said.

~

The company made camp outside the village. Byon pointed to where Alex, Nancy and Emily should pitch their tents, a spot close to the officers' tents, which were large and trimmed with bright colors. The village men brought several heavy, ceramic jugs and two pigs. The pigs were promptly slaughtered, gutted and skinned. There would be meat tonight, Emily thought.

It was well after dark before the feast was ready. Nancy, Alex and Emily sat with the officers, the boys, and a few others, including Byon. Emily wished she could understand what they talked about. They were served rib meat in broad bowls mixed with various greens and a kind of tuber. The meal was good if not overly flavorful. Emily ate as much as she could. In the wine bowls they were served thick, dark beer. It was spiced with fennel, she thought, and something else.

Soon the mood turned merry and the men talked loudly and laughed. The beer was good, especially the second bowl. Emily was feeling flushed and reminded herself that she wouldn't be able to handle as much alcohol as *he* could. Nancy put a hand on her shoulder.

"You sure made a spectacle of yourself this morning," she said. "You have a pretty singing voice."

"It was a surprise to me," Emily said. "It felt ... weird."

Nancy gave her a gentle push. "You are who you are now. Better get used to it."

Who was she, she wondered. Perhaps a better question was who was she becoming. She had no idea. She didn't even know what her choices were.

The old man with the leopard-skin tunic appeared at the campfire with two other village men. Emily had seen no women. They must be hiding in the houses. Was that the fate of women in this age, to be kept out of sight when strangers were around?

Callias invited the village men to sit and talk. The tone was business-like at first but, when they seemed to come to an agreement on things, the talking became more convivial. Callias started telling a story, referring to Nancy, Alex and Emily.

"He's talking about the fight in the meadow and how Hank and whats-his-name killed each other," Nancy whispered.

"Hydakoles," Emily said.

"I want to set the record straight," Nancy said. "Hank wasn't the only hero."

Nancy stood up.

"I don't know if it's such a good idea," Alex said.

Nancy ignored him and the men's eyes became fixed on her. She started speaking in her limited Greek and going into a kind of charades act. Emily couldn't tell if the others understood, but they paid rapt attention regardless. Nancy used her deepest voice and exaggerated gestures as if telling a story to children. She grabbed Byon's hand and pulled him up to use as a prop, indicating he was to play Hydakoles. She emphasized Emily's role and showed how she had struck Hydokoles with a stick and stabbed another man in the leg. The performance caught the attention of the whole camp and most everybody had gathered around.

"And that's just how it happened," Nancy concluded.

She bowed and sat back down.

"Talk about a spectacle," Emily whispered.

Callias nodded slowly. Whatever he understood must have rung true for him. Then he clapped and everyone else joined in. The act was over and the gathering broke up. Byon stood before Emily and squeezed her shoulders with his strong hands.

"Gonnayo koritsa," he said.

~

In the morning, Nancy and Emily had hangovers. They gulped down aspirin tablets with water from their bottles.

"What was in that beer?" Nancy asked. "I really made a fool of myself, didn't I?"

"Yes, but thank you," Emily said.

The company wasted no time and moved out as soon as the sun was rising. The road continued through the valley, following the course of a river on their left. About mid-morning they came to another village, very similar to the one they had left. The column stopped while the officers talked with the village men. The news was good, Hydakoles was dead, and the column moved on.

The road branched and they turned left, heading southwest. The road came to a wide, shallow part of the river and they forded it. The water came up to Emily's knees. It was slow, heavy work getting the wagons across. On the other side, after a quick lunch, they continued into the hills. The forest was mostly larches with a few maple stands here and there. Emily saw an apple tree, its fruit small and green.

Emily and Byon continued their language game and Alex joined in. Byon sang another song, this one sadder and more complicated. Emily sang her lines as best she could. No one seemed to mind when she struggled with the words. Nancy and Callias continued their attempts at conversation.

Near the top of a ridge, a peak jutted above the trees. Callias ordered the column to stop. He dismounted and helped Nancy down from the wagon. He signaled for Alex and Emily to join them and led them up a deep water-cut formed in sandstone. Byon followed. At the peak, Emily got her second view of the sea. They were much closer now. It was Nancy's first view.

"Oh my god ...," was all she could say.

It seemed like an infinity of blue bordered by rugged hills and even taller mountains that loomed to the southeast. Looking down at the closest part of the slope, not more than a few miles, they could see a river flowing into a natural harbor framed by a curving peninsula and two small islands. Straddling the mouth of the river was a town. Two wooden ships lay at anchor in its harbor.

Callias stretched out his hand.

"Artemios," he said. "Artemios sta Euxine."

Chapter 9 | Strangers

ALEX broke down and wept. Callias and Byon looked befuddled. Emily put her arm around Alex. It was some time before he regained a degree of composure.

"I'm sorry," Alex said. "It just hit me. I mean, I already knew, but now I really know. We can't go home. Home doesn't even exist. Ah, God, Emily, what are we going to do? You were right. 'Euxine' is the ancient Greek name for the Black Sea. When he said it, I felt like I was poleaxed."

Emily had no words to console him with. She just held him. Nancy sat on a rock and stared out at the sea. Callias indicated they should be getting back to the column. As they headed down, he put a hand on Alex's shoulder and spoke in a comforting tone, as if to say, "You're safe with us."

~

The column descended into an area of low, rolling hills where much of the ground was cultivated with grain and orchards. They passed several farm houses made of wood and stone. The houses were square and larger than the huts of the villages. Most had thatched roofs, a few had tile.

People lined up along the road. One of the peltasts fetched Hydakoles' head from its bag and mounted it on a spear. The onlookers were mostly men. Many wore felt hats with wide brims.

The road converged with one from the northeast then the column made a long turn around a big hill and headed toward the town. Emily could see the outlines of a stone structure built on a wooded plateau about half way to the top of the hill. The structure had a peaked roof tiled with ceramic shingles. Not much further on, and also on the left, was a large two-story house. The walls were stone at the first level and wood at the second. Its tiled roof slanted one way. A stone wall defined a large yard around it and there were several outbuildings.

Another road that stretched to the northwest converged on theirs. The town's ramparts were made of split logs and rose up perhaps twelve feet. The wall had square towers spaced about 50 yards apart, one straddled a river that flowed in from the southeast. Callias shouted and the soldiers formed themselves into orderly ranks. They marched or trotted smartly toward the open gate. Before the gate, on the right side of the road, stood a tall, elaborately carved pole. It had wings at the top and two serpents coiling up its height, one painted red, the other green.

Guarding the gate were two soldiers holding long spears, carrying large, round shields, and armored with bronze breastplates and greaves. Their full-faced helmets had orange crests of painted horse-hair. Their arms and legs rippled with well-developed muscles. Hoplites, Emily thought. Depending on just when they were, hoplites could be the most formidable fighting men on earth. A few hundred of them held off a Persian army of many thousands for days at Thermopylae. The sight of them made Emily want to be a man again.

The column entered a wide compound that appeared to be a military marshalling yard. There were stables and long wooden buildings that looked like barracks. There was a broad, single-level stone building and near it were two massive stacks billowing smoke. Emily could hear the clanking of metal on metal. Callias called for a halt. He and Cosmas dismounted.

A stout man strode toward the officers. He wore a white tunic bordered with red and carried a sword in a wooden scabbard. Bald with a gray beard, he looked a little like Bob except he had powerful limbs and a ruddy complexion. Two younger men followed in his wake. By the way Callias addressed him, it was clear that the bald man was the senior officer. They talked at length while the soldiers stayed at attention.

Callias turned and barked orders to the foot soldiers who dispersed and headed for the barracks. Callias motioned for Nancy, Alex and Emily to come forward. Two slaves removed their backpacks from the wagon and set them on the ground while another assisted Nancy down from her seat.

Nancy took Emily's hand and squeezed as they approached the officers. The bald man looked them over slowly, betraying no emotion. He waved Byon over and asked something. Byon announced their names. The bald man continued to scrutinize them. Finally he spoke.

"I am Agathon. Welcome to Artemios" is what Emily gathered he'd said along with other words she didn't understand.

Agathon shook hands with each of them, smiling as he did so.

~

Apparently they needed to wait. Slaves brought stools to sit on and refreshments -- dried fruit, nuts and wine. The riders under Callias' command dismounted, brushed their horses and straightened their gear.

The afternoon sun was casting long shadows when Agathon returned, wearing a red, hoodless cloak. The party formed into a procession with Agathon at the head, flanked by two hoplites. Nancy, Emily and Alex walked behind them, followed by Callias and his troop of horsemen, Hydakoles' head again held high.

They crossed a sturdy wooden bridge with stone foundations and entered the city proper. The road was paved with stones and went through an open area with closed up tents and stalls that Emily supposed must be a marketplace. From there an intersecting road headed toward the harbor. The street they were on wound its way up a gradual slope, passing buildings that looked like artisans' shops. People lining the street cheered and waved. Curious eyes gazed at the strange trio that walked among the soldiers.

"I wish I'd had a chance to clean up," Nancy said.

"You wouldn't want to dazzle them too much," Alex said. "You might cause a riot."

All the buildings looked new and several were under construction. They passed through a residential area of modest houses. Radiating from the road were narrow avenues that went into dense neighborhoods. They were walking on the peninsula they had seen from the hilltop. The houses got bigger as they went, many enclosed small courtyards.

The street ended at a very large, two-story house. Two long, rectangular wings defined a courtyard that was sheltered from view by a stone wall. The first-floor walls were stone and the second floor walls were made of wood stained a light brown. The tiled roofs slanted toward the courtyard. Broad stone steps led up to the gate. The air was cool and fresh with a breeze blowing in from the sea.

A soldier in the column blew a horn. After a few moments, the gate opened and a man and a woman appeared. The woman had dark hair worn in braided strands that hung about her shoulders. She wore a flowing white gown with a gilded belt and a blue cloak. Her eyes were brown and flanked by deep wrinkles. Emily guessed she was in her fifties. She seemed healthy and was pleasing to look at. The man didn't look so healthy. He was older and gray-haired. He wore a generous white robe and burgundy cloak. One of his arms was exposed and Emily could see sores on it.

Agathon spoke in a loud, commanding tone so everyone who had gathered could hear. It was clear he was talking of Hydakoles' death. Then he referred to Nancy, Alex and Emily. The gray-haired man replied with a short speech of his own. A congratulatory one, Emily assumed.

The man and the woman walked down the steps and greeted the newcomers. Their names were Philocrates and Berenike. Berenike bade them to come inside. As they walked through the gate, Emily looked back and saw Byon on his horse. He was looking at her.

~

Philocrates, Agathon and two slaves carrying the backpacks followed them in. Someone shut the gate and the riders clomped off.

The courtyard was spacious and floored with colored stones. On the front end, there were two large cisterns to collect rainwater flowing from the roof. Two garden plots were alive with flowering plants. A tree grew in the center of the courtyard. An ash, Emily thought. Near it were two rectangular tables with benches.

The slave carrying Alex's pack led him away to the north wing. A woman, about the same age as Berenike but dressed in a plain flax gown, led Nancy and Emily up a stairway and into a bedroom on the second level of the south wing. It had a bed, roughly queen-sized, a table, a large rug, and two chairs. Its window was shuddered. A slave set their packs down in the back of the room.

"I guess this is where our new life begins," Nancy said. "What I wouldn't give for a hot shower."

The woman in the plain dress introduced herself as Gaina. She spoke words they couldn't understand then motioned for them to follow her again. She led them to a back stair descending to the rear part of the house that connected the two wings. They came to a room with a large wooden tub in it. There were tables and chairs and poles with pegs to hang clothes and towels. A plump, teenage girl entered, carrying a large jug with steam rising from it. She poured its hot water into the tub.

"How about a hot bath instead?" Emily asked.

"I'll take it."

Gaina issued orders to the plump girl and left the room. The plump girl said her name was Hagne and she nodded toward the tub. Nancy and Emily took off their clothes, hung them on pegs and climbed in. The warm water felt heavenly. Hagne handed them a sponge, set a ceramic bottle on a ledge within reach, and left the room.

"Only one sponge," Nancy said. "If you wash me, I'll wash you."

"Deal," Emily said.

Emily was sponging Nancy's back when Hagne brought in another jug of hot water.

"Thank you, darling," Nancy said.

Hagne smiled then left the room again. After washing each other, they sat back and relaxed, realizing just how tired they were.

"How long has it been since the crash?" Nancy asked. "I've lost track."

"This is the tenth day," Emily said. "Our sixth day of traveling."

"We must have gone a hundred miles."

"Not that far, I don't think, but plenty far."

"I wonder what they're going to do with us?" Nancy asked.

"Probably try to figure out who we are, then decide," Emily said.

"They have slaves. That scares me."

"Me too."

∼

They got out of the tub and dried themselves with linen cloths that served as towels. The bottle by the bathtub had liquid in it that smelled like lavender. Nancy rubbed some on herself.

"You should too," she said.

Reluctantly, Emily did so. As she was applying the liquid, she looked at the pegs where they had hung their clothes.

"They're gone. Our clothes are gone," she said.

Her stomach knotted. Her puukko! She was relieved to see it on the table.

"Well, we can't traipse around naked," Nancy said.

Hagne returned carrying a bundle of garments.

"Where are our clothes?" Nancy asked, pointing to the pegs. She asked again using her childhood Greek.

Hagne answered and made rubbing motions with her hand.

"They're being washed, I guess," Emily said. "Can't blame them. They had to have been pretty ripe."

Hagne laid the garments on the table. For Emily, there was a simple tunic dress, similar to what Hagne wore except that it was died a pale blue and had a yellow stripe near the hem. She also was given a short cloak or shawl made of thin, gray wool. Nancy was given a long white gown with a red cloak.

"I think they call this a chiton," Nancy said when she held up her gown.

Hagne helped Nancy put on the garments. Emily's clothes were quite simple. The tunic was sleeveless and hung just below her calves. She cinched it with an yellow cloth belt after sliding her knife onto it. The belt had a felt pouch to hold things.

Nancy's clothes were more elaborate and the ensemble was put together with a lot of folding. Hagne talked while she did so, clearly wanting them both to pay attention to how it was done.

"You look cute," Nancy said to Emily.

"Thanks," Emily said dryly.

"How do I look?" Nancy asked.

"Like a goddess, of course," Emily said.

They had been given no shoes or sandals. It was clear to Emily that they thought of her as subordinate to Nancy. Was it that they thought she was just a girl? A handmaiden? A slave? She didn't want to be cast as a servant, but what could she do?

Hagne led them out to the courtyard where Alex sat at one of the tables. The sun had set and four torches were lit around the table. Alex wore a man's tunic, similar to what Agathon had been wearing.

"Holy cow, Nancy, you wear it well," Alex said.

Nancy blushed. "Could I launch a thousand ships?"

"Five hundred, at least," Alex said.

They were fed a meal of sweetmeats, bread, grapes, plums and wine. Berenike came out and sat down. They thanked her for the meal and clothes as best they could. Berenike tried to communicate something to them. About all Emily could discern was that there would be someone coming to help them learn Greek. Berenike bade them good night and went up the stairs.

~

Alex: "Any thoughts, Emily, about where we are or when we are?"

Emily: "This must be a Greek colony. A new one by the look of it. I know the Greeks colonized the southern coast pretty early and the north coast later on. I'm guessing we're before the Roman period but that still leaves us between 700 and 200 B.C."

Alex: "That pole outside the town's gate is a caduceus. If I remember right, they're associated with Hermes and represent trade and negotiation."

Emily: "That makes sense. I think the colonies were more for trade than conquest."

Alex: "Maybe that's why they're treating us so well."

Emily: "I suppose they might think we're from a distant land or kingdom and they want to establish good relations. I bet our clothes, our packs, our shoes, even our water bottles make them think we have desirable things to trade."

Nancy: "What happens when they realize we have no country they can trade with? They won't make us slaves, will they?"

Emily: "I don't know. If they've accepted us as guests, I don't think they could honorably turn us into slaves. We did kill one of their enemies. That should count for something."

Emily's feet were getting cold. She pulled them up and sat cross-legged on the bench.

Alex: "And we have knowledge we can parley. You mentioned they don't use stirrups. We could invent stirrups. Metallurgy isn't my specialty, but I'm sure I could help them make better steel for weapons and tools."

Emily: "Or a compass. Could you fashion a compass?"

Alex: "Yes, that would be pretty straight forward. And I could teach them math techniques, like calculus, which would vault them ahead centuries."

Emily's mind began to spin with the possibilities.

Nancy: "Should we do that? Wouldn't we be changing history? Wouldn't it change our time?"

Alex: "I doubt it. It's good fodder for science fiction but I don't think time works like that. I'm not a theoretical guy but I try to stay on top of current thinking. In quantum mechanics there's a lot of weird stuff that goes on that's difficult to explain like wave-particle duality and Heisenberg uncertainty. One explanation for it all is called the Many Worlds Interpretation.

"The implication is that the universe contains all that's possible, past, present and future. When we perceive ourselves moving through time, we perceive only one line of possibility. But, according to Many Worlds, all lines of possibility exist. There's a 'world,' so to speak, for each line, and the worlds don't interact with each other, generally. Pretty much by necessity we have to be on a different line now. Our line going forward won't affect the one we left."

Emily: "It seems like there must be a lot of worlds."

Alex: "Yes, many worlds."

Nancy: "Okay, fellas, this is all over my head."

Emily: "I suspect Alex is right. Our actions now won't affect people back home. And if they did, the damage may already be done. We killed Hydakoles. If we hadn't, he might have gotten away. He could have gone on to kill other people, people who now will live. What impact does that have?"

Alex: "Good point. I didn't think about that. We're already in for a penny."

Nancy: "It still doesn't seem right to me. Wouldn't we be tampering with these people's natural development?"

A not-quite full moon illuminated wispy clouds in the night sky. Nancy poured more wine into their bowls. It was sweeter and richer than the wine they drank while traveling with the column.

Emily: "Maybe Nancy's right. Maybe it's a question of ethics, not physics. Should we really interfere?"

Nancy: "We should probably turn in. I hate to think we're keeping these people up with our talking."

Alex: "Okay, perhaps we shouldn't start any technological revolutions. Let's just consider it our ace in the hole if things get dicey."

Emily: "Fair enough."

Emily wondered if Alex -- an engineer, a builder -- would be able to help himself. She wondered if she could.

Chapter 10 | Greek Lessons

EMILY opened the shutters and morning sunlight poured into the bedroom. The view was to the southeast. They were at the end of the peninsula and the house was situated near cliffs that overlooked the sea. Beyond the town was a broad beach. Distant mountains reached skyward. The other side of the house must overlook the harbor, she thought. In the backyard smoke rose from a hemispherical stone structure. She could smell bread baking.

The bed had been surprisingly comfortable. At some point, a small bed had been brought in -- for her, apparently -- but she had slept with Nancy on the big one. The mattress was like a futon and had linen sheets and feather pillows. It felt good after sleeping for days on hard ground. Emily ruffled the sheets on the small bed to keep up appearances. She didn't think the ancient Greeks were too shy about homosexuality but she didn't want to push her luck.

She fetched toilet paper from her pack and used the chamber pot. When she finished, she covered it with its wooden lid. She washed her hands in a large pot filled with water that served as a basin. She wetted her hair and combed it. Nancy got up and went through the same routine.

"We should shave our legs before we turn into wild women," she said.

"I'm guessing the natives don't," Emily said. "Why should we bother?"

She put her fingers to the smooth skin of her face. That was one thing she no longer had to worry about -- shaving every day. She put on her tunic-dress and cloak. She slipped the puukko onto her belt. If she always wore it, she thought, they would think it was normal for her. Into the pouch she put the canister of pepper-spray and a wash cloth.

Nancy was struggling to get her gown arranged when Hagne knocked and entered with a tray of food and pitcher of wine. She set the items down and helped Nancy. She indicated that Emily should help, too, so she did.

The small table had a polished bronze mirror on it, oval and about two feet long. Nancy primped in front of it. The reflection was surprisingly clear.

"All dressed and ready to go. What do we do now?" Emily asked.

The question was answered shortly after they ate breakfast. Emily was brushing her teeth when Gaina came to the door. She beckoned Nancy and Emily to follow her and led them to the courtyard. Alex was sitting on one of the tables, looking uncomfortable in his Greek tunic. Berenike and another woman were with him.

"Kolamara," Berenike said.

Berenike introduced Nancy and Emily to the other woman who rose to her feet. Her name was Kallisto. She was tall, nearly as tall as Nancy, and wore a simple brown chiton. She was thin in contrast to Berenike's plumpness and had light brown skin. Her dark hair hung long in intricately woven braids. She wore a light blue cloak similar to Emily's. On her head was a felt hat of deep blue with a rim of twisted cloth colored green and red. Hanging from her neck was a gold pendant shaped like a crescent moon with a blue stone set in its widest part.

Kallisto's face was angular with deep-set brown eyes. She greeted them each with a smile and shook their hands with both of hers -- first Alex, then Nancy. She lingered on Emily. Crow's feet betrayed her age but didn't diminish her beauty.

She released Emily's hand and started talking, using well-practiced gestures. It became clear that her purpose was to learn how to communicate with them. They all sat down and Kallisto spoke phrases from a dozen different languages, apparently hoping they might understand one of them. They didn't.

Kallisto seemed to resign herself to the fact that they would have to do this the hard way. A male slave brought over a broad but shallow wooden box and set it on the table. The box had sand in it along with a dowel and a little rake. Kallisto used it to draw pictures and give the appropriate words for the images. She also asked for the English words.

She used gestures and pantomime, spoke phrases and had them repeat them back to her. Emily felt like she was in kindergarten. Kallisto's teaching skills were remarkable as was her retention of English words. She was a master of languages, Emily figured, and a master of teaching and learning them.

While they were engaged learning Greek, Berenike, Gaina and Hagne sat at the other table cutting and sewing bits of cloth, for what purpose Emily couldn't tell. At noon, a man was let into the gate. He wore a simple brown robe with a hemp belt and carried a lyre. Kallisto embraced him and introduced him as her husband, Nikanor.

Three ladies also came through the gate. Berenike greeted them and they wore clothing similar to hers. One was about Berenike's age, the other two were younger. Berenike introduced them to Alex, Nancy and Emily. They did their best to greet the ladies with their newly learned phrases.

The tables were cleared and lunch brought out. After eating, they were served wine and Nikanor strummed a few notes on his lyre then began speaking in verses. Emily couldn't make out much of it but she thought the story had something to do with Persephone, the goddess doomed to be Hades' wife. Nikanor had a long, salt-and-pepper beard and a deep voice that entranced Emily even though she didn't understand what he said.

He finished and everyone clapped. Kallisto said goodbye, indicating that her lessons would resume tomorrow. Nikanor stayed, helping himself to more wine.

~

Agathon and several men came through the gate. They were unarmed but wore fine tunics and cloaks. Philocrates emerged to meet them.

The slaves scurried to clear the tables. Berenike stood and indicated to Nancy and Emily that they should follow her. It was time for the women to make themselves absent. Alex, however, could stay.

Emily was beset with a strong feeling that her place was with the men. She yearned for that camaraderie, that easy rapport *he* had had with *his* male friends and acquaintances. She felt deprived of something she could no longer have as she was ushered into a richly furnished room with the other women.

The shutters of the room's two windows were open, allowing the breeze to come in and offering a view of the sea. The room had patterned rugs on the stone floor, two divans, chairs and pillows. In the corners were large black and orange vases with figures and scenes painted on them. On one end of the room was a loom. A pair of slaves brought in a box filled with raw wool. From a chest, the women retrieved spindle whorls. They sat and spun thread while they talked. One of the younger women offered to show Emily how to do it. The other young woman showed Nancy. Berenike and the older woman talked between themselves.

Emily's efforts were clumsy at first but she started to get the hang of it. Once a certain length of thread was created, they would spool it neatly on a dowel. She presumed the thread would later be worked into fabric on the loom. It was a laborious process but it did pass the time. The women seemed to enjoy it as they chatted.

She worked out that this room was called the gynaeceum and men were not allowed in. They had their own rooms, called androns, where women were forbidden to go.

~

That evening Alex, Nancy and Emily were served supper in the courtyard and left to themselves except for a slave who tended to them. It was a welcome break from the awkwardness of being with people you could not converse with except for the simplest expressions. The main course was fish served on ceramic plates with sea creatures painted on them. The plates were indented at their centers and the little bowls thus formed served as containers for sauce. The sauce was mustardy and tasty.

Alex had had the more interesting afternoon, Emily thought. While Philocrates, Agathon and the other men talked business, Nikanor, the storyteller, took Alex for a tour of the city.

"The market was open," Alex said, "and filled with goods -- rugs, cloth, jewelry, tools, weapons, pottery, knick-knacks. If I'd had money or something to trade, I'd have bought presents."

"Did you see the ships?" Emily asked.

"Yes, we went to the pier," Alex said. "The ships are amazing. We saw one arrive. It was narrow and sleek and glided on the water. It had a sail up until it reached the harbor then they switched to oars.

"It looks like they trade slaves here, too. It's pretty disturbing. I saw one being punished. They put him over a barrel and beat the back of his legs with a rod."

"That's terrible," Nancy said.

Berenike and Philocrates joined them for an after-dinner drink. They exchanged pleasantries as best they could. From small, ceramic cups, they drank a thick, undiluted wine spiced with fennel. Using simple words and gestures, Berenike conveyed that tomorrow they would bury Hank and Tim and there would be a ceremony. Philocrates started coughing and had trouble controlling it. He excused himself and Berenike went with him.

"I think he has tuberculosis," Nancy said.

"I bet we could clear it up," Alex said. "Hank collected a bunch of prescription medicines and put them in his pack. I know there's some strong antibiotics in there."

"I don't think that's a good idea," Emily said. "If we cure him, we'll be expected to cure others. We're not doctors and we don't have that many drugs. It'd be a recipe for trouble, I think."

"I suppose you're right," Alex said. "Keep our aces in the hole."

~

The next morning's routine was similar to the previous one. They met Kallisto in the courtyard and continued their Greek lessons. Nancy was doing the best, probably because of her childhood Greek. The conjugations and inflections came more naturally to her. Alex did well with grammar, too, while Emily had a hard time with it. She remembered words well, however, better than Nancy or Alex. Words seemed to stick after a couple of repetitions. She remembered *his* German courses in college and how *he* struggled with vocabulary (mainly because of laziness). But it felt like she was soaking up words like a sponge. Did her brain have an aptitude now that *his* did not?

Near the end of the session, her mind growing weary from the exercises, Emily asked Kallisto where she lived.

"I am a priestess," Kallisto said. "I serve the temple of Artemis. My home is near there."

"You Greek are not," Emily said, enunciating the words as well as she could.

"No, I am not Greek. I am Lydian. My husband, Nikanor, is Greek. He comes from Miletus. We met in Trapezus."

There was a story behind those simple statements, Emily realized. Kallisto stayed for lunch. She and Berenike let them know they would need to get ready for the funeral.

"Your friends will be buried with three soldiers," Kallisto said. "Can you tell me their names?"

"The one with the beard is Henry and the other is Timothy," Nancy said.

~

Alex was ushered to the men's wing while Nancy and Emily were taken to their bedroom where they found their clothes neatly laid out on their respective beds. Their shoes were on the floor at the feet of the beds.

"I get the impression they want us to wear these to the funeral," Emily said.

"It would seem so," Nancy said. "I just wish I wasn't so sick of that dress."

They began to change clothes. Emily pulled on the now clean and lavender smelling t-shirt.

"Don't wear that," Nancy said. "This is a formal occasion. Let's do it up right, or as best we can."

Emily put the dress on without the t-shirt. Nancy was sitting in front of the bronze mirror, applying makeup. Emily started putting on her sneakers.

"Wear the flats, not those silly things," Nancy said. "And you should wear the stockings. They go well with the dress."

Emily found the stockings and put them on. The flats were buried deep in the pack. She pulled them out along with the jewelry box. She supposed if there were an appropriate time to wear the necklace and earrings, this was it. She put the hematite necklace on, removed the studs from her earlobes and slid in the hanging-globe earrings. What was the point of the of the earrings, she wondered. Her hair covered them up.

"Get the barrette out," Nancy said.

She stood in front of Emily, pulled her hair back, exposing the earrings, and clasped the barrette on behind her head. Nancy undid the top button of the dress and spread the fabric out a little to show more of the necklace.

"There, that's how it's done. Now all you need is a little makeup."

"I'm not wearing makeup," Emily said.

"C'mon sweetie, it's for Hank. And Tim. He had a crush on you, you know. He went after that awful man to protect you, not me."

That hadn't occurred to Emily but when Nancy said it, she knew it was true. Tim had given his life for her. It aroused feelings she couldn't name or grasp. She felt a little dizzy.

"Just sit here. It'll be fine. You'll see."

Emily was so lost in thought she hardly realized what Nancy was doing as she applied mascara, eyeliner, lipstick and a touch of rouge to her cheeks.

"There. A little bit is all you need and, voila, pretty as a picture," Nancy said as she held the mirror in front of Emily.

It did make a difference. Her eyes looked bigger, her cheeks more prominent, her lips fuller. It was nice but not overdone. It looked natural. Nancy knew what she was doing. Still, she felt awkward. She almost wished Nancy had overdone it. She would have an excuse to wipe the makeup off.

"It's okay, I guess," Emily said.

Instead of running shoes, Nancy put on a pair of sandals she had kept in her pack.

"Well, you're dressed better for the occasion than I am," Nancy said.

"You'll outshine everyone regardless," Emily said.

"Thank you, dear, I just wish I had some jewelry to wear."

Emily slipped the puukko onto her dress's belt.

"Do you have to wear that thing?" Nancy asked.

"Yes."

~

They went down to the courtyard and met Alex who was wearing his jeans and polo shirt.

"You two are looking good," he said. "I'm feeling underdressed to say the least."

Later, Berenike appeared with Gaina. Berenike wore a kind of silver web-work, glittering with crystals of blue and green, that enveloped her neck and shoulders. It was mesmerizing.

"You look lovely," Nancy said in Greek.

Berenike returned the compliment. She whispered something to Gaina who left the courtyard. She returned carrying a necklace and two earrings that she offered to Nancy. The necklace was a gold chain with a polished red stone hanging as a pendant. The earrings were red agates.

"You may wear these if you wish," Berenike said.

"Thank you," Nancy said as Gaina put them on her.

They went well with the blue dress, Emily thought. She was happy to be wearing gray tones and let Nancy attract the looks.

Outside the gate, they mounted chariots that were painted red and black and had polished bronze fittings and trim. Each had a driver and two people could stand behind them. Philocrates and Berenike were in the lead chariot, followed by Nancy and Alex, then Emily and Nikanor in the last one. They advanced down the street at a walking pace followed by a small train of slaves.

"Your mistress is beautiful," Nikanor said to Emily, speaking slowly.

"Not mistress," Emily replied in Greek.

Nikanor looked puzzled.

"Friend," she said. "Nancy is friend."

"Ah," he said, smiling. "Kallisto is right."

"Kallisto right?"

"Always," Nikanor said.

He laughed out loud and the others looked back at him.

~

They trotted through the bustling market area. People lined the streets to get a view of the strangers. Emily supposed word of their arrival had spread through town. She imagined their speculations. Were they sent by the Gods? Were they an omen? Were they from a distant land? India? Did they think the fabric of their clothes was a kind of silk?

At the rampart's gate, they were met by a dozen hoplites who assembled in a column in front of them. Agathon and other dignitaries joined the procession, riding chariots, and the column moved through the gate.

About a half mile northwest of town, they came to an open area of cut grass. There was a large mound with a simple altar on it. To the east, were several smaller mounds marked by stones. In their midst were five freshly dug graves with corpses wrapped in cloth beside them. Emily supposed two of the corpses were Hank and Tim's.

South of the altar mound were several large fire pits. Around them were many long, rough-hewn tables and benches. A canvas pavilion covered a much finer table. Nearby was a large tent and its flaps were shut. Many slaves scurried around, making preparations among the myriad jugs, barrels and crates of foodstuffs.

West of the altar mound was an open field where a hundred or more men were engaged in athletic contests.

The chariots stopped. Nikanor took Emily's hand and helped her off. It wasn't necessary, she thought. Members of the procession walked to the pavilion. Apparently, they were to wait there until the ceremonies began. Slaves served wine for refreshment.

"Is this all for Hank and Tim?" Nancy asked.

"I suspect it's part funeral and part victory celebration," Alex said.

Nikanor apparently intuited what they were talking about. "Thracians. This is for the Thracians," he said.

"Thracians? What does he mean?" Nancy asked.

"It's for the Thracian mercenaries," Emily said. "I'm guessing three of them were killed fighting Hydakoles' band. This event is to honor their dead and their efforts."

"Kind of throwing them a bone to keep them happy," Alex said.

"Exactly."

"But Hank and Tim aren't Thracians," Nancy said.

"No, but they're not Greek," Emily said. "Anybody who's not Greek is pretty much a barbarian."

"So, we're barbarians to them?"

"I'd bet yes."

~

Nikanor pointed to the Thracian men playing games.

"Do you want to watch?" He asked.

"Yes," Emily said.

The four of them walked toward the field. Agathon whistled and barked a command. Two hoplites broke ranks and followed them over. With their helmets covering their faces, they seemed like androids of science fiction.

The Thracians were engaged in a javelin throwing contest. The men standing around watching stood aside so the visitors could get a good view. They spoke welcoming words, apparently happy to have the newcomers in their midst.

"Now they have an audience to show off to," Nancy said.

Emily saw a couple of the younger Thracians making faces at the hoplites behind their backs. She winked at them. They seemed delighted and surprised by her reaction but ran off in case the hoplites grew wise to their antics. The hoplites remained impassive, however.

"What are you laughing at?" Nancy asked Emily.

"Nothing."

The contestants threw their javelins like athletes did in the Olympics. They'd get a running start then go into a sidestep before launching their missiles with a long, arcing throwing motion. One of the competitors was Byon. He saw Emily and nodded. She nodded back. The contest came down to two men, Byon and a tall, lanky fellow with red hair and a shaggy beard.

The lanky man come over to Nancy, knelt before her and offered his javelin. His smile revealed a missing front tooth. Nancy was uncertain. Nikanor showed her that she should kiss it.

"For luck," he said.

"This is ridiculous," she said, but took the javelin, kissed it and handed it back.

The lanky man howled and hooted and danced around.

Byon offered his javelin to Emily who kissed it and handed it back. Byon let out a war cry and the two men went to their starting positions.

Byon went first. His throw was a study in athletic precision and his javelin flew high and long. The lanky man's technique, however, was almost unnatural in the way his body bent back and the way he threw himself to the ground after his release. The lanky man's javelin outdistanced Byon's by about two feet.

Cheers erupted and the lanky man ran around with his arms in the air. Byon looked at Emily and shrugged. She shrugged back.

~

The sun descended from a clear blue sky and afternoon shadows grew long. A horn sounded and all the people present, except the slaves preparing the feast, queued in a long line. A drummer began beating a slow rhythm and a flutist blew a sorrowful melody on a set of large Pan pipes.

The line of people, led by Philocrates, walked around a mound and filed passed the corpses and graves. It was a viewing, Emily thought. She, Alex and Nancy walked behind the Greeks followed by the Thracians, most of whom had donned colorful wool cloaks.

The bodies were wrapped in rough flax cloth. Only their faces were visible and copper coins covered their eyes. Hank and Tim's faces were sunken but still recognizable. Emily felt sad but no tears came. What were the odds that Hank and Tim would end up dead and buried along the Black Sea coast two or three thousand years before they were born? She felt helpless, like a falling leaf that has no choice but to float in the wind.

~

The music stopped when the procession ended and a horn sounded again. The flaps of the enclosed tent opened and out walked Kallisto, magnificent in the amber rays of the setting sun. Resting on her head was a ring of gold from which gold chains descended, mingling with the braids of her hair. She wore quilted, multi-colored trousers tucked into leather boots and a burgundy tunic that came down to her thighs. From her neck hung a gold pendant in the shape of a horse and rider with bow and arrow. Over her shoulders was a black cloak similar to what the Thracians wore, dyed with different colored swirls and starbursts. She wore a knife at her hip. Hank's knife.

The Thracians made way for her and she ascended the altar mound. Two Thracians followed, one leading a lamb that trotted beside them. At the altar Kallisto raised her arms and she began to speak in a loud, clear voice. The language wasn't Greek. It must be Thracian, Emily thought.

Kallisto picked up a large pitcher and poured its liquid contents onto the altar. The men put the lamb on top of the altar and held it down. It bleated and struggled. Kallisto drew Hank's knife.

Nancy whispered: "Oh my God, she's going to kill it."

"The lamb is for Sabazios," Nikanor said.

"Who Sabazios?" Emily asked.

"God" and "Sky" were the words Nikanor used that she could comprehend.

Kallisto grabbed the lamb's head and sliced open its throat. She held the lamb up by its hind legs and let the blood pour onto the altar. A large, round moon rose behind her.

∼

The ceremony ended and supper was served: pork, mutton, yams, bread, greens, grapes, plums, green apples, and oddly shaped red berries that were sour to the taste. The wine flowed freely and the Thracians ate hungrily.

Kallisto walked solemnly back through the crowd and into her tent, closing the flap. She emerged later wearing only her brown chiton and the Thracian cloak. At the pavilion she inserted herself between Nikanor and Emily. She produced Hank's knife and handed it to Emily.

"This belongs to you," she said. "Thank you. We honor Henry, slayer of Hydakoles.."

Emily unsheathed it. Its blade had been wiped clean and oiled, although, being stainless steel, oiling was unnecessary. She returned it to its sheath and handed it back to Kallisto.

"You keep it," she said.

Kallisto shook her head. "No, do not give it to me," she said along with other words. "Give it to Oikist Philocrates."

Emily conferred with Nancy and Alex.

"I told Kallisto to keep Hank's knife but she thinks we should give it to Philocrates."

"I think that's a good idea," Nancy said. "It's nothing beyond what they don't already have."

Alex asked to see the knife and looked it over.

"It's higher tech than you think," he said. "The precision machining is not something the Greeks can do."

"I don't think it will upset the culture," Emily said. "It's just a knife. It will simply be a mystery to them how it was made."

"And it has meaning for them," Nancy said. "It would show appreciation for their hospitality."

"I suppose it's okay," Alex said. "You do the honors, Emily."

Emily turned to Kallisto: "We give it to Philocrates."

~

Soon it was time for toasts and speeches. Agathon spoke first. The gist was clear enough. He thundered out words of praise for the Thracians' bravery and skill in battle. He thanked them for their service to the polis and offered condolences for those who had died in battle. He spoke the names of the dead including Henry and Timothy. Emily couldn't make out what he said about them but it was positive.

Philocrates spoke, too, but kept his speech short. His voice quickly became hoarse. When he finished, Kallisto stood and gestured for Emily, Nancy and Alex to stand with her. She spoke a few words in Greek and Thracian then nudged Emily.

Emily walked approached Philocrates and, with two hands, offered him Hank's knife.

"Please take gift," she said in Greek.

Philocrates smiled and accepted the knife.

"Thank you dear one," he said, and other words she didn't understand.

He unsheathed the knife and raised it above his head, its blade glimmered in the torchlight. The Greeks clapped. The Thracians hooted and pounded their tables. When Emily sat down, Kallisto put her hand on her shoulder and said in English, "Good job."

Emily could tell Philocrates was happy with the knife. At one point, she saw him slice a cucumber to test its sharpness.

"Philocrates!" His wife scolded.

Music started again, the drum's tempo faster now, and a few Thracians performed war dances. The dances looked like real combat moves and Emily watched with interest. The other Thracians shouted cheers and catcalls. She saw Byon performing flourishes with a spear, drawing hoots and whistles from his comrades. It was then that Kallisto indicated it was time to leave.

"I gather the Thracians will get pretty rowdy before the night is over," Alex said. "I guess it's not something for civilized company."

Emily longed to stay, and be a man again, and drink and boast and laugh with the warriors from the land of Thrace.

Chapter 11 | Rough Period

LIFE over the next few days fell into a homebound routine. Emily, Nancy and Alex took their lessons in the morning and, when visitors came to talk business, the women would retreat to the gynaeceum to spin thread, make fabric and chat. Berenike would keep it interesting for herself by entertaining different women friends from neighboring houses. She liked to talk about her vase collection, the scenes painted on them, and the artists who created them. The funeral ceremonies were a source of considerable conversation. Some of the Greek women were scandalized that Kallisto had worn trousers. It was too barbaric, even out here.

Emily envied Alex who would go for walks with Nikanor in the afternoons. She wasn't invited. There was nothing keeping her from leaving the house. The gate was neither locked nor guarded but it was clear that, if she did so, it would create a stir. She decided her top priority was to learn the language so she would put up with the homebound life for now. What other life was there?

Berenike did say that someday soon they would visit the market then forage nearby woods for herbs and roots, just as soon as Agathon could spare the men to watch over them. During quiet times, when others napped, Emily would wander around the house. Once she ventured into the main andron to have a look. The floors had bear and lion-skin rugs. Animal skulls hung on the walls. On a side table, lay Hank's knife, unsheathed, on a piece of felt. It was a showoff item, she thought. A male slave saw her and gently urged her to leave. She did so. She did get a glimpse of the adjoining andron. It was smaller and had shelves of papyrus scrolls. A central table had what appeared to be maps on it. She wanted to look at them but didn't venture in.

~

One morning Emily asked Kallisto why she hadn't inquired more about who the three of them were and where they came from. Kallisto managed to get across that Philocrates and Agathon were waiting until they had learned Greek well enough to be able to tell their story in full and with no misunderstanding. Kallisto would determine when the time was right.

That evening Alex, Nancy and Emily relaxed in the courtyard before bed. Emily brought up the subject.

Emily: "What are we going to tell them?"

Nancy: "We could just tell them the truth."

Alex: "Would they believe that?"

Emily: "We've got stuff to show that would be pretty convincing. A flashlight, for example."

Alex: "Yes, I suppose, but it seems problematic. If they believe we're from the future, what would they expect of us? Would they think we could tell them their fates?"

Emily: "What other story could we tell them? The most plausible thing I can come up with is to say that we are from the far east or far north. But I don't think such a story would hold up. How do we explain how we got here? What was our purpose? How did we plan to get home? We all know how sharp Kallisto is. We're not going to pull one over on her. We'd be breeding distrust. I don't think it would end well."

Alex: "I suppose you're right. We just don't know enough to plausibly pretend we're from somewhere in their time."

Nancy: "The truth, then, for better or worse."

∼

The next morning Nancy asked Kallisto why such a big house didn't have more children around. Kallisto said Philocrates and Berenike had two daughters and a son. The daughters, Apollonia and Pelagia, were married. One lived in Miletus, the other in Trapezus. The son, Pantheras, was studying in Athens and would come to Artemios the following spring. Pantheras was expected to marry soon and take over leadership of the colony. If the gods favored it, Kallisto said, the house would be filled with children then.

Emily did find she could wander out to the backyard without agitating the household too much. She would sit on the low stone wall and look out over the cliffs toward the harbor. Two small islands extended from the point of the peninsula. The larger of the two islands had a tall, pyramid-shaped pile of stones. She assumed it served as a lighthouse.

That afternoon, while Nancy and the other women were dying wool for cloaks, she saw a long ship heading into the harbor. It was much bigger than the trading vessels and fishing boats that came and went. It had three decks of oars and a ram at its bow. It was painted like a great sea serpent and its stern flared up like a huge fish tail. It was a trireme, a warship. It resembled ships *he* had seen in picture books that the Greeks had used to battle the Persians. Had the Persian wars happened yet? She wasn't sure. Horns blew, initiating a bustle of activity near the pier.

~

The house became noisy with voices. Emily went inside. Berenike and Gaina were giving orders to slaves. Nancy was putting things away in the gyneaceum.

"What's going on?" Emily asked.

"Unexpected visitors," Nancy said. "Important people."

Berenike asked Emily and Nancy to stay out of sight, apologizing profusely for having to make the request. Whoever the visitors were, Berenike didn't want them to see the exotic strangers. Nancy did her best to say that it was okay and that it was the least they could do in return for her hospitality.

Emily and Nancy retreated to their bedroom. Nancy fetched a deck of cards from her pack.

"Might as well play some rummy. Looks like we're cooped up here tonight," she said.

After Nancy won the second game -- her luck was astonishing -- someone knocked on the door. Emily quickly put a cloth over the cards and the score pad. It was Alex. He had been out walking with Nikanor who had hurried him back to the house when they had heard news of the ship's arrival.

"Did you learn who they are?" Emily asked.

"I gathered they're dignitaries from another colony called Novorosa. It's up the coast. I don't know how far. I think it's a rival colony. And there's something else. Nikanor used a word I think means 'Persian.' He seemed worried about it."

"The Greeks and the Persians fought bloody wars," Emily said.

"Do you think we're in danger?" Nancy asked.

"Not from one warship," Emily said. "There are too many hoplites and Thracians around. But, in general, maybe. As I recall, at one point, the Persians controlled most of the Black Sea coast."

"So we may not be safe here?"

"I'm not sure we can be safe anywhere, not safe like back home," Emily said. "Life was much more precarious in ancient times."

"On that score," Alex said. "I think I learned something useful. We paid a visit to the harbor master, who was reviewing plans for a shipyard. I saw some of his calculations and remarked he must be good with his numbers. The harbor master -- Midaleus, I think was his name -- said he had studied under a man who himself had been a student of Thales."

"Who's Thales?"

"He was an early philosopher and mathematician who came up with the first known geometric proofs. If I remember right, he died in the middle of the sixth century B.C."

"That narrows things," Emily said. "If the Persians are active around the Black Sea, it means the time we're in is before Alexander the Great. He conquered the Persians. So that puts us between, say, 520 B.C. and 350 B.C., something like that."

"We'd have to be on the early side of that if the harbor master's teacher studied under Thales."

"True, so right around 500 B.C. then," Emily said. "And that puts us on the cusp of the Ionian Rebellion."

"What does that mean?" Nancy asked.

"It means the Greek city states in Anatolia, a.k.a. Turkey, are under Persian control. With help from Athens, they rose up against the Persians."

"What happened?"

"The rebellion was crushed."

~

Hagne brought up a light meal and wine. She was nonplussed that Alex was in the room with Nancy and Emily. They assured her that it was all right and Alex would sleep in his own room when the time came. Emily found that Hagne's rapid speech was almost unintelligible. She couldn't seem to bring herself to speak slowly and enunciate her words. How old was Hagne -- sixteen, seventeen, Emily wondered. Could she only look forward to a life of servitude? Were there no other prospects for her? She seemed happy enough but the question depressed Emily. What were *her* prospects?

While they ate, they could hear the guests coming in. Loud talking carried from the courtyard. After eating they lit candles and Emily taught Alex and Nancy how to play pitch, a card game *he* had learned as a kid. There was more strategy in pitch than rummy so Emily tended to win, that is when Nancy's luck wasn't too overwhelming. Alex picked up the tactics quickly and seemed to enjoy himself.

"I have to admit, it gets pretty lonely in that room by myself," he said.

"I bet it does," Nancy said.

The noise coming from the courtyard grew more boisterous as the evening progressed and often sounded like arguing.

"I better get to my room," Alex said. "We don't want to push our luck too much."

~

Despite the noise, Nancy went to sleep quickly. Emily dozed off for a time then woke and couldn't get back to sleep. She was thirsty and hungry. She could still hear talking coming from the courtyard, though more subdued. If she took the back way to the kitchen, she thought, she could grab a piece of bread and a bowl of water without being seen.

She got up, put on her Greek tunic and cinched it with the rope belt. She had taken to wearing it most of the time unless it was being washed. She hadn't worn shoes for days and her feet were growing callused. She found she liked going barefoot and being able to feel the textures and temperatures of the surfaces she walked on. She yearned to be able to explore the city and the countryside.

She moved slowly and quietly down the stairs, through the dark gynaeceum and into the kitchen where candles were still lit. She dipped a bowl into the water barrel and took a drink. She couldn't find any bread but did find almonds. She slipped a handful into her pouch.

Someone came into the room. She turned to see a man dressed in a blue tunic trimmed with gold. He had dark hair, a roundish face and a day's worth of stubble. He stopped momentarily when he saw Emily then walked toward her, smiling.

"Hello," Emily said to him in Greek.

The man spoke. Emily understood only parts of what he said. "Bad girl. You should not [something] at night."

He slurred his speech. He was drunk. He moved closer to her, still smiling and talking. She could make out the word for "kiss." He was a little shorter than Alex but much stouter. A soldier, she thought, an officer probably. Her heart beat wildly.

She sidestepped toward the door of the gynaeceum but the man grabbed her right arm. She tried to yank herself free but his grip was too strong. He pulled her close and grabbed her other arm. Terror gripped her. She couldn't think of what to do.

"Shhh." Then the man spoke soothing words.

He released her left arm, pulled her close and started groping her backside. She tried to push him away but didn't have the strength. Her puukko! But with his body pressed against hers, she couldn't reach it. Then she remembered. She put her free hand into her pouch and amid the almonds felt the smooth aluminum of the canister. He was trying to kiss her now. Her terror turned to rage. She bit his lip. The man's head snapped back and she gave him a blast of pepper spray.

"Ahh!" He staggered back and put his hands to his face.

Emily drew her puukko and assumed a defensive stance, left arm forward, the knife cocked at her hip. She bared her teeth and hissed.

"Nyfitsa!" The man yelled.

She eyed his inner thigh. A quick cut would kill him. Another man walked in. Now outnumbered, she backed into the gynaeceum, moved quickly through it and up the stairs.

~

Emily slipped into her room and inserted the wooden peg that served to lock the door. She sat in darkness on one of the chairs and took deep breaths. She heard shouts coming from the courtyard. She recognized Agathon's voice among them. What would happen? Would they come for her?

Nancy sat up.

"Emily, are you here?" she asked.

"Yes, I'm here."

Nancy's naked form was silhouetted against the moonlight coming in from the window. The sight of her and the sound of her voice calmed Emily.

"Sounds like they're at it again," Nancy said. "Are they ever going to sleep? Why are you up?"

"Couldn't sleep. I went to get a drink."

She imagined what it would be like if she was still a man and here with Nancy, how aroused *he* would be, how much *he* would want to hold her, absorb her womanliness, and make her feel *his* strength.

"Come to bed," Nancy said.

The courtyard had gone quiet. Emily heard the gate open and close. She slipped off her tunic. She crawled on the bed toward Nancy in a kind of stalk. She seized Nancy's head and kissed her, a long and probing kiss. She slid her lips down Nancy's neck, kissing and lightly scraping her skin with her teeth like *he* would do, slowly moving downward.

"You're frisky tonight," Nancy said. "What's got you worked up?"

Emily pushed Nancy to her back and moved her mouth to Nancy's breasts, filling her mouth with their pliant, soft skin. She moved down to Nancy's navel, taking her time. She could feel Nancy's heart beating and the heave of her breathing. She moved through her pubic hair and to her clitoris, using her tongue to lick and probe.

"Mmm, there you go, that's it, baby," Nancy said.

Emily dwelled there for a time then moved back up, parting Nancy's thighs as she did so, slowly, like *he* would do, back to her breasts, up her throat and to her mouth, while slipping *his* penis into her vagina.

But *his* penis wasn't there.

"You don't have the equipment for that, honey," Nancy said.

Emily was overcome by a wave of revulsion. She rolled over onto her side, her back to Nancy.

"What's wrong?" Nancy asked.

"I'm a fucking girl, that's what's wrong."

"I'm sorry. You've been doing so well."

Nancy started petting Emily's hair.

"Don't touch me," Emily said.

She got out of the large bed, went to the smaller one and slid into the sheets.

~

Two soldiers stood on either side of Emily as she faced the oikist who looked down on her with a frown.

"I'm sorry but the only sensible course is that you should become a slave," the oikist said.

"What? What do you mean?" Emily asked.

"The colony can't afford to support unproductive members. It's really the only role you're suited for. So, from this moment on you are slave of the household. With grandchildren coming, Berenike needs more help. Believe me, I do not make this decision lightly. This is as good an assignment as you could hope for."

"You can't do this. I'm a free person," Emily pleaded.

"I can and I have. The documents have been duly registered and accepted."

"I won't be a slave."

"It is not your decision. You will have to undergo the initiation and the banding but, after that, if you do as you're told and perform well, life will be comfortable for you here."

The soldiers took her to a back room and forced her to bend over on a table, her arms spread out. Another man came over with a bronze bracelet, put it on her left wrist and clamped it with a plier-like tool. He slid a thin piece of wood between the underside of her wrist and the bracelet. With metal tongs holding a ceramic cup, he carefully dripped molten solder onto the overlapping ends of the bracelet. Despite the piece of wood, the heat burned her wrist.

"You can't do this! Let me go!" She screamed.

Gaina appeared before her. The soldiers still held her to the table.

"The bracelet marks you as a slave of the Ampeliosian family. It is a high honor and you will wear it as long as you live," Gaina said.

Gaina nodded to the soldiers, who then lifted her tunic to expose her thighs and buttocks. Emily felt the piercing sting of a rod slapping against the back of her legs.

"Ahh! What are you doing?" She screamed.

They beat her again and again, ten times, until she sobbed uncontrollably.

"Stop, please stop. Why are you doing this?"

"This is what happens when you disobey orders or shirk a task or try to run away," Gaina said. "Will you obey?"

Emily glared at her. They beat her again, ten more times, until she was blubbering and nearly senseless.

"Will you obey?"

Anything to make it stop.

"Yes, I'll obey. I'll do whatever you want. I'll obey."

$\sim$

Nancy nudged Emily's shoulder. "Wake up. You're having a nightmare."

Emily reached for her wrist. The bracelet wasn't there. She sighed. It was the first time she had dreamed since the crash where she was a woman in the dream and not *him*. She hoped they wouldn't all be like this.

There was something wet and sticky between her thighs. She felt for whatever it was.

"Nancy, I'm bleeding," she said.

"Where?"

Emily threw off the covers.

"Oh, you're just having your period," Nancy said.

"What do I do?"

"Wash up and use one of your tampons. I'll show you."

Emily shook her head in disbelief.

"Welcome to the wonderful world of being a woman," Nancy said.

Chapter 12 | On the Farm

HAGNE brought up breakfast. She was upset about something but Emily and Nancy couldn't understand her babbling. She saw the stained sheets on the small bed, removed them, and took them away.

"Hagne's in a tiz this morning," Nancy said. "I wonder why."

"I have an idea," Emily said.

"What? What happened?"

A knock at the door. It was Kallisto. She said they needed to pack their things. They were being moved.

"You will be going to Agathon's farm outside the polis," Kallisto said. "You will like it there, I think, better than here. It is close to my house."

"Why are we moved?" Nancy asked in Greek.

"Last night," Emily said in English, "when I was in the kitchen, a man tried to rape me. I think it was one of the visitors from the other colony."

"My God. You're kidding."

"No. He was drunk. I think he thought I was a slave."

"What did you do?"

"I squirted him with pepper spray."

"Oh dear."

~

Emily and Nancy packed their things. Two slaves came up to carry the packs. In the courtyard, they met Alex.

"I'm not sure what's going on. Looks like we're moving," he said.

"Some bastard tried to rape Emily last night," Nancy said. "She zapped him with pepper spray."

"Oh, shit. That can't be good," he said. "Are you okay, Emily?"

"Yeah, just shaken up a little."

"Fuck, that's awful."

Philocrates emerged and greeted Emily. He seemed distressed and struggled to begin what he wanted to say.

"I am sorry," he said, and spoke more words that Emily did not understand.

"Thank you," was all she could think of to say in Greek.

They were ushered out of the gate into a wagon waiting at the bottom of the steps. Berenike did not come out to see them off.

Kallisto sat with them in the wagon which was hitched to a team of two mules. The driver was waiting for something and did not move off right away. Two riders approached, one leading an unsaddled horse. When they neared, Emily recognized Callias with his red plume and Byon who wore his bronze helmet.

Byon's face was serious and he held himself stiffly upright while Callias issued an order to the driver. But when Byon's eyes met Emily's, he winked. The gesture was like a soothing balm. She had never been so glad to see someone.

The wagon moved out and Callias and Byon rode ahead of it. As they clopped along the cobbled street, Emily turned to Kallisto.

"What is 'Nyfitsa?'" She asked.

Kallisto searched the air for a way to explain.

"A small animal," she said. "It has sharp teeth. It eats rabbits and snakes."

"She must mean a weasel," Nancy said. "Where did you hear that word?"

"That's what the man called me last night after I sprayed him," Emily said. She recalled that a weasel could emit a nasty musk like a skunk to defend itself.

"That's horrible. The man should be shot," Nancy said.

It didn't bother Emily at all to be thought of as a fierce little predator with a vicious bite. Kallisto looked at her with those deep-set eyes. Her expression seemed to say, I know what you're thinking, I know who you are. If only I knew who I was, Emily thought.

~

They had seen Agathon's house before when they first came to Artemios. It was the two-story one with the stone wall around it, along

117

with several outbuildings which included two barns, a stable, and a smaller house. To the north on a mild slope was a large orchard of apple trees. To the east was an orchard of plum trees situated on a steeper slope. To the south was level ground with fields of wheat, barley and oats. To the west across the road were the burial mounds. The morning had brought a stiff breeze in from the sea and clouds rolled overhead.

Bumping along the drive to the wall's gate, Emily wondered about the time of year. She guessed it was late August, a Roman month. She didn't know how the Greeks divided the year.

Agathon greeted them at the gate. His chariot was at the ready nearby.

"Welcome to my home," he said. "You will be safe here."

Alex, Nancy and Emily offered their thanks. Agathon introduced them to two men and two women standing with him.

"This is Cleon and his son, Timon."

Both were short and stocky with dark hair and ruddy skin. They wore flax tunics and broad felt hats. Cleon's beard was thick and flecked with gray. Timon's was sparse.

"This is Zosima and Phoibe."

Slaves, Emily thought. They wore similar kinds of simple chitons that Gaina and Hagne wore. Zosima was the older one. She was short and her braided black hair was tied into a bun behind her head. Phoibe was thin and tall, almost as tall as Nancy, and had dishwater hair braided into two long tails.

Agathon spoke a few words to Kallisto and Byon before he mounted his chariot and rode away with Callias beside him. Byon stayed behind.

"I think we got our watchdog back," Nancy said.

Cleon, the older man, headed for the stable with Byon and his two horses. Timon, along with Zosima and Phoibe, helped carry the packs into the house. The design was similar to the other house but only the size of one wing. It was not so richly furnished and lacked Berenike's fineries. The wall enclosed a lawn of cut grass. There was a garden plot, a flower bed and a brick stove. The place was an unfinished project, Emily thought. She and Nancy were taken upstairs to a room with furnishings similar to their previous room, though it was smaller and had no mirror.

"This is a nice house," Nancy said. "But it needs decorating. Agathon must be a bachelor."

Kallisto said they should resume their lessons before she had to return to the temple. Nancy, Alex and Emily plied her with questions about Agathon and the farm.

Agathon was a widower. His wife had died of some kind of sickness. He had a daughter and two sons. The daughter was married and lived in Trapezus. The latest news was that she was pregnant with her first child. The younger of the two sons commanded a merchant ship. The eldest ran the old family farm near Trapezus and a was a hoplite officer. Agathon was the polemarch, or military commander, of Artemios, second in rank only to the oikist.

The colony was a joint venture between wealthy families in Trapezus and Miletus. The farm was part of the deal to induce Agathon to serve as military commander. Cleon was the farm's foreman and lived with his family in the smaller house. He had a wife, Thais, and a young daughter, Agape, whom they met at lunch. Thais was not much taller than Emily and beefier. She kept her hair short and in braids that dangled around her neck. Agape, a toddler, was naturally awed and fascinated by the strange visitors, especially Nancy.

Nancy scooped her up.

"Why you're just about the cutest thing in the world," she said, making Agape giggle with tickles.

Cleon, Timon and Byon joined them while Zosima and Phoibe served the meal. Apparently the division of sexes wasn't so rigid on the farm. The lunch was amiable if awkward because of the language barrier. Kallisto did what she could to further communication but departed when she had finished eating.

Cleon and Timon returned to their work. Nancy went off with Thais and her daughter to look at their small house. Alex, Byon and Emily were left sitting at the table.

"Now what do we do?" Alex asked.

"I suppose anything we want," Emily said.

She looked at Byon and made a motion with her arm as if throwing a javelin.

"Yes, we can practice," he said.

~

Kallisto had been right. They did like it better on the farm than in the oikist's house. In the mornings, Kallisto would come down from her home near the temple and continue their language lessons. In the afternoons, they would pursue their own activities.

Nancy took charge of the household. Zosima and Phoibe seemed to resent her presence at first but Nancy won them over with humor, kindness and by not talking down to them. Nancy helped with the cooking and the laundry. She tended the garden and the flower bed. She would also babysit Agape at times and acted like a kindly aunt to the child.

Alex helped Cleon and Timon with various chores. Alex was especially good at fixing things. He learned that the stone patio in the courtyard was meant to have a gazebo so he took on the project of building it while Cleon advised and assisted.

Emily and Byon practiced throwing javelins, using the space behind the barns. Byon also taught Emily how to use a sling and they hurled pebbles at a target. She wanted to know more, so Byon taught her the rudiments of spear fighting. They set up a wooden dummy to use for practice.

He had trained a little in Japanese bo-stick fighting and kendo. She pestered Byon to spar with her. He was reluctant at first but when he saw that she could handle a staff with some proficiency, he agreed. Byon's skill was far superior but she could occasionally surprise him with a clever move or feint. She realized she had quicker reflexes and quicker feet than *he* had had. She also noticed she had better balance; a low center of gravity was helpful. She chopped wood to build strength in her arms and shoulders. She was getting stronger but she would never have anything like *his* strength. Her legs were strong, though, so she focused on using her hips and thighs to generate power.

Byon took on the job of tending the stable and Emily helped -- brushing and feeding the horses and cleaning the stalls. This freed Timon to do other things like practice weapons with Byon and Emily. Sometimes Alex and Cleon would participate, too. Emily took to being a general assistant, not only helping Byon and Cleon but Alex and Nancy as needed.

Agathon, at first, didn't spend much time on the farm. He had quarters in Artemios. Callias, or another officer, would come daily to check on them. After a few days absence, Agathon rode up and declared he would be spending the night. He seemed to approve of the activities, even the training ground that was growing up behind the barns.

They all ate supper together that evening and Kallisto and Nikanor joined them. Nancy sat close to Agathon and, after the meal and a couple of bowls of wine, she explained she wanted to practice her Greek on him. He obliged and they chatted merrily. She would occasionally touch his arm when she laughed at something he said.

Agathon returned more often after that evening.

~

One day Cleon announced that the wheat was ready to harvest. The next day a column of slaves, soldiers and wagons arrived. Sickles were distributed and most everyone went to work cutting grain. Zosima, Phoibe and a few other women slaves distributed water and food to workers in the fields. Nancy and Kallisto directed the effort from the house. Emily worked in the fields and, in the evening, helped sharpen the sickles.

Cleon and Timon, along with a few slaves, would do the threshing and the winnowing. When the kernels were mostly separated from the stalks, they would scoop them into wagons which were driven off to the mills outside of town. There the grain would be sieved and ground into flour or stored for later use.

At night Emily would collapse into bed. *He* had been lazy and didn't relish this kind of work. She didn't mind it and found it therapeutic. The skin on her arms had taken on a deep tan and her hair was longer. She wanted to cut it but Nancy braided a tail instead.

The wheat harvest took a few days then the crew moved on to another farm. They had hardly recovered from that effort when the oats were ready, then the barley, then the apples (the plums had already been picked).

The days grew shorter and the nights chillier. She wondered how cold it would get during winter and how they would cope. When the harvest was over, Emily counted off the 57th day since the crash. Leaves were turning and beginning to fall from the trees.

~

One day Agathon did not go to Artemios but stayed on the farm. Byon got the day off and he mounted one of his horses and rode away. Agathon walked around the farm with Cleon discussing various things. He spent time with Alex whose gazebo project was coming along. He went through the house with Nancy who made suggestions about how to finish and decorate it.

Emily busied herself in the stable, watering and feeding the animals. She knew Byon treasured his horses and was very protective of them. The only time he had been short with her was when she once made a tangled mess of a bridle. She had learned that Byon came from a noble family in Thrace. As a horse warrior, he drew more pay and commanded more respect from his Greek employers. His horses were expensive and critical to his livelihood.

It was late in the morning and she was brushing down the horse with one white sock when Agathon appeared beside her.

"You work well with horses, I see," he said.

"Yes, I like them very much," she said.

"I want to thank you for all your help with the harvest," he said. "Cleon says you outworked most of the men and were not even asked."

"Thank you, I try to ...," but she couldn't find words.

"I understand, You are not a freeloader."

"Yes, freeloader. I do not want to be a freeloader."

"Neither do I," Agathon said. "The farm did well this year so in payment I give you this."

He produced a small pouch and handed it to Emily.

"It contains 50 silver drachmas," he continued. "It is a freeman's wage and a little extra."

"Thank you," Emily said and bowed.

"You bow like a Persian, yet act like a Thracian girl," he said. "Very strange. I am curious to know where you come from. We all are."

"If you like, I will do my best to tell you," Emily said.

"No. Not yet. Kallisto says the time is not right. I respect her judgment. I will cheat just a little and ask, do you plan to return home someday."

"We have no home to return to," Emily said.

Agathon seemed puzzled by her answer but went no further with the subject. He put a hand on her shoulder.

"Take me out back and show me what you and Byon have been up to," he said.

She showed him the straw bundles they used for javelin targets, the scrap wood they erected as sling targets, the dummy made from a log and pieces of deadwood. She pointed to an area that Byon wanted to make into a horse run so he could practice using weapons from horseback.

Agathon took off his red cloak and draped it over a simple rack erected to hold javelins and other weapons. He took a long pole and a shield and started performing drills, using the pole like a spear.

"A Greek warrior fights differently than a Thracian, you will see," he said.

His style was tighter than Byon's, his movements compact, efficient and deadly. He dropped the spear, drew his sword and attacked the dummy. His footwork was adroit but, at the same time, sturdy. He would be very difficult to knock off his feet. The way he angled himself toward the dummy, and the way he used his shield, offered his imagined foe few openings to attack. He would thrust, snipe and occasionally slash with the sword. Emily realized he was fighting like a hoplite, accustomed to tight formations and constricted spaces.

Nancy came around the corner of the barn.

"There you are ..."

She stopped when she saw Agathon and watched his performance with Emily. When he finished, Emily offered him a cloth and he wiped sweat from his forehead.

"I need to practice more often," Agathon said.

"I wager you could defeat any opponent," Nancy said.

Agathon laughed. "In my youth, I might have thought so but I know better now."

Nancy took his arm.

"Come, it is time for lunch."

~

Late that afternoon Agathon returned from a long visit with Cleon's family at their house. Alex was planing boards for the gazebo. Emily and Nancy were at the table in the courtyard sewing a pair of wool trousers. The Greeks considered trousers barbaric but their utility in cold weather was undeniable. Agathon marched up to Nancy and took her hand.

"Come with me. I have something to show you," he said. "You too, Alex and Emily."

They followed him southeast through the orchard and to a trail that went up the hillside into a stand of oaks. Their feet crunched newly fallen leaves. Emily remembered her first climb with Hank and how out-of-breath she had become. She was in much better shape now. Near the top were steps carved into a rocky slope. They went up the steps to a ledge sheltered by an overhang of rock. There was a crude bench to sit on.

The ledge offered a panoramic view of the Black Sea and Artemios below. The sun was descending upon the sea's blue swells and silhouetted a merchant ship heading into harbor. The golden light set the forested hills and mountains aglow with reds, yellows, greens and browns. Below their feet was the stone structure they had seen when they first arrived. It was the Temple of Artemis, Kallisto's temple. Behind it was a pool of water ringed with stones.

"It is all so beautiful," Nancy said.

"The most beautiful place I know," Agathon said. "I have chosen to make it my home and defend it to the last. You may consider it your home, too, if you choose."

Chapter 13 | Marketing

THAT night Emily slept by herself. It was the first time she had done so since the crash. *He* had been accustomed to sleeping alone but Emily had grown used to Nancy's presence -- her smell, her late-night farts, her cute snore, the feel of her soft skin. The ache of her absence made Emily realize how much of a comfort Nancy had been. She wondered what kind of wreck she would be without her. Would she have even survived? Emily knew it couldn't go on forever. She didn't want it to go on forever.

In the morning Emily was sitting up in bed, thinking, when Nancy entered the room.

"I'm sorry, honey. I don't know what to say."

"You don't need to say anything," Emily said. "I need to say something, though."

Her eyes moistened.

"What, baby?" Nancy asked.

"Thank you. Thank you for everything you've done for me. I don't think I could have made it this far without you."

Nancy and Emily embraced.

"Oh, honey, I know I couldn't have made it without you," Nancy said. "You'll always be my hero, my mighty mouse."

Eventually they separated and dried their tears. Nancy went about changing her clothes while Emily dressed.

"I think my boobs have gotten bigger," Emily said.

"You've put on some weight, in a good way, you're more womanly now. You probably eat better than the old Emily did."

Womanly was better than girly, Emily supposed.

"How is Agathon?" Emily asked.

"Oh, he's fine. He's going into town today. He says he's going to take us shopping tomorrow."

"I meant how is he in bed."

"Oh, he's a teddy bear, a little rusty, but I'll get him trained soon enough."

"I'm sure you will."

~

Kallisto kept the lesson short that morning. She said she would need to do so for the next several days because she was preparing for Thesmophoria, a festival for Greek women.

"Is Novorosa a danger to Artemios?" Emily asked, carefully phrasing her words.

Kallisto scrutinized her. Emily could see the question had struck something.

"Perhaps," Kallisto said. "Novorosa, and Trapezus, and many other cities are ruled by the Persians. Artemios is not. But Artemios is ... useful."

"Artemios can trade under Persian ... nose?"

"Yes, that is a way to say it. And Artemios has friends ... Scythians, horse warriors ... the Lion Tribe."

"The Lion Tribe trades with Artemios?" Emily asked.

"Yes."

"The Lion Tribe protects Artemios?"

"Yes."

Kallisto cut the conversation short, saying she needed to go.

~

Nancy: "What was that all about?"

Alex: "I think Emily just got some insight into the political situation here. This pretty little city is in a precarious situation."

Nancy: "I'm not sure I understand."

Emily: "The Persians control most of the Black Sea coast but their reach does not extend to Artemios. Artemios is useful to the other colonies as a trading hub where merchants can avoid Persian taxes. I'm guessing, but I bet Novorosa resents this because Artemios attracts trade that would otherwise go there."

Alex: "Novorosa might be tempted to take over Artemios or shut it down by force."

Nancy: "But Agathon commands an army to protect us."

Emily: "From what I've seen, the force here is small, relatively speaking. An army of a few thousand could probably take the city pretty easily."

Nancy: "That's not very comforting."

Emily: "No, but it seems Artemios has an alliance with a band of Scythians -- the Lion Tribe. Scythians are known as fierce warriors. That makes Novorosa, and even the Persians, I bet, hesitate to attack."

Nancy: "So, we're safe then?"

Alex: "As long as the alliance holds."

Emily: "That's the picture I'm getting."

~

Byon returned that day. He seemed a little down but happy enough to see Emily when they met in the stable.

"Did you enjoy visiting your fellow warriors?" She asked.

"Yes," he said. "They are my brothers. I like riding with them."

"You do not like being on the farm?"

"It is ... easy duty, but ... not exciting."

He was bored. Emily couldn't blame him. She knew he normally would be out patrolling the countryside with his comrades, watching for approaching enemies, gathering news, sometimes catching a criminal. Playing watchdog to three strangers was getting old.

Byon led One-sock out of the stable to exercise him. It was a beautiful horse, lean and swift and hard to tire. He leaped up on it with a practiced, scissor-kick motion. Without stirrups, mounting a horse was not a trivial task. Byon patted the horse's back behind him, offering Emily a ride.

"Yes, I would like that."

Byon grasped her arm.

"Jump and I will pull."

She did, and almost went over the other side but he kept her from falling. She put her arms around his waist and he kicked the horse into motion. The skirt of her tunic dress was not ideally suited for riding but she arranged it as best she could. Being on a horse felt familiar.

They made two circuits of the barns at a trot before he kicked the horse into a gallop and headed into the orchards. Her feet wanted to slip into stirrups but they weren't there. She had to squeeze her knees to keep herself on and keep her rump from bouncing too much against the horse's spine. At the end of the row, he slowed to a canter to make the turn then resumed the gallop.

"Too fast?" He asked.

"No. Faster," Emily said.

They picked up speed and came to the end of the row.

"Hang on," he said.

He made an abrupt turn at speed. Emily leaned into it and they raced down another row. It was exhilarating. Byon slowed the horse to a trot and headed for the stable. When they stopped, she swung a leg over and slid down. Byon did the same.

"Have you ridden before?" he asked.

"Yes," she said. Her answer didn't feel like a lie even though *he* had never been on a horse.

They brushed and stabled One-sock then headed out back. They threw javelins for a while. Emily had become fairly accurate but couldn't throw one much further than thirty paces. She practiced left handed as well but her accuracy wasn't as good. She had become a decent slinger, though it had taken effort to get the hang of it. She was amazed at the speed a sling could propel stones. They took chips out of the target board when they hit. Byon once used a lead war bullet and punched a hole clean through.

They started sparring with staves, going through a few drills to warm up. Emily liked doing this the best -- the contest of it, the tactics, the test of reflexes. Byon wasn't very enthusiastic. She tried to encourage him but he wasn't staying focused. He presented an opening and she whacked him hard on the shoulder.

"C'mon fight!" she shouted in English.

Byon's eyes grew hard and he circled her menacingly. She tried a series of attacks. He parried them easily but didn't counter attack. She tried feints, ruses and jabs but to no avail. It was like he knew what she was going to do before she did it. He was in "the zone," she realized. She tried a rapid series of strikes. Byon countered them all, then, wump! Emily yelped and went to the ground holding her side.

Byon's face became one of blanched dismay. He knelt down beside her.

"I am sorry, Emily. I did not want to strike you that hard."

"It is all right," she said, grimacing. "I earned it."

"Let me feel," he said.

Byon put his hand on her side and applied a little pressure. His fingers probed her ribs.

"Nothing broken," he said. "Tough girl."

"Thank you," she said. "You are a good friend."

"I will always be your friend," he said.

He lifted her to her feet.

"You are like my sister. She is a fighter, too."

"Really? Is she a horse warrior?"

"Yes."

"Does she fight for the Greeks?"

"No, the Greeks do not hire female fighters."

"Figures," she muttered in English.

~

The next morning, Nancy came into the room while Emily dozed in bed. The bruise on her side throbbed.

"Better get up," Nancy said. "We're going into town."

Emily sat up and swung her feet to the floor, wincing as she did so.

"My God, what happened to you?" Nancy asked.

"I sparred with Byon. It got a little rough."

"He should know better. I should give him a piece of my mind."

"Don't. It was my fault. I started the rough play and egged him on. He was beside himself afterward."

Nancy fetched her makeup case from her pack.

"I want to buy a mirror at the market if we can find one," she said.

Emily put on the blue tunic-dress she had received when they first arrived at the oikist's house. She didn't wear it much anymore. A plain flax tunic was more suitable for farm work. She also put on her short wool cloak.

"Here, sit down. Your tail's getting frazzled," Nancy said.

Nancy unbraided her hair and brushed it straight.

"Do you really like Agathon?" Emily asked.

"Sure, he's strong and smart and not bad looking for a bald guy," she said.

"And happens to be the polemarch, and rich by Greek standards," Emily said.

"The opportunity was there. It seemed like a good idea to take it."

"Does he want to marry you?"

"I don't know. He hasn't said as much. I'm guessing it would be complicated, me being an outsider."

Nancy pulled Emily's hair back and began braiding it.

"I'm okay with being his concubine and seeing where it goes," Nancy continued.

"Practical to the last," Emily said.

"A woman's got to do what a woman's got to do."

"What happens if you get pregnant?"

"My tubes are tied, honey."

The feeling of Nancy handling her hair was pleasant. She realized she preferred the warmth of friendship over the heat of being lovers. That time had passed. She thought about what life here had to offer. Was a woman's choice essentially limited to what man she could find to attach herself to? Or what man was found for her? What if she didn't want a man?

"You and Byon get along nicely," Nancy said. "He really likes you. That's clear."

"He says I remind him of his sister," Emily said. "I think that's how he thinks of me, a kind of younger sister."

"Hmm."

~

Timon drove the wagon toward town with Emily sitting next to him. Alex, Nancy and Nikanor rode in back. Agathon rode ahead in his chariot. Byon trotted alongside on One-sock. He wore his helmet and carried his weapons. It would take more than a few bandits to get passed him and Agathon, Emily thought.

The day was cloudy and cool but so far the rain held off. They went through the gate, stopped and got out of the wagon. Agathon said he had business to take care of. He assigned two hoplites to escort them in town. Byon would escort them home when they were ready.

The market was crowded and people seemed to be rushing. Perhaps they wanted to conclude their business before rain came. Entering the midst of the crowd, people did take notice and curious eyes watched them. Small-time hawkers tried to get their attention, displaying jewelry and baubles. Emily supposed they would have been more aggressive if not for the presence of the hoplites and their hefty spears. The odors of food and spices filled the air.

Nikanor led them to a broad tent with a large, overhanging canopy that sheltered stacks of rugs. The merchant greeted them warmly, offered wine and little almond cakes for refreshment. Emily declined the wine but nibbled on a cake. The rugs were colorful. Some had flowery designs, some had abstract geometric patterns. Nancy looked them over carefully.

"What do you think of this one?" Nancy asked. "I think it would go well in the gynaeceum."

"Looks fine to me," Emily said.

"I can tell you're going to be a fat lot of help," Nancy said.

"They look expensive," Emily said. "How much did Agathon pay you?"

"He didn't pay me anything. He told me to pick up whatever I thought was needed for the house plus some nice things for myself if I wanted. It'll go on his tab."

"He gave you a blank check? Agathon's not as smart as I thought."

"That's enough out of you."

Emily finished her second cake and Nancy was still deciding. She had compelled Alex to pick out a rug for the andron which he did in less than a minute. Next to the tent was a pavilion displaying weapons and several men and boys were browsing its wares. Emily decided to go take a look but a hoplite stepped in front of her.

"Apologies. You need to stay together. Orders," the hoplite said, his voice emanating from the narrow vertical slit of his full-faced helmet.

Emily felt a flash of irritation. She didn't like being constrained yet she didn't want to cause trouble. She couldn't force her way passed him.

What else could she do? She remembered the time when *he* had escorted *his* niece around an amusement park and how she invariably got what she wanted.

"Please," Emily said. "It is only a few paces away. I just want to look at the weapons. You can come with me."

She smiled and looked up at him as doe-eyed as could. The cold metal face of the helmet stared back at her. She blinked a couple of times deliberately. He turned to his comrade, muttered a few words, then waved her on. He followed close behind. It rankled something inside her to use the tactic but one couldn't argue with results.

The pavilion had an array of spears, javelins, swords, knives, shields and other war gear. A man limped toward her. He had one arm and a patch over one eye.

"May I help you, my lady?" He asked.

"I need to buy javelins," she said.

She did actually need them. She had been wearing out Byon's and some needed replacing. The man showed her his selection. She picked one up. Its shaft was straight and true and its leaf-shaped head was even and sharp. She handed it to the hoplite.

"What do you think?"

The hoplite lifted his helmet back, revealing a young, clean-shaven face that seemed the opposite of the menacing visage of the helmet. He looked the javelin over, thumped its shaft with a fingernail, tested its rigidity, felt the edge of the blade, worked it back and forth to test the mounting.

"It is good," he said.

"Highest quality," the one-armed man said. "All made in Thrace."

"How much?" Emily asked.

"Three drachmas. Highest quality. None better."

The hoplite scoffed. The one-eyed man shot him an irritated look.

"One drachma," Emily said. "I will take six."

The one-armed man looked aghast. "No, no, I cannot sell for that. For six I ask fifteen drachmas."

"I don't know. I will think about it."

"Twelve drachmas. Lowest price."

Emily went to look at the swords and knives. Three boys hanging around got out of her way and whispered among themselves. She picked up a sword. It felt heavy in her hand. She put it back. She saw a dagger that intrigued her. It had a finely carved wooden handle and a polished double-edged blade that was about a foot long. It reminded her of a "pig-sticker" that *he* had owned. It had a thick spine and a strong, sharp point. It felt good in her hand.

"How much?" She asked.

"Sixty drachmas. Corinthian made. Best in the world."

Even if she could talk him down to half that, it would be more than she wanted to spend.

Alex appeared in the pavilion. "C'mon, Emily, Nancy wants to look at pots now."

She told the one-armed man she would pay twelve drachmas for the javelins if he threw in fifty sling bullets. He agreed to twenty-five and she paid him the amount. She told him they would be back later to pick up the items.

~

They went to an area for vendors of pots, vases and other ceramic items. The three boys followed them. Nancy was particularly interested in the large vases which were popular among the Greeks. Nikanor explained the stories behind the scenes painted on them. One showed Odysseus and three of his men poking out the eye of the cyclops with a great spear. Another depicted Heracles battling Geryon, the three-headed giant.

Emily lost interest after a while and took a seat on a nearby bench. Her hoplite companion stayed close at hand. She got the feeling that she was the one they thought most needed watching. So, apparently, did the boys from the weapons pavilion. She figured they were nine or ten years old. They huddled, shooting glances at her. She heard the word, "Nyfitsa." The story had gotten around.

After some nudging and pushing from his friends, one of the boys approached. He had dark hair, wore sandals and a white tunic bordered with blue.

"Are you a witch?" The boy asked.

"What is your name?" Emily asked as sternly as she could.

"Markos," he said.

"Do you think I am a witch?" She asked.

"Yes," he said, and with a quick motion touched her knee and tried to run off.

But Emily's reflexes were too quick. She caught his wrist with her left hand and put her right hand on her puukko but did not draw it. The boy's face went red.

"You are right. I am a witch and I like to eat little boys," she said slowly.

"Sorry, sorry!" The boy pleaded.

She let him go. The boy ran off after his friends who were already running away. The hoplite laughed aloud and had to take off his helmet to wipe spittle from the inside.

~

Emily watched the comings and goings of the marketplace. People carried goods, chatted, haggled, ate snacks purchased from vendors' carts, and drank wine. The majority were men, although a few were women -- mostly slaves, Emily supposed -- buying food and wares for the households they were bound to. It was strange in a way. The slave women had more freedom of movement than the wealthy ladies who did not venture out unescorted.

She noticed a man, dressed in rags, who eyed her and slunk toward her in increments. His tunic was tattered, hair matted and beard unkempt. He carried a small box. When he got to within a few paces, the hoplite intervened.

"Get out of here, maggot," he said. "She wants nothing from you."

"My humble apologies," the man said. "I just want a brief word with the lady."

The hoplite looked back at Emily. She shrugged and waved the man forward. What now, she wondered. The hoplite stepped aside. The man came close to Emily and went to his knees. He stank.

"Many pardons," he said. He had few teeth. "They say you are strong with Artemis, protector of women's virtue."

Emily couldn't think of a reply, even an English one.

"I do not wish to offend and I submit to your mercy," he continued. "I have some small trifles. I humbly ask that you bless them."

He opened the box. It contained a dozen or so wooden figurines. He took one out and handed it to her. It was a carving of a weasel sitting up on its haunches. It was about four inches long. Its tail wrapped around its feet and served as a base. It had tiny red stones for eyes. The workmanship was good, not life-like detail, but clear what it was meant to be. Emily was overcome by an emotion she couldn't place. It was one thing to have a reputation for fierceness, another to have become a kind of cult figure associated with a goddess. She was getting an inkling of the depth of these people's superstition and it made her nervous.

It also flattered her. And it was clear the pathetic man before her was making a bid to profit from her notoriety.

"I cannot say if I am strong with Artemis. Only Artemis knows," she said, concentrating on her words. "But I will try ... to bless them. May I keep one?"

"Yes, please, you may keep one, thank you, please."

She put the figurine into her pouch and cupped the pepper-spray canister. Trying to reveal as little as possible of the canister, she gave each figure in the box a brief squirt. When she was done, the man sniffed the box with the now anointed weasels. The peppery chemical smell must have been something new to him. He beamed, his smile painful to look at.

"Thank you, thank you, you are very kind," he groveled. "May the gods favor your every step, ah ..."

"Emily. My name is Emily."

"Emm-ee-lee, thank you, thank you, gracious one."

The man closed the lid of the box and scurried off.

~

The breeze from the sea freshened and the clouds broke up. There would be no rain today. When Nancy was done with the pots, they moved on to other stalls where she bought cloth, plates, bowls, and other utensils, plus a bronze mirror, gifts for Zosima and Phoibe, and a necklace, bracelets, and earrings for herself. Alex bought an assortment of tools and measuring devices. Emily bought a pair of soft, fur-lined boots, said to be Scythian made. They cost ten drachmas but she thought they would be worth it when winter came. She also bought a hooded Thracian cloak made of raw wool. It was too long for her but she figured she could cut it to size and have Phoibe dye it. She bought a leather satchel and stuffed the boots and cloak inside it.

Lunch consisted of eating tidbits offered by the merchants they visited. By midafternoon they were ready to go home. Nikanor arranged for an agent to have their stuff hauled to the wagon parked near the gate. Walking toward the bridge, they saw Timon playing a dice game with other young men. Nikanor waved for him to come along.

Emily's hoplite stayed close beside her.

"What is your name?" She asked.

"Drakon," he said.

"Thank you, Drakon, for watching over us today."

"You are welcome," he said. "I like the ribbon in your hair."

"What ribbon?" Her speech slipped into English.

Emily reached back and felt a strip of cloth tied to her ponytail in what she assumed was a bow. Nancy had done it again. She untied the knot and saw the ribbon was orange. She handed it to Drakon.

"Keep it," she said. "May it bring you luck."

"Thank you," Drakon said. "When you come back to the market, I would be happy to escort you again."

Maybe she shouldn't have done that, she thought. She realized how naive she was in reading these situations. But good will was good will.

"That would be nice," she said.

~

The stuff Nancy had purchased filled the wagon and meant they would have to walk back to the farm. Emily took one of the javelins to use as a walking stick and stuffed the pouch of sling pellets into her satchel.

"Agathon's going to choke when he gets the bill," Emily said to Nancy.

"I was being frugal," she said. "Just the things the house needs to have."

"I wonder how we got along without them."

"I see you took off the ribbon," Nancy said.

"About that ..."

"It was nice. Just the right touch, I thought. What did you do with it?"

"I gave it to the hoplite."

Nancy laughed. "Better be careful, girl, or you'll have to beat him off with a stick."

The piercing blare of a horn cut their conversation short. A man on a watchtower shouted and the message got relayed along the ramparts. Soon the marshaling area was alive with activity and the gate was closed.

"What is going on?" Emily asked Drakon.

"Scythian warriors approaching," he said. "Our allies ... most likely."

She saw Agathon climb up to the ramparts followed by a detail of bowmen. A group of maybe 100 hoplites were forming into a phalanx in the middle of the yard.

Tense moments passed before she heard Agathon shouting, followed by a distant reply. Agathon then shouted down to the yard. Men still hurried to their battle stations but the atmosphere relaxed considerably.

"Our allies," Drakon said. "A party of Lions."

The gate opened. Its two guards stepped outside and assumed their usual posts. Agathon came down to the yard. He shouted orders and a dozen hoplites broke from the phalanx and followed him to the road where they lined up in an orderly rank in front of the wagon. Emily, still clutching a javelin, stood on the driver's bench to get a better view.

Twenty Scythian warriors rode through the gate on lean, long-legged horses. Unlike the uniformity of the hoplites, they seemed to want to outdo each other with the variety of their attire. Many wore pointed hats of red felt with leather rims. Some had cloaks with colorful patterns. They rode in a column two abreast. One of the lead pair of warriors was clad in armor of bronze scales and wore a bronze helmet, open at the face and a red tail of horsehair flowing behind it. His beard was thick and brown and he carried a shield and a spear.

The warrior beside him wore a dark leather cuirass with a red starburst at the chest. The armor flared to a kind of short skirt of leather strips and fitted over a quilted, long-sleeved tunic of deep red. The warrior wore black leggings with red, zigzagging stripes. The warrior's dark hair was woven into two long, thick braids. The warrior wore a red felt hat like the others but, being a woman, she had no beard.

Emily was transfixed. The woman had a long sword at her hip and strapped to her saddle was an elaborately decorated quiver that held a bow and many arrows. Her arms rested on her lap and she viewed the line of hoplites with a look that bordered on contempt. The woman's blue eyes found Emily's and they briefly held each other's gaze.

Two other warriors also were women. One was quite small and looked no older than a teenager. Her red cap had studded flaps that hung to her shoulders. The top of the cap had a snake-like protrusion that curved forward to a knob at the end. On her broad belt was a knife and what looked like a tomahawk with a long, thin handle. She too had a quiver with a bow and arrows. She carried herself like the others and bore the same contemptuous look.

The lead male warrior raised his spear and the troop stopped. They turned their horses to face Agathon and the hoplites. Without a word or any apparent signal, the lead female warrior's horse knelt. She swung a leg over and dismounted. The other warriors dismounted in similar fashion. They were all bow-legged. Agathon shook hands with the woman. She was tall, taller than Nancy, and lean. Her cheek bore a deep scar.

Agathon dismissed the hoplites and walked with the Scythian warriors and their horses toward the stables. Emily hopped down from the wagon and watched them walk away.

"There's something you don't see every day," Alex said.

"My God, what a spectacle, it hardly seems real," Nancy said.

"Drakon, who is the tall one?" Emily asked.

"Kydoime," he said. "They say she will one day be queen of the Lion Tribe."

"I wouldn't want to meet her in a dark alley," Alex said.

"I'm glad they're on our side," Nancy said.

The Greek soldiers stood down from their battle readiness and began to resume their normal routines. Byon approached leading One-sock. He saw the hoplite standing close to Emily.

"You are relieved now," Byon said, an edge in his voice. "I will escort them home."

Chapter 14 | Happy Hunting

PLEASED with the new javelins, Byon added them to his war kit. He and Emily used the old ones for practice. After they had gone through their routine, they sat on a bench and drank spring water brought down from the temple.

"Do you know the Scythians?" Emily asked.

"I have ridden with them, yes," Byon said. "Back home, they would raid our farms and steal horses and cattle. We would raid their herds back. It was fun, sometimes deadly."

"What about the ones we saw yesterday? Do you know them?"

"I have not met them. Everyone knows who Kydoime is and her husband, Uratan. They have fought many battles."

"What about the small woman. Do you know who she is?"

"I think she is Aella. She is a dasher. She leads the chase on hunts. They say she can hit a man 50 paces away with her bow at full gallop. She is very dangerous."

"I want to ride One-sock by myself," Emily said.

She had to settle for Byon's other horse, a small but sturdy brown mare with a thick tan mane. Emily called her Shaggy. It felt good riding her but Emily's feet still searched for stirrups that weren't there. She was doing well but didn't realize Shaggy could turn so sharply. She flew off, rolling on the grassy turf. Byon ran up to her.

"Are you hurt?"

"My pride is wounded," she said, picking herself up.

It occurred to her that the fall would have been much harder on *him*. Byon whistled and the mare returned.

"Done for the day?"

"No," she said. "One more go-round. I do not want to end this way."

She mounted Shaggy by jumping so her stomach was on the horse's back then pivoting and swinging her legs around. Byon chuckled at the awkward procedure but it was the first time she'd been able to mount the horse herself. She trotted Shaggy once around the barns and slid off.

"Do you like to hunt?" She asked.

"Yes, very much," Byon said.

"We should go hunting."

"I do not know if Agathon would allow it."

"I will talk to him."

~

A day later the Thesmophoria festival began. Nearly all the Greek women in the area were camped out in tents near the temple. Nancy and Emily weren't invited. Kallisto had said the festival involved secret rites and it was rare for foreigners to attend. Even she was something of an outsider and not a full participant. In the evening they could hear the women laughing and carousing. It sounded bawdy and raucous and went on late into the night. Emily lay in bed wishing the bitches would shut up.

Agathon had not returned to the farm since their day at the market. Apparently he was discussing business with the Scythians. Emily wished she could be a part of it and learn the details of the strategic situation. What threats loomed? What aid were the Scythians prepared to give and at what cost?

Nancy knocked and came in carrying a candle.

"Sorry. Agape's got a fever. I want to get some aspirin."

Nancy was caring for the young Agape while her mother, Thais, attended the festival.

"Are you sure it's a good idea?" Emily asked.

"It's just some aspirin. No one will know."

The next day Agape's fever abated and she seemed to feel better, but she had developed a bad cough. The day after that, her cough worsened and her breathing became wheezy and labored. Zosima prepared a concoction that soothed Agape's throat but did little else.

Nancy approached Emily and Alex who were working on the gazebo. Alex had erected six bases of mortared stone. Each supported a thick wooden beam and the beams supported the roof. It was nearing completion and almost ready for the tile shingles.

"I think Agape's got pneumonia or a really bad case of bronchitis," Nancy said. "I want to use antibiotics."

"Remember what we talked about," Alex said.

"I know but I'm not going to let her die. Not if I can help it," Nancy said. "Thais came back from the festival. She's out of her mind. Zosima says when it gets this bad, children rarely live."

"We're not doctors. She's a child. We don't know the dosage," Alex said.

"If it works, word will spread," Emily said. "We can't cure everybody."

"You would let her die? I don't believe you two," Nancy said. "Just listen to yourselves."

Emily knew that Nancy would have her way. So did Alex. They went upstairs to Emily's room and fetched the bag of prescription pill bottles from Hank's pack.

"Here, this is a fairly mild antibiotic," Alex said. "I have a hunch it will work. It says one pill twice daily. If we cut the dose in half, that should be about right."

He emptied the bottle onto the table and Emily used her sharp puukko to split the pills.

"Wouldn't pneumonia need something stronger?" Emily asked.

"My hunch is that infections of this time will not be resistant to antibiotics," Alex said. "And, being mild, there's less danger of side effects."

Nancy said she would make Thais swear not to tell anybody.

"Remember, she's got to do the full regimen," Alex said.

~

The following day, Agathon returned and Agape's cough improved. Folks attributed it to Demeter's divine intervention, a sign that she was pleased with the festival and the land would be bountiful in the coming year.

The sky was clear and the air unseasonably warm. Emily worked on her Thracian cloak in the courtyard. She had cut it to knee length and was sewing the hem. Phoibe was mixing a dark green dye using indigo and a yellow substance pressed from pomegranate rinds. They had decided to fringe the cloak with a dragon's tooth pattern of burnt orange cloth.

Phoibe didn't talk much but seemed to enjoy being with Emily. Sometimes Emily would turn around and there Phoibe was, looking sheepish and wanting to help with whatever she was doing.

Emily saw Cleon, Timon and Alex riding away on the wagon with Byon trotting beside them on Shaggy. They all laughed at something. Alex must have cracked a joke. The men were going into town.

Agathon sat at the table across from Emily.

"It is so relaxing here," he said. "I wish I could get away from the polis more."

"Did it go well with the Lion Tribe?" Emily asked.

"Yes, I think so, you never know with those people. They are so different. I suppose I should be used to them by now."

"Is there any trouble?"

"Persian patrols have been spotted south of Novorosa," he said. He seemed like he was going to continue along that line but checked himself. "Nothing to worry about, though."

"I have something to ask you," Emily said.

"Yes?"

"Byon and I would like to go hunting, with your permission."

"Hmm, I would like to do that myself but I want Byon here to look after you folks."

"It would be safe. Cleon and Timon are still here," Emily said.

"Perhaps you are right. I do not worry as much as I used to," Agathon said. "Byon says you would be dangerous in a fight, quick and sneaky."

"Nyfitsa?"

"No, I did not mean that. I am warming to the Spartan practice of training women to fight so they can protect their homes in need."

"A good idea," Emily said.

"Nyfitsa, ha! You are something else, my young friend. Are you sure you are not Scythian?"

"No, not Scythian," she said, though it occurred to her that she might like to be.

"You and Byon get along well," Agathon said. "He is fond of you."

"I am fond of him."

"You know, if you two wanted to settle here, you would be very welcome," Agathon said. "There is land we can clear. You could start your own farm, perhaps raise horses. You could start a family and become full-fledged citizens. I am sure any children you two had would be healthy and strong."

Agathon winked and rubbed her head. He must have seen that the blood had drained from her face.

"My apologies. I get ahead of myself. Just an old man thinking out loud."

~

Agathon stayed on the farm for a couple of days, spending a lot of time with Nancy. On the second day, the two went for a long walk in the forest. Byon was with his Thracian comrades, doing what, Emily didn't know. Probably out on patrol. It was the first time since coming to the farm that neither Byon nor Agathon was around. Emily hoped it meant that they thought she could take care of herself.

Rain came the next day. Emily was doing chores in the stable when Byon led Shaggy into her stall.

"I have something for you," Byon said.

He handed Emily a cloth bundle. She pulled back the folds. It was the Corinthian dagger she had admired at the market.

"Byon, it is too much. You cannot give me this."

"It is not a gift. You earned it," he said.

"Earned it?"

Byon explained that the Greek paymasters had finally distributed the booty taken from Hydakoles and his bandits. Byon had asked his fellow riders to each give up a small amount for Emily because she had played a role in killing Hydakoles.

"They agreed to that?"

"After ... convincing," he said.

"What did you say to them? You did not tell them I was a witch."

"No, they already believe that."

"What then?"

"I said if they did so, they would gain favor with Artemis because you are favored by her."

"Do you believe I am favored by Artemis?"

"Yes, it is plain to see."

The dagger had a wooden sheath wrapped in black leather and tipped with bronze. Emily withdrew the polished blade and felt its edge. It wasn't razor sharp but it didn't need to be. Its heft would do the work and it was primarily a thrusting weapon. She sheathed it and hooked the sheath to her belt on the left side, opposite her puukko.

"How does it look?"

"Like it was made for you."

"Thank you."

Without thinking she hugged him. He didn't put his arms around her immediately but when he did, he squeezed her tight. Emily suddenly felt self-conscious and backed away.

"Tell your friends I will ask Artemis to look after them in battle," she said.

"I will."

"I wish I could ride and fight with your fellow warriors," Emily said.

"Perhaps you can some day when you are ready," Byon said. "I have two years left with the Greeks. Come back to Thrace with me. There you are free to ride and fight with the men. You will enjoy my sister and my family and they will enjoy you."

"I would like that, I think, but ... I am not like other women. I am not who you think I am."

"You are who you are. I like who you are."

"I am not ready. I do not know when I will be," Emily said. She wondered if she would ever be ready to be with a man.

"Two years. Maybe you are ready then."

"Maybe. I cannot promise anything."

"Maybe is enough."

His willingness to be patient was unnerving. She realized he was playing a long game and probably knew more than he let on.

"Agathon told me we can go hunting if we want," Emily said.

"Yes, he told me this morning. When the rain stops, we will go."

~

The rain didn't stop, not for two days. People on the farm busied themselves with indoor chores. Kallisto and Nikanor came to visit and stayed for two nights. They resumed their language lessons with renewed vigor. Nikanor participated, telling stories and myths, asking Alex, Nancy and Emily questions afterward. Emily liked the story of Atalanta, the tomboy huntress who would only marry the man who could beat her in a foot race. Those who didn't she would kill with her spear. She was very fast and many men died trying, until Melanion, with help from Aphrodite, finally bested her.

Byon let everyone know that Emily could sing. After much goading, Nikanor taught her a song that featured Atalanta. She sang while he strummed his lyre.

That evening the men went to the andron to play dice games. In the gynaeceum Emily and Phoibe were finishing the cloak, sewing on the orange dragon's teeth. The dying had turned out well, a couple of uneven spots but otherwise it was the dark green Emily wanted. It was going to be her stalking cloak. Nancy played Itsy Bitsy Spider with Agape while Thais, Zosima and Kallisto spun thread. Emily was nearly done sewing the dragon's teeth on the hood when Phoibe pushed her hands away.

"Let me finish," she said.

In ways, Phoibe's mind wasn't much beyond grade school, Emily thought, but she was amazed at the array of skills she possessed: sewing, weaving, dying, skinning, butchering, cooking, and many others. She wasn't stupid -- it was just the way her brain had developed, perhaps the only way it could develop. Phoibe tied off the last stitch and secured it.

"Stand up," she told Emily.

Such a direct instruction from a slave would have been unthinkable at Bereneke's house. It pleased Emily that Phoibe felt comfortable enough to talk to her like a friend instead of a master. Phoibe put the cloak on her shoulders and fastened it with a bronze clasp.

Emily spun around.

"You look like an elf," Nancy said.

Emily pulled up the generous hood and raised the cloak to the bridge of her nose like a vampire in an old horror movie. She glared at the other women with mock menace. With a quick motion, she drew her Corinthian dagger.

"Aimay Nyfitsa!" she hissed.

Zosima cackled and bent over. Phoibe clapped and hopped up and down. Agape copied her. Kallisto and Thais laughed, too. Nancy shook her head.

"Girl, you're a bad seed."

~

The rain stopped the next day. Emily and Byon went hunting but without much success. They hiked east below the temple and into the forest beyond. Byon knew what he was doing. He could identify tracks, read scat and spot other signs. Byon's woodcraft was far better than *his* had been. Emily paid close attention, soaking up all the knowledge she could. She carried a javelin, her sling, ten sling pellets, her dagger and her puukko. In her satchel, she carried a water skin, cloth rags, twine, a bag of nuts and two apples. Unbeknownst to Byon, she also had her multi-tool, flashlight, magnesium fire starter and first aid kit.

They tracked a deer for a while but couldn't get close. One advantage she did have was stealth. She could step more quietly than Byon. Emily was going to wear her sneakers but, when she put them on, they felt weird and heavy. She had grown used to going barefoot and had developed tough calluses, so she went without shoes. The weather was not cold enough yet to need her fur-lined boots.

After some lunch, they spent most of the afternoon familiarizing themselves with the forest and discussing possible strategies for future hunts. Byon did kill two rabbits with his sling. Emily missed her shot. Being accurate on the practice ground was different than being accurate in the field. When they returned to the farm, Phoibe took the rabbits. She knew how to prepare the fur for later use and cut up the meat to supplement meals.

~

It was two days before they had a chance to go out again. They had not traveled far when Emily heard a rustling sound ahead. She stopped, looked at Byon and pointed to her ear. He shook his head. She signaled him to wait.

Slowly, quietly, she advanced. The sound moved away and was further off than she thought. She was perhaps 200 paces ahead of Byon when she saw what it was -- a wild pig, a sow by the look of it. Emily's heart pumped rapidly. She couched low and began her stalk. She hoped no breeze would come and give her away. She got within 20 paces, not close enough for a sure throw. Patience, she reminded herself. She inched forward.

At 15 paces, the pig looked up from its foraging and sniffed the air. Now or never. She hurled the javelin. It struck the pig's haunches and sunk deep into its flesh. The pig squealed and ran off. She chased after it. The animal hobbled as it ran but still moved rapidly. It was all Emily could do to keep up. She was amazed at its stamina. A deer would have gone down far sooner.

Finally it slowed and was barely able to keep its feet. She heard a hissing sound. An arrow struck the animal's head and it collapsed.

"Got it!" Someone shouted.

Emily stopped ten paces from the pig and looked around. Two men emerged from the trees. One had a bow. He was youngish, bearded and wore the tunic and cloak of a Greek citizen, as did his companion who carried a hunting spear. They approached the dead pig but did not notice Emily.

"Whose javelin is that?" The man with the spear asked.

"It is mine," Emily said. "And that is my kill."

The two men were startled at first then the man with the bow grinned.

"Ah, what do we have here? A forest maiden?"

The man took in Emily with his eyes.

"Not the prettiest nymph but we could make do. We could take her back to the lodge. Would you like that, little hen?"

He started walking toward Emily.

"Leave her alone, Hermus," the man with the spear said. "She is right. She scored the first shot."

"I am just having a little fun."

The bearded man continued toward Emily. She drew her dagger.

"The pig is mine. Now be off!"

"The girl has a temper and likes to play with knives," the man said and drew his sword. "But sweetie, your dagger is no match for a xiphos."

Emily assumed a fighting stance. She was at a disadvantage against his greater size and larger weapon but, if he underestimated her, her quickness might win out. Unexpectedly the man stopped and looked beyond Emily. A strong hand gripped her wrist. It was Byon and he had his sword drawn.

"I offer you my apologies," Byon said to the two men. "We do not want any trouble."

He spoke with a low, calm tone but his eyes betrayed an undercurrent of fury.

"I am Byon, lieutenant of the hipparch, Callias. This is Emily, guest of the polemarch, Agathon. I am charged with her safekeeping and will defend her with my life if need be. You may take the pig if you wish. It is not worth fighting over."

Both men backed away. The bearded man, Hermus, sheathed his sword.

"I am sorry. I meant no offense. I got carried away. I would not have hurt her."

"I accept your apology," Byon said. "And you should know you were in more danger than you think. She fights like a Scythian."

"Nyfitsa," the man with the spear whispered.

"With your pardon we will be on our way," Hermus said. "The pig is yours, of course."

~

Byon didn't say anything when the men left. Emily could tell he was angry with her. He turned the pig on its back and she gutted it with her puukko. Byon found a large branch and hacked the smaller branches off with his sword. They lashed the pig's legs to the branch and started carrying it back home.

"I am sorry, Byon," she said. "I was foolish."

"You are brave and you are smart but you need to be brave and smart together," he said.

He was right. Anger had overwhelmed her good sense. She should have remained hidden until Byon arrived, then they could have resolved the matter of the pig. It was unsettling because *he* would not have been so rash.

The pig was heavy and they set it down to take a break. She drank water from her skin. Byon put his arm around her. She rested her head on his shoulder, relieved he had not stayed angry for long.

"It was not your first kill," Byon said.

"My first pig. I have killed deer before," she said.

"How did you kill the deer? With a bow?" he asked.

"With a rifle," she said. "I cannot easily explain. Someday, when I have the words, I will tell you everything. You will not believe it and you may not want to be my friend anymore."

"You are honest. I will believe it and remain your friend."

~

On their return, everyone came out to see the pig Emily had killed. She and Byon had decided to keep quiet about their encounter with the Greek men. She recounted the story of her stalk, throw and chase.

"She moves like a panther through the forest," Byon added.

"I think you are an elf," Nancy said.

~

They hung the pig in one of the barns to let it age a few days. Phoibe skinned it and worked on processing the hide. It amused Emily to think they could make a football out of it.

Agathon returned one afternoon and talked at length with Byon under the now finished gazebo. It was well done with its stone pillars, thick beams, precisely fitted supports, and maroon tile shingles. Its generous eaves would keep rain water well away from the stone patio beneath.

Emily was exercising One-sock (Byon had finally let her ride him) when Agathon waved her over. She slid down and handed the reins to Byon. She hopped over the courtyard wall instead of using the gate.

"Congratulations on your kill," Agathon said. "I understand you are quite the huntress. I am beginning to believe what they say about you and Artemis."

"Thank you," Emily said. "Byon is the better woodsman. I am learning much from him."

"Yes, Thracians are good woodsman," he said. "We will have to celebrate with a pig roast and inaugurate the new gazebo."

"I would like that."

"About Byon," Agathon said. "I am going to have to take him away from you for a time. I am sending Callias and his squadron north to keep an eye on the Persians. Callias needs Byon. He is one of our best men and a leader among the Thracians."

"When will he have to go?" Emily asked.

"The day after tomorrow. We will have that pig roast tomorrow night to send him off."

"How long will he be gone?"

"Hard to say. A few months. He could come back sooner if the Persians back off. We shall see."

"Will there be fighting?"

"A skirmish or two would not surprise me. I do not expect war. The Persians and the Novorosians are not strong enough to attack us and the Lion Tribe."

"Cannot the Persian Empire field a very large army?" Emily asked.

"Yes. But we are too far out of the way and too small for the Persians to send the Immortals."

The Immortals, Emily knew, represented the empire's elite fighting force, 10,000 strong, and greatly feared.

"We will be safe, I am sure," Agathon continued. "And from the whispers I am hearing, the Immortals will soon have their hands full down south."

She was about to ask if the whispers meant there would be an uprising of Greek city states against the Persians but she checked herself. Such a question could create suspicion. She didn't want him to think she had knowledge she shouldn't have. Agathon's words did support what she suspected. They were on the verge of the Ionian Rebellion.

"I will worry about Byon," Emily said. "And I worry about Artemios."

"Byon will be fine," Agathon said. "And I will make sure Artemios is safe."

~

Emily could tell Byon was eager to ride north. He was a warrior and desired action. She couldn't blame him. She wished she could go. Would he ever come back, she wondered. Would he even want to?

Shortly before the pig roast, as everyone was getting ready, Emily knocked at Nancy's door. Nancy had taken over the dressing room meant for the lady of the house. Zosima was with her, helping arrange her garments. Nancy wore her hair Greek style now, her blond locks woven into fine braids that dangled delicately on her shoulders.

"Why are you looking so sheepish?" Nancy asked.

Emily felt like saying, "never mind," and leaving.

"C'mon. Out with it."

From her pouch, Emily produced her makeup kit and lipstick.

"Could you show me how to put this on?" She asked.

"Why of course," Nancy said. "It's about time you learned."

Emily sat in front of the mirror while Nancy guided her hand with the brushes.

"We should undo your braid and fix your hair up right but it's too late for that."

Emily fished out a burnt-orange ribbon from her pouch.

"Phoibe made a few of these from the leftover cloth."

Nancy tied the ribbon to the end of Emily's ponytail.

"There you go, cuter than a button."

~

The party ate outside under the gazebo. Fires were lit in broad ceramic pots which kept the air reasonably warm. Byon had come with Callias who brought his wife, toddler son, and a slave woman who helped with the food preparations. Callias's wife, Ariadne, was young and very pretty with silky dark hair and big brown eyes. She wore a white chiton with a blue cloak and clearly was eager to meet the farm's strange residents. She was in awe of Nancy who charmed her with big smiles and silly jokes. She seemed nervous around Emily and watched her closely throughout the evening.

Kallisto and Nikanor were there, too. Emily pulled Kallisto aside.

"I promised Byon I would ask Artemis to favor him and his men in battle, but that is your role. Could you do it for me?"

"I will dedicate the meal to Artemis and then you will ask her."

They all sat down at a long table. Phoibe and Zosima served bowls of nuts and dried fruit. Agathon stood.

"Tonight we eat Thracian style, men and women together. It will be like ancient times."

Since coming to the farm, they had always eaten meals together. Emily guessed Agathon's words were for Callias and Ariadne's benefit. Alex and Timon carried in the roasted pig on a bronze platter. Nikanor carved it. Kallisto went through her formal dedication to Artemis then gestured toward Emily who stood and raised her wine bowl.

"I humbly ask Artemis to keep Callias, Byon and their fellow warriors safe and guide them to victory in all their battles so Artemios will remain safe from its enemies."

"Well spoken, my dear," Agathon said. He raised his bowl to Callias and Byon. "And happy hunting to you both."

The evening was a merry one. Nikanor played his lyre and told the story of the time when Mother Earth disgorged two giants with serpents for feet. The giants laid siege to Mount Olympus. It was said no god or person could kill them. In the end, the cunning and swift-footed Artemis maneuvered the giants so when they threw their spears, instead of killing her, they struck and killed each other. Emily found it interesting that most of the gods, even Zeus, cowered during the attack but it was Athena who kept her cool and, with Apollo and Artemis, devised a plan to defeat the monsters.

When the story was over, Agathon announced they would have to leave. The squadron was setting out tomorrow and they had to be ready to ride at first light. Byon shook hands with Alex. Nancy gave him a hug which took him by surprise. Emily and Byon hesitated then just shook hands.

"I will miss our hunts and our sparring, but I will be back before long," Byon said.

"Be brave and smart," Emily said. "But, mostly, be smart."

Byon smiled and squeezed her shoulder.

Callias and Byon took the leftovers of the pig with them to feed to their men the next day.

Chapter 15 | Confessions

LIFE on the farm fell into a winter routine. The air grew cold and rain came frequently. Emily tended to the stable. She missed Shaggy and One-sock. The draft horses and mules weren't much fun to ride. She practiced with her weapons. Sometimes Alex or Timon would practice with her. She hunted often but Agathon asked her not to stray too far and she respectfully minded him. Her sling accuracy improved and she brought home rabbits from time to time. Phoibe would shave the fur and save it. With enough fur they could make a soft felt with it.

Kallisto continued their language lessons. Emily's Greek was becoming second nature. She sometimes would think in Greek and dream in Greek.

Nancy had the house looking like it should for a man of Agathon's status. She aspired to rival Berenike's house but had a long way to go. One day Agathon brought the harbor master, Midaleus, and his wife to the farm. Nancy was delighted to play the hostess. Alex, Agathon and Midaleus talked in the andron late into the night.

Alex made frequent visits to town after that, helping the harbor master build the shipyard. Otherwise, when not helping repair things on the farm, he set about making a chess set from scraps of wood.

Emily missed Byon but, in ways, was relieved he was gone. She realized just how strong the expectations had been for their friendship to turn to romance. Part of her longed to embrace him but she tensed up at the thought of kissing him or having sex with him. The thought of getting pregnant still horrified her. Would it ever not horrify her? Should she accept the fact that her condition made her a lesbian and that was that? Phoibe's attentions didn't help dissuade her.

One night, after bathing, Phoibe had brushed Emily's hair and was braiding it. As usual, she said little as her long fingers skillfully did their work.

"Thank you, Phoibe, you are a good person," Emily said when the braid was finished.

From behind, while Emily still sat in her chair, Phoibe threw her arms around her and pressed her cheek against hers.

"I love you, Emily. I would do anything for you."

Emily felt that tingling in her nethers. She sighed. Phoibe's hand was squeezing her ribs. Emily gently pushed it up to her breast and Phoibe started rubbing it. The action confirmed what Phoibe had meant by "anything."

Emily stood, took Phoibe's hands, and looked up at her hazel eyes. She saw a longing to love and be loved. The relationship could not be equitable, Emily thought. Phoibe was a slave and she was not. She decided that it would be best, as gently as possible, to call a halt to going any further. But it dawned on her that Phoibe was making her bid, that it might be her only real opportunity for love making. Would denying her really be the right thing to do?

Emily undid the cords of Phoibe's chiton and slipped it off. Her skinny body was not so alluring as Nancy's and her breasts were small like her own. She had hairy legs but, then, so did Emily. Phoibe crouched down and put her hands on Emily's calves, sliding them up her thighs and hips, taking her tunic with them. Emily raised her arms and let Phoibe pull the tunic over her head and off.

Emily snuffed the candles and they crawled into bed. Phoibe's long limbs entwined Emily like an octopus. It was as if she wanted to press herself into Emily and become a part of her. Emily decided the right thing to do was to pleasure Phoibe until she couldn't stand it anymore.

~

Time rolled on at the farm and entered the month of Gamelion. It was the 188th day since the crash. A cold wind had blown in from the north, bringing a coating of snow. Greek houses were not particularly well designed for winter weather. They kept reasonably warm until temperatures dipped below freezing. Emily wore wool trousers, fur-lined boots, and two cloaks over a wool tunic. Kallisto came for the language lesson and wore a fur robe she said was from lands northwest of Thrace. Celtic perhaps, Emily thought.

Kallisto asked Emily to come to the temple and spend the night. She eagerly accepted. Their breath steamed and snow crunched as they padded through the orchard and up the hill.

"I really do not like this weather. It is hard to get used to," Kallisto said. "Does it get cold like this where you come from?"

"Yes, often much colder," Emily said.

"I suppose it is cleansing in a way. The snow is starkly beautiful on the land."

"Why have you asked me to come with you today?"

"There are many things I would like to discuss," Kallisto said. "I have told Philocrates and Agathon that you are ready to tell your stories."

"And you want a first hearing?"

"Yes, and more as well," Kallisto said.

"Why me instead of Nancy or Alex?"

"Nancy is radiant, a beauty among beauties. Many women admire her, some are envious. Do you know that a few have even fashioned gowns for themselves that resemble the tunic Nancy wore when she first came to town? And Alex, I know he possesses deep knowledge of things, knowledge he wants to share but restrains himself. Perhaps it is dangerous knowledge. I do not know. But you, Emily, interest me the most, and you are the one most talked of in Artemios."

The path from the farm merged into a wider one that ran from the temple to the road that leads to town. The main path paralleled a gurgling brook and, approaching the temple, it entered a stand of tall oaks that formed a kind of natural cathedral. Snow clung to dark branches which seemed in motion against the passing gray clouds.

The temple itself was an open stone structure. Twelve pillars of carefully fitted rocks supported a peaked tile roof now covered with snow. It somewhat resembled Alex's gazebo but was much larger. The brook coursed around the temple and a flat, stone bridge crossed the brook and led to the entrance. The temple had a stone floor with a trough that carried a rivulet of water into the brook.

At the back of the temple was an altar and behind it was a wall. A spout protruded from the wall and water trickled from it into a basin that looked a little like a birdbath. Water flowed from the basin into the trough on the floor. Painted on the wall above the spout was a woman drawing a bow and arrow and riding a lion. On the altar was a golden pitcher, a bowl and a small object. Emily stood with Kallisto at the entrance, taking in the temple's rough-hewn beauty.

"Why a temple to Artemis?" Emily asked. "Why not Athena, or Apollo, or Zeus?"

"Such a thing to ask when confronting the holy altar of Artemis. People say you are strong with her. For your sake, you had better be. Artemis can be unforgiving."

"I am sorry if I gave offense."

"No, your question is pertinent," Kallisto said. "Artemis is a goddess our Scythian allies honor and worship, though by another name. We built the temple, in part, as a token to cement the alliance. It is also why we named the colony Artemios."

"The Scythians do not worship other Greek gods?"

"No, they have their own gods. Some link Ares to their war god or Zeus to their sky god but that is Greek doing. Artemis, the huntress, is worshiped by many people other than the Greeks. The Thracians call her Bendis. She is an aspect of the Great Mother."

"She is not the daughter of Zeus and Leto, sister of Apollo?"

"Only to the Greeks."

A gust of wind blew snow from the branches and enveloped them in a white, crystalline mist.

"I have something to confess," Emily said. "And you probably will not like it."

"Tell me."

"I do not believe in gods. Many people I know back home believe in one supreme God. I don't believe that either."

Kallisto laughed.

"I thought as much but belief is not so important. It is the doing that is important. Artemis and the other gods are faces we put on forces we do not really understand. The gods are a way to connect with them, similar to the way I would connect with another person. As I connect with you, I connect with Artemis. She is the face of forces I do not fully know, as you are the face of forces I do not fully know. It is a way different than the philosophers who see these forces as faceless objects to examine. I will not say it is a better way but it is my way."

Her words reminded Emily of a certain philosophy she had read about but couldn't place. It was clear that Kallisto's depth of mind was beyond common superstition. And her words were compelling. Even *he,* the arch-skeptic, would not have dismissed them.

"To my eyes," Kallisto continued. "The forces that surround you and the forces that surround Artemis are entwined. To what end, I do not know."

Kallisto raised her hands to the sky and intoned words in a language Emily didn't understand. She put an arm around Emily.

"Come. Approach the altar with me. You do not have to believe," Kallisto said.

Emily felt anxious and strangely thrilled. Kallisto's charisma was magnetic, she had to give her that. When they got to the altar, Emily stood before it while Kallisto went around to the other side. Emily couldn't help but smile at the small object on the altar next to the bowl. It was a wooden weasel figurine.

"I see you recognize it," Kallisto said. "It still smells of pepper, a rare and expensive spice. Do you know who owns it?"

Emily shook her head.

"Berenike. She paid a tidy price for it, too. She loaned it to me but wants to give it to her granddaughter."

"It's just a piece of wood," Emily said. "I was trying to help an old beggar."

"It was an act of the heart. Such acts have strong ripples," Kallisto said. "Sometimes it does not matter what you believe. It matters what others believe."

"I am sorry if it caused a problem."

"There is no problem. I just wanted to show you the regard people have for you."

"I have done little to deserve it," Emily said.

"Hmm. Tell me about that night at the oikist's house."

Emily described what happened when the man from Novorosa accosted her. She tried to explain how she used pepper spray to ward him off.

"Can you show me?" Kallisto asked.

"I can but I do not know if I should," Emily said.

"What I see will go no further than here."

Emily produced the canister of pepper spray from her pouch. She handed it to Kallisto who felt its smooth aluminum sides. Emily took it back, pointed it at the floor and depressed the nozzle. A stream of fluid hissed out.

"A device. It is not magic," Kallisto said.

"No, not magic," Emily said. "Do you know what happened to the man afterward?"

"His name is Euneus. He is a nephew of the oikist at Novorosa. At first he claimed that you attacked him but Agathon did not believe it. Euneus then said he thought you were a slave and apologized for being drunk. Agathon was furious and threw him out of the house. If Euneus had not been so high ranking, Agathon would have had him flogged. Philocrates was furious, too, when he heard the news."

"Did it sour negotiations?" Emily asked.

"The delegates from Novorosa left without reaching an agreement," Kallisto said. "I am told an agreement was unlikely in any event."

"Another ripple."

"Yes."

The memory of that night remained painful for Emily. She felt small and couldn't help but wish she were a man again. Kallisto seemed to notice her anxiety. She took the golden pitcher and dipped it into the basin. She spoke more words in the strange language and poured the water into the bowl.

"A maelstrom swirls inside you. Currents of different directions fight each other," Kallisto said. "Drink. Let the water of Artemis unite the currents and calm the sea."

Emily hesitated. She couldn't understand why she felt tears welling up.

"It is funny," Kallisto continued. "Sometimes you seem to me like a man, the swing of your arms when you walk, the way you talk to your friends, the way they look to you. Even Byon and Agathon act differently toward you than other women. And, yet, sometimes you seem like a girl, the way you would look at Byon when he was riding his horse, or the way you giggle with Phoibe over seemingly nothing."

Emily picked up the bowl and drank the cold water. Some of it dribbled down her cheeks. She set the bowl down on the altar. She took deep breaths, letting the indefinable torrent of emotions flow through her. When her breathing slowed, she looked up at Kallisto.

"I was a man, a large man," she said. "The gods turned me into a small woman. I do not know why, or if there is a why."

Kallisto's face was struck with wonder. Emily looked beyond Kallisto to the painting of Artemis. The goddess's fierce eyes seemed intent on Emily, seemed to say this is my will, this is my doing. Come on now, she thought, don't get caught up in that kind of thinking.

Kallisto came around the altar and took Emily's hand. She appeared elated.

"Do not see it as a curse," Kallisto said. "It is a gift, a marvelous gift."

"A gift? Are you saying it is better to be a woman than a man?"

"No, not better. The gift is to have lived as one and then the other, to know both from the inside. It is an opportunity for wisdom."

The notion hadn't occurred to Emily but there was sense to it.

"Live as a woman now and be happy you were once a man," Kallisto continued. "Do not be angry you no longer are one. That would squander the gift."

"I do not think I could ever be a woman like you are a woman, or Nancy," Emily said.

"Perhaps not. Perhaps it is enough to let the currents merge and flow together."

"Where will the currents take me?"

"I do not know but I am eager to find out."

$\sim$

Kallisto put the weasel figurine into her pouch and put the pitcher and bowl into a box. She led Emily out of the temple to a side path that went into the woods to the south. They came to a clearing which was mostly open pasture but had a few structures. One structure looked like an elongated shed, its entrances closed up. Another was a chicken coop. A small barn had an adjoining corral that contained a few goats and sheep. There was a house with a tile roof, not large but well built. Beside it were two conical huts with thatched roofs, each had smoke rising from their peaks. A large, hairy dog barked and ran to Kallisto, greeting her with a wagging tail.

"This is our protector, Otus," Kallisto said. "Though I cannot imagine him hurting even an insect."

Emily scratched Otus's ears. She missed *his* dog.

Kallisto bypassed the house and took Emily into one of the huts instead. A fire crackled in a circular pit made of stones. Four thick poles supported the roof that had a smoke hole in its center. A hammock was strung between two of the poles. The hut contained a bed, a long table with benches, and crates and chests that seemed haphazardly placed. The floor was made of wide wooden planks that were hard to see because of the rugs that covered them. The rugs were well worn, some tattered, but clean. The hut was quite warm.

"We stay in here when it gets cold so I can heat my old bones," Kallisto said. "Take off your cloaks and your boots and be comfortable."

They reclined on divans near the fire, drank wine, and nibbled nuts.

"Nikanor is entertaining at the Philocrates' house today and will spend the night there," Kallisto said. "Next door live Lotai and Mucha. They take care of the place and the temple. Mucha will serve supper soon."

"Are they slaves?" Emily asked.

"No, they were here when we started the colony. They are hill people. Bandits burned their village many years ago. They were very poor when Nikanor and I found them. All their children had died. They seem content with the arrangement here. I had a house slave but she died of fever a year and half ago. Berenike would send another if I asked."

"Do you have children?"

"We have a son, Kyrillos. He is a trader. Right now he should be in Libya buying gold to bring here to sell to the Scythians. The Scythians do wonderful things with gold."

"Does your son have his own ship?"

"He has a stake in one. Someday he will have his own."

They talked of small things until Mucha brought supper -- chicken, barley meal and dried fruit. It was bland but fortifying. Mucha was a squat woman, no taller than Emily. Her hair was mostly gray. Kallisto and she talked with each other in a different language. Mucha left as soon has she had laid out the meal.

They drank beer with their supper. Emily told Kallisto it tasted like the beer she had drunk while traveling with Callias' column and staying at the village.

"Those are hill people, too, the last remnants of their tribe. They trade hides and furs with us."

"Their beer is potent," Emily said.

"Yes, it has a way of opening the mind," Kallisto said.

Emily told her of Nancy's performance that night at the village.

"I had heard. She enchanted everyone though they understood little of what she said, except that you had a hand in killing Hydakoles. What kind of man were you, Emily?"

Kallisto's question deflected her train of thought. How could she describe the man *he* had been? There was so much context that would be alien to Kallisto. Keep it simple, she thought.

"I was a tall man, taller than anybody I have seen in Artemios. I was bald like Agathon but not as gray. My eyes were blue. I was prosperous, I suppose, with plenty of time to pursue various interests. I was married for a short time. I had no children."

"No children. Berenike would say you were a selfish man."

"I suppose that I was," Emily said. "I was at home with myself and led a contemplative life."

"Were you strong?"

"Yes, very. I exercised and stayed in good shape."

"What did you contemplate?"

"Many things. I was especially fond of military history. I played games that depicted warfare. I was quite good at them, to be honest."

"You should counsel Agathon," Kallisto said.

"Agathon is a real soldier. I played games and read about war."

Emily sipped more beer. Kallisto lit a small brazier and added incense. The aroma was soothing. Emily felt warm and relaxed. Kallisto had cast her spell. She knew she would tell her anything she wanted to know.

"Where did you come from?" Kallisto asked. "How did you get here?"

"I come from a city called Detroit in a land called America."

"Where is America?"

"It will be a great empire on a continent that lies beyond the western ocean."

"Will be?"

"Nancy, Alex and I are from the future."

Kallisto sat up, still holding her bowl of beer.

"How can that be?" She asked. "The future does not yet exist."

"It does and it doesn't," Emily said. "I do not have the words to explain. Alex might do better but even he does not understand what happened. It is as if the gods transported you back to the time of the Trojan War, so we were transported back to your time."

"You do not know how?"

"We have no real idea. We could tell a story that might be true but one story would not be much better than another."

"From how far in the future do you come?"

"Two and half thousand years."

~

Kallisto seemed staggered by the idea. She set her bowl down. It was the first time Emily had seen her agitated.

"Do you know what happens to Artemios?" Kallisto asked.

"I do not. Of the three of us, I know the most about history but I had never heard of Artemios. That does not mean much. The world is a big place. I know only a tiny fraction of all that happened."

"Do you know what happens between the Greeks and the Persians?"

"Only in the broadest strokes. Do you really want to know?"

Kallisto picked up her bowl and drank. She took her time, gathering her thoughts. Emily began to wonder if the decision to tell the truth was the right one. Kallisto stood then paced around the hut.

"Tell me what happened that brought you here."

"In our time, we have many devices that you would find wondrous. One such device is called an aircraft. It is a ship that flies through the air like a bird and can carry people to distant places very quickly. Nancy, Alex and I were on such a craft, along with many others who perished ..." Emily began the story, talking about the cloud, the music, how the plane crashed in the wilderness, how she woke up finding herself in the body of a woman. She told how she killed a hyena with a rifle and her encounter with the tiger.

"It means something that the tiger did not kill you," Kallisto said. "You should remember that."

Emily told how they set out on their journey, their encounter with Hydakoles, and how they were found by Callias and his men.

"I cannot blame you if you do not believe me," Emily said when she finished.

"It is a fabulous story," Kallisto said.

They needed more wood for the fire. They put on their boots and went outside, taking the opportunity to urinate. The sky had cleared and the temperature had dropped. They picked up armloads of chopped logs from a stack near the house and hurried back inside. Kallisto rinsed their beer bowls and poured fresh spring water into them, saying the water would ease their morning hangovers.

"I have always believed that the future was not etched in stone," Kallisto said. "Strong currents, yes, going in certain directions, but many different things are possible. What you said distressed me because it seemed to say that events are etched in stone. Now I am not so sure what you say means that."

Emily felt admiration for Kallisto that bordered on awe. The way her eyes seemed to see beyond the surface of things, the clarity of her words and the care she took speaking them. Her understanding of the world was more sophisticated than most of the people *he* had known in *his* time. Her intelligence was uncanny.

"Alex thinks, and I agree," Emily said, "that different lines of history exist at the same time. Which one we travel on is not etched in stone. Our coming has already changed history, if only in a small way."

"Yes, that is just what I was thinking," Kallisto said. "So tell me, I think it is all right for me to know, what happens between the Persians and the Greeks in the line of history that you know?"

"There will be war. Things will look bleak for the Greeks but they will prevail."

"Thank you. I do not think I want to know more. You have opened your mind to me and I will always be grateful," Kallisto said. "My mind is weary and we should go to bed. I will sleep in the hammock."

"I do not want to deprive you of your bed," Emily said.

"I prefer the hammock and sleep in it when Nikanor is not here and sometimes when he is."

Emily didn't have her toothbrush so she brushed her teeth in the Greek way, with a piece of felt and a minty paste. She got into the bed and Kallisto got into the hammock.

"Do you like being a woman?" Kallisto asked.

The question caught Emily off guard. She was a little surprised she didn't answer with an immediate "no."

"I don't know. It frustrates me," Emily said. "When I try to lift something and cannot because I am not strong enough, when I try to reach something and cannot because I am short, when people treat me like a child, when the men go to the andron and I feel like I should be with them. But tonight, I admit, has been a good time that I don't think I could have had if I were a man."

"That is true," Kallisto said. "Have you had other good times as a woman?"

"Yes."

"That is excellent to hear. Good night."

~

After breakfast Kallisto and Emily headed back to the farm. Otus followed them to the edge of the clearing and barked when they continued on. The morning was cold but the sun was up, promising a warming and a melting of snow.

"It was you who cured Agape of the coughing sickness. Am I right?" Kallisto asked.

"Not me," Emily said. "We had some medicine that Nancy gave to Agape. It helped clear her lungs of the disease."

"Do you have more of the medicine?"

"Only a small amount," Emily said. "We had decided not to give any to others because we did not want to become known as healers with magic power. We do do not have any magic power."

"You gave it to Agape, regardless."

"Yes. Nancy insisted."

"Can you make more of the medicine?"

"No. It requires knowledge and devices we do not possess."

"Where you come from can you cure all diseases?"

"No. Only some," Emily said. "And everybody dies sooner or later, just like here."

Descending the hill, the trail was slippery. They walked slowly and minded their footing, holding each other's hands for support.

"What will you tell Agathon and Philocrates?" Emily asked.

"Nothing much. What you said to me is between you and me," Kallisto said. "You can tell them what you wish. I think Philocrates and others will be disappointed there can be no trade with your people. Agathon will not mind. He loves Nancy. He enjoys Alex's company and is fond of you like a daughter. He will not cast you aside."

The slope leveled off as they entered the orchard. They saw a deer, a large buck by the look of it, though it had shed its antlers. It saw them and trotted away.

~

Kallisto gave her language lesson and left before lunch. Emily, Alex and Nancy ate in the kitchen. Emily liked dried apple slices and Phoibe always made sure she had extra on her plate.

"I swear, Emily, you could tell that girl to fly to the moon and she'd flap her arms until she expired," Nancy said. "So how was your evening with Kallisto?"

"I enjoyed it," Emily said. "And I need to apologize. I sort of spilled the beans."

"What did you tell her?" Alex asked.

"Everything. More or less."

"Did she believe you?"

"Yes, I think so. She knows I was being honest."

"How did she take it?"

"In stride, like the wise woman she is."

"I have a confession, too," Nancy said. "I've pretty much told Agathon everything."

Emily laughed. She had a giggly cackle that kind of embarrassed her when it came forth but she stopped trying to suppress it. It was her laugh now. Alex shook his head.

"What's the saying? Up to three people can keep a secret if two of them are dead."

"And you, Alex, have kept the faith?" Nancy asked.

Alex shrugged. "I suppose I've told Midaleus some stuff I shouldn't have."

Chapter 16 | The Prince

THE month of Gamelion passed into Anthesterion. The weather warmed but rain fell frequently. News came that Callias' squadron had skirmished with the Persians. One Thracian was killed and another wounded. Agathon told Emily personally that Byon was unharmed. The Persians retreated to Novorosa to wait out the rains. Callias would remain on patrol in case it was a ruse.

"Are the Persian probes a prelude to attack?" Emily asked.

"Just testing our resolve, I think," Agathon replied.

An infrequent merchant ship arriving at the harbor brought word that Philocrates' son, Pantheras, was in Trapezus and would be coming to Artemios when the weather improved. Philocrates himself was bed-ridden and weak. Kallisto feared he might die before long.

Emily, Alex and Nancy had expected to have to tell their story to Philocrates, Agathon and other high-ranking members of the community, but the meeting kept getting postponed because of Philocrates' health. Agathon, it was clear, was not eager to have the meeting.

On an unusually sunny afternoon, Emily returned to the house after exercising the horses to find Alex and Agathon playing chess under the gazebo. The set was crudely beautiful. The board was a painted panel of wood, the squares red and black. The pieces were simple geometric shapes that only vaguely resembled standard chess pieces. Alex was no wood carver. The Pawns Alex called hoplites, the knights were hipparchs, the bishops were priests and the rooks were polemarches. Alex had just announced "checkmate" when Emily arrived.

"Beaten again," Agathon said. "I do feel I am getting the hang of it. What an excellent game. Let us play another."

Emily thought about asking if she could play but thought better of it. After supper Alex and Agathon took the chess set into the andron and resumed play.

In the gynaeceum, Nancy and Zozima worked the loom while Emily and Phoibe spun flax into thread, striving to make it as fine as possible. Emily had become quite skilled with a spindle whorl and found she enjoyed the work. It was meditative and soothing.

Agathon knocked at the open door.

"Sorry to disturb you, ladies, but I would like to borrow Emily for a while," he said.

Emily set her spindle down and went out to the common room where Agathon stood.

"Alex tells me you know how to play chess," he said.

"Yes, I do."

"Good. Come and give Alex a game. He keeps beating me and I would like to watch two people who know the game play each other. Perhaps I can detect some weakness in his tactics. He is very smart, as you know, so I don't expect you to win."

"I will do my best to make it interesting," Emily said. "Are we playing in the andron?"

"Yes, why not? We can bend the rules now and again."

She had been in the andron before when no one else was around but this was the first time she had been in it with the men. It was the first time any woman had been in the room with the men that she knew of. It was what she so often wanted but now she felt out of place and almost would rather be back in the gynaeceum. The feeling irritated her.

She sat down facing Alex over the board. She would play black and Alex white. Alex deployed his pieces quickly and moved aggressively. She could tell he was tactically sharp but only in a narrow sense. He had little notion of pawn structure or the importance of controlling the center of the board. She deflected his attacks with a strong pawn formation supported by her bishops and knights while she patiently maneuvered her rooks and queen for a counter attack.

Frustrated, Alex sacrificed a knight to break her wall of pawns but the move created more openings for her than him and soon he was down three pieces. When he blundered his queen away, he conceded.

"Well played, Emily," Agathon said. "Alex, you must be getting tired."

"No, I think I was just getting careless," Alex said. "Do you mind playing again, Emily?"

"No."

She took white this time. Something told her that she should deliberately lose but her gaming blood was up. She opened with a very aggressive King's Gambit. It was a risky opening against a quality player but she knew Alex wasn't up to it. She moved her pieces quickly. Soon Alex's king was under tremendous pressure and he took longer and longer to make his moves. He became so focused on defending one angle of attack, he neglected Emily's other, more potent, angle. Alex made a poor move. Emily pounced with a three-move combination that led to checkmate.

"Wow, clearly I'm overmatched," Alex said in English. "I'm not even sure what happened."

"I see this game has depths I have yet to fathom," Agathon said. "I am impressed, Emily."

"Thank you."

"Well, I think it's about time for bed," he said. "Shall we call it a night?"

~

The days moved from Anthesterion to Elaphebolion and Emily no longer needed to wear her boots. The chess set remained idle. Agathon was busy most days in Artemios and so was Alex who helped with the construction of the shipyard. The goal was to build triremes to use in defense of the harbor.

One evening, Alex returned to the farm and explained over supper that Pantheras had arrived along with another dignitary named Linus. He was a member of the Phocasian clan, one of the wealthiest families of Miletus and a primary backer of the Artemios colony. Philocrates remained deathly ill and there was much discussion over who would take over when he died, Alex reported.

"Midaleus told me Pantheras isn't all that interested, but Berenike is nagging him to assume leadership of the colony and take a wife."

"I suppose," Emily said, "if Pantheras is used to Miletus and Athens, both great cities, this would be like Siberia."

"Maybe your prince has come, Emily, and Pantheras will sweep you away," Nancy said.

"Shut up."

"I believe Berenike has a nice rich Greek girl lined up for him," Alex said.

"Of course she does," Nancy said.

~

Despite an afternoon drizzle, Emily worked on her weapons skills behind the barns. She was making practice thrusts at the log dummy with an old spear, its tip broken and edge dull. She performed a few flourishes Byon had taught her, twirling the spear and whirling it around her shoulders and waist. Such flourishes had no real combat value but they could be intimidating and encouraged physical intimacy with the weapon. Practicing her footwork, she finished a twirl and pivoted around into a fighting stance. Before her stood a man she did not know.

"Peace, I am unarmed," the man said. A grin stretched across his face, revealing healthy, straight teeth. "You could be no other than Emily Nyfitsa, the nymph of Artemis."

Lean and clean shaven, the man was tall, as tall as Hank had been. His hair was black, curly and long for a man. He wore a cloak of deep blue over a white tunic trimmed with gold. His brown eyes under thick eyebrows gleamed with amusement.

Emily straightened up and set the spear on the rack. With a cloth she wiped moisture from her brow and hands. She reached out a hand to the man.

"You must be Pantheras, son of Philocrates," she said.

"Why, I am indeed," he said and took her hand. With his other hand, he clutched her forearm, not hard but with enough pressure to let her know his tightly muscled frame possessed considerable strength.

"There is steel in your arms," he said. "It is a refreshing change from the pampered rich girls who can hardly lift their gold cups to their mouths. I am delighted to meet you, Emily."

He released her hand.

"The honor is mine," Emily said.

"Ho! Let us be friends. I am sorry I used that vile word, 'Nyfitsa.'"

"In truth, I do not mind."

Pantheras laughed at that.

"You know, I dreaded coming to this forsaken place. The only thing I looked forward to was meeting you and your friends, the strangers from where, only the gods know. Now that I meet you, I am glad I am here."

Another man came around the barn. He was smallish and thin and wore a long blue tunic with a brown cloak. His hair was curly and face boyish.

"There you are, Pantheras. We wondered where you had disappeared to," the man said, his alto voice clear and smooth.

"Emily, let me introduce you to my beloved friend, Acasius, the wisest man this side of the Euxine Sea. Of course, that is not saying much."

Emily and Acasius greeted each other cordially.

"I suppose we should go to the house," Pantheras said. "I am here with Agathon and that old ninny, Linus. We plan to have it out with the three of you and milk you of all your secrets."

They walked side by side toward the house. Pantheras moved with smooth, athletic surety as if there were nothing in the world with which he could not contend.

"You must excuse Pantheras," Acasius said to Emily. "He can ladle it out thick at times."

"Acasius! You wound me."

~

They met the others in the common room of the house. Alex and Nancy were there along with Agathon and another man -- old, tall and bony with a narrow gray beard that hung to his chest. He wore a long blue tunic and a burgundy cloak. Agathon introduced him as Linus of Miletus.

Pantheras shook hands with Alex.

"I am pleased to meet you. I hear your knowledge of mathematics is second to none. Thales himself would be your pupil."

He turned to Nancy.

"The rumors do not do your beauty justice. Aphrodite must seethe with envy. I am smitten and humbled before you."

Emily could tell Nancy savored his words.

"Tonight," Agathon said, "we shall have our little visit and you can tell us about yourselves, but not before we have dined."

Linus, Pantheras and Acasius were shown to their rooms. Alex, Nancy and Emily met in Emily's room.

"I guess this is it," Alex said. "Are we still agreed the truth is best?"

"Yes," Nancy said.

"What choice do we have? Kallisto and Agathon already know," Emily said.

"I don't like the look of that Linus. He doesn't seem friendly," Nancy said.

"I imagine he's looking out for the family interest and will evaluate us in those terms," Emily said. "The question is do we threaten or aid the investment."

"Are you up for doing most of the talking, Alex?" Nancy asked.

"I think so," he said. "I've given a lot of thought to what I will say."

"That Pantheras is a charmer," Nancy said. "And handsome. I almost melt looking at him."

"I hope you're not thinking of abandoning Agathon," Alex said.

"Not to worry," Nancy said. "Pantheras is gay."

~

The three decided to wear their old clothes for the occasion. Emily put on the gray dress, stockings, flats, necklace and earrings. She put on a touch of makeup and tied an orange ribbon to her braid.

Kallisto arrived and they all dined in the common room. Zosima had prepared a mutton roast. Pantheras dominated the conversation, telling anecdotes about his visit to Athens and how he drove his tutors crazy.

"It is a wonderful place," he said. "So many people and so many new ideas in the air. It makes one's head spin."

After eating, they went into the andron with jugs of wine and water and bowls of nuts and dried fruit. Agathon closed the door. Most sat in chairs or reclined on divans. Present in the room were Agathon, Linus, Pantheras, Acasius, Kallisto, Alex, Nancy and Emily, who sat cross-legged on a pillow on the floor. When everyone was comfortable, Alex stood.

"First we want to thank the good people of Artemios for their kindness and willingness to treat as honored guests three strangers such as ourselves. We especially would like to thank Agathon for taking us in and treating us like family, and Kallisto for her tireless efforts to help us learn your language. She is a magnificent teacher. We are honored by the noble presence of Linus, Pantheras and Acasius. Thank you for coming to hear what we have to say."

"I wouldn't miss it for all the gold in Persia," Pantheras said. He reclined while Acasius sat on the floor in front of him, leaning his back against the divan.

"So, where to start?" Alex continued. "I suppose I will come right out with it. We are from the future, the distant future. How many years do you suppose it is, Emily?"

"Two and half thousand," she said.

Acasius and Pantheras laughed.

"This is going to be better than I thought," Pantheras said.

Linus looked annoyed, whether at Pantheras or the preposterous idea of coming from the future, Emily couldn't tell. Perhaps both. Alex took a deep breath.

"I know it is outrageous but it is the truth. I do not know what strange forces aligned to bring us here but I will tell you what we experienced."

Alex told of the "flying ship," the storm cloud, the crash, the hyena, the tiger, their journey through the wilderness, their encounter with Hydakoles and finally meeting Callias and his men. Nancy interjected now and then. Emily mostly kept quiet. When Alex finished, even Pantheras remained silent for a time, but not for long.

"I do not think even old Homer could come up with a tale like that," he said. "If you are not telling the truth, you deserve great honors for creativity."

"It is the truth as I know it," Alex said. "Though, if I were in your place, I would not believe it."

Linus stroked his beard.

"Can you substantiate your story?" He asked, his voice low and gritty. "A ship that can fly and carry scores of people is simply impossible."

Alex went over to the table and picked up a blank sheet of papyrus.

"I know it is expensive, but may I use it?" Alex asked Agathon.

"Yes, of course," he said.

Alex folded the papyrus into a paper airplane, went to one side of the room and tossed it. The airplane dipped and floated across the room's length before hitting a wall and falling to the floor. Pantheras and Acasius laughed again. Kallisto joined them. Acasius got up, retrieved the airplane and threw it back toward Alex who caught it in the air.

"What do you think of that, Linus of the Phocasian clan?" Pantheras asked.

"A clever trick," Linus said. "It is not much different than a feather or an arrow."

"Good point, Linus," Acasius said. "Birds can fly, of course, but they have hollow bones and are very light in weight."

"Why Acasius, how can such a beautiful young man be such a skeptic?" Pantheras asked.

"We must use logic and consider the evidence," Acasius said.

"With large enough wings and sufficient force to push them, heavier things can be made to fly," Alex said.

"Could you build such an aircraft?" Pantheras asked. "I would love to ride in one."

"No, I am afraid not," Alex said.

"Pity."

"He cannot build one because one cannot be built," Linus said. "This is foolishness."

"These are honest folks, Linus," Kallisto said. "I have worked with them closely for months. They are not liars or charlatans."

Agathon appeared angry but held his tongue. Pantheras appeared amused. Alex put out a hand.

"Linus' opinion is reasonable. I do not take offense," he said. "I cannot build an aircraft such as the one we rode in. In time I might be able to fashion something more convincing than folded papyrus."

Emily stood and retrieved an item from her pouch. With all eyes upon her, she walked up to Pantheras.

"Here, take this," she said.

Pantheras held the object in his hand. It was a smooth cylinder that widened at one end.

"What is this?" he asked.

"It is something that may help convince you that what we say is true," Emily said. "It is not dangerous. It is not magic. Agathon, with your permission, I would like to put out all the candles but one."

He nodded and Emily snuffed the candles except the one in a carrier by the door.

"Pantheras, please depress the button on the object you hold," she said.

Using an exaggerated gesture, he pressed it with his index finger. The button clicked and a beam of light shot forth, creating a bright spot on the ceiling. A moment of silence turned to awed murmurs.

"What an utterly marvelous thing," Pantheras said. He waved the object around, putting the beam on everything and everyone in the room. He shined it on his own face.

"It is so bright," he said. "Yet it is not hot."

He handed the object to Acasius who now looked like a boy with a new toy. He pressed the button and the beam went dark. He pressed again and it came back on.

"What do you say now, Linus?" Pantheras asked. "Even your hardened mind must be softening a bit."

"Emily," Linus said. "I would like to examine the item, if I may."

"Yes, please do so."

Acasius reluctantly gave the object to Linus who looked at it closely, turning it off and on, running his fingers over the plastic surface.

"We call it a flashlight," Emily said.

"How does it work?" Linus asked.

"Inside are two objects we call batteries. They provide power for the light."

"Would it shine forever if you let it?"

"No. The batteries would wear out. In time the batteries will wear out even if it is not shining."

Emily used the candle by the door to relight the other candles.

"It is a wondrous device to be sure," Acasius said. "And very useful without question, but it does not logically prove you came from the future."

"What more proof do you need, my dear one?" Pantheras asked.

"Acasius is correct," Linus said. "I admit I am impressed by this device. It is clearly beyond our knowledge and skill, but there are tales of wondrous devices made in the far eastern lands of India and beyond. It is more reasonable to think our visitors come from there rather than the future."

"I have heard a smattering of Indian tongues," Kallisto said. "Our guests' language does not resemble them at all."

Nancy went around and poured wine, starting with Linus. She smiled and gave him a curtsy when he said thank you. Emily sat down on her pillow and spread her skirt flat over her lap. She looked up and spoke, her voice as clear and calm as she could make it.

"Alex, Nancy and I discussed what we would say to you when the time came. We decided the truth would be best, even though we worried you would not believe it. We made that decision mainly because honesty is our way. We did briefly consider claiming we were from a distant land. But this would raise questions that would require more lies. How did we cross vast deserts and wilderness unarmed and unescorted? Why would we have made such a journey? How would we get home? And when asked to talk about the land we said we came from, we would have to make up stories. Before long my stories would not match Alex's and his would not match Nancy's and hers would not match mine. You would come to distrust us."

Emily moved her gaze around the room while she talked, making eye contact with everyone, finishing with Linus.

"We are stranded in your time," she said. "We cannot go home. We depend on your hospitality and we strive to repay it as best we can."

Linus stroked his beard. The anger had faded from his face. Agathon stood.

"As long as I live, you will be welcome here," he said.

"Of course, we bear you no ill will," Linus said.

"I can hardly believe my eyes and ears," Pantheras said. "The hardy little maiden's sweet voice has melted the heart of crusty old Linus."

"Be silent for once," Linus snapped.

Linus turned to Alex.

"You say you cannot build an aircraft but is there anything of your advanced ways that you could show us that might be useful?"

"Perhaps," Alex said. "The question is do you really want us to. Is it right for us to influence the natural course of your history?"

"That is a deep question," Linus said. "We will have to think about it and discuss it further."

Acasius rose to his feet and straightened his cloak.

"My heart tells me these strangers are good people and do not seek to deceive us," he said. "But I am committed first and foremost to the muse of reason, and my reason tells me I need more proof than a magical lamp and sincere words. Sometimes people can be honest but also mistaken, or they are themselves deceived."

Emily had thought that Linus was the one they needed to win over, but now it seemed that Acasius' opinion carried weight. It occurred to her that he must be more than just Pantheras' boyfriend or he wouldn't be in the room at all.

"What proof could they give that would satisfy the muse of reason you are so devoted to?" Pantheras asked. "Do we not simply have to decide whether to believe them or not, and decide knowing our doubts may never be fully satisfied?"

"My dear Pantheras, you of all people should see that our doubts can be satisfied," Acasius said.

"My apologies. I am an oaf. Please tell me."

"Our honorable guests said that their aircraft crashed in the wilderness east of here. We simply go there and see for ourselves."

When the suggestion sank in, Pantheras clapped his hands and sat up.

"What a splendid idea, Acasius," he said. "I knew there was something more to you than good looks."

Acasius' idea struck Emily like a thunderbolt. She suddenly knew what she wanted to do, what she needed to do. She stood and all eyes were on her again. She went to Pantheras and Acasius.

"I will take you there," she said.

"Ha! The nymph of Artemis will show us the way," Pantheras exclaimed. "The gods are with us! Soon old Nikanor will have new material for his songs."

The others in the room looked less enthusiastic.

~

Agathon: "I simply cannot spare the men needed for such an expedition."

Pantheras: "Just give us a handful of peltasts and a few mules and we will be fine. Emily, how far would you say it is?"

Emily: "About five or six days on foot."

Pantheras: "See, we will be there and back before you know we are gone."

Agathon: "It is wild country. There are dangerous animals and there could be bandits."

Pantheras: "You slaughtered the bandits last year. I am sure there will be nothing we can't handle. I know how to lead men and you know I am a good fighter. There are few who can match me."

Agathon: "You would be out of the territory of the Lion Tribe. You would not have their protection. There are other Scythian tribes not so friendly with us."

Pantheras: "The Scythians roam the plains. We will be in the forest. All we are likely to meet are hill people and they are allies."

Agathon: "Emily has become dear to me. I would not see her harmed."

Pantheras: "Anybody with eyes can see she can take care of herself. You are the one who told me she moves through the forest like a phantom."

Agathon: "The colony cannot risk losing you."

Pantheras: "The colony can do fine without me. You are the real leader here, anyway."

Agathon: "And if something happened to Acasius, I would face the wrath of the most powerful families in Miletus and Athens."

Pantheras: "There is that. Acasius, perhaps you should stay behind. I will be your eyes and give a full account of what I see."

Acasius: "I want to see it for myself. I will fund the expedition. If you send me away, I will hire men to take me there by another route."

Pantheras: "See, Agathon, Acasius is determined to go. We do not have the authority to stop him."

Agathon: "What do you say, Kallisto?"

Kallisto: "The mother in me wants them to stay safe here in Artemios. In my mind, there is no need for further proof. I know what our visitors say is true. I think everyone here knows what they say is true. Why risk life and limb to find out what we already know?"

Linus: "So you oppose the journey?"

Kallisto: "No. I favor it."

Nancy: "But why? You just said there is no point to it."

Kallisto: "There is no point in getting further proof. But the journey does have a point, I am sure of that, though I cannot say what it is. When Emily offered to guide Pantheras and Acasius, what I saw in her eyes moved me. I knew then that Artemis wants the journey to take place. I serve the goddess so I support the endeavor."

Nancy: "That is just silly. I do not believe what I am hearing. From you of all people."

Linus: "I also favor the journey. While I defer to Kallisto as to the will of Artemis, I disagree with her on the matter of proof. I now believe our visitors. I apologize for doubting them. However, there may come a time when others need to be convinced. A firsthand report from Acasius would be very helpful to that end. I do not like risking the jewels of Greek youth but it is their time for bold action. We should not restrain them when such action has clear purpose. I do not like risking one of our visitors but from what I hear, Emily is well suited to the task and offers the best chance of getting the expedition to its destination quickly so it may return quickly."

Pantheras rubbed both Acasius and Emily's heads and put his arms around them. "Well, my friends, it looks like we are going for a little stroll in the hills."

~

"We will discuss the matter further tomorrow," Agathon said. "It is late and we should get some sleep."

Linus approached Emily and handed back the flashlight.

"You may keep it if you wish," Emily said.

"I should like to have it," Linus said. "But I would be tempted to show it off and I do not think that would be a good idea. I am, however, moved by your generosity. I think your people must share much in common with mine."

"More than you know," Emily said. "Our people owe much to yours."

"You are sweet to flatter an old man's pride," he said.

Chapter 17 | Partings

EMILY woke to Nancy sitting at the foot of her bed.

"Do you really have to go?" Nancy asked.

"Yes."

"But why? They can find the plane themselves. Alex can draw them a map."

"I need to go. I need to get away from here for a while."

"You'll be alone with a bunch of men."

"I'll be fine. I was man once, remember."

"I'll worry about you terribly. It'll be lonely without you. You're my strength."

"You have your own strength, Nancy, more strength than me, I suspect."

"Promise me you'll come back."

"I'll come back. I promise."

~

Agathon, Pantheras, Acasius, Alex and Emily met that evening in the andron to discuss plans. Alex worked on a map, consulting his field sketches. Acasius stood over him, fascinated with the paper of Alex's notebook and the felt pen he used to draw on a large sheet of papyrus.

They decided they would leave in ten days on the first day of Mounichion. They hoped the weather would be warmer and not as wet. If all went well, the expedition would be back in time to help with the planting. Now that Agathon was on board with the trip, he talked of giving them a full complement of 40 peltasts.

"No, that is too many," Pantheras said. "We would need supply wagons, drivers and porters. It would slow us down and attract attention. Word might spread that we were up to something."

"I agree," Emily said. "We should keep it small."

They decided on six hand-picked peltasts, two slaves and four mules.

"My dear Acasius, are you sure you are up to it?" Pantheras asked. "It will be hard going for someone not used to the rigors of the road."

"I will suffer whatever I need to," Acasius said.

"We should exercise," Emily said. "We can climb the temple hill daily to strengthen our legs and harden our feet."

~

The next morning, Pantheras bounded up the hill like a mountain goat. Emily walked with Acasius who became winded half way and had to stop.

"I feel like I am going to lose my breakfast," he said. "Perhaps I am not cut out for such a journey."

"Just stick with it," Emily said. "Your wind will get better, even by tomorrow. In nine days you will be running up the hill like Pantheras."

Pantheras skipped back down.

"Get going you sluggards," he said. "The view up there is fantastic."

Acasius was flushed and panting when he finally made it to the top. The three of them sat on the crude bench and gazed out over the sea and Artemios below.

"Are you looking forward to taking over as oikist someday?" Emily asked Pantheras.

"I fear there will be nothing to take over," he said. "Artemios is doomed."

"Why do you say that?"

"Too many enemies -- the Persians, the Novorosians, the Phanagorians, the Bosporans."

"The Lion Tribe is strong, it seems," Emily said.

"As long as King Huraslan lives, Artemios is safe, but he is old and will die soon."

"I hear Kydoime would become queen. Would she not support Artemios?"

"She would, yes, I believe, but there are others who would vie for kingship. When succession is up in the air, Novorosa will strike and with Persian help. That is what Agathon fears most."

"Trapezus and Miletus would not help?"

"You must remember they are under the Persian yoke as well. And there are things going on that make Artemios a minor consideration."

Acasius' color returned and his breathing slowed. Emily changed the subject. "Alex wants to go with us but Agathon insists that he stay."

"Oh, they won't let Alex out of their sight," Pantheras said. "Linus wants to take him to Athens to make sure he does not fall into Persian hands. They worry he has dangerous knowledge."

"Will they take him to Athens?"

"There is no route that does not pass through Persian controlled lands," Acasius said. "They would have to smuggle him there and that would be risky."

"I think Alex would like it in Athens," Emily said.

"He would be treated well and would meet the most learned of men," Acasius said.

"I do not think it would be the place for me," she said.

"Where is the place for you?" Acasius asked.

"I am trying to figure that out?"

~

That evening, after supper, the men headed for the andron. Pantheras glanced at Emily, indicating she was welcome to come. She gave a little shake of her head and went into the gynaeceum with the women. She was working with Phoibe on two traveling tunics, one blue and one brown. The conversations of the men in the andron were more interesting to her but she felt more relaxed in the gynaeceum. As they worked on the garments, Phoibe stroked Emily's foot with her own under the table.

~

One afternoon, Pantheras stayed to practice weapons with Emily. He could throw a javelin nearly as far as Byon. He said he once took third place during games in Trapezus. He didn't know how to use a sling but he brought his bow which he could shoot accurately. The bow was long with a mild recurve. He pulled arrows back by pinching with his thumb and forefinger instead of the three-fingered loose Emily was familiar with. From what she could tell, the draw weight of Pantheras' bow was light, yet it was clear he could be quite deadly with it.

Pantheras set the bow down and picked up one of the staves from the rack.

"Agathon tells me you often sparred with that Thracian fellow, what's-his-name."

"Byon, yes. You could say I was his pupil."

"Then we shall go a round and see what he has taught you."

Each warmed up with a few flourishes, assumed ready positions then circled each other. Pantheras made a few probing attacks which Emily parried but he would jump back before she could counter. He was testing her and using his greater reach to keep her at a safe distance. She decided to test him and rushed in with a quick combination. He parried the attacks and they both jumped back. She knew then that he was the better fighter and not just because of his greater size. He had an easy smoothness about him and his movements were compact and efficient. He had grown up doing this sort of thing, she thought, while she had only been at it a few months.

Pantheras attacked with a quick combination that put her in an awkward position. He took advantage with a thrust that she just barely deflected with the back of her staff. Had it been a full speed attack with live steel she would have been dead.

"The point is yours," Emily said.

She did wonder whether or not his confidence might be his undoing in a real fight if his opponent did something unexpected. Despite his skill, she suspected he lacked Byon's scrappiness and battle sense.

"Nyfitsa fights well," Pantheras said. "You made me work for that point. I hope we do meet some bandits. Your scheming eyes tell me there is more in your bag of tricks."

He set his staff on the rack and wiped sweat from his brow. Emily did the same.

"I am wound up," he said. "Let us race to the top of the hill."

He took off and she ran after him. She knew she couldn't win but was glad she kept the pace and wasn't flagging when they reached the top. They were both winded, however, and bent over to catch their breaths.

"Can Acasius fight?" Emily asked.

"He went through the training as a boy. He did not like it and had no talent for it. He is a creature of the mind."

"We shall have to look after him," she said.

"With my life, Emily, with my life."

~

As suppertime neared the next day, Agathon found Emily finishing up chores in the stable.

"Timon is not going to be happy when you leave. He will have to do this job."

"It should not be for long," Emily said.

"I hope so. I'm counting on you to make it a quick trip," Agathon said. "Come out back, I want to show you something."

They walked around to the practice area and Emily immediately noticed a spear on the rack that hadn't been there before. Agathon picked it up.

"It is a throwing spear, heavier than a javelin and good for punching through shields at short range. We keep a supply on hand along the ramparts."

The spear was short, a little longer than Emily was tall. It had a bronze butt cap and wicker covering over the head with a wooden knob at the tip. Agathon pulled off the cover. The head was not the typical leaf type. It had narrow blades running along its long, conical head. The steel had a patina that suggested age but there was no rust or pock marks. It must have been kept well oiled. Agathon ran his fingers along the head.

"This one is special," he said. "The steel has a remarkable temper. Many years ago I was leading my men against a bandit stronghold when this came down and went right through a soldier's shield, punctured his armor and killed him. After the battle, I had to break the shaft to remove the spear. I noticed the head was unscathed. Once in a while, by chance it seems, one finds steel of this quality. I kept the head, thinking I would use it to make a spear for my own use. I never got around to it until now."

"It looks like an excellent weapon," Emily said.

"I want you to have it," Agathon said. "I had the shaft made with you in mind. Here, try it out."

Emily took the spear. Its ash shaft, stained a dark brown, was thicker than a javelin's but not so hefty as a hoplite's spear. It felt good in her hands. She performed a few flourishes. The butt cap balanced it so it could be used like a staff as well as a lethal thrusting weapon. With a grunt she drove it into the log dummy. It penetrated deeply and she had to press her foot against the log to pull it out.

"It is perfect," she said. "More than I deserve. Thank you."

"Just make sure you do deserve it," Agathon said.

~

That evening Emily laid out her things on her bed and thought about what she would need to bring. She ruled the jeans out. They fit too snug now. She decided to take the swimsuit as an extra layer in case the weather got cold. Her thoughts were interrupted by a knock on the door.

Alex came in carrying a blanket. He unrolled it on the bed, revealing the binoculars and the compass.

"I thought you might want to take these," he said.

"Thank you," Emily said. "I was going to ask but I hadn't gotten around to it."

"You should pack some antibiotics and painkillers," Alex said.

"That wouldn't leave much for you and Nancy."

"They won't last forever and they will be gone sooner or later."

Alex got the drugs out of Hank's pack.

"Thanks," she said. "Alex?"

"Yes."

"Pantheras thinks Artemios could be doomed in the near future if the Scythian king dies. While the Scythians are busy deciding who their next leader will be, Novorosa and the Persians will strike."

"That's not a pleasant prospect."

"I think you should help Agathon," Emily said.

"What could I do?"

"I was thinking catapults. They won't be invented for a couple of centuries. I bet an attack will come by both land and sea. Catapults would be particularly useful against ships trying to force the harbor."

Alex nodded. "It would take a lot of experimenting but I'm sure I could get something to work."

Emily told him all she knew about catapults from reading about them in books. It wasn't much.

~

On the day before they planned to leave, Kallisto appeared and found Emily brushing the four mules that would be used for the journey. The sky was clear and a cool breeze blew in from the sea.

"Will you accompany me to the temple?" Kallisto asked.

"Yes, of course."

Approaching the entrance, the cathedral of oaks was even more impressive than Emily's last visit. The leaves were not fully grown and the sky could still be seen through them. Flowers resembling pansies lined the walkway in an array of yellows, oranges and reds. In the temple, Emily saw a blanket spread on the stone floor and on it was a large basket. A bronze brazier smoldered on the altar.

"Today we break bread with Artemis," Kallisto said. "But first we must purify ourselves."

Kallisto took two towels from the basket and led Emily around the back of the temple to the spring-fed pool ringed with stones. Near it was a stone table placed close to steps that led into the pool. Kallisto undressed and Emily followed suit. Kallisto's hips and breasts sagged some with age but her skin was smooth and her form remained beautiful. They set their clothes on the table.

"Here, let me undo your braid," Kallisto said.

She did and brushed Emily's hair out with her fingers. It hung longer now, a few inches beyond her shoulders. Emily remembered the day after the crash and the shock of when she first felt it. Kallisto intoned words in the strange language she had used before then guided Emily down the steps and into the pool.

The air was chilly to her naked skin but the pool was ice cold. Kallisto seemed unperturbed. The depth came to Emily's shoulders. Kallisto spoke more words then said in Greek, "Now we go under."

They crouched so they were fully submerged. The cold water was numbing. Emily stayed under until Kallisto came up.

"Let us get out before we freeze to death," Kallisto said.

They went back up the steps and shivered as they dried themselves.

"That language you speak, what is it?" Emily asked.

"It is an ancient tongue, spoken by people who lived in Ionia a long time ago," Kallisto said. "It is the language of Artemis and other goddesses absorbed by the Greek religion. It is not a living language but is still spoken by priestesses who know the ancient rites."

"What did you say?"

"I asked Artemis to purify you and give you strength for what lies ahead."

"What lies ahead?"

"I am a priestess, not a seer."

~

They dressed and went back into the temple. From the basket, Kallisto fetched three plates, placed one on the altar and two on the blanket. She did the same with three bowls. On the plates she placed bread, dried fruit and pickled meats. She poured wine into the bowls. She put a cube of something in the brazier and soon the temple was filled with the aroma of frankincense. She intoned more words and sat on the blanket. Emily joined her.

They ate their food under the painted image of the goddess. Emily wondered if she were pleased. Kallisto seemed to be.

"When you find your aircraft, will Pantheras and Acasius be impressed?" Kallisto asked.

"I am certain they will be. Even though it is mangled and in pieces, it will be an awesome sight to their eyes," Emily said.

"Excellent. Those two could use a dose of humility."

"I was not so different when I was a man and their age."

"Some things do not change."

"And you were always humble?"

"No. I was a brash girl who thought she could play everyone like a set of pipes."

~

After eating, Kallisto withdrew an item from her pouch. It was a simple stone pendant attached to a leather cord.

"I want you to have this," she said. "I thought you might like it."

It was a flat, oval shaped stone, orange in color, with black specks and two ragged black stripes. Its surface was smooth and rounded. Gold wire hid the peg that secured the cord. Emily immediately liked it. It felt comfortable in her hand and she stroked it like a worry stone.

"I found it in the brook when they were building the temple," Kallisto said. "I call it the Tiger Stone. Nikanor put the cord on it for me but I never felt the occasion right to wear it. When you told me the story of your encounter with the tiger, I knew it belonged to you."

"It is beautiful. Thank you," Emily said.

Emily put the cord around her neck. The stone rested comfortably on her chest.

"I have something else," Kallisto said. She retrieved a small wicker box from the basket and handed it to Emily.

"This is a gift from Berenike," Kallisto said. "She hopes it will help make amends for what happened to you at her house."

"I never blamed her," Emily said.

"I know but she was deeply ashamed. She wanted to come to the farm and give it to you herself but Philocrates is too sick."

Emily opened the box. Inside was a pair of earrings. She inspected one of them closely. It was like a gold hook. One end of the hook attached to the ear. The other end curled around and up to a delicate gold flower. The center of the flower had a sky-blue stone. Dangling from the lowest point of the hook's curve was a tiny golden songbird.

"They are very pretty," Emily said.

"There is a Scythian goldsmith who lives in town. He does wonderful work," Kallisto said. "You do not like them?"

"Yes, but ... they are a little too feminine for me. I do not think I would ever wear them."

"Perhaps there will be a time when you will want to bring that side out," Kallisto said. "I know you can. like the other night when you sat on the floor and spoke so beautifully."

Emily blushed, took a drink of wine.

"You act, and others too, like I won't be back in a few days," Emily said.

"Will you be back so soon?" Kallisto asked.

Kallisto's question cut to the core. Assuming everything went smoothly, would she march right back to take up whatever life awaited her here? She didn't know. But what else could she do? Live like a hermit in the wilderness?

"The trip you are taking has a feeling of something larger -- for you at least, if not for us all -- than satisfying Acasius' curiosity," Kallisto said.

~

That evening was a festive one. Pantheras and Acasius had arrived with the six peltasts and two slaves who were part of the adventuring party. They slaughtered a sheep, dedicated it to Artemis and ate under the gazebo. Nikanor told another story of Atalanta and how she helped hunt and kill the great Calydonian boar with the hero, Meleager. He ended the story by telling about how Atalanta volunteered to join Jason and his Argonaughts. Jason refused her because he feared a woman would sow discord amongst the men.

"Pity," Pantheras said. "They could have used her."

Nikanor strummed a lively melody and the Thracian men pounded a steady pulse on the table. One of the warriors, Dokaris, performed a war dance. He was the tall, lanky man who had defeated Byon in the javelin contest at the funerary games. His spear dance was all weird angles and serpentine motions. He would be a very difficult opponent, Emily thought. His movements would mesmerize and distract and then, out of rhythm, he would strike.

When Phoibe poured wine into Pantheras' bowl, he whispered something in her ear. Phoibe brought him his shield and sword and he performed his own dance. It was slow, elegant and precise. The movements seemed effortless but Emily knew they required considerable strength and suppleness. When he stopped, he turned to Emily.

"Now it is your turn," Pantheras said.

Phoibe had appeared beside Emily holding her new spear. She shook her head but the crowd would not be denied. She grabbed the spear and went to the open area. She took a deep breath and bowed to her imaginary opponent.

"Time for the dance of Nyfitsa!" Pantheras shouted.

Nancy slugged him in the shoulder.

Emily crouched in an overly wide stance. She used her light weight and strong legs to keep herself as low to the ground as possible, performing flourishes with the spear around her shoulders. At certain moments, she thrust the spear, holding it with one hand at the butt end and fully extending her arm and body, then pulled it back quickly with a jump, assuming a low defensive stance, almost hugging the ground. She finished with a standard thrust, letting out a cry as she did so, sticking her tongue out and wagging it like a Maori warrior from New Zealand.

The crowd was silent for a moment before erupting with laughter, cheers and table pounding. Dokaris raised Emily's arm as if she were the winner, almost pulling her off her feet, and howled at the sky.

"My dear, Acasius," Pantheras said. "Please remind me to wear my greaves if ever I have to fight that girl."

~

Emily was glad Agathon called an early halt to the revelry. They finished with farewell toasts and Emily went to her room. The Thracians had set up tents for themselves in the courtyard.

Emily thought about what Kallisto had said during their lunch and decided to pack the earrings Berenike had given her as well as her makeup case. When going through her things, she came across the plastic horse. She packed that too.

Phoibe came up later and, in the candlelight, rewove Emily's braid.

"I will miss you," Phoibe said. "I love you more than anything."

From her pouch, Emily produced the weasel figurine the beggar had given her months ago at the market. She handed it to Phoibe.

"It is yours to keep," Emily said.

Phoibe clutched it with both hands as if it were the most precious thing in the world.

"If the need arises," Emily said. "You could sell it for quite a bit, enough probably to buy your freedom."

"I would never sell it," Phoibe said.

Phoibe hugged Emily as if she would never let go. Eventually their lips found each other and Phoibe's hand found its way up Emily's thigh.

Chapter 18 | Bloody Meadow

AFTER a quiet breakfast, Alex presented Emily with a leather tube that contained his map. Nancy gave her a prolonged hug.

A westerly breeze brought clouds and a mist from the sea. The traveling company assembled near the road. Pantheras took the lead, wearing a red cloak and an open-faced helmet with a red plume. He had a cuirass of leather armor over his tunic. Emily and Acasius walked behind him. Acasius wore a blue cloak, a broad felt hat and carried a walking stick that was well polished and stained dark brown. The peltasts followed, each carrying a light spear in one hand and a shield and two javelins in the other. Following them were the two slaves leading the mules.

"Do not tarry," Agathon said as they marched onto the road. "There and back as quickly as you can."

Pantheras set a fast pace and the peltasts marched smartly until they had gone around the bend and were behind the hill. At that point, Pantheras signaled them to be at ease and they walked at a more normal pace.

"Thank the gods, we are finally on our way," Pantheras said. "All these farewells were getting tedious."

Emily handed Acasius the map tube.

"You should have this," she said. "I do not need it. If something happens to me, you can still find your way."

"Thank you," he said. "Why do I get the feeling you are someone older than you are?"

"Mine is a tale you would not believe, and it would make you laugh."

"When you have a mind to tell the story, I promise not to laugh, even if I do not believe it," Acasius said.

"I will believe it and I will laugh," Pantheras said.

~

The road wound its way through the farmsteads and orchards. They saw a few people who looked at them with curiosity. Emily used her new spear as a walking stick. She was glad it had a wicker cover. It meant she didn't have to be as wary of cutting or poking herself. The mist receded as they climbed into the hills. Pantheras took off his helmet and stowed it on one of the mules with his shield and bow.

The road reached its high point near where Callias had shown Alex, Nancy and Emily their first view of Artemios. Acasius was breathing heavily but his wind was much better than it had been a few days ago. By late morning the road came to the river she had forded many months earlier. The water was much deeper now and flowed swiftly. Pantheras halted the company. On the far bank, they could see a raft and a coil of rope.

"It figures the villagers would keep the raft on their side," Pantheras said. "We will have to go get it. Dokaris, Coystus, come with me."

Pantheras and the two men set aside their gear, took off their cloaks and waded across. The current came up to their chests and they had to lean into it to keep from being swept away. It depressed Emily that she was too small to do what they were doing. The water would be up to her neck.

The men reached the other side. Pantheras tied one end of the rope around his waist and headed back. Dokaris and Coystus readied the raft. Pantheras stepped out of the water, breathing hard and shivering. The other peltasts pulled the rope taught and tied it to a tree. Dokaris and Coystus pulled the raft over along the rope.

"The rest of you unload the mules," Pantheras ordered. "No reason to get our things wet. The mules can wade across."

Emily and Acasius rode in the raft along with the gear. Coystus, a barrel-chested man, did the pulling while the others waded across. His thick limbs made it seem easy. Emily wondered if she had the strength to do it. She supposed she would find a way if really necessary. The mules snorted and shook themselves when they climbed out of the water. A peltast went across again, untied the rope, and came back.

The two slaves fetched a couple of linen cloths and passed them around as towels while the others took their tunics off and wrung them out. Emily felt small and out of place among the naked men.

"You chose to travel with us," Pantheras said. "We are not going to be too discrete out here."

Moisture made his taught, well-defined muscles glisten. He could have been a model for the cover of a romance novel, except perhaps for his hairy chest. He bore no scars, however, while most of the peltasts did.

"Do not mind me," Emily said. "Do what you need to do."

The work had made them hungry so they ate an early lunch of bread and dried fruit. They repacked the mules and followed the road upstream. Emily walked beside Dokaris who stroked his damp beard.

"Are you friends with Byon, by chance?" She asked.

"Yes, we are friends. We are also cousins," Dokaris said. "His family is rich. Mine is not."

That would explain why Dokaris was a foot soldier and Byon a horseman.

"Are you the same age?"

"I am older. I used to beat him up when we were children."

Emily laughed. "Could you beat him up now?"

"Yes, but it would not be so easy." Dokaris looked down at Emily and smiled, displaying his missing front tooth.

"Byon says he has a sister. Did you beat her up, too?"

"Lussia? No, she was older than me and too tough."

~

By midafternoon, the party came to one of the villages of the hill people. Pantheras spoke briefly with a couple of the elders. They moved on, planning to camp at the second village. The sky remained cloudy but there was no rain.

"No reports of bandits or other trouble," Pantheras said.

"Where do the bandits come from?" Emily asked.

"I do not know. They are like weeds. They just sprout up," Pantheras said.

"Do you know anything about who Hydakoles was?"

"I believe he was from Colchis. He was a soldier, a great warrior some say, but he murdered his commander and fled into the mountains. There he raised his band and tormented the hill people and coastal villages."

"Bandits are like wild dogs running together," Acasius said. "Murderers and thieves fleeing to the wilderness. Once in a while a strong leader emerges, like Hydakoles, and they become formidable. They prey on remote villages, extracting loot. Hydakoles was greedy and tried to put the villages of this valley into his orbit. That is when Agathon sent Callias to lay a trap for him."

~

By late afternoon, they reached the second village. Pantheras met with the leopard-skinned elder and paid him for two jugs of beer and a few chickens. The old man eyed Emily with interest. He clearly recognized her. Pantheras told him the party was on an extended patrol to check for bandits or Persian spies who might come by way of the mountain passes.

The slaves set up Pantheras and Acasius' large tent. Emily set up her own as did the peltasts. She caught sight of her first village woman, or child rather. The girl was looking at Emily through the entryway of one of the huts. She was round faced and cute with dark hair and features that reminded her of Kallisto's servant, Mucha. Emily waved at her. The girl ducked back into the hut.

When the large tent was set up, the slaves slaughtered the chickens and cooked dinner. Emily passed the time by slinging stones at a large rock. Soon the Thracians joined her and they made a contest of trying to knock a small rock off the large one. Emily didn't win but she was happy she held her own.

~

Pantheras, Acasius and Emily ate around one campfire, the Thracians around another, and the slaves made a third for themselves. The company ate chicken off the bone, toasted yams and leafy greens. They washed it down with the villager's thick, black beer. When Emily had finished eating, she rinsed her hands in a bowl of water and wiped them with the cloth she kept in her pouch.

"Outside of Artemios, do many people know about Alex, Nancy and me?" Emily asked.

"I am afraid so," Pantheras said. "Even in Miletus some talk of the 'mysterious strangers.' It is part of why Linus is fretting over you. The Persian tyrant of Trapezus almost certainly knows."

"And Novorosa?"

"That goes without saying."

"Do they think we are anything more than a curiosity?" Emily asked.

"The priests of Trapezus think you might have been sent by the gods," Acasius said. "They want to consult the Oracle at Delphi to find out and determine your purpose."

"Do you believe we were sent by the gods?"

"It is a bunch of rubbish," Pantheras said. "Superstitious men who pander to superstitious people."

The cloud cover had broken up and stars peeked through the gaps. The air was chilly and Emily wrapped herself in her cloak. A slave came by and poured more beer into her bowl.

"What about our expedition?" Emily asked. "Do other people know about it?"

"I doubt it. We have kept it quiet," Pantheras said.

"If, say, the polemarch of Novorosa knew, or the Persians, would they be inclined to do something?"

"The young woman asks a good question," Acasius said. "Novorosa must have informants in Artemios."

Pantheras had his sword out and was wiping the blade with an oiled cloth.

"Hmm, I suppose I would be curious," he said.

"I would have someone follow us," Acasius said.

"There would not be enough time to set that up," Pantheras said.

"Just enough time, I should think, if they acted quickly," Acasius said.

"Who knows our purpose other than Agathon, Linus and Kallisto?" Emily asked.

"No one," Pantheras said. "Except my mother and father. We are on a hunting expedition. The young prince, that is to say myself, wants to bag a leopard for the andron. Who better to come with us than the huntress upon whom Artemis smiles?"

It was a reasonable cover story, Emily thought. Hunting was the kind of thing Pantheras would be expected to do while visiting a remote outpost like Artemios.

"Enough of this talk," Pantheras said. "Acasius, use your lovely voice and give us a song."

Acasius sang about Theseus and his defeat of the Minotaur of Crete and his subsequent love affair with King Minos' daughter, Ariadne. The song had a chorus which Pantheras sang badly. Acasius said a woman's voice was more appropriate for the chorus and they cajoled Emily into singing it. She was on her third bowl of beer. She giggled as she stumbled through the lines. By the third run-through, she had it down and the song took on a magical quality that attracted the attention of the Thracians. They clapped and hooted when Acasius and Emily had finished.

She sipped the last of the beer in her bowl. Pantheras got up to refill it and started pacing around the fire.

"Tell us, Emily, something of your homeland," he said. "Had your people accomplished any great feats?"

Three bowls of beer were too much, Emily thought, a fourth was silly but she sipped from it anyway.

"We put a man on the moon," she said, slurring her words a little. "It took years and thousands of people but we built a giant flying craft, a special kind, called a 'rocket.'"

"Fantastic," Pantheras said. "Tell us all about it."

Emily did her best to recount the Apollo program and Neil Armstrong's first steps on the moon. Pantheras reclined on the ground and put his head in Acasius' lap. Acasius petted his hair.

When she had finished she realized that, at some point during the telling, she had lapsed into English. She looked over to Pantheras and Acasius to apologize but saw that they were kissing and hadn't been paying attention. Her head was swimming and she watched with woozy fascination. She wondered what it would be like to kiss them -- Acasius and his boyish delicateness, or Pantheras and his smooth, sculpted masculinity. She wasn't tensing up at the thought of kissing a man. Too drunk, she supposed. She wished Phoibe were around.

Acasius and Pantheras stood up and, without a word, went into their tent. She decided she should do the same. She got up and the world started spinning. She took a couple of wobbly steps toward her tent and collapsed.

"Oops, I guess I had too much beer," she said in English to no one in particular.

She lay on her back watching a passing cloud obscure the stars. Maybe I'll just sleep out here, she thought. Then a face appeared in the sky, a large face with a beard and a tooth missing from its smile. The face came nearer and nearer to hers. Oh no, she worried, I'm going to have to kiss that face. She closed her eyes but the kiss never came. She felt arms slide underneath her and pick her up.

She opened her eyes and realized it was Dokaris. Was he going to rape her? She tried to reach for her pepper spray but her pouch was covered by her cloak. Dokaris set her on her feet near her tent, his arm around her shoulders to keep her upright. He opened the flap and guided her in. He crawled in far enough to put the blanket over her. He patted her hip and crawled out.

"You're not going to rape me?" Emily asked.

She soon slipped into unconsciousness.

~

The corpses that littered the battlefield where the main body of Hydakoles' bandits had been routed were now mostly skeletons, their flesh eaten away by wolves, carrion birds and other scavengers. The sight added more nausea to Emily's horrible hangover. That damn beer, she thought. One quality it didn't have was that of making her forget the night before. The party trudged on. Only the slaves seemed energetic.

"I would love to fight bandits on our trip," Pantheras said. "But I hope we do not meet any this morning."

A drizzle dampened the mood further as they climbed a craggy hill covered with stunted junipers. They stopped at the top of the ridge to rest and eat a belated breakfast. Emily skipped the wine, drank spring water from one of her bottles and took three aspirin tablets. Acasius looked peaked and Pantheras helped him mount a mule.

By the time they reached the crest of the next ridge, the drizzle had stopped and the sky cleared. Their moods improved and Emily began to feel like herself again. Pantheras walked beside her.

"I was thinking about what we talked about yesterday," he said. "I wonder if we are being followed."

"It is only a possibility," she said.

"If we were, how close would they be, do you think?" He asked.

"With some tracking skill, they wouldn't have to follow very close, half a day back perhaps."

"I would like to know for sure," Pantheras said.

"We could lay a trap but it would delay our journey," Emily said. "Do you think it is worth it?"

"Let me think on it."

~

They came to more level ground. Oaks replaced the larches and they stopped for lunch.

"If we want to make the meadow by nightfall, we will need to pick up the pace," Emily said.

Pantheras ordered everybody up. Emily walked ahead about 100 paces with Dokaris. They were in the wilderness now and needed to stay alert. The terrain offered ripe opportunities for ambushes. At a muddy spot, Emily pointed to tracks. They looked like the pads of a large dog except there were no claw marks in front of the toes.

"A leopard," Dokaris said. "It came through this morning."

Late in the afternoon, Emily and Dokaris slowed as they approached the meadow and saw a flock of guinea fowl pecking the ground. They both loaded their slings and twirled off shots. Dokaris missed but Emily's pellet struck home. There would be fresh meat for the barely gruel.

By nightfall they had the tents up and the slaves served the meal. Emily thought of Hank and Tim. Their encounter here with Hydakoles seemed so long ago, yet it hadn't even been a year. She didn't really miss them -- she had hardly known them -- but the bond with Hank had been strong at the time and the grief she felt when he died left a residue.

"This is where Hydakoles killed your friends," Acasius said.

"Yes."

"How did it happen?"

Emily told the story as best she could remember.

"The girl is a fighter," Dokaris said. "You must have Thracian blood."

"Perhaps I do."

"Hydokoles' was a fool," Pantheras said. "He should not have let Nancy's looks stop him. Now we have no bandits to fight."

~

Clear skies prevailed the next morning. The sun was well up in the sky and all the gear packed except Pantheras and Acasius' tent. They were sleeping late. Emily and the Thracians idly sharpened or oiled their weapons. The two slaves played a dice and stick game like they always did when they had the opportunity. Emily was sitting near Coystus who muttered something in Thracian. She didn't know the words but the gist was clear enough: "Bloody, lazy, rich Greeks."

Emily got up and paced around the camp. She found a javelin in a bush. It was the one that a bandit had thrown when Hank was fighting Hydakoles, the throw that Emily disrupted with her walking stick. Rust coated its head. It was still usable but she had three new ones stowed on a mule and didn't think she needed another.

A raven croaked and flew up from the west side of the meadow. She left the javelin in the bush and walked over to Coystus.

"I am going into the woods like I am going to wash myself, then circle around to the trail," she said.

"Do you think someone is there?" He asked.

"Probably not, but it will not hurt to look."

She made an obvious show of taking a bowl of water and a cloth with her. She walked about fifty paces into the forest and set the bowl and cloth down. She took the cover off her spear, pulled her hood over her head and began her stalk. She moved from cover to cover, crouching low, feeling the ground with her bare feet before putting any weight on them. She could hear Pantheras who was finally up.

"Where's our little maiden this morning?" he asked.

"She went to wash up," Coystus told him.

"Ah, lesser men than ourselves might be tempted to go have a peek."

Pantheras rambled on in that vein, talking louder than he needed to. Coystus must have let him know her plan.

She took a wide arc around toward the trail they had come from. As she drew close, she saw a hobbled donkey. It was laden with two large bags, a small bow and a quiver of arrows. Someone was here. She got low to the ground and crawled away, paralleling the trail back toward the meadow. Out of sight of the donkey, she slowly raised herself into a crouch and advanced.

A large oak provided a good approach to the point where the trail entered the meadow. She pressed herself up against it and looked around. She saw the back of a man, about 15 paces off, crouched in shadow, looking out at the meadow and holding a spear. She was glad he didn't have his bow. She might dodge or deflect a spear throw. She inched closer, wondering how close she could get.

Pantheras yelled.

"Emily! It is time to go now. You do not have to make yourself pretty for us. You are not that pretty anyway."

She used Pantheras' voice as cover and moved up quickly, getting within range of a long thrust.

"Do not move or I will run you through," she said to the man.

The man flinched and jumped forward. Emily's thrust just nicked his backside. She pulled her spear back quickly. The man wheeled around. His eyes were full of fear, but he had the longer spear. He lunged with it. Emily parried the thrust, forcing his point into the ground. He was overextended and off balance. She stepped in and, with a strong pivot of her hips, swung the butt end of her spear around, clocking the man's jaw. He went down. Emily pressed the point of her spear into the man's side. Blood dripped from his mouth.

"Get up and put your hands behind your head," Emily said. "Move!"

The man complied but was unsteady on his feet. He was bearded and young, about her own age. He wore a dark gray cloak over a brown tunic. A knife hung at his belt.

"Turn around."

He did so and she put the point of her spear into his back.

"Walk," she ordered.

Emily followed the man into the meadow. She could hardly believe what she had just done. She was glad that not everyone possessed Pantheras or Byon's skill at arms.

~

Pantheras, Coystus and two peltasts ran toward Emily and her prisoner. The peltasts carried their spears and Pantheras had his sword drawn. They stopped when they got within thrusting range, spears aimed at the man's torso. Coystus gave Emily a nod.

"My, my, look at the bird our cat has caught," Pantheras said. He sheathed his sword and looked the man over. "You should be more careful. Do you not know there are dangerous creatures in the forest?"

"I mean no harm," the man said. "I am just passing through."

"Why were you skulking in shadow watching us?" Emily asked.

"I ... I did not know if you were friendly. I ..."

"Coystus, get him on his knees," Pantheras ordered.

Coystus planted his spear in the ground but before he could act, the man went to his knees of his own accord. Coystus took the knife from the man's belt. By now, Acasius, Dokaris and the other peltasts had come up. Emily raised her spear and put the cover back on.

"What is your name?" Pantheras asked.

"Charis, son of Straton."

"Who sent you to spy on us, Charis, son of Straton?"

The man hesitated.

"Uh, no one. I am a hunter seeking game," the man said. He was in obvious pain. Emily suspected his jaw was broken.

"It is a little late in the season for collecting furs," Pantheras said.

"He has a hobbled donkey down the trail," Emily said.

Pantheras ordered a peltast to go get the animal. Pantheras yanked the man's pouch from his belt. Fishing through its contents, he produced a handful of silver coins.

"You must have had a good year," Pantheras said. "Why are you not back in Artemios enjoying the barbarian whores it is so famous for?"

"I don't know. I ... I like to hunt."

Pantheras gripped the man's jaw. The man shuddered with pain.

"Tell us who sent you, Charis. If you do not, things will go very badly for you."

The man, Charis, didn't reply.

"Coystus, would you do the honors?"

Coystus stood close to the man, closed his thick hand into a fist and cocked it back.

"No, please," Charis said. "It was Hermesthenes who hired me."

"Hermesthenes? Who is he?" Pantheras asked.

"I do not know. A merchant, I think."

"What did he want you to do?"

"Just to follow you, see where you went, and report back."

"How much did he pay you?"

"Two hundred drachmas up front, two hundred more when I get back."

"Who else is with you?"

"No one. No one else, I swear."

"Hermesthenes is a stupid man, and so are you."

Pantheras drew his sword and, with a quick backhand stroke, sliced open the man's throat. Blood gurgled from the cut. Charis put his hands to his neck and collapsed on the ground.

"Pantheras!" Acasius screamed. "Why did you do that?"

Emily was stunned and looked on with horror at the man bleeding out on the ground. He shuddered and went still.

"He was a spy and an agent of our enemies," Pantheras said. "The poor sap probably did not know it but the consequence is the same nonetheless. Dokaris, you and your men bury the body. We will leave as soon as you are done."

He put his arm around Acasius.

"Come, I am sorry you had to see this."

The Thracians appeared unmoved by the event. They went about the business of digging the grave as if it were just another chore. Emily looked on and Dokaris stood beside her.

"Would you have killed him?" Emily asked.

"Yes. It needed to be done," Dokaris said. "The man died quickly and did not suffer long. He was lucky."

The killing made clear how much closer to death she now lived. It was terrifying, and exhilarating. She saw a raven perched on a branch nearby. Soon another joined it.

~

When the hole was finished, Emily put two silver coins on the dead man's eyelids. Coystus planted a stick in the ground as a marker. Two peltasts lowered the body into the hole and filled it in with earth.

"He paid for his mistake. May the gods see him safely to the Underworld," Emily said.

Dokaris, Coystus and the other peltasts were looking at her.

"We should get going," she said.

A name for this place occurred to her: Bloody Meadow. She walked toward the mules and the Thracians followed.

Chapter 19 | Ground Zero

EMILY walked beside Pantheras at the head of the party. A sullen Acasius walked behind them. The forest was quiet and still.

"Are you angry with me for killing that man?" Pantheras asked.

"No, just sad that it had to be done," Emily said.

"You understand, then, that it had to be done."

"I suppose, yes, in this time and place."

"You caught the spy," Pantheras said. "You have the right of plunder. His goods and coins are yours."

Emily thought for a moment. She didn't want any of it, though the bow did interest her.

"Give thirty coins each to the peltasts and ten each to the slaves," Emily said. "The donkey and the rest of the items we should give back to the man's next of kin."

"As you wish."

~

They came to a fork where a smaller trail diverged from the main road. The company stopped and Emily looked around. The trees were familiar. This was where they wanted to turn.

"Where does the main road go?" She asked.

"I believe it leads to a pass through the mountains," Acasius said.

They turned up the smaller trail and soon they were amid stands of towering beech trees. Pantheras and Acasius marveled at their size. The trail led up a gradual slope and they stopped to rest at the crest, mainly for Acasius' benefit. The descent, Emily knew, would be steep.

She took the lead down the rocky trail, followed closely by Pantheras. Soon she could hear the rush of water. The rapids that led into a narrow ravine had become a torrent. The trail that flanked the stream remained dry, however, and the party got safely down to it. Acasius' face was flushed.

"You had better ride for a time," Pantheras said, nearly shouting to be heard over the whoosh.

The trail was level at the base of the ridge and the going easier. The noise of the rapids receded behind them as they walked through what seemed a tunnel of closely growing oaks and hackberries. Emily pointed out fresh deer tracks. Pantheras retrieved his bow in case they got lucky and flushed one. When they had walked the better part of two hours, Emily raised her hand and halted the company.

"There is a valley about a half mile on," she said. "I should scout ahead and make sure the area is clear."

Pantheras agreed and followed about fifty paces behind. Soon Emily could see where the trees opened to the sun-brightened valley. She stayed in shadows as she approached the edge of the forest. The valley was as serene and beautiful as she remembered, the distant mountains visible through the gap in the ridges. The grass was not so tall now, a few inches of green striving for sunlight through the previous year's dried and flattened stalks.

She saw no sign of people but saw four deer at the edge of the stream -- three does and a fawn -- about forty paces away. They pranced at the stream's edge, looking as if they wanted to cross the swift current. With the breeze in her face, she could smell the deer. Part of her didn't want to disturb the beauty of the moment but her hunting instincts prevailed. The opportunity was too good to pass up.

She was well out of range of her spear and a sling bullet would not do. She looked back at Pantheras, put a finger to her lips and waved him up.

Suddenly, the largest doe jumped into the stream and waded across. The fawn jumped in after it. The other two snorted and stamped. The big doe made it to the other side, turned and looked back. It must have seen Pantheras. Its white tail went up and it ran away, the fawn following close behind. The two smaller does, alerted to danger, leaped into the stream, splashing their way across. Pantheras loosed an arrow and just missed. He nocked another and loosed again at the trailing one hoofing its way up the far bank. This time the arrow found its mark and lodged itself into the doe's back. It slid into the stream. It tried to struggle up but its rear legs were not moving. Pantheras shot another arrow, missed, tried a fourth and struck its neck. The deer's life quickly ebbed away and it went still.

Pantheras shouldered his bow, grasped Emily's head and kissed her.

"Mmm-whah, you are a gem. Thank you. We are eating venison tonight!"

~

Emily ate one of the tenderloins and Pantheras the other. Everyone, including the slaves, enjoyed venison steaks. roasting them in the stone oven that stood in the midst of the ruined village. The meat was tender and tasty, the doe being quite young.

The slaves cut the remaining meat into strips, salted them and put them into flax bags. Two peltasts worked on the hide, scraping fat off the underside and applying a mixture of oil and a mash of the deer's brains. This would help keep the hide supple. They stretched it between two sticks stuck in the ground and supported by lengths of twine.

The mood was festive. Pantheras had distributed the silver coins to the peltasts and the slaves. They praised and toasted to Emily's hunting prowess, generosity and good luck. Coystus gave her a bear hug and Dokaris rubbed her head. Despite lingering dread over the morning's killing, she was enjoying herself.

As the evening wore on, Emily asked about the village that once stood in the valley. "Did Hydakoles burn it down?"

"No, it is too old," Acasius said. "Looking at the shape of that oven, I would say the village was Cimmerian. The Scythians drove the Cimmerians out of this region a long time ago. The Scythians then crossed the passes and raided the cities of the Median Empire before eventually being driven back across the mountains."

~

The morning brought rain and Pantheras and Acasius showed no inclination to get out of their tent. The slaves brought Emily a bowl of nuts and dried fruit then scurried back to their own tent. Only the mules and the donkey seemed unirritated by the weather, happy to graze on the fresh grass. Emily stretched, meditated, sharpened and oiled her knives. Fortunately the rain didn't last long and they were on their way by midmorning, the mules complaining about the extra weight of the wet tents.

By noon they reached the swamp Emily had named Willow Bog. It was more like a lake now, its waters reaching up to the trail's edge, covering parts of it. The cool air kept the bugs at bay but it was a slow, muddy trudge around the swamp and all were glad when they finally ascended the ridge on the other side. They stopped and rested on the slope. Dokaris suggested they check their feet and ankles for leeches but they found none. Too early in the year, Emily thought.

"We should be going," she said. "There is a clearing some miles ahead where we can dry out the tents if the weather holds."

"Yes, we have wasted enough time already," Acasius said.

"My dear, I believe you will be a seasoned woodsman by the time we are done," Pantheras said.

They made the clearing by the time the sun dipped behind the western ridge. They set up camp, ate and turned in early.

~

The morning brought sunshine and even Pantheras and Acasius were up to greet it.

"How much further?" Acasius asked. His complexion had ruddied, making him seem less fragile and roughing his baby-faced looks.

"We are getting close," Emily said. "But even if we push hard, I doubt we could make it today."

"We should let the tents dry in the sun," Pantheras said.

To pass the time, Acasius sat in on the slaves' dice games and seemed to enjoy it. The Thracians busied themselves with weapons practice and a slinging contest. Pantheras and Emily decided to climb the nearby peak and have a look around. Coystus eyed them as they headed up. He had been staying close to Emily as much as he could. It felt to her like the behavior of a loyal hound. She sensed that he did not trust Pantheras.

The view from the peak was even more striking than when she and Alex had climbed it. The plains were green and sprinkled with the yellows, reds and whites of blooming prairie flowers. There were no bison to be seen, only a few antelope, and no Scythian hunters.

"I am beginning to like this country," Pantheras said. "It is so vast and beautiful. Perhaps Artemios is worth fighting for."

"If you stayed, would Acasius stay with you?" Emily asked.

"For a time, but he belongs in Miletus or Athens. He would leave sooner or later. We both know we cannot always be together."

"Would you marry the girl your mother wants you to?"

"I do not know. It makes me ill to think about it," he said. "Now you, on the other hand, I think I could stomach marrying you."

Emily tensed up, the comment took her off guard.

"Why me? I am neither rich nor beautiful, and I am a barbarian."

"I could be friends with you. You like women in your bed and I like men in mine. In some ways, it would be the perfect match. We would have to do our duty and churn out a couple of children, of course -- the little rodents -- but otherwise we could live our lives as we wanted."

"Or you could," Emily said. "I would be stuck spinning thread in the gynaeceum."

"You seemed to want to go there the other night, rather than the andron," Pantheras said.

"The women are my friends. I like being with them but I also want to hunt, and I want to visit the market when I please, and I want to fight with the warriors, and other things that women are forbidden to do."

Pantheras chuckled. "I am reminded of something the great Thales said: 'There are three things for which I am grateful, that I was born human and not animal, that I was born a man and not a woman, and that I was born Greek and not barbarian.'"

"Thales was an ass."

Pantheras bent double. "Oh, Emily, if Acasius heard you say that, he would faint."

~

By the time Emily and Pantheras had climbed down, the tents were dry. The party packed up and continued on. They made good progress and, by late afternoon, arrived at the campsite near the small stream where Emily and Tim had found the old sandal. At Emily's suggestion, they camped there. Tomorrow they would find the crash site.

Emily retrieved a towel, a cloth and her brown tunic from her pack.

"I am going to wash," she said.

She went to the spot where she and Nancy had bathed together and she had wondered whether Tim was looking on. Would one of the Thracians look now? She undressed and set her things against a tree. She stepped into the stream, now much deeper, and began to wash herself. The muscles in her thighs and calves had swelled over the months and she actually had grown proud of her legs. Her small body was serviceable and healthy. She was thankful for that.

The water was cold but she took her time. Her braid had become frazzled so she unwove it and combed her hair out straight before dunking her head in the water. While rinsing her blue tunic, she was startled to see Coystus standing near her things. His back was turned to her. His spear and shield were at the ready. He was protecting her, she realized, though it didn't seem necessary. What did it mean? Was he in love with her? Or perhaps it was another kind of devotion. She couldn't fathom the source of it but she sensed Coystus would happily do her bidding. Should she acknowledge it?

"Coystus, please give me a hand up the bank?" She asked. "It is all right. I am sure you have seen women before."

Tentatively, Coystus approached the bank, keeping his eyes down. He stole a quick glance to get her location, reached out a hand and pulled her up.

"Thank you. I am glad to have you as a traveling companion."

Coystus didn't reply but resumed his station with his back turned. Emily dried herself, put on her brown tunic, belt and cloak.

"I am dressed now," she said.

Coystus nodded and went back to the camp. She wrung out her blue tunic, shook it and headed back herself.

The men decided to wash, too, and went to the stream. Emily tended the fire and hung the wet tunic from a branch. Listening to their laughter, she felt alone and apart. She had earned their respect to the point of being a leader but she could never be one of them, it seemed. Was it simply the way things had to be? She supposed that it was and she just needed to resign herself to it. She wondered how the Scythian warriors, the men and the women, got along. Did they bathe together?

~

The trail narrowed and the party marched single file. Emily took the lead with Dokaris close behind. He was the best woodsman of the group and helped her make sure they kept to the path. Three peltasts brought up the rear behind the pack animals. They were in tiger country, Emily had warned, and they didn't want to get a mule snatched from them.

"I would like to see that tiger," Pantheras said. "Would it not be something if we brought home its pelt?"

Emily had no wish to kill the tiger. She wondered if Pantheras would change his tune if he actually saw it.

"We should leave it alone if it leaves us alone," she said.

By late morning they reached the diminutive stone hut with a small, round hole for an opening. The tiger's face painted on it seemed to smile at their arrival. Pantheras was fascinated, circling the hut and feeling its flat, granite slabs.

"This is most peculiar," he said. "Acasius, do you think the hill people made it?"

"No," Acasius replied. "It is too old. I have heard talk of such structures. They are ancient and no one knows who built them or why. There are said to be scores of them throughout these hills and mountains."

The Thracians were nervous. Only Dokaris would come near the hut. It was a reminder of how old the world was. How many people had come and gone in this area over the millennia? Emily knew that human beings themselves were new creatures on the earth. From nature's point of view, the hut was built a brief moment ago. Even so it conveyed a sense of the great depths of time. She felt small but realized, in the scheme of things, they all were small.

"We are close to our destination," Emily said, "but the trail ends here."

"Can you find the way?" Pantheras asked.

"Yes. I think so."

Acasius spread the map on the roof of the hut.

"Do you want to look, Emily? Alex has drawn it out rather clearly with figures and lines."

"No, my heart says I should use my instincts and not the map."

"Then lead the way," Pantheras said.

~

The party resumed its single-file march. Emily was confident of her direction. The forests were becoming a book she could read, at least in part. Nevertheless, as a precaution, she peeked at the compass in her pouch. Descending into a flat area between ridges, the forest grew dark, the high canopy thick with new foliage.

"Our sixth day out from Artemios, our fifth day from any human habitation," Pantheras commented. "We are in the deep wilderness now, my friends."

The party stopped for a quick bite. Emily checked her compass. They moved on. About half an hour later, she turned the party up the ridge to the east. When they reached the top, the far slope was too steep to climb down. Emily had overshot her turn, but it was what she expected to find if she had. They backtracked north along the crest.

"Are you sure you know where you are going?" Pantheras asked.

"Yes."

Before long the slope down became traversable and they descended, turning southeast again at the bottom. In another half hour, Emily recognized a large outcropping of rock to their right. She knew for sure now that the ridge to the left helped frame the valley where the plane had crashed. She led the party up the slope. At the top, they rested.

Emily knew if they descended here, they would emerge close to the campsite. Instead she led them south along the crest for a few hundred paces before making the descent.

"How many more damn ridges will we have to climb?" Acasius asked.

Emily didn't answer. She didn't need to. The party emerged into a verdant, sunlit valley.

"We are here," she said.

Before them, only a few paces away, was a mangled wing broken off from the fuselage. They stared at the massive cylinder that was the engine, and at the nosecone and turbine blades within. Pantheras moved his mouth as if to speak but no words came out.

~

The men became like boys, unsupervised, and in a museum filled with race cars. They felt the metal of the engine, tugged at wires and lines, climbed onto the wing, peered inside the fuselage. They seemed oblivious to the decomposing corpses within. Emily had no desire to participate. She kept back from the wreckage and just pointed out the major segments like the cockpit where the pilots had guided the plane.

She and the slaves led the mules to the old campsite. While one slave unloaded the gear, she took the other to the spring so they knew where to get water.

She saw no sign that anybody else had been here. The little mound where they had buried food and equipment remained undisturbed except for weeds growing on it. She saw no reason to disturb it now. She helped the slaves prepare the camp.

When the tents were up and the fire going, she sat on the rock where she had eaten a bad Danish, had first contemplated her new existence as a woman and, a day later, had accepted Emily as her name. It had happened fast, that first acceptance, but subsequent events had shown her how short she had fallen. Real acceptance eluded her still.

Did she hope that by returning to her point of origin, the gods might see fit to restore her manhood? No, she thought, she harbored no such hope. It would be like hoping a rescue helicopter would fly in and take her back to Detroit. This was *her* time and place now. She would have to find a way to belong, find a way to belong to herself.

She felt close to something out here. Whereas in Artemios, she felt far away, even when surrounded by people who loved her. Part of her wanted to go back and receive the comfort they offered, give into the currents, maybe hook up with Byon and raise horses. She imagined employing Phoibe as housemaid. It was an idyllic vision that she sensed would lead, even if it worked out, to a kind of drowning.

A drowning of what? The part of her that still longed to be a man? No, that would hardly be a tragedy. It would be the drowning of a possibility, a possibility she could feel but could not see, a possibility

Kallisto had alluded to, a possibility that was reflected in the eyes of Coystus, Dokaris and even Pantheras. Pantheras sensed it. He wanted to fold it into himself. But it was not his to possess. It was Emily's. She took hold of her pendant, the Tiger Stone, and rubbed it with her thumb. Suddenly she giggled. The slaves gave her perplexed looks. She was amused that Kallisto had already put a name to the possibility: Artemis.

Chapter 20 | Claws

BY sunset the camp had become littered with assorted junk the men had scrounged from the wreckage -- bags, cameras, bottles, toys, a blow dryer, etc. But what interested them most were the magazines. Acasius intently studied the pictures in a news magazine while the peltasts jostled each other for glimpses of a fashion catalog. The detail and realness of the images were miraculous to them.

Acasius pointed out to Emily a picture of Chicago's spectacular skyline along the shores of Lake Michigan.

"Is this the city where you lived?" He asked.

"No, but one similar if not as large."

"And that is an aircraft?"

"Yes."

The questions came faster than she could answer them. The excitement abated some when the sun set and they could no longer easily see the pictures. Pantheras sat down next to Emily, holding a cardboard tube. It was dark blue and embossed with gold lettering. He pulled off its top and extracted a bottle filled with brown liquid.

"This looks like something expensive that one might drink," Pantheras said.

"Yes, but you may not want to try."

It was a bottle of whiskey, 100 proof, aged 18 years, probably purchased at the airport's duty-free shop.

"What is it called?"

"Whiskey."

"How do you open it?"

"Twist the cap."

He did so and sniffed the opening.

"Whew! By the gods, that is strong," he said. "You can actually drink it?"

Emily took a small sip, savored the stinging woody flavor, and recalled pleasant moments with people she had once known. Pantheras took a drink, too much, and spat it out.

"That is awful. It is like fire."

"More like fire than you know," Emily said. "A similar kind of liquid fueled the aircraft's engines."

She picked up a small stick from the campfire, poured some whiskey into her mouth and blew it out on the stick's burning end. It ignited into a ball of flame. The slaves and a few of the peltasts cowered back.

"Prometheus walks among us in the form of a woman," Pantheras said.

"It is not magic," Emily said. "It is the same substance found in wine, only much purer."

They passed the bottle around and each man took a sip. They all agreed it was horrible stuff.

"It's an acquired taste," Emily said.

~

She was glad the men were not inclined to drink more of the whiskey. They were worked up enough as it was.

"It is a wondrous world you come from," Acasius said.

"It has wonderful things, yes, but horrible things, too. In a way it is killing itself with its things. Is it a better place than here and now? I am not so sure."

Pantheras wanted to spend a day at the crash site before heading back to Artemios. That made sense, Emily thought, let them get their fill. She considered telling him that she had decided not to return with the party. She wondered how that would play out. Would he object enough to try to force her to return with them? She decided she would tell them tomorrow. If they were determined not to let her go, she would contemplate other plans.

~

Emily woke late. The sun's rays made the nylon of her red tent glow. She put on her brown tunic and buckled her belt. She crawled out to find Coystus sitting nearby, thumbing through the news magazine.

"Here," he said, handing her a bowl. "Breakfast."

"Thank you," she said.

"I saw a hyena pelt hanging from a line on a tree," he said. "Is that the one you killed?"

"Yes."

"Too bad the pelt is ruined now."

"It is a shame."

Acasius came out of his tent, rubbing his eyes.

"Where is Pantheras?" He asked.

"He found tracks," Coystus said. "He took his bow and went to follow them."

"Which way did he go?" Emily asked.

Coystus pointed toward the north ridge. She set her bowl down and grabbed her satchel.

"I am going to look at those tracks myself," she said.

She headed toward the north ridge, walking the perimeter of the forest, scanning the ground. There was a muddy spot at the head of a game trail and she saw a giant paw print. It looked fresh. The tiger must have come through during the night and headed up the hill. Shit, she thought, Pantheras went after it.

She moved as quickly as she could up the trail without making a lot of noise. Two bad things could happen: Pantheras could kill the tiger or it could kill him. She felt a desperate urgency. She had to stop him. She stifled an urge to shout, thinking it would not be helpful. Cougars, she knew, were wary predators and could be scared off. But a tiger, being so large, might, like a grizzly, attack instead of slink away.

She reached the crest, finding no sign of either Pantheras or the tiger. The slope became steep as she followed the game trail down and she had to be careful with her footing. She was annoyed she hadn't brought her spear. She came to the edge of a broad, shallow ravine. She saw no tracks. She crouched low, trying to think of what to do next. She could hear something coming from the ravine. She skirted its edge to her left.

Then she saw it, or part of it. The tiger was down in the ravine, gnawing on carcass, but a tree obscured most of its body. She hoped it wasn't eating Pantheras. She continued along the rim and was able to see the half-eaten hind quarters of a tur.

Then she saw Pantheras. He was crouched on the rim, looking at the tiger. He had an arrow nocked but not drawn. He probably had a decent shooting angle there, she thought. He seemed to be contemplating something. She waved silently but he didn't notice her. She picked up a stick of deadwood and moved closer. Pantheras drew his arrow back. Emily threw the stick at him.

"No! Pantheras, don't!" She shouted.

The stick struck his arm just as he released. The arrow sailed wide. Pantheras' face contorted with fury.

"You bloody little cunt!" He yelled.

He nocked another arrow and this time aimed at Emily. She dove to the ground and the arrow missed. She scrambled up the hill. Pantheras pursued her.

"I am going to kill you, you bitch!"

Pantheras was catching up. She couldn't outrun him. She ducked behind a tree and heard the thud of an arrow striking its bark. She slipped her sling out of her pouch and loaded a pellet. Pantheras's footsteps drew closer. She exposed herself on the left side of the tree and quickly ducked back. An arrow hissed by. She stepped out from the right side while Pantheras nocked another arrow. She was going to sling him but shouted instead.

"Pantheras! Look out!"

Pantheras turned but was too late. The tiger lashed out with its huge paw. The blow caught Pantheras on the side, spinning him and hurling him to the ground. The bow and arrows scattered in different directions. The tiger reared back to pounce. Emily twirled her sling and hurled a shot that struck the tiger in the ribs. It flinched and jumped back, snarling. Emily drew her Corinthian dagger, ran to Pantheras and stood over him. She locked eyes with the tiger for the second time in her life. The tiger roared. It seemed to ponder what to do next. It decided to turn and bound down the hill.

~

Emily sunk to the ground, trembling. The dagger dropped from her hand. Her vision had narrowed, her hearing had numbed. She breathed deeply and her senses slowly returned. She could hear Pantheras struggling for breath. She looked at him. Blood pooled on the ground. There were four gashes in his leather armor at his lower abdomen. A claw protruded from one of the gashes, yanked from the tiger's paw by the force of the blow. Blood trickled from the wound.

She needed to stop the bleeding. The trauma pad in her first-aid kit might work but she had to get the claw out and the armor off. She pinched the claw between her fingers and thumb but it was too slippery with blood.

"I think this is it," Pantheras rasped. "I am glad I got to see your aircraft, and the tiger."

"Shut up. You are not going to die," Emily said.

From her satchel, she got out the multi-tool and the first-aid kit. She unfolded the tool, gripped the claw with its pliers and pulled. Pantheras groaned. The claw came out. The size of it seemed unreal.

"I am sorry you will not get your pelt but you can have this as consolation," Emily said.

Pantheras laughed then groaned from the pain of laughing. Emily drew her puukko and cut a section of the armor away, exposing the wounds. Only the one looked deep. She unwrapped the trauma pad and pressed it hard against the cut. Pantheras let out an anguished yell. She hoped the pad's clotting agents would be enough to stop the bleeding.

After about a minute, it appeared to be working. With one hand, she unscrewed the cap of a small bottle of alcohol.

"This will probably be unpleasant," she said.

Pantheras grimaced and grunted as she poured alcohol on the cuts. She continued to keep the pressure on the deep one. She hoped the others would find them soon.

"You are a better man than I, or woman, or, you know what I mean," Pantheras said. "I tried to kill you. Why did you save me?"

"I do not know. I did not have time to think. I just acted."

"You did it because you love me," Pantheras said, smiling.

"Maybe a little," Emily said.

"I knew it."

"You are an ass."

Pantheras groaned again as she pressed harder on the trauma pad.

~

Coystus found them first. He shouted to the others who had fanned out in the forest. He instructed two peltasts to go make a stretcher. Acasius arrived and almost fainted when he saw Pantheras.

"Pantheras, what has happened?"

"I got into an argument with a tiger and lost," Pantheras said. "Emily saved me. She drove it off."

Acasius knelt beside him and held his hand. "You are so stupid sometimes."

Dokaris had experience treating battle wounds. After they carried Pantheras back to camp, he began the process of stitching the cuts. Emily gave Pantheras a prescription painkiller while Dokaris worked. Pantheras slipped into unconsciousness.

~

The mood was somber around the campfire that evening. Acasius was in his tent, tending to Pantheras. The men wanted to know the story of the tiger. Emily said Pantheras should tell the tale when he was able and she only told them that she had driven the tiger off with her sling.

"We will probably have to carry him home," Dokaris said. "But we should wait a few days first."

"I will stay until you are ready to leave," Emily said. "Then I will be going my own way."

Dokaris appeared puzzled. Coystus looked up from a stick he was whittling.

"You will not lead us back to Artemios?" Dokaris asked.

"You can lead them. You know the way as well as I do."

"Where will you go?"

"East, perhaps, wander the forest."

"But why?"

"I do not know if I can put it into words. I need to be out here. Artemis wants me out here. Perhaps I will find a place with the Scythians. I do not know."

The men regarded her with what seemed like awe. She had invoked Artemis and they really believed she was tied to the goddess. She realized they would not try to stop her. She was free to choose and that, strangely, made her afraid of her choice.

"I will go with you," Coystus said. "I will follow you anywhere."

"No," Emily said. "You have a contract with Agathon and Artemios needs you. I must do this alone."

~

They spent the following days playing games and hunting. Emily scrounged the debris for toothbrushes, toothpaste and dental floss. She kept some for herself, put the rest in a bag and gave it to Acasius, telling him to give it to Nancy.

The Thracians put on a javelin throwing contest. Emily won the accuracy contest at twenty paces. Dokaris, of course, won the distance throwing.

Pantheras' wounds did not fester but he grew feverish. Emily gave the bottle of antibiotics to Acasius.

"Have Pantheras swallow one tablet twice a day," she said. "Keep doing it until the bottle is empty, even if he is feeling better."

The day after Pantheras' fever broke, they decided to leave in the morning. Pantheras sat against a rock, soaking up the afternoon sun. The weather had been generous and little rain had fallen. Emily sat cross-legged next to him.

"Acasius tells me you are not going back with us," Pantheras said. "You are a stupid girl."

"I have been called that before," Emily said.

"I have a mind to order the men to force you to come back," he said.

"I am not sure they would heed you," she said.

"I see. They are under your spell. But, then, so am I. Agathon will be furious and your Nancy will kill me."

"Kallisto will understand," Emily said. "I promised Nancy I would return and I will, when I am ready. Tell her that. Tell Byon, too."

Coystus and another Thracian emerged from the trees of the western ridge, running toward the camp.

"Hmm. Is the tiger prowling again?" Pantheras asked.

Emily stood up as they approached.

"Persians," Coystas gasped. "Persian soldiers. They are coming. They must have found our trail."

"How many?" Pantheras asked.

"Twenty, at least, probably more."

"Did they see you?"

"They could have. I am not certain."

"Ah, hell," Pantheras said. "The bastards must think there's something important out here."

"Maybe they are after you," Emily said.

"And they shall have me. I can neither fight nor flee," he said. "But it may be you they really want. You must run. How long before they are here, Coystus?"

"Not long. A fraction of an hour."

"Get your things together and go," Pantheras told Emily.

"What about you, and Acasius, and the others?"

"Acasius and I will be fine. We are too valuable as hostages."

"But the Thracians. They are my friends. I will fight beside them."

The other men had crowded around. Acasius came out of his tent. Coystus seized Emily by the shoulders.

"No. Pantheras is right. You must flee. We will fight them and buy you time. It is the will of Artemis. I know this."

Emily was dumbstruck that he really believed what he was saying, believed his life had divine purpose, and that purpose was to save her. She hugged him.

"Hurry! Get your things."

Emily's pack was essentially ready. All she needed to do was fold up her tent. While she did, the peltasts gathered up their weapons and shields. Acasius and the slaves moved Pantheras into the copse near the camp. When she had stuffed the tent into her pack and had strapped on the bedroll, she could hear arrows whistling in from the trees. The Thracians had formed a battle line, protecting themselves with their shields. She hoisted her pack and went into the copse.

She hugged the slaves and Acasius. "May you all fare well."

She went to Pantheras who was sitting up against a tree. She took his hand and shook it.

"Goodbye, Pantheras."

He gripped her forearm.

"Tell me your secret," he said. "The one we would laugh at and not believe."

She leaned down and whispered in his ear. Pantheras grinned and his chest shook.

"Damn, that hurts. You will slay me yet, Emily. That is too rich. Goodbye, my friend. You are the Tiresias of our time."

~

Emily headed for the trees to the east, using the copse to hide her movement. She walked with her spear in one hand and javelin in the other. Entering the forest, she heard Dokaris let loose a piercing howl. He and his comrades were doing what they were born to do.

PART TWO
SCYTHIA

Chapter 21 | Solitaire

SHE padded through the forest as fast as she could with the weight she carried. She hoped she wouldn't have to ditch her backpack and run. She used her spear and javelin like walking poles. From the crash site behind her, she heard shouting -- loud, angry, but, she thought, not battle cries. Perhaps it was a parley. She didn't want her Thracian friends to die. The fact that they were willing to die for her was something she knew but didn't comprehend. How could one live up to such a thing?

The eastern slope was not steep. There was little ground clutter and she moved in the dark shade of the ancient oaks. Even in haste, and with extra weight, her footfalls were quiet. She strove to be just a shadow moving among the trees.

She was surprised the Persians had come in such force. What were they after? What did they hope to find? Did they want to capture Pantheras and Acasius, use them to force harsh terms on Artemios or extract high payment. Sending a spy to follow them made practical sense, but a large armed party suggested a significant play. Had word got out about the story of Nancy, Alex and herself being from the future. Were the Persians after her? What value did they think she would have?

She set a steady pace, creating a rhythm between her walking and breathing. She could keep up this pace a long time if needed. The mid-spring air was chilly in the forest. She could see the vapor of her breath.

Would the Persians pursue her? That was the immediate question. Pantheras would probably tell some lie as to her whereabouts. The crash site itself might be so awesome to them that they would think they found what they wanted and not pursue her at all. Nevertheless she had to assume they would.

She rested briefly at the crest then started her descent. She knew she was heading for an open plain where she had seen the bison herd many months ago. It would be dangerous to cross it, especially in the daytime. She checked her compass. She decided to turn southeast which, she hoped, would keep her in the forest. She made her turn at a large deadfall, walking along its trunk, trying to mislead anybody who might be tracking her.

She hopped down from the trunk, set her direction and resumed her walking rhythm. Less than an hour later, her rhythm was interrupted by a small stream that flowed in a northeasterly direction. She stepped into it and walked about 100 paces upstream. She came to a large boulder that the stream flowed around. She climbed up and over it and continued southeast.

After about another hour, she stopped, drank water and ate an energy bar. Daylight was beginning to fade. Had she gone far enough? She couldn't be sure. Her legs burned and she would like nothing more than to make camp and rest. She couldn't really travel at night through the forest, not without using her flashlight. But, she thought, if she could keep going, it would greatly improve her chances of getting away clean. She turned eastward down the slope. Perhaps the plain would be narrow enough to risk a crossing.

The trees thinned out at the bottom of the slope and were replaced by thick brush. She skirted the edges and found a game trail which she followed. It was twilight when the brush thinned and she could see the plain. Five or six miles to the next ridge, she figured. It would be dangerous to cross at night -- lions and hyenas, she knew, would be active -- but it might give her the edge she needed.

She sat and waited for nightfall, eating dried fruit and nuts. She had seen no bison or antelope on the plain. She hoped that meant no large predators were around. When it was dark, she started across.

Soon the grass was chafing her bare feet and calves. They would be raw and bloody before she reached the other side. "Fuck," she whispered. The stars of the moonless night provided some light but not enough to see into her pack. Her boots were at the bottom and she didn't want to pull everything out to get them. She couldn't risk using her flashlight in the open.

She remembered her leather flats and argyle stockings. She had packed them but where? She found them in a side pocket, put them on, and hoisted the pack. It was then she caught the dim reflection of two yellow marbles floating in the grass. Except they weren't marbles.

The terror *he* had felt when he had encountered a bear in Montana was a shadow of the terror she felt now. Her legs felt weak and her arms didn't want to move. The marbles were gone but she knew the creature was not. Whatever it was, she couldn't outrun it. She willed herself to pick up her spear. She charged forward with a grunt.

"I see you. Don't fuck with me," she hissed.

There was a sudden rustle in the grass and the creature moved off. A brief shadowy glimpse of a long tail let her know the animal was probably a leopard. She hoped she had dissuaded it from stalking her further. She picked up her javelin and continued across the plain.

~

Her legs were beyond burning and became almost numb with fatigue. She guessed she had walked two hours or more. The dark slope of the ridge was closer but she had misjudged the distance. She had to keep going. She didn't want to be caught out on the plain in the daytime.

She trudged on, her vision narrowing to the grass just in front of her. Her sense of time disappeared. She had no idea how long she had been out on the plain when she nearly ran into a tree. It took an effort of will to stop before colliding with it. It was a larch. There were others around. She moved deeper into their midst, stumbling as she went. She knew she would not be able to resume her walking rhythm. She could go no further. She set her pack against a tree, wrapped herself in her blanket, and sunk into the sleep of exhaustion.

~

The sun was already well up when she woke. A woodpecker knocked on the tree trunk above. She did not feel rested. Her limbs ached with stiffness and it took her a moment to realize where she was. What the hell am I doing out here, she thought. She was alone now, about as alone as a person could be. She remembered the Persians might be pursuing. So what? Would being taken by them be so terrible? No, she didn't want that, even if they treated her well.

She found a spot to relieve herself and drank nearly a liter of water. She had one liter left and a skin of diluted wine. She ate another energy bar. She carried perhaps four days of food. Soon she would have to start foraging and hunting but she felt she needed to put more distance between her and the crash site. She headed up the ridge, her legs complaining that they had to be put to work again so soon.

The rocky slope only supported scattered junipers. She came to a spot where she could see down to the plain. She took the binoculars from her satchel, scanned the area carefully and saw no sign of pursuit. If her nighttime hike across the plain had left a trail, she saw no evidence of it.

A plan formed in her mind. She would hike as far as she could for a day. Tomorrow, if there were no indications she was being followed, she would look for a suitable place to settle in for a time. She would still have a couple of days of food left while she foraged and hunted and got the lay of the land. If things got desperate, she was close enough to the crash site that she could return and dig up the buried camp supplies.

~

The terrain became one of craggy hills, scrubby junipers and tough shrubs. She stayed off the peaks as much as she could. The going was slow navigating around patches of sharp rock and loose slate. She kept her flats on to protect her feet.

In a crease between hills, she found a spring surrounded by a stand of larches. She filled her water bottles and kept going. She flushed a tur that was bedded down in a patch of grass. The sight of the animal reminded her of the hike up the peak with Hank on her second day as a woman. What a day it was. She remembered how afraid and alive she felt. She felt much the same way now.

By late afternoon, a long ridge loomed in front of her. Its tree cover was light. She climbed it to have a look around. In front of her was an area of tall beeches and oaks. To the north, she could see the plains of the Caucasian steppe and to the south were snow-peaked mountains. She descended into the forest and set up a cold camp, not wanting to risk a fire yet. The sun was hardly down when she crawled into her tent and slept.

In the morning, leaving her pack against a tree, she grabbed her spear and satchel and ascended the slope she had come down from. She sat next to a juniper and peered through the binoculars. She stayed on the crest about two hours but saw no sign of pursuit. She decided the Persians weren't following her. She also decided that, for the time being, she would make this forest her home.

~

She retrieved her pack and headed into the forest. She walked up and down a low hill then another. At the bottom of the second hill she came to a river flowing roughly south to north. Its banks were steep and it was about 40 paces across. The current was swift and appeared deep. She knew she couldn't cross it, not here, not without planning and effort.

She walked upriver until she came to a small feeder stream that angled in from the southwest. She followed the steam a few hundred paces to a point where it cascaded out of a small ravine. Water pooled at the bottom of the cascade. This, she thought, was a good spot. She set up her tent about 50 paces away at the base of a slope, out of sight of the pool and far enough away that the rush of the cascade wouldn't mask the sound of something approaching.

She gathered deadwood, bathed, rinsed her brown tunic, hung it from a branch near the camp. She put on her blue tunic and started a fire. The canopy above would act like a filter, keeping smoke from being visible as long as the fire was not too big. She boiled some barley and roasted a piece of salted venison.

The hot meal felt good in her stomach and she drank a little wine with it. Camp Nyfitsa, she would call this place. She felt strangely elated to be out here, proud she had the skills and strength to survive. But she knew she couldn't stay here for long. She wasn't a hermit. She also knew that surviving the winter was beyond her abilities. She supposed she would have to return to Artemios and take up whatever life waited for her there. Two weeks, she thought, a good long camping trip and then she would go home. Except Artemios did not feel like home, a refuge perhaps, but not home.

~

She crawled out of her tent into the dawn light of a new day. A pleasant cacophony of birds tweeted above her. With javelin in hand, she snuck up on the pool, hoping to catch a passing animal taking a drink. No animals were there. She returned to her camp, ate a cold breakfast, cleaned and oiled her weapons.

She thought about how dependent she was on them. Their sharp points and edges made up for the claws and fangs she lacked. Without them, she was so much more vulnerable. It occurred to her that human beings were new to the game of being top predators, immature even, compared to the finely-honed instincts of the leopard that had stalked her. It had chosen not to attack, probably wisely. The quarry was unknown and the risk too great. Not that she was a match for a leopard but she could very well have wounded it, possibly to the extent that it would not have survived. Pride did not get in the leopard's way. It would watch and learn and wait until the odds were stacked in its favor or desperation forced its hand. It had nothing to prove.

She heard something moving through the trees. She stood up and readied her spear. Soon she saw it -- a large brown bear, its nose in the air, ambling toward her. When it saw her, it stopped, the lips of its lower jaw drooped as it sniffed. The bear dwarfed her. She raised the spear and shouted, "Ahrrr!"

The bear cocked its head and looked at her quizzically. She made jabbing motions with her spear.

"Go away! This is my camp. Begone!"

The bear rocked its head back and forth and stood up. It roared. She felt like a mouse, not mighty, but tiny. She wished she had a hole to scurry down.

"You don't scare me," she lied. "Go away or you will feel the bite of my spear."

The bear's front paws slumped and it dropped to all fours, looking as if the noisy creature in front of it could offer no further amusement. It turned and walked toward the pool. She moved so she could watch it through the trees. It took a long drink, defecated, and ambled up the slope.

She giggled nervously.

"I'm a top predator. Yeah, right."

~

She decided to do a little scouting and foraging. She grabbed her satchel and spear, and headed north, walking slowly, often looking behind her, trying to get a feel for the land and the woods. The forest is never really the same from one spot to the next. To those not used to it, however, it can all look the same and that's why it's so easy to get lost. She didn't completely trust her abilities but she knew she could always find the river and get back to camp that way.

The air was still and nothing moved so when something twitched in the corner of her eye, she looked closely in that direction. It was a rabbit sitting in shadow near a tree. She loaded her sling and took a shot. Missed. The rabbit hopped away. She was irked by her poor aim but she at least was able to find the pellet. She kept going north.

It was beyond midday when she thought she ought to head back. She sat on a fallen limb and ate an energy bar. She heard rustling and snorting to the northwest. A pig, she thought. She put up the hood of her cloak and stalked toward the sound.

After about 30 paces, the animal came into view -- a large boar with formidable tusks. It had overturned a log and was gobbling up grubs and insects underneath. She inched to the side, putting a tree between the pig and her, and crept forward. Reaching the tree, she readied her spear, the range about 10 paces. She stepped out, focused on her target and threw.

The spear struck the animal's neck, the point going through and out the other side. The boar squealed and took off. She ran after it. The boar would have easily outpaced her except the spear's shaft knocked against trees and other objects, slowing it down. She kept after it, hoping it would bleed out soon.

The pig was running for a clearing ahead. The shaft struck a tree as it emerged into the open and the beast stumbled to the ground, struggling to right itself. She drew her dagger and stood at the edge of the clearing, hoping it would cease struggling and die where it was. But the boar found its feet again and ran off. Slower now. It was weakening. She sprinted and caught up. She grabbed the shaft of the spear. With renewed energy, the boar grunted and wheeled around to attack her. They danced a strange pirouette, spinning around each other, the boar trying to close the distance. Then it tried to get away and the spear started to come out. She let go and the boar flopped to the ground on its side.

She pounced and drove her Corinthian dagger into its side. The boar tried to slash her with its tusks but the spear in its neck protected her. She moved the dagger side to side, pulled it out and jumped back. Blood poured from the wound. The boar struggled briefly but couldn't gain its feet. Soon it was still.

~

She plopped to the ground and lay flat on her back, chest heaving. She had been lucky, she thought. She could have lost her spear, or worse, been gored by the thing.

"Sorry, Mr. Boar, I probably shouldn't have killed you," she said.

She sat up. The boar was big, 200 pounds at least. What was she going to do with it? She looked around. The clearing wasn't really a clearing but rather the edge of the grasslands. Before her was a low, grassy hill and her eyes went to the crest. There Emily saw a man on a horse looking down at her.

The man's form was silhouetted against the blue of the sky. He had long dark hair and wore no hat. His beard was full but not unkempt. He wore a cloak of checkered browns and blues that partially covered a long-sleeved tunic of dark orange. Blue trousers with yellow spots covered his legs. A sword was sheathed at his hip and, hanging from his saddle, was an elaborately decorated quiver that contained a bow and several arrows. Emily wasn't sure if the man was very tall or his horse was small. His feet hung far enough to be hidden by the grass.

Emily and the man looked at each other. He was not far off, a hundred paces or so, but too far to read his expression. She felt self-conscious. She must look a jumbled mess. She realized then what had been so refreshing about being alone in this forest -- here she had been neither a man nor a woman, simply another creature trying to survive. But the gaze of the strange man had transformed her back into a woman.

Emily stood, straightened her tunic and cloak, brushed off dirt and grass. She put a foot on the boar's neck and yanked out her spear. She looked up and met the man's eyes again. After a moment the man turned his horse and disappeared down the other side of the hill.

Chapter 22 | Hitched

EMILY set about field dressing the boar. It took all her strength to get it on its back. She kept the rear legs spread apart with pieces of twine tied to stakes in the ground. When she had it gutted, she cut out the tenderloins and put them in the bag that had contained the dried venison. To get the pig turned over on its belly, she had to lean her back against its torso and push with her legs.

She clutched its forelegs and began to drag it toward the forest, doing it in heaves, a couple of feet at a time. She stopped when she was in the shade of the trees. She decided she would return tomorrow and salvage what meat she could, provided a tiger or bear didn't get it first.

Emily needed to hustle back to camp to get there before dark. She decided not to risk dead reckoning and, instead, went to the river and followed its course upstream.

She wondered who the man was she had seen. He must be Scythian. That type of quiver, she had learned, was called a gorytos. It was distinctive to Scythians who were known as expert archers. The man could have killed her if he had wanted to. Did that mean he was friendly? He hadn't tried to communicate. Perhaps he had more pressing things to do than mess around with a lone woman in the wilderness. She was just a passing curiosity.

A wind had picked up, the forest canopy swayed with its blowing. Occasionally she could hear the crack of a dead branch breaking. At the river's edge, she picked some chickweed and put it in her satchel.

She arrived at camp with enough light left to wash. When she was drying herself, she felt self-conscious again, like someone was watching her. She had been thinking of the man again, conceiving herself through his eyes. Was her body one that would arouse his passions -- short with muscular thighs, narrow shoulders, lean arms and small breasts. She was no comic book heroine. Just as well, she thought, she could be passed up and not haunt a man's erotic dreams. She combed her hair and let it lay straight to dry.

She got a fire going and cooked one of the tenderloins. The other she put in a nylon bag and buried it in a shallow hole. She would eat it later. Through a gap in the canopy, she saw the stars disappear behind dark clouds. She could hear distant thunder.

She cleaned and oiled her weapons. The storm grew closer. She had positioned her tent so rain water would flow around it, provided it was not too much. She heard the patter of drops on the leaves above. She went inside and closed the flap. She dreamt of riding horses with Byon. Phoibe rode behind her, arms hugging tightly. A thunderclap broke the dream. It was some time before she fell back to sleep.

~

She strapped on her belt and crawled out of the tent carrying her spear. The ground was wet and mist hung in the morning air. She drank water and ate an energy bar. She scolded herself for eating it. She should save the few she had for emergencies. Today, she figured, she would go back to the boar's carcass and get more meat. She tried to think of ways she might preserve it but did not have many ideas. She shouldn't have killed it. She should just stick to small game. There was plenty around.

She also thought she might climb the grassy hill and see if there was any sign of Scythians. If so, should she risk making contact? How would that go?

She went a ways from camp to relieve herself. While walking back to get her satchel, suddenly, as if from nowhere, a rope appeared and cinched itself around her chest and arms.

"What the ..."

Emily felt herself yanked off her feet. She landed hard on her back and lost her grip on her spear. She was being dragged up the slope. She struggled to get to her feet but couldn't. Her puukko. She was just able to reach it with her left hand. She drew it and slipped the blade under the rope in the gap between her chest and right arm. The sharp edge did its work and the rope snapped. She tumbled down the slope. She tucked into a ball with the blade pressed flat against her chest to keep from stabbing herself.

She bounced off a tree, which spun her, then did a backward somersault and staggered to her feet. She looked up the slope and saw a man sliding down feet first on his back. He must have fallen when she cut the rope. The man dug his heels into the ground and stopped himself before he reached Emily. She was waiting with her knife, ready to stab him.

He stood up and was maybe ten steps away. He was tall and lean, a giant in an orange tunic and blue trousers. A broad grin revealed yellow teeth through a thick, dark beard. His silvery eyes were hypnotic.

"Vasha kiz, im par chup tu," he said, reeling in the rope and coiling it.

Emily looked around, saw her spear and made a dash for it. The man bounded after her. Just as she was grabbing for it, he pushed her. She rolled on the ground and back to her feet. He approached her slowly, hands out, leading with the coiled rope. He had not drawn his sword.

With her left hand, she reached for her Corinthian dagger but it wasn't there. It must have fallen out when she tumbled down the slope. He kept coming closer. He was using the rope as a shield. If she attacked, she might stick him but then he would have her. She would not survive if his intent was to kill.

Emily ran. If she could get far enough ahead, she might have time to load her sling. The man ran after her. She dodged and weaved between the trees but couldn't gain any distance. At some point, he anticipated her move and intercepted her on the other side of a large oak. She ducked his grasp but lost her footing and went to the ground.

She got on her feet and faced him. There was nothing for it. She would have to fight him with her puukko. She kept low to the ground, circling him, hissing. His reach was too long to get inside and stab his body. Attack the hands, she thought. She made quick thrusts and slashes but he was quick, too, very quick, almost catching her arm at one point.

She decided she would have to charge berserker style and hope she could cut something vital before he killed her. Just before she made her lunge, the man threw the rope in her face. She flinched and that was enough. He snatched the wrist that held the puukko. His hand gripped her like a steel clamp. She could see the bulging cords of his wrist muscles. She was caught.

Vainly she tried to yank herself free. She clawed at his hand but he grabbed her other wrist. She wriggled and kicked but he twisted her around and pressed her to the ground. He put her in a headlock. Her hands were free now but there was nothing she could do. She was in the snug embrace of a sleeper hold.

Emily, you fucking idiot, she thought before she passed out.

~

Emily's vision slowly returned from blackness. She was sitting against a tree and her arms, knees and ankles were tied with rough twine cords. The man's rawhide lariat secured her to the tree. She saw the man leaning over her backpack, stuffing the tent into it. The cooking utensils were gone. Apparently he had packed them away. He played with one of the pack's zippers, moving it back and forth, smiling. His blue trousers fit loosely and had yellow dots arranged in triangular groups. His orange tunic was cut in a kind of double-breasted fashion and cinched with a blue sash. His feet were covered with what looked like leather socks tied at the ankles.

The man wrung his soaked cloak out then tied it to the pack. Emily gathered he had used it for a rain shelter during the night. He must have followed her or tracked her back to camp and then waited out the storm nearby. What did he want with her? Was he taking her as a slave? Would he sell her at a slave market? Would he have his way with her first? Was he contemplating some cruelty to sate his violent passions? He hadn't done so yet. Perhaps that was a good sign.

The man hoisted the pack and picked up her spear which looked like a javelin in his hands. He was as tall or taller than *he* had been.

Emily pointed to a spot on the ground.

"There is good meat there," she said in Greek.

He dug out the nylon pouch, looked inside then stuffed it into his satchel.

"Mmm, ash havas," he said. He had a tenor voice with a deep undertone.

He came over to her and untied the rope that held her to the tree.

"Mar haja tee," he said, wagging a finger at her. "Pul avan kiz."

He lifted her to her feet, put her over his shoulder and began to walk due north.

His long strides carried them quickly through the forest. His movements seemed relaxed and unstrained despite the weight he carried. She had to weigh more than 100 pounds and the other gear must add up to 40 or so. She watched the forest floor and trees moving away from her. Maybe that bear would come by and attack, give her a chance to escape. Not likely. Maybe a chance would come. She would have to be ready for it.

But the rhythmic jostle of the man's walking lulled her into a torpor. When he set her down, she had no idea how long it had been. Coming back to her senses, she realized they were on top of the grassy hill where she had first seen him. She looked at the spot where she had dragged the boar. It was gone. Who or what had taken it?

The man stuck a thumb and finger into his mouth and whistled, the sound clear and piercing. He handed her a water skin which she drank from greedily. With his back turned to her, he pissed on the ground. She managed to get into a squatting position, pull up her tunic, and do the same.

Soon a horse trotted up. It was a stocky brown gelding that looked a bit like Shaggy only with a dark mane. The man strapped the gear onto the horse's saddle. He lifted Emily up and placed her belly down over the front of the saddle. He hitched her with a length of rope. He grabbed the reins and, with some silent signal, the horse knelt and he mounted it. They cantered off in a northwesterly direction.

What did life have in store for her now? She shuddered, trying not to think about it.

~

They rode all day. At one point in the afternoon, the man stopped, set Emily on the ground and untied the bonds around her wrists. She had no feeling in her hands and could do nothing with them. He rubbed them then retied the cords. He did the same with the bonds around her knees and ankles. She was too groggy to struggle or protest. He fed her a few pieces jerked meat and let her drink from her wine skin.

Soon they were on their way again. Dusk came and they rode into the night. She lost her sense of time and was barely conscious when he stopped. She blinked and tried to rouse herself.

People were gathering around them -- man shapes and woman shapes in the darkness, backlit by a few fires. She could make out several tents. The man unhitched her from the horse and put her over his shoulder. She could hear people chattering but she could make nothing out.

He carried her inside one of the tents and set her down on something soft. He went back outside but left the flap open. All was shadow in the tent and she could see little. There was a slight musty smell that seemed homey. What she would give to be in her bed back at Agathon's house.

She could hear the man's voice, loud and forceful like he was booming out a proclamation. A woman's voice answered, strong and clear. It must have been a joke because people laughed. The man said something in return then there was much talking all around. It was some time before the talking faded. She was tired and wanted to sleep. She fought it off. She needed to stay awake.

Emily saw the man's legs through the entrance. He threw a spear into the ground, her spear. He came inside carrying a burning ember. He lit a candle with it and went back outside. The tent was spacious and high enough that even the man could stand upright. A large rug covered much of the floor. Four poles supported the roof. The candle burned in a holder attached to one of the poles. In the middle of the tent was a brazier on a simple tripod. Emily was sitting on one side of a large mattress. There were pillows and sheets and a wool blanket, blue with a yellow zigzag pattern. Near the entrance she noticed a tear in the tent's felt.

She could see a chest and a few crates. A line strung between two poles suspended a tunic and a pair of trousers. Looking behind her, she saw a cuirass covered with bronze scales, a helmet and a shield.

The man came back in and closed the flap. He looked down at Emily and smiled. She tried her best to look as fierce as possible. The man undid his sash and removed his tunic. Sinewy muscles rippled over his lean frame. He had a hairy chest. She saw tattoos on his sides -- a wolf, a stag, a lightning bolt and a spiral. From a pocket on his tunic, he withdrew her puukko.

He pulled the knife from its sheath and ran a finger along its edge, admiring its sharpness. His smile widened. His silvery eyes gleamed. He stepped toward her.

A lump formed in Emily's throat. Her heart raced. Goddammit, there was nothing she could do.

The man knelt in front of her, holding the knife between them. He mulled her for a few moments then sheathed the knife and set it beside her. Starting with her feet, he untied her bonds, rubbing her numb flesh like he did out on the plain. When he finished with her hands, he stood, fetched a skin from a crate, took a long drink and set it next to the knife.

He went around to the other side of the mattress and took off his trousers. She saw a small scar on his hip and a long one on his thigh. He snuffed the candle then slid under the covers beside her.

~

It was dark now and she was confused. Feeling returned to her hands and feet. The prickly pain of it was intense. The first thing she did was grab her puukko and draw it. If he tried anything now, he would regret it. But he had to have known this. Was he playing a game, goading her to attack so he would have a pretext to punish her?

She bided her time, breathing deeply to calm herself so she could think. She could try to run for it but where would she go? These were horse people. Unless she could find forest to hide in, they could easily catch her in the morning. Her confusion deepened when she heard the man snoring. She listened to it for a while and decided it wasn't faked. The man shifted and grunted.

She lay on her back, holding the knife to her chest, trying to think of what to do. Before she could decide, she fell asleep.

~

The first thing she noticed was the knife was no longer in her hand. She sat up. The puukko was in its sheath beside her. A small blanket had been put over her while she slept. The man was gone.

The flap was open and morning light poured in. Her spear was still stuck in the ground just outside. She took a drink from the skin next to her knife. It was water. Folded at the foot of the mattress was a pair of quilted trousers and a plain flax tunic. She still had on her blue tunic which was grimy and sweat-stained. She stood, stretched, ran her fingers through her hair, and took a deep breath. It was time to see what the day had in store. She stepped out of the tent.

~

She was in a large encampment. There were dozens of tents. Hers was on the periphery. Just outside the tent she saw her pack, satchel and belt. Everything seemed to be there except that the scabbard that held her Corinthian dagger was empty. To the south she could see hills and mountains. To the east was a line of poplar trees. Otherwise they were on a plain, like a vast, green lawn. She could see horses grazing in the distance.

There were people around, men and women, going about chores. They mostly wore plain tunics, trousers and caps. None looked like warriors. Not far from her was a woman sitting in the shade of a lean-to. She was working a kind of loom. One end was tied to a pole while the other was strapped around her waist. The weight of her body kept the tension on the threads. She used a cigar-shaped implement to help guide the cross-threads. She used a comb-like board to secure them in place. Seeing Emily, she disengaged herself from the device and walked over.

She was a little taller than Emily, had generous hips, a full bosom and brown hair tied up under a blue cap. Her face was round and weathered with prominent cheeks and big brown eyes.

"Do you speak Greek?" She asked.

Emily nodded.

"Hello, then, my name is Chunya. What is yours?"

"Emily."

"Pleased to meet you, Emily," the woman said, reaching out a hand. Emily shook it.

"We should get you breakfast," Chunya said.

They walked toward a smoldering fire pit.

"Why am I here?" Emily asked. "Why did ... that man kidnap me?"

"That man is Taval. He took you because he wants you to be his wife."

"Wife? But why?"

"He fancies you. Why else? Last night he told us he watched you kill a warthog. He said Tavapa, the sky god, gave him a vision and he knew he must make you his wife."

"Why would I want to be his wife?" Emily asked.

"I do not know. That is up to you. There are plenty of women who would be happy for the opportunity. Taval is our war leader, one of them."

"Up to me? Am I not a prisoner?"

"No. Taval kidnapped you to impress you. You are free to go if you choose. He told me, if you want to leave, to give you a horse as payment for your trouble."

At the fire pit, they sat on a mat and ate flatbread with wild onions and cheese. She drank a bowl of a pungent, fermented milk brew. The taste would take some getting used to.

"Your Greek has a strange accent," Chunya said. "Where are you from?"

"A land called America, but lately I am from Artemios."

"Ah, I have heard of Artemios, the upstart city that the Lion Tribe protects."

"Yes. Are you not Scythians yourselves?"

"Scythians? Well, yes, I suppose. It is a word the Greeks use for all sorts of people. But we are not part of the Lion Tribe. We are part of the Wolf Tribe and our band here is called the Storm Wolves."

"Are you enemies with the Lion Tribe?"

"We steal their horses. They steal ours. Sometimes there is bloodshed but I would not say we are enemies. We trade with them. We will be heading that way soon."

"Does the Wolf Tribe have a king, like Huraslan?" Emily asked.

"No. We have no king. Sometimes, like when the Persians invaded, we rally around a strong war leader. We are on the move too much to have a kingdom. The Lion Tribe stays in one area, mostly, so they have a king. Huraslan would like us to join his kingdom but the Wolves are not interested in swearing oaths to that old conniver."

"Months ago, I saw a party of Lions in Artemios," Emily said. "Some of the warriors were women. Do women fight for the Wolves?"

"We all fight for the Wolves if there is need," Chunya said. "And yes, some of our best warriors are women."

"Are you a warrior?"

"No. I do not like to fight and I am not very good at it."

Chunya began to clean up and rinse the breakfast dishes. Emily helped her. They walked back to where the loom was and Chunya resumed her work. Other people were eyeing Emily, not hostile, but not exactly friendly. They seemed to deliberately keep their distance. She noticed a large pig hide stretched between two poles.

"That is your warthog," Chunya said. "Taval said you were alone. What were you going to do with such a large beast?"

"I do not know. The opportunity was there. I got excited," Emily said. "I am glad it is being put to good use."

"Why were you in the forest by yourself?" Chunya asked. "People say you are a niava, a forest nymph. They worry it is bad luck for Taval to have taken you. It will upset Samvi, the goddess of the forest and animals."

"I had not been alone for long," Emily said. "I was with a party of Greeks and Thracians when we were waylaid by Persians. My friends did not want me to be captured so I fled into the forest."

"Persians? This is news. How far away are they?"

"From here I am not sure," Emily said. "From where Taval took me, it would be about two days walk to the place where they attacked. The direction would be west by northwest."

"I will tell Taval if you are not here to tell him yourself."

"Where is Taval now?" Emily asked.

"Out hunting. They are tracking a bison herd," Chunya said. "He should be back later today or this evening. If you are going to leave, it would be best if you went before he returns. If he sees your spear at his tent, he will assume you have decided to stay and be his wife."

Emily paced in front of the tent, thinking about what to do. The thought of having her own horse excited her but where would she go with it? The forest is no place for a horse. Maybe she could skirt the forest's edge and work her way around to Artemios. She would be in the Lion Tribe's country. If she met them, she would tell them she was a friend of Agathon's and they likely would let her pass or take her back to Artemios themselves. That seemed like a good plan.

"I will be leaving," she said.

"All right," Chunya said. "We shall find you a horse from Taval's stock. Do you know how to ride?"

"Yes, but I am no expert."

Emily put on her belt, hoisted her pack and swung the satchel across her shoulders. She grabbed her spear and pulled it out of the ground. She hesitated. Her stomach tightened. The homey smell of the tent caught her nose. She stared at the ground where the spear had been.

"Are you coming?" Chunya asked.

Emily felt fixed to the spot, two wills pulling in opposite directions. She recalled the drowning she wanted to avoid. She realized it was the man inside her who was afraid, who was choosing to flee, who was seeking out the drowning.

"Is Taval a good man?" Emily asked.

"Yes," Chunya said. "He will treat you well if you treat him well. But if you stay it will not be all cherry juice. Even as Taval's wife, your status will be low. You will have to earn the tribe's respect and acceptance. The warthog is a good start, though."

Emily recalled the time when she had seen Kydoime and Aella, the Scythian warriors, and how she wanted to be like them.

"What the hell," she whispered in English.

She raised her spear and threw it back into the ground. She slipped the pack from her shoulders and let it fall. She felt free to move again.

"I will stay and be Taval's wife," she said in Greek.

Chapter 23 | Animal Husbandry

EMILY set her pack and satchel inside the tent and picked up the tunic and trousers. She went back outside to see Chunya looking perplexed.

"I should wash up and change," Emily said. "Is there a place to do that?"

Chunya pointed to the poplars. "The river is just there."

Emily started toward it and Chunya walked beside her.

"I am surprised you chose to stay," she said.

"So am I."

"Taval told me to keep you company until he returned," Chunya said. "But I do have chores to do."

"Then I will help you with them," Emily said.

"I suppose I should start teaching you the Lovta language."

"I should like to learn it. You speak Greek very well, like a native."

"I am half Greek. My mother was Lovta but my father was Greek. He was killed by the Persians, she was taken as a slave. I escaped and the Wolf Tribe took me in."

"Do others here speak Greek?" Emily asked.

"Most know a little Greek, some speak it well."

"What about Taval?"

"He knows some Greek."

At the river, Emily undressed and waded in. It was wide here; the current was slow and there was a sandy beach. Clothes hung from lines strung between the poplars. Emily rinsed her blue tunic, wetted her hair and combed it. She stepped out onto the beach and let herself drip dry in the sun.

"You are short but strong," Chunya said. "I see why Taval fancies you. It is known he likes small women. Opposites attract, they say."

"Has Taval had other women?"

"He was married but his wife died two years ago giving birth. The child died, too. Since then, he had not been much interested in anyone until now."

"Are you married?"

"Yes, my husband is Arlav."

"Is he a warrior?"

"No, but he is a leader. He runs the camp, keeps track of supplies and the livestock. He often is the one who decides where to go next and when. He knows the land very well. He has seen sixty winters and remains strong."

Emily put on the trousers. They hugged her hips but fit well enough. She tied the waist cord and put on the tunic. It was cut like a karate gi and was the light khaki color of raw flax. Working clothes, she thought. The tunic came with a blue cloth belt. She put her puukko, pouch and sling on the belt and cinched it up.

"Those clothes were made for a boy who died a while back," Chunya said. "I hope they fit well enough. In time we will make you better ones."

"They are fine, thank you," Emily said. "Do you know how to braid a tail?"

Emily retrieved an orange ribbon and they sat in the shade of the lean-to while Chunya worked on her hair. When it was done, Chunya returned to her loom while Emily spun flax into thread with Chunya's spindle whorl.

"I want to be a warrior," Emily said.

"That is a hard path, especially for outsiders. You will have to earn it and prove yourself," Chunya said. "To be a warrior for the Wolf Tribe, you have to be able to fight from horseback. It is very difficult for those not born to it."

"I will learn. What will be expected of me as Taval's wife?"

"It will not be a marriage of equals. That may come later. You will be expected to see to his tent, see to his horses, care for his weapons and otherwise do his bidding. And, like everyone, you will have other duties around camp as well."

"Marriage of equals? How does that happen?"

"You perform a great deed or kill an enemy in battle or, like me, put in years of good service to the tribe."

Emily wondered what she was getting herself into. She wasn't averse to hard work but she didn't want to be Taval's slave either. She could still leave. The tent fluttered in the wind. She could see the tear in its side flapping. No, she would bide her time and see what happens. This tent was her tent now.

"I would like to fix that tear," she said. "Are there any scraps of felt to be used as a patch?"

"Yes, let me show you."

~

To patch the tear, Emily used thread and a needle she had found in one of Taval's crates. His sewing kit was well stocked and included a couple of spindles. That surprised her. She applied lard to the seams as a sealant. In the afternoon she helped Chunya with laundry. The others in the camp continued to avoid her.

"Do they not want to meet me?" Emily asked.

"They will in time," Chunya said. "They are keeping their distance until Taval returns."

As the afternoon wore on, Emily grew anxious. By suppertime Taval had not returned. Emily and Chunya ate apart from the others.

"Thank you for keeping me company," Emily said.

"I was an outsider, too," Chunya said.

"When will Taval come back?"

"Hard to say."

Emily's anxiety mounted. When Chunya returned from rinsing the dinner bowls, she was shaking.

"You look scared," Chunya said. "Are you all right?"

"I am scared. I do not know why."

"Have you ever been with a man?"

Emily shook her head.

Chunya laughed. "You poor girl. But do not worry. Taval is our fiercest warrior, except perhaps for Kaplea, but under the blankets, I am told, he is as gentle as a lamb. Trust me, you will like it."

"Who is Kaplea?"

"You will meet her soon enough. You do not want to cross her. She is not so gentle as Taval."

Chunya talked on for a while but Emily wasn't paying much attention. She breathed deeply, trying to calm herself. Part of her wanted to run away.

"I should get back to my tent," Chunya said. "I have my own husband to look after."

Emily went into her tent and lit a candle. Nancy, she supposed, would have ideas about how to spruce up the space. She had none. She sat cross-legged on the mattress and tried to meditate. It didn't do much to calm her. Where was Taval? She wanted to get this over with.

She thought about leaving, just disappear into the night and follow the river back to the forest. No. She had made her choice. She wished she could take control of the situation, turn her dread into anticipation. She undressed, snuffed the candle and slid under the covers. Eventually she fell into a fitful sleep.

~

She heard men talking outside the tent. She was curled up on her side. Someone came in and she tensed up. She kept her eyes closed and pretended to sleep. There was man's odor in the air now, Taval's odor. After a few moments, he got into bed beside her. He lightly rubbed the curve of her hip then lay back on his pillow.

She was annoyed at feeling like a trembling child. She had made a choice, act like it. She turned on her back. She found his hand with hers. Their fingers intertwined and he squeezed. Somehow the tension eased from her limbs and the knot faded from her stomach. He didn't do anything more. He must be tired. Soon his hand relaxed and she could hear the breathing of sleep. It struck her as odd that she now felt safe in the bed of a man she hardly knew. She fell asleep to the sound of a stiff wind buffeting the tent.

~

Emily woke to Nancy fondling one of her breasts. Except it wasn't Nancy. A large, rough hand was rubbing her and her nipples had grown hard. Her limbs tensed up. It was still night. She could see no light seeping in from the seams of the tent's flap. She turned her head. She was going to tell Taval she wasn't ready but his lips found hers and her mouth was enveloped in a hairy kiss. She forgot what she was going to say.

She slid her hands behind his head, holding him as if to keep him from withdrawing. His tongue went into her mouth and hers into his. Time seemed to stop for a moment. Then she could feel Taval's hand sliding down her belly and over her pubic hair until his palm covered her vagina. He rubbed it slowly at first and then faster. She could feel his callouses. It was a firm stroke, not precise and delicate like Nancy or Phoibe's fingering. Her head arched back from the electric pleasure of it.

He kissed her forehead, her nose, her chin, her neck, caressing her with his beard. He kept rubbing her with his palm which became smoother with a coating of vaginal fluid. Her groin ached with desire.

He stopped rubbing and pushed her legs apart with his hand and knee. They spread willingly and he pressed her on her back, crawling on top of her. He kissed her breasts, moved up to her neck and to her mouth. She could feel his penis against her thigh.

Through the strong current of pleasure, she was caught by a wave of panic. She could get pregnant! A warrior can't be pregnant. She started to try to squirm away but it was too late. Taval's penis had found its home. A wave of sensation washed away her panic. The ache in her groin had found the relief it was seeking.

Taval pumped harder and harder, grunting as he did so while Emily emitted little involuntary chirps. Then Taval stopped pumping, his pelvis shuddered and he let out a high-pitched groan.

It was over. So soon? Taval disengaged and lay on his back, breathing heavily. She felt strangely frustrated. The frustration ebbed, however, replaced with warmth. She slid her arm under his neck and laid her head on his chest. One of his arms squeezed her tight and the other petted her head. Before long, he was asleep again.

~

Sunlight seeped through the tent flap. Taval was on his side, snoring. Apparently he was sleeping in today. Mrs. Taval. The thought made her chuckle. She thought about modern ideas of relationships, how one should evaluate compatibility before plunging into marriage.

Kidnapping wasn't part of the process, nor visions from gods, nor forest spirits, nor spears at the threshold. Taval didn't even know her name. She didn't care. It felt right somehow being the wife, or wife-to-be, of the man lying next to her.

She was hungry. She got up, stretched, put on her new clothes, and went outside. Something smelled good coming from the cooking fire. She walked over to it. A dozen or so warriors sat or squatted in the area, eating from bowls. A black pot steamed over the fire. The warriors looked at her, showing mild interest. There were two women among them. One whispered to the other. A man got up and greeted Emily.

"Good morning," the man said in Greek.

"Good morning," Emily said. "I would like to get some breakfast for Taval and myself."

"Help yourself," the man said.

He was a smallish and wiry. He sported a long mustache with an otherwise sparse beard.

"My name is Halaba," he continued. "You have decided to become Taval's woman, yes?"

"Yes," Emily said.

Halaba grinned and swatted her on the shoulder. He turned to the other warriors, speaking the Scythian language, Lovta. He went around collecting payment for what must have been a bet.

She went to the cooking pot and ladled some of its contents into two bowls. It was oatmeal, she realized, cooked in milk and spiced with cinnamon. The Greeks didn't have cinnamon. Where had it come from?

"You are my good luck charm," Halaba said. "Two bets I have won because of you."

"Two bets?"

"That you would stay and be Taval's wife and that you would not kill him in his sleep."

He pointed to one of the women.

"Koia there said she would have killed him."

The woman named Koia squinted at Emily. Her light brown hair was braided into two long tails. She wore a pointed felt cap, blue with an orange stripe. She was thin and had pale blue eyes staring from a ruddy, weathered complexion.

"You can kill a warthog but perhaps you do not have what it takes to kill a man," Halaba said.

Emily finished filling the second bowl and put the ladle back in the pot.

"Dead men do not make good husbands," she said.

Halaba laughed. A few others did too.

"Some women think dead men make the best husbands," he said.

She took the bowls back to her tent. Halaba must have translated the exchange. Soon there was more laughter.

Taval was still asleep. The sun was warming the inside of the tent and he had pushed the covers back, revealing his upper body which was not so athletically chiseled as Pantheras' but radiated a sinewy animal strength. Emily felt the ache in her groin. She set the steaming bowls down on a crate and lay down beside him. She caressed his hairy belly and slid her hand down to his penis, gently grasping it.

Taval murmured and stirred. He took a deep breath through his nose. The smell of cinnamon filled the tent. His penis grew and hardened in her hand. Emily swung her leg over and mounted him, guiding his penis to its home. They looked into each other's eyes.

"I am Emily," she said.

"I am Taval," he said.

"Pleased to meet you," she said.

~

Emily and Taval ate cold oatmeal. They didn't say much, just eyed each other and smiled from time to time. When they finished, she took the bowls to the cooking area and rinsed them in a bucket of water. The warriors were gone but Chunya was there.

"You look unharmed," she said. "Did things go well last night?"

"Yes. You were right," Emily said.

"We feast tonight on your pig. Zandra, the priestess, will tie the knot."

Emily returned to the tent and saw her spear was missing from the threshold. She went inside. Taval had removed the cover from the tent's smoke hole. Light filled the space and cool air was being drawn in from the entrance. He sat on a crate, oiling her spear.

"Good weapon," he said in Greek.

"Yes."

"Made by Greeks?"

"Yes, but the blade was forged in Persia," Emily said. "It was given to me by Agathon of Artemios."

"I heard of Agathon. Greek warrior. Your father?"

"No, but like a father."

Taval nodded. Emily wasn't sure how much of her Greek he understood.

"Why were you in forest?" He asked.

She explained as best she could and told him how she had fled from the Persians. He looked frustrated and concerned.

"Come. We find Chunya."

Chunya was back at her loom. She translated what Emily told her about the Persians.

"Taval wants to know how long ago they attacked your party."

Emily had to think about it for a moment.

"Six days," she said.

Taval shrugged and spoke to Chunya.

"He says it has been too long to hunt them down now. He is concerned the Persians have ventured out so far, even if they were staying in the forest. He wants to know why they pursued you."

"It is a long story. I will do my best to tell it if he wants."

Chunya spoke to Taval. He shook his head.

"Later," he said. "Now we ride together. Be happy today."

Taval took Emily's hand and they walked toward the grazing horses. She felt a chill as she walked beside him, her short legs seemingly taking double the steps of his long strides. She didn't mind. It was where she wanted to be, what she wanted to be doing.

~

They stopped by a simple but long tent, open at both sides, that sheltered saddles, bridles and other gear including spears, javelins and arrows. He loaded her arms with a saddle and horse tack. He grabbed some for himself along with his gorytos and a few javelins.

They carried the stuff to the herd. A boy on a horse rode up to them. Emily guessed his job was to keep an eye on the remuda. Taval gave him instructions and he rode off. She stepped in horse manure but, out here, she figured, it was something that couldn't be helped. The horses of the remuda seemed to be of two varieties -- lean, long-legged ones and short, long-haired ones.

A group of horses trotted toward them, the boy riding in their midst. The group was led by a large stallion, chestnut colored with a dark, braided mane. It trotted up to Taval and the other horses, three mares and four geldings, surrounded them.

Taval patted the stallion's snout, speaking sweet words to it.

"Skolov," he said. "King horse."

He put the saddle and bridle on it and strapped the gorytos to the saddle. He pulled out the bow and strung it. The bow was shorter than Pantheras' but was highly recurved. By the way Taval strained to string it, she could tell it was very powerful. Its limbs were wrapped in white leather with black stitching. He slipped the bow back into the gorytos. He went over to another horse, the smallest of the group. It was a light brown gelding with an unbraided mane.

"Hurlov," he said. "Gold horse. For you."

He started putting the bridle on.

"I can do it," Emily said.

The tack was similar to what Byon used -- a bitless bridle and cloth saddle. She put the saddle on, spoke soothing words, adjusted the straps so everything fit snug. Taval strapped to her saddle a leather tube and put the javelins in it.

The stallion kneeled down for Taval and he mounted. Emily pulled at the reins of the gelding but it did not respond. There must be a signal she did not know. Taval watched her with a smirk on his face. The gelding was a little smaller than One-sock. She went to its side, jumped up and mounted belly first. Taval laughed.

He turned the stallion to the west and trotted off. Emily didn't have to do anything but hold on. Hurlov followed the stallion's lead. Taval gradually worked the horses into a gallop. They raced up a mild grade. Taval slowed Skolov to a walk as they reached the crest. The other side dropped off steeply into a sandy blowout. The place offered a broad view of a landscape that reminded Emily of parts of Wyoming. Taval slowly peered around, seeing what he could see. A few antelope grazed in the distance. An eagle soared overhead.

"You ride not bad for a Greek," Taval said.

"I am not Greek," she said. "I am American."

"American?"

"Yes, American."

"Hmm"

They rode south along the crest, playing the word game like she had done with Byon so many months ago, learning words for horse, hoof, bridle, saddle, grass and so on. They turned east toward the river. When they got to the line of poplars, they headed back toward camp.

Taval grabbed a javelin from the quiver on Emily's saddle. He kicked Skolov into a gallop and, as he approached a tree, threw the javelin into it. He circled back around.

"You try," he said.

Emily readied a javelin and urged Hurlov into a gallop toward the tree. She hurled it but, in the effort, she lost her balance and slid off, rolling on the ground. She lay on her back, staring at the sky. Nothing felt broken. Soon she saw Taval's towering figure standing over her.

"Hurt?"

"No."

He pulled her up, put his arm around her and pointed to the tree. The two javelins were only inches apart.

"Good throw," he said. "Next time stay on horse."

~

They rode back to the remuda and unsaddled the horses. As they did so, they saw large group of riders approaching from the plain. By the hats and colors, Emily figured they were Scythian. Taval was not alarmed.

"Kaplea returns. Good," he said.

The riders were armed but did not wear armor. They dispersed when they reached the remuda. Most dismounted and tended to their saddles and gear. A woman rode over to Taval on a tall black gelding. She wore a sleeveless orange tunic with a broad leather belt and brown trousers. She and Taval greeted each other with a cross-armed handshake. A war hammer with a cruel-looking spike hung on her belt. The woman was broad-shouldered and had long arms. Her hips were wide and powerful. Hazel eyes looked out sternly from a square-jawed face. Most striking was her long, red hair that flowed from her head in waves. It was the kind of hair that suffered no hat, Emily thought.

The woman and Taval talked at length in Lovta before he introduced her to Emily. Kaplea smiled politely but she looked at Emily with what seemed like suspicion or contempt or both.

"You are the wild girl Taval has taken for a bride?" She said to Emily. Her Greek had polish, if heavily accented. Emily held her gaze but it filled her with trepidation.

"Yes, that is true," Emily said. "I am honored to meet you, Kaplea."

She offered her hand. Kaplea took it and gripped it firmly. She squeezed Emily's arm above the elbow.

"You are no soft Greek girl," Kaplea said. "Are you Thracian?"

"No, west of Thrace. America."

"Hmm. Are the Persians after you?"

"Perhaps. I do not know. If they were pursuing me, I lost them in the forest."

"Not now, Kaplea," Taval interrupted. He then spoke in Lovta. Kaplea smiled and slapped his shoulder. She finally released Emily's hand.

"Taval says the Persians would not follow you out here, and if they did, we would have some real fun," Kaplea said to Emily. "But I will be watching you."

Kaplea walked away. Taval and Emily carried their gear back to the supply tent.

"She seems like an angry woman," Emily said.

Taval shrugged. "She is Kaplea."

~

That afternoon, the Storm Wolves played games. Emily figured there were about a hundred warriors all told and about the same number of non-warriors plus about 20 children of various ages. Of the warriors, she surmised, about two in ten were women. The ratio was reversed for the non-warriors. Most of the games were played mounted including a free-for-all race where it was fair to try to unseat one's opponent. A few of the warriors and non-warriors got a slinging contest going. Emily participated and finished fourth out of twenty.

The warrior named Koia won the contest, barely edging out her friend, Donya, a stocky woman remarkable for her blonde hair. The three of them stood together to watch the most prestigious contest -- horseback archery where contestants shot arrows into a target at full gallop. Halaba, the warrior she met that morning, placed third. She hadn't met the man that won.

"Kaplea would win easily if she had played," Koia said to Emily. She spoke decent Greek, better than Taval.

"In Artemios, I saw a warrior named Aella who is supposed to be a very good archer," Emily said.

"We have heard of her. She is said to have divine skill. She is an oiorpata like Kaplea."

"Oiorpata?" Emily found the word difficult to pronounce.

"Man-killer."

Emily wondered what one had to do to win that moniker.

"I see not everyone has bows. Do you, Koia?"

"Bows are expensive and take a long time to make. Taval is having one made for me. I will owe him for a long time," Koia said. "I borrow Halaba's or Donya's as often as they let me."

"Taval will not lend you his bow?"

"Taval's is too strong. He can shoot an arrow farther than anybody."

Taval did not enter any of the games but watched and judged and gave prizes to the winners. For a while he had disappeared but reappeared to judge the archery contest. Players earned extra points for riding fast and were docked for riding too slow. As the afternoon waned, Chunya pulled Emily aside.

"Come help me chop onions and I will tell you the words you need to know for tonight."

There was only one line she needed to speak and she learned it quickly. She found herself doing one chore after another to help prepare for the feast.

"Are there special clothes I need to wear?" Emily asked.

"No special clothes," Chunya said. "I would wear the clothes Taval first saw you in."

Emily went to the river to bathe. Others were there, too, men and women. They weren't averse to sneaking glances at one another but they respected each other's space. She returned to her tent and put on her black leggings, blue tunic and green cloak. Tonight she would play the forest spirit.

~

They feasted on boar and bison meat and drank undiluted wine. Before the meal, a strange priest, or priestess, sacrificed a lamb to Samvi, goddess of the animals and the hunt. Chunya said Samvi was the equivalent to the Greeks' Artemis. Normally, they would sacrifice to Tabiti, goddess of the hearth and home but the priestess must have decided Samvi was more in need of appeasing.

The priestess was a man but acted and dressed like a woman. He was old in comparison to most of the others, fifties, Emily guessed. He wore a long red gown and was bedecked with gold jewelry. His gray hair was braided and he wore thick makeup that made his lips bright and eyes feline. He slaughtered the lamb on a tree stump while making intonations to the goddess.

Emily sat with Taval before the stump along with a dozen others including Kaplea, Chunya and her husband, Arlav, who appeared to be the oldest person present. Taval stood and spoke. From his gestures, Emily could tell he was recounting her killing of the boar. People laughed when he described how she had gone around in circles with the animal, holding the spear stuck in its neck, before plunging her dagger into its heart. When Taval finished the tale, he pulled Emily to her feet and they approached the priestess.

Taval drank lamb's blood from a gold cup and handed it to Emily. It took an effort not to gag when she sipped it. Taval looked her in the eye and spoke his vow. Emily then spoke hers.

"Par ne ge mo hal, par ne ge mo chon, par ne ge mo gi."

"I give you my strength, I give you my truth, I give you my heart," was what Chunya had told her the words meant.

The priestess produced two pendants that were the warthog's tusks - - the base of each wrapped in gold wire and attached to leather cords - - and put them around Taval and Emily's necks. The others shouted and howled. Emily had to stand on her toes to kiss her new husband. He seemed surprised by the gesture.

~

The priestess led Emily and Taval to an open area ringed with torches and others followed. At the perimeter was a small tent shaped like a tepee. Smoke seeped from its top and out of its entrance. The smell was familiar -- marijuana. The priestess opened the flap and ushered Emily and Taval in. The smoke was thick and she closed her eyes. She struggled not to cough but failed. Mercifully, Taval stepped out after only a short time. Taval led her to the other side of the ring where they sat on a log.

Others filed in and out of the tent while the priestess chanted. A boy brought Taval a wineskin which he shared with Emily. It wasn't what she would have preferred to sooth her raw throat. Two men, after standing in the hemp tent, began playing instruments -- a small drum shaped like an hourglass and a flute made of raptor bones. Donya, the blonde warrior, joined them and sang. She had a beautiful, strong voice, a diva's voice. The melody and syncopations were simple and soothing. Emily welcomed the sound as something to latch onto as the marijuana took effect. She found herself swaying with the music.

Soon a crowd of people were sitting or standing around the ring. Many were dancing in the middle -- sinuous, flowing, individual dances. Taval joined them, staying close to Emily, performing for her, showing off his strength and suppleness. He looked good in his blue tunic and quilted trousers of many colors. Chunya sat beside her and helped herself to wine.

"Look," Chunya said. "Kaplea has got her hammer."

Kaplea had entered the ring, dancing slowly, almost serenely, except that it resembled a prowl or a stalk. She had on an orange tunic trimmed with black and orange leggings with wavy black stripes. Her fiery hair shimmered in the torchlight. A tingle ran up Emily's spine. A feeling formed into an idea -- Kaplea was the tiger. They were the same spirit.

Others on the dance ground moved out of her way. Soon she was alone. She stood on one leg, raising her other leg high and holding the long-handled hammer over her head. Then she backed into a low crouch, her eyes wild and teeth flaring. She leaped forward and lashed out with her hammer and began a whirlwind of figure-eight twirls assisted by the weapon's lanyard. Impossibly, while she did this, she ran and hopped and spun her body. She moved around the ring then back to the center where she turned and looked at Emily and Taval. She ran toward them, still twirling the hammer. She leaped and landed in a crouch, the hammer's spike punching into the ground a few feet away. She snarled at Emily.

Taval howled and rose in response. Kaplea retreated from the dance ground. Taval drew his sword. Emily figured he was going to dance in response. She grabbed his hand.

"No, Taval," she said. "I will do this. Chunya, get my spear from the tent."

Chunya ran off. Emily put her hood up and entered the dance area, moving slowly as if stalking in the forest, pretending to move around trees and push away brush with her hands. When she reached the center, Chunya had returned with her spear. Taval took it, removed the cover and tossed it to Emily. She caught it and pivoted into a low stance.

She proceeded to repeat the dance she had performed back in Artemios, executing flourishes around her shoulders and waist and making low, long jabs. She finished facing Kaplea with a lunge-thrust and her Maori tongue waggle. Taval howled again and others followed suit. Kaplea eyed her menacingly.

~

Emily returned to Taval and the priestess shouted. Everyone became quiet and he entered the hemp tent. He emerged after an unusually long stay and started his own weird dance, shouting at the sky and waving a felt cap.

"Now you will get a name, a Lovta name," Chunya said.

People shouted out suggestions while the priestess danced. Chunya translated for Emily.

Niava, some said. "Forest spirit."

Jumakiz. "Mystery girl."

Vashakiz, Taval thundered. "Wild girl."

Pakshakiz, Kaplea shouted. "Squirrel girl."

The crowd laughed at that. Many hooted their approval. Taval looked annoyed.

The priestess stopped, raised his hands in the air then gave Emily a wild-eyed look. The crowd was silent. He came over to her and brought her out to the center. He put the pointed cap on her head. It was blue with an orange stripe like Koia's.

"Tilkya!" The priestess shouted.

Everyone cheered and hooted, pounding or stomping the ground. Taval ran over to her, picked her up and twirled her around. He put her over his shoulder and headed for the tent, picking up Emily's spear on the way.

"Tilkya?" Emily said as they passed Chunya.

"She-fox," she replied.

There was a flash of lighting in the distance followed many seconds later by crack and rumble of thunder. A storm brewed in the west.

~

Taval set Emily down on the mattress. Four candles were already lit. He opened the chest, pulled out a long dagger, and handed it to Emily.

"For you, Tilkya," he said. "I took it from a Persian warrior, an Immortal."

It was beautiful. Its wooden sheath had swirling gold inlay and tiny green gems embedded in it. The hilt was polished bronze with a fine leather wrap. Emily withdrew it. The blade was longer and narrower than her Corinthian dagger had been.

"Thank you, Taval," she said. "I wish I had something to give to you."

"You are my gift," he said.

Then she thought of something. She rummaged through her pack until she found the plastic horse, the sorrel mare.

"For you, Taval," she said.

Taval looked at it with fascination. Its life-like detail would be like nothing he'd ever seen. He started playing with it, making galloping noises as he did so. My husband is a bit of a dork, she thought. She undressed before him. His attention was distracted and he set the horse aside.

"What does Taval mean?" She asked.

"An old word," he said, silver eyes twinkling in the candlelight. "It means storm."

As if on cue, she heard another thunderclap.

Chapter 24 | Gambit

EMILY wanted to ride and hunt with Taval's warriors but she had to content herself with chores around camp. Taval agreed her skills with spear, javelin and sling were sufficient but said her riding skills were inadequate. He worked with her when he could, as did Koia, but she struggled to stay in the saddle when using weapons or ropes. It was sobering to think she may be too old to ever get the knack of it. These people were born in the saddle.

She did get a tattoo, a red fox on her side. Halaba did the work which involved a painful session of getting pricked with a bronze needle. The fox was her totem and it stood for cleverness, foresight, agility and fierceness when cornered. Tilkya, her name now, was a high name. She wondered how she would live up to it if she couldn't ride with the warriors.

Taval's troop, called an arim, patrolled the edge lands of the foothills and forests, looking for signs of Persians. They found none. He was gone for two days and she was giddy when he returned. In the evenings people sat around fires, telling stories. She didn't understand much of the language yet but she liked how the men and women, warriors and non-warriors, mingled freely. Everyone spun thread. Taval was proud of his spindle whorl like he might be proud of a good weapon. The Lovta language had a peculiar cadence compared to Greek or English. Most of the words were pronounced emphasizing the first syllable.

Chunya, she learned, possessed considerable authority. She was in charge of clothing and decided who had priority in getting new trousers, tunics and cloaks. Even Taval or Kaplea had to wait their turns or make the garments themselves.

One chore Emily pursued was fixing Taval's lariat, the one she had cut the morning he had captured her. Cutting a rope was not trivial, particularly a lariat. The boar she killed came in handy. She worked with a man named Kavad to cut the hide into strips, soak and stretch them, and then weave them into the rope. Taval was quite pleased when they were finished.

Life in the camp could be pleasant, if unexciting, except for Kaplea. She saw to it that Emily was assigned to arduous tasks, like digging latrine pits and filling them in. Kaplea would squeeze the back of Emily's neck and say, "I have a special job for you, squirrel girl." Emily endured it. She was too proud to tell Taval and Kaplea knew it.

One morning after scrubbing a large cooking pot, Emily was walking to her tent when Kaplea grabbed her ponytail from behind, yanked her back to the cooking area and threw her to the ground.

"This pot is dirty. Do your job right or I will knock out a few of your pretty white teeth."

Emily picked herself up. Chunya was nearby, working her loom.

"Leave her alone, Kaplea," Chunya said. "She is a hard worker."

Emily looked Kaplea in the eye. "You are right. The pot is still dirty. I will tend to it."

Kaplea growled and walked away.

"You got on her bad side," Chunya said. "Perhaps it was that spear dance of yours."

"Is she jealous of Taval and me?" Emily asked.

"She did not act that way around his last wife. She and Taval are friends. They have been since childhood. She has forsworn the company of men to keep her warrior edge and to keep from getting pregnant."

Emily worried about getting pregnant herself. It seemed inevitable. She couldn't get enough of Taval when he was around. Her body's drives were strong and she had no desire to check them. Most women gave up the warrior life when they had children, Chunya had said. Not all, however. Donya had a 12-year-old son who tended the remuda and trained to be a warrior himself. There was a cadre of women who looked after the children so their mothers didn't always have to tend to them. It wasn't clear to Emily exactly how all that worked. Older children mostly fended for themselves, playing, fighting and working together unless receiving training or instruction.

~

About a week after Emily's marriage, the band broke camp. She found it remarkable how quickly and efficiently everything was packed and readied. There were a dozen wagons pulled by mules. Both mules and horses were used as pack animals. Moving northwest they headed into Lion country to trade. Emily rode Hurlov, the light brown gelding Taval had given her. The pace was about fifteen miles per day. They could go faster but there was no pressing need to stress the animals.

Emily got saddle sore quickly. She often dismounted and walked. No one else did this and it made Emily feel like an outsider. She would get scornful looks from Kaplea who, of course, rode a horse like it was an extension of her body. Emily used petroleum jelly from her pack to sooth the chafing but it did little to relieve her her aching hind quarters.

Scouting parties ranged out in all directions, wary of the danger that one of the Lion Tribe's arims would try to raid the remuda. The Wolves would have to refrain from retaliating until trading was concluded. On the second day out, Emily rode beside Taval at the head of the column. On the crest of a hillock, they saw a small herd of bison. Halaba and Koia wanted to put a hunting party together. They figured lions might be around and wanted to try to bag one. Taval said no, they needed to be on good behavior while in the Lion Tribe's country. Emily told him how last year she had seen a giant herd of bison, miles long, south of here near the foothills.

"Yes, we got word of that herd," Taval said. "Once in a while they gather in great numbers."

That evening the band's leaders -- Taval, Kaplea and Arlav -- conferred and decided Taval should ride ahead with half his arim, taking Arlav with him, to a trading settlement known as Sinki on a large river called the Jumasin. There Arlav and Taval would begin trade negotiations and prepare for the arrival of the band.

The weather was clear and most people slept in the open. A few set up small tents. Emily set up her nylon tent, preferring to have some privacy with Taval. Chunya asked Emily about the fabric.

"It is made in the land I come from, far to the west," Emily said. "Someday, I will tell you the whole story but Taval should hear it first when I know your language well enough."

"Then I shall work harder to teach you," Chunya said.

"Do you think at Sinki, I could get word to Artemios?" Emily asked. "I want my friends to know I am safe."

Chunya explained what she wanted to Taval. He said it could be done and he would look into it.

~

With Taval gone Kaplea rode Emily relentlessly. Nothing Emily did was good enough. The physical manhandling stopped short of real violence but it grated on Emily. Others noticed, too, and avoided her, not wanting to risk Kaplea's wrath themselves. It seemed beyond hazing. Emily needed to do something. But what? Tell Taval? That might just make things worse in the long run. No, she had to handle this herself.

Emily observed that Kaplea was generally friendly with the non-warriors and occasionally played games with the children. She could be hard, though, on the warriors of her arim. Once she beat a man senseless for falling asleep on night watch. The man was larger than Kaplea but seemed powerless against her. Not only was she strong, and not only were her fighting skills first rate, she possessed a combative energy that came across as indomitable.

Emily could try to fight her. She knew she would lose. Perhaps just the act of standing up to Kaplea would be enough. But Emily had no desire to get the crap kicked out her. Even if she survived, it might drive a wedge between Taval and Kaplea. Emily didn't want to see them fighting. Any outcome of that could only be bad. But what other course did she have other than to simply endure Kaplea's bullying and hope it abated over time?

Late one afternoon, a storm loomed on the horizon. The band unpacked most of the tents and set them up. After supper and cleaning chores, Emily sat by herself outside her tent, sharpening her puukko. Her mind dwelled on ways to get Kaplea to back off and earn her respect but nothing made much sense. She could wait for a chance to prove herself in battle or on a hunt but, since she could not ride with the warriors, that chance may not come for a long time. She didn't think she could put up with the harassment much longer.

She thought about that second day after the crash, how she had gained the respect of the others with an act of violence -- shooting the hyena. It amused her to think that, in a way, she had vaulted up to the position of alpha male -- the one who could protect the group, the one who could kill. And, naturally, Nancy's instincts were to play the alpha female and bond with the alpha male. They were people, of course, not baboons, but the metaphor mapped pretty well. Emily remembered how powerless she had been when Nancy seduced her.

She saw Koia and Donya duck into a tent, holding hands. The storm had moved closer. It would rain soon. She realized she had been thinking in terms of handling the situation with Kaplea as if she were a man. But what would Nancy do, or Kallisto? There were tools other than spears or blades or fists. She dug through her pack and pulled out the wicker box that contained Berenike's gift -- the golden earrings with delicate flowers and dangling songbirds. She looked up at a sickle moon and watched it disappear behind thick clouds.

~

Emily took a candle over to the cooking fire and lit it on the smoldering embers. She filled a large bowl with water and carried the items back to her tent where she undressed and washed herself. She unbraided her hair, combed it, then put on the orange swimsuit. It stretched tightly around her hips and thighs. The way it accentuated her breasts was disconcerting but that was what it was supposed to do. Her hairy legs, however, did not go well with it. She rubbed oil on her legs, shaved them with her puukko and did the same with her armpits. She got out her makeup case and lipstick and went to work on her face. It was a challenge in low light but she took her time. She used the barrette to hold her hair back then put on the earrings. She applied deodorant, a dab of perfume and put the Tiger Stone around her neck.

Emily used the makeup case's mirror to look herself over as best she could. This was a gamble, she thought, and she could end up dead. She was no Nancy but she hoped she was pretty enough. Maybe with a little help from Artemis this would work.

She sat cross legged in her tent, breathing deeply, feeling the chill of the air on her skin. The wind blew and the rain came down.

Thunderclaps accentuated the downpour. She was happy to have the storm -- it worked in her favor -- but she hoped it wouldn't be too bad. She waited about a half hour then wrapped herself in her cloak, put up the hood and crawled outside. She left her puukko behind.

~

Emily stood before the entry flap of Kaplea's tent. It was large like Taval's. Wind buffeted its felt walls but the guy wires held it firm.

"Kaplea. It is Tilkya."

"What do you want, Pakshakiz?"

"I need to speak with you. May I come in?"

A moment passed before Kaplea answered.

"Yes, but make it quick."

Emily lifted the flap and stepped in. Four candles illuminated Kaplea who stood brushing her long red hair streaked with sun-bleached orange.

"What is it? Do not think I will let you shirk any task that needs doing."

Kaplea wore trousers. A small knife and sheath hung from its waist cord. Her torso was bare. Her breasts were fuller than Emily expected but not so shapely as Nancy's. She bore several tattoos including a tiger, a wolf, a stag and a spiral. She had a small scar on her belly and a long one at her side that traced across one of her breasts. The effect was strangely beautiful and terrifying at the same time.

"You are my leader. I will do what you require of me," Emily said.

"Good. Say what you have to say."

"I believe Artemis sent me to your tribe. I do not know why but when I saw you, I knew we were bound to each other."

"What nonsense is this?"

"We are bound by the spirit of the tiger," Emily said. She let her wet cloak fall to the tent's floor. "I have seen the tiger, twice I have been in its presence, close enough to touch, and yet I live."

Kaplea blinked and her arms fell to her side. Emily moved closer.

"The spirit of the tiger moves through us both and draws us together. I know you feel it."

Kaplea moved her mouth but said nothing. Emily sensed the warrior was on unfamiliar ground. Emily stepped closer, holding the pendant in her hand.

"This is the Tiger Stone, unearthed at the Temple of Artemis and given to me by her priestess, Kallisto. It has found its home."

Suddenly Kaplea's face turned to one of fury and she growled. She drew her knife, shoved Emily against a support pole, pinned her there, and put the knife to her throat.

"You try to put a spell on me, witch, but it will not work."

Emily's gaze locked with Kaplea's, their faces inches apart. Emily took a deep breath.

"I looked down the Tiger's throat when it roared. It was no further from me than you are. It did not kill me then. You will not kill me now."

Slowly, Emily moved her head forward. She could feel the sharpness of the blade against her skin. She kissed Kaplea on the tip of her nose.

The fury drained from Kaplea's face which took on the aspect of a confused child. Emily clutched Kaplea's wrist and slowly pulled it and the knife away from her throat. Kaplea did not resist. The knife dropped from her hand. Emily kissed her lightly on the lips and then her chin. She put the pendant around Kaplea's neck.

"Kallisto told me the Tiger Stone belonged to me. She was wrong. I am only its carrier. It belongs to you."

Emily kissed Kaplea's chest and her breasts and moved her way down, kissing the scar on her belly and untying the waist cord. Kaplea stood motionless as Emily pulled the trousers down, revealing thickly muscled legs. She nuzzled Kaplea's pubic hair then her lips and tongue found her clitoris. Kaplea let out a girlish whine.

Checkmate, Emily thought.

Chapter 25 | Bagged

KAPLEA continued to razz Emily and put her to work on unpleasant tasks (she was becoming an expert latrine digger) but the edge was gone. Not only was it clear to Emily, it was clear to others. They stopped avoiding her and became friendly. Kaplea became less of a tyrant and the mood of the band became happier.

In the late afternoons, when the column stopped, Emily would dig the latrine pit then go spar with Koia and Donya. They had impressive skills and she was learning from them. They learned from her, too, mainly about good footwork, which was a testament to Byon's skill and knowledge.

"We heard whispers that you visited Kaplea's tent during the storm," Koia said to Emily after a practice session.

"Did you put a spell on her?" Donya asked in her broken Greek.

"I did no such thing," Emily said. "You should not listen to rumors."

"No, not a spell," Koia said. "Just a little cherry juice."

Donya and Koia giggled at that. Emily blushed and couldn't help but giggle too.

When fighting on foot, Emily could hold her own but she continued to struggle on horseback. Koia did her best to help her and even Kaplea had offered pointers, yet the knack eluded her. Part of the problem was the habit of generating power with her hips. It worked so well on foot but undermined her balance on the saddle. She did know of a solution. Giver her feet what they longed for: stirrups.

"I want to make a saddle," Emily said to Chunya one evening at the fire.

"Why? The one Taval gave you is perfectly fine."

"I want to make a special saddle, one that will help me ride better. I would need to use leather. I know what I want but I do not know how to make it."

"What did you have in mind?"

Emily explained what she wanted. Chunya seemed dubious.

"Did you think of this yourself?"

"No. It is the kind of saddle people use where I come from."

"We have no master leather worker in our band. Kavad might have some ideas. We can try but you will owe me."

Emily rubbed Chunya's back. At that moment she felt she had moved another step closer to achieving belonging with the tribe. Everybody owed Chunya.

~

The following day the column came to an area where the plain descended into wooded bluffs. At times, they could see the Jumasin River as they skirted the bluffs heading west. Kaplea halted the column. She said they would make Sinki by midday tomorrow.

Emily grabbed a shovel from one of the wagons and looked for a good spot to dig the latrine pit. She had just started digging when two boys approached.

"Kaplea says we are to dig the latrine today," one of them said.

Only some of the Lovta words clicked for Emily but the gist was clear. She handed the boy the shovel. She was at a momentary loss as to what to do. Did Kaplea have a more onerous task in mind? She bided her time helping two women unload cooking gear.

"Pakshakiz, come here!" Kaplea shouted.

Kaplea had her bow out and strung. She had a small wicker quiver at her hip with three arrows in it.

"I feel like fresh meat tonight," Kaplea said. "Get your cloak and we will hunt together."

Emily ran over to her pack, slipped on her belt, grabbed her satchel and cloak. The two headed into the woods. The trees were smaller and more densely spaced than the primeval forests of the mountain foothills, mostly maples and poplars with a few stands of gnarled oaks. The ground descended until they came to a small stream. Kaplea made entirely too much noise for hunting.

"I have been here before," she said. "This leads to a small meadow ahead."

"How far?" Emily asked.

"A few hundred steps."

They walked a ways then Emily put a hand on Kaplea's shoulder. "Wait here," she whispered. "I will see if anything is there."

Emily approached the meadow at a stalking pace. There she saw three pheasants, a rooster and two hens, bedded down in the grass. They seemed content to stay where they were.

She backed away slowly. An impish idea occurred to her. As quietly as she could, though with some hustle, she circled around. From behind, she approached Kaplea who had not noticed her movements.

"Pakshakiz, what is taking so long," Kaplea hissed.

Putting a tree between her and Kaplea, Emily poked her head out.

"I am here," she whispered.

Kaplea spun around. In an instant, she had an arrow nocked and the string stretched to shoot. Emily ducked behind the tree. No arrow came.

"It is me," Emily said. "Do not shoot."

She stepped out. Kaplea lowered her bow.

"There are three pheasants in the meadow. If you approach slowly, like a prowling tiger, you may get a shot," Emily said.

"I should just kill you and be done with it," Kaplea said.

"You cannot kill me. I am niava."

Kaplea grunted, turned and stalked as quietly as she could toward the meadow. Emily followed. When Kaplea saw the pheasants, she pulled the string back. The limbs of her bow were covered with black leather and had red lacing. Instead of a finger-pinch draw, she hooked her thumb on the string, locking it with her forefinger. She loosed and the arrow struck the rooster dead center. The hens fluttered off.

"Got it!" Kaplea shouted. She ran to the struggling rooster and wrung its neck. Emily joined her in the meadow. Kaplea put an arm around her.

~

The bluffs leveled off as the band approached the settlement of Sinki. Smoke rose from stone furnaces. It was a town of many tents lining the banks of the Jumasin. There were some permanent structures, round and made of earth, wood and thatch. They resembled Kallisto's winter sleeping hut.

"Pakshakiz, take Donya and Koia and go find your husband," Kaplea ordered. "We need to know where we should camp."

The three rode off together, Emily riding Hurlov as usual. She donned her pointed blue cap to mark her as a member of the Wolf Tribe. The town was ringed with scattered, irregular fields of newly sprouting grain and assorted garden plots. She looked forward to eating fresh vegetables. They saw dozens of wagons, some full, some empty, and corrals of mules and horses. Goats and sheep wandered freely.

An open area near the river served as a marketplace where goods were exchanged. It didn't resemble the market of Artemios with its tents and stalls serving individual buyers. This was a place for wholesale buying and selling. Boats lined the river which meandered its way westward along the plain.

They spotted warriors from Taval's arim. They loitered with what appeared to be Lion Tribe warriors in red caps. Halaba was among them.

"Hello, good, the rest of you are here," he said.

"Kaplea wants to know where to camp," Koia said.

Halaba ordered the warriors to fetch their horses. They seemed happy to have something to do.

"Where is Taval?" Emily asked.

"I will take you to him," Halaba replied.

Emily dismounted and handed the reins to Koia. Halaba led her to a round building. Inside were several tables situated around a smoldering fire pit. Taval sat awkwardly in a chair, his long legs seemed not to know where to go. Arlav was next to him pouring over sheets of papyrus with a man who sat across the table. The man was bald and bearded and dressed like a Greek.

"Taval, your wife is here," Halaba said.

Taval looked up and his face brightened when he saw Emily. He almost knocked the chair over when he stood.

"It is good to see you, Tilkya," he said. "You have not run off yet."

"Not yet," she said.

Taval introduced her to the Greek man whose name was Thaos. He looked at her with curiosity.

"You are Taval's new wife. My best wishes," he said in Greek.

"Thank you," she said.

~

Taval gathered his warriors and they all rode back to the column. Conversation between him and Emily remained halting because of the language gap but their ability to communicate was improving. They left Arlav behind to continue the trade accounting. Thaos, she learned, was an agent hired by the Lion Tribe to conduct business for them. He regularly traveled to other settlements in Huraslan's kingdom and to Artemios. She wondered if he suspected who she was.

Taval said a caravan had left for Artemios the previous day and the caravan's leader had agreed to take Emily's message to Agathon. Emily felt relieved. She knew Nancy and Phoibe would be beside themselves with worry.

"Any news from Artemios?" Emily asked.

"Their leader died, not Agathon, the other one," Taval said.

"Philocrates?"

"Yes, that was his name. They say his son was out hunting and has not returned."

"The son's name is Pantheras. He was the one I traveled with," Emily said. "I fear he was captured or killed by the Persians."

"Was Pantheras a friend?" Taval asked.

"Yes, but do not worry. He loves a man named Acasius who traveled with us."

"Ah," Taval said. "I hear no news Pantheras is hostage. We will stay here many days. We may learn more."

When they reached the column, Taval and Kaplea spoke at length. They moved the band to a spot close to the river and everyone started making camp. Taval left Kaplea to do the directing while he and Emily set up Taval's large tent as quickly as they could. When it was up, they didn't wait to move in any rugs, bedding or other gear. They went right to work on sex.

"You shaved your legs. Why?" Taval asked.

"It is what women do where I come from," Emily said. "I thought you would like it."

Taval stroked and squeezed the muscles of her thigh.

"You have good, strong legs. I like them hairy."

"Then they will be hairy again."

"You and Kaplea? No trouble between you?"

"Some trouble," Emily said. "But we ... reached an agreement. I am now the best latrine digger in the tribe."

Taval smiled then enveloped one of her breasts with his mouth while she ran her fingers through his long hair.

~

The trading took several days. What the Storm Wolves had to offer for the most part were horses, rugs, hides, jewelry and spices. The band had spent the previous year traveling in eastern lands, raiding and trading. They had happened along a large caravan heading for Persia. It had a sizable escort so instead of risking a fight, Taval negotiated a deal. In exchange for rugs and spices, the Storm Wolves escorted them through bandit-rich country to the mountain passes leading to Persia. Later, the band tracked several bandits to their hideout and plundered their stolen goods.

With this accumulated booty, the Storm Wolves traded for grain, oats, wine, gold, silver, tin and copper. These goods they would later trade at a gathering spot of the Wolf Tribe where they would refresh their stock of horses. They also called on the local smiths and craftsmen to repair weapons and tools. Individually they bought clothes, tools, jewelry, and other goods. It had been a prosperous year for the Storm Wolves.

Sinki was protected by an arim of Lion Tribe warriors serving under an old veteran named Kusapa. He in turn served a warlord named Takahal. Takahal rivaled Kydoime in terms of power and prestige within the Lion Tribe. Both were seen as potential successors to Huraslan's throne.

Emily also learned that Novorosa was about 40 miles west and closer to Sinki than Artemios. By agreement and Huraslan's decree, the Lions only traded with Artemios (though Emily figured the restriction was probably rather loose). At Sinki, the Jumansin River represented a border of sorts but the Lions routinely crossed unless the Persians were out in force.

The Persians hired horse warriors from the Scyth tribes who dwell on the plains north of the Black Sea and west to the frontiers of the Thracian tribes. Rumor was they were coming in large numbers and the Lions were wary.

~

One afternoon Emily and Chunya visited a tanner, looking for a suitable piece of leather for Emily's saddle. Inside Emily found the stench intolerable so she loitered outside while Chunya talked with the man.

"Emily," she heard someone say.

She turned her head but no one was there. She looked around but others in the vicinity seemed not to be paying her any attention. She went around to the side of the building and saw only a few people going about their business. She quickly went back to the entrance. The skin on her neck tingled. She had her Persian dagger. She wished she had her spear.

Chunya came outside.

"He will cut the leather we need," she said. "We can pick it up tomorrow."

Emily grabbed her arm.

"Someone called my name, my old name, Emily, but I did not see him," she said. "I think he lost himself in the market square."

"Why would someone do that?"

"Too learn if I am who they think I am."

"To call your name and disappear is a child's game."

"I think I am in danger, Chunya. Go find Taval, quickly. It is me they are after, not you."

Chunya ran off. A woman leading a goat and carrying a chicken walked by. Emily kept her back to the tanner's hut. Two men walked by dressed in plain flax tunics and trousers. They carried bundles tied to staves. They went around the hut toward the market area.

Two more men appeared and walked toward her. Like the others, they wore plain clothes. One was tall and lean, the other stocky. The stocky man had a cudgel in one hand and an empty hemp bag in the other. The lean man carried a staff. The lean man smiled at her.

"You are Emily, late of Artemios, are you not?" He spoke in Greek.

Emily drew her dagger.

"Do not come any closer," she said, her voice high and wavering. The lean man stopped and motioned his companion to do likewise.

"All you have to do is come with us. We have friends who want to talk with you," the lean man said. "You can make it easy or difficult. If you make it easy, I assure you that you will be well rewarded. Trust me when I say a life of luxury and high honor awaits you."

"Who are you?"

"Just a humble servant."

"Who's servant?"

"I serve the one we all will sooner or later," he said. "Please, put your knife away. We do not have much time."

Emily feinted an attack. The man raised his staff quickly to defend. She bolted away around the hut but two men with staves awaited, cutting off her retreat. She wheeled around. The lean man was upon her, swinging his staff. She ducked and lunged at him. The man was startled by her quickness and she managed to grab the staff and thrust the dagger into his side.

The man yelled but the dagger did not penetrate deeply. He had armor on under his tunic. She yanked the dagger out then the world went dark as a bag went over her head. She struggled and kicked. Someone grabbed her from behind, pinning her arms, while another pried the dagger out of her hand. Then someone had her legs and she was being carried.

"Quickly, get her to the ..."

The lean man's voice was cut off by a piercing yell. Emily heard a whoosh and a thud. She dropped to the ground. There was yelling and commotion. She rolled away and pulled the bag off her head.

The stocky man and another were down, motionless. The lean man was clutching his side and getting up. The fourth man was trying to fend off a red-haired fury with his staff. The red-haired fury was Kaplea and her hammer blows rained down on him. With one of the blows, she hooked the staff then yanked back so the hammer's head slid along the shaft and caught the man's hand. He yelped and let go. With a smooth, efficient motion, Kaplea looped the hammer around and struck the man's skull. He crumpled to the ground.

The lean man was running away. Emily got up and started after him but the hammer whirled passed, flying end over end. Its spike stuck in the man's back. The man staggered then fell to his knees. Kaplea strode over to him, grabbed his hair, yanked his head back and cut his throat with her knife.

~

Emily stood in wonder and horror at the death around her. People gathered, looking just as awed. Kaplea pulled her hammer from the lean man's back and wiped the blood off its spike. She walked toward Emily and, on the way, picked up the Persian dagger. She looked at its tip.

"You drew blood, I see," she said. "Pakshakiz has a bite, at least."

She handed the dagger to Emily who wiped the blade and sheathed it.

"I knew you would be trouble," Kaplea said. "I do not know why I bothered to save you."

"You wear the Tiger Stone. You are bound to save me."

Kaplea growled. "And why did these men want you? I thought only Taval liked squirrelly girls."

"I am not certain. I will tell you what I think -- you and Taval -- but not here."

Kaplea took her hand and squeezed. Soon they heard the galloping of horses. It was Taval with Chunya, Halaba and three other warriors. Their bows were out or spears ready. Taval dismounted and embraced Emily.

"You are unharmed," he said. "Thank Pava and the gods."

"Thank Kaplea," Emily said.

He turned to Kaplea.

"Thank you, my friend. I owe you."

"You owe me nothing," Kaplea said. "The Wolves protect each other."

Taval surveyed the carnage while Emily explained what happened.

"You do your work too well, Kaplea," he said. "Dead men cannot tell us their purpose."

"It is not my nature to leave my enemies alive," Kaplea said.

About a dozen warriors from the Lion Tribe rode to the scene, led by a man with a long, gray beard and hair. He carried a hefty spear and wore a red cloak. He dismounted and greeted Taval and Kaplea respectfully. The man was Kusapa, leader of the arim that protected Sinki.

"These men waylaid my wife," Taval said. "Are they your men, Kusapa?"

Kusapa looked at each one closely. "I do not know them."

With his spear, he opened a dead man's tunic. The torso bore several tattoos.

"Western Scyth, hirelings of the Persians, or slave hunters."

The lean man's torso had no tattoos.

"This one must be Greek. Slave hunters, I wager." Kusapa turned to Taval and Kaplea. "This is a grievous insult to your tribe and mine. If there is anything that will serve justice, I will do it."

"Kaplea has dispensed justice well enough, I think," Taval said.

"That she has," Kusapa said. "War is brewing. This is yet another sign."

"What other signs?" Emily asked.

"We have word that the Greeks of Artemios fought a small battle with the Persians along the coast southeast of the city."

"What happened?"

"The Greeks won. I do not know more."

Chapter 26 | Lions and Wolves

EMILY rode back to camp on Taval's horse, her arms wrapped around his waist, her face pressed against his back. The feeling of his breathing and beating heart was a tonic her body drank in like ambrosia.

"Taval, there are things I need to tell you," she said. "I wanted to wait until I spoke Lovta better but I think I need to tell you now, or soon."

When they got back to camp, Taval and Kaplea informed the band that no one should go into town unarmed and unescorted. Slave hunters were about, looking for easy targets.

At supper Taval told the story of the attack on Emily and how Kaplea killed the assailants. No one seemed surprised that she could fell four men in such short order. Of course she could. She was Kaplea.

~

That night Emily, Taval, Kaplea, Arlav and Zandra, the he-priestess, met in Kaplea's tent. Taval had said Emily should say what she had to say before the band's leaders. Kaplea could translate any Greek he did not understand. They sat around a large bronze brazier stoked with charcoal. Zandra added incense and hemp and invoked Pava, the god of wisdom, seeing and justice. Emily had brought her satchel. She stood and faced the others.

"What I have to say will be difficult to believe but I swear to Samvi, known to me as Artemis, that all of it is true. I am from the future ..."

She told the story much as Alex had back in Artemios. The account of the tiger seemed to please Kaplea. She talked of her stay in Artemios, the expedition to the crash site, the second encounter with the tiger, the attack by the Persians and her escape into the forest.

She had brought her satchel because she intended to use the flashlight to substantiate her story. But, as she talked, she saw no incredulous looks and heard no objections to flying ships or going back in time. Even Arlav, the pragmatic man whose main concern was seeing to the physical needs of the tribe, expressed no skepticism. Were they gullible? Was she missing something? She decided to leave the flashlight in the bag. There was no need to bring it out. Doing so, it seemed, would only demean the trust they were granting her. She was struck by a wave of emotion. Her lip started to quiver.

"My friends and I are stranded in this world," she concluded. "The good people of Artemios welcomed us and offered us a home there. For that I will always be grateful. But I believe I have found my home. It is here with you, with Taval, with the Lovta."

A tear dripped down Zandra's face, streaking his copious makeup. He made exaggerated feminine gestures with his hands. Taval frowned while Kaplea translated what Emily just said. Arlav simply nodded.

"I fear I have become a danger to you. The Persians, I think, want to capture me," Emily went on. "I do not wish to leave but perhaps I should for the benefit of the tribe."

Kaplea started to translate but Taval understood well enough. He stood, silver eyes gleaming fiercely in the candlelight.

"No! You will stay. You are my wife."

"If the Persians come for you, I will welcome them with my hammer," Kaplea said.

Arlav remained silent.

Zandra stood and went into a twirling dance, waving his hands in the air. He stopped suddenly and spoke in Lovta, gesturing broadly. He went on at some length and when he was done, he sat down.

"What did he say?" Emily asked.

Kaplea translated: "Apma, the Earth, the Mother of All Things, brought Tilkya to us. Apma willed Tavapa, the storm god, to open the sky and draw the flying ship through. Apma bid Samvi to guide Tilkya to safety and lead her to us. Apma bid Argimi, the love goddess, to touch Taval's heart when he looked upon Tilkya. Apma willed Pava to grant Taval the guile and strength to capture Tilkya in a fair contest. Apma bid Tabiti to touch Tilkya's heart so she would know her home was with us. Apma invoked the spirit of the Tiger to protect Tilkya and the spirit of the Fox to guide her. Apma will bid Kurapa, the war god, to ride into battle with us when the time comes. This is the truth. I, Zandra, have seen it."

Emily shook her head in bewilderment. Did they really believe all that? Taval turned to Arlav who was brooding, arms folded, looking into the embers of the brazier.

"Arlav, my friend," Taval said. "You have not spoken. We should hear your thoughts."

Arlav stood and straightened his tunic.

"I am going to bed before Chunya becomes upset," he said and stepped to the tent's flap. He lifted the flap and paused. "We should find Tilkya some armor. And someone should teach her how to ride that damned horse properly."

~

Emily and Taval sat on a blanket near the river in the shade of a large poplar. The afternoon was warm and the freshening breeze felt good. Emily was applying an oily balm to a broad leather girdle that Taval had found for her. It was doubly thick and designed to protect a person's midsection. Taval had also found a diminutive hoplite helmet in the armorer's pile of junk. It apparently had been made for a boy or a small man. It fit Emily about right and Taval added padding to make it snug. He was straightening its horsehair crest which was dyed with maroon and white stripes that were quite faded.

The helmet offered good protection and allowed good visibility side to side and upward but poor visibility downward. It wasn't ideal for fighting on horseback. Taval made clear, that for now, Emily would have to content herself with being a foot warrior. She told him about the saddle she and Chunya were making and that she would be a better rider when it was done. He seemed skeptical.

To go along with the helmet, Taval had found a small wooden shield. It was round, rimmed with bronze and backed with leather. The paint was chipped and faded but otherwise it was in good shape.

They traded words back and forth, Emily working on her Lovta while Taval tried to improve his Greek.

"Do you really believe all those words Zandra said about Apma and the other gods, that they guided me to you?" Emily asked.

Taval looked puzzled. Emily regretted her question. Questioning religious beliefs could be dangerous, she thought, and she didn't want to upset him. Taval seemed to sense her consternation.

"When the hemp is on the brazier and Zandra speaks, I believe," he said. "Now the water flows in the river, the wind blows in the trees and my wife sits before me. That is what I believe."

~

A warrior galloped into camp shouting, "Taval! Riders approach!"

Taval hurried to the man. Emily followed.

"From where? How many?" Taval asked.

"From the west. Five hundred or more."

"Lions?"

"I cannot say. Halaba is getting a closer look."

Taval put his fingers to his mouth and whistled three screeching bursts that set the camp into motion.

"Fetch Hurlov," he told Emily. "We may need to flee."

When she had found her horse and saddled it, most of Taval and Kaplea's warriors were mounted and ready. Taval had donned his scale armor, strung his bow and mounted Skolov, his large stallion. The non-warriors had gathered horses for themselves and were packing essentials onto others. If forced to flee, they would have to leave much behind. Emily followed Chunya's lead and helped as best she could.

The arims of Taval and Kaplea moved as two separate units. Chunya explained that, if forced to retreat, they would do so in stages. One arim would cover the rear, firing arrows at the enemy and running off as they approached. The other arim would do the same when the first had retreated past. This tactic could break up an attack and might offer the opportunity to counterattack, though not likely against 500. Chunya was confident they could outrun them because the approaching force would already be fatigued. Emily was glad Kaplea and Taval were diligent about using scouts. Without ample warning, they could easily be overrun by such a force.

Emily spotted Halaba riding in. He reined his horse to a stop beside Taval. The two talked for a moment then Taval rode over to Kaplea.

After speaking with her, he rode out by himself toward the riders, just visible now on the horizon.

"They must be Lions or Taval would not go off alone," Chunya said.

The Wolf warriors appeared at ease but were not standing down. Emily mounted Hurlov. Chunya handed Emily her spear and then she mounted her own horse, a long-legged mare. At a word the non-warriors were ready to take flight.

Emily could make out the distinctive red caps of the approaching force. It halted several hundred paces away as Taval met them. He stayed out there for what seemed like a long time. Hurlov grew fidgety along with other horses. Finally, Taval returned. He spoke briefly with Kaplea then shouted, "Tilkya! Come here!"

Emily rode to him.

"It is Kydoime," he said. "She wants to speak with you."

"With me? Why?"

Too excited to talk in understandable Greek, Taval spoke rapidly to Kaplea who translated:

"Agathon has asked Kydoime to bring you back to Artemios. Taval told her you are a Wolf now and do not want to go. Kydoime wants to hear it from you."

"Ride to Kydoime," Taval said. "Tell her you wish to stay. Or go if you wish to go."

"I want to be with you, Taval, always," Emily said.

"Ride to her and say so," Kaplea said.

"By myself?"

"Yes, there must be no question in Kydoime's mind that you freely choose to stay with us."

"What if she takes me by force?"

"She gave Taval her word that she would not."

Emily took Taval's hand and looked at him. She felt afraid.

"Go, Vashakiz, go," Taval said.

It was clear he wanted to get this over with. Emily turned her horse and trotted toward the bristling spears and nocked arrows of the broad array of Lion warriors.

~

Kydoime rode out to meet her about fifty paces from the line.

"I am Kydoime. Are you the one known to Agathon as Emily?" She asked in fluent Greek.

"Yes. The Wolves call me Tilkya."

"'Tilkya,' she-fox, it is a noble name for one not born to the Wolves."

"It is the name Zandra the priestess gave me. Though Kaplea calls me Pakshakiz."

Kydoime's smile wrinkled the scar on her face. She had remarkably deep blue eyes.

"I am told you would be wearing a green cloak with orange at the hem and would have a pack of peculiar design and fabric."

Emily pointed to the pack lashed to her saddle. "This is my pack. The cloak is inside. It is too warm to wear it now."

"That must be the throwing spear Agathon gave you."

"Yes. It serves me well."

"What did Agathon say when he gave it to you?"

It seemed like a strange question. Emily was puzzled for a moment then realized Kydoime was verifying her identity.

"He said the head had an excellent temper and he had the shaft specially made for me. I told him I didn't deserve it. He told me to make sure I did deserve it."

Kydoime dismounted.

"Come," she said. "Let us sit on the grass and talk."

Emily slid off her horse.

Kydoime was taller and leaner than Kaplea and looked every bit a queen in her leather cuirass, leather skirt, red cap, red sleeves and black trousers. The pommel of her long-bladed sword was a golden serpent's head. She took Emily's hand. Her long fingers were callused. They sat cross-legged facing each other.

"We have not met but I feel like I have seen you before," Kydoime said.

"Our eyes met once, last year, when you rode into Artemios. I was standing on a wagon holding a javelin."

"And a knife at your belt. Yes, I remember. It was strange to see a Greek girl so armed."

"I want to be a warrior," Emily said. "When I saw you, I knew it was possible."

Kydoime nodded.

"Agathon asked me to return you to him. Taval says you do not want to go."

"My place is here with the Wolves."

"There are those who love you in Artemios. You do not wish to see them?"

"I do but I wish to stay with Taval more. I am sworn to him. He is my husband."

Kydomie raised an eyebrow.

"Husband? Taval did not say that."

Emily fingered the boar's tusk hanging from her neck.

"This is a token of our bond. He wears the other. When I was in the forest alone, I killed the boar. Taval watched me from a distance and decided he wanted me as his wife."

"This is a tale I would like to hear," Kydomie said. "For now I ask you this: Do you want to stay with him? Before you answer let me say that you are in no danger here with me. I can see you safely back to Artemios and the Wolves can exert no hold over you. There is no reason to be afraid."

Emily looked Kydoime in the eye.

"I appreciate your assurances but I want more than anything to stay with Taval and the Storm Wolves. I do not wish to live the life of a Greek woman. I want to be a warrior and a leader like Kaplea or you. I may well fail but with the Wolves I have the chance. With the Greeks I do not. I love Agathon like a father. I would gladly serve him as a soldier but he cannot grant me that."

Kydoime touched Emily's face. She seemed to be churning things over in her mind.

"Agathon has told me something of you and your friends, Alex and Nancy. You do not wish to be with them?"

"I miss them, yes, but they are better suited to life with the Greeks. I will return to Artemios someday but on my own terms at my own choosing."

"Very well," Kydoime said. "Agathon will be disappointed and so will Pantheras. He seemed most anxious about you when we talked."

"Patheras? He is safe?"

"Yes. As you may know, he was captured by a band of Persians in the wilderness. Agathon got word of the incursion and waylaid the Persians along the coast before they could board their ship."

"And Acasius? Dokaris? Coystus?"

"I do not know the names."

"How about Byon? He is a Thracian horse warrior who serves under Callias."

"I have met him. He is well, so far as I know."

Kydoime stood and pulled Emily up with her.

"We can talk more later," Kydoime said. "I think we have kept our arims on edge long enough. Go back to Taval. Tell him we will camp here tonight. We shall talk then feast and sing to the gods."

Emily mounted Hurlov and returned to the Storm Wolves. Taval listened stoically as she relayed what Kydoime had told her. She could tell by the twitch in his eye that he was relieved she had come back to him. Kaplea clamped a firm hand on his shoulder.

"There is no getting rid of your squirrel girl," she said.

~

Three days later, the Storm Wolves left Sinki. They rode east following the main course of the Jumasin. They had added two wagons and several mules to their train. Emily rode Hurlov and, at Chunya's suggestion, sat on the sheet of leather that would become her saddle. It was a way of fitting it to the horse's back but it was uncomfortable for both of them. She patted Hurlov's neck.

"Trust me. It will be wonderful when it is done," she said.

Hurlov snorted.

The plan was to head east to a spot where they could ford the river then head north looking for good hunting or raiding opportunities. Kydoime had encouraged them to swing back west and raid Persian controlled lands near the coast. Emily hadn't been part of the council but she guessed Kydoime's intent was to have the Wolves distract the Persians from the Lion Tribe and Artemios.

During the day of feasting and revelry, Kydoime spoke highly of the Wolves, calling them the heart of the Lovta people and said that the

Lions looked to them as brothers and sisters. She encouraged fraternization between the tribes.

Kydoime and Kaplea were friendly and often seen together. Taval told Emily that they were cousins of a sort though she didn't understand the lineage. She did find it interesting that they traced their ancestry through their mothers and not their fathers.

Aella, the famed archer, had been there, too. She was small, smaller than Emily, younger, and leaner in legs and hips. On the second afternoon, she showed off her skills. She would gallop passed a target and shoot three arrows in rapid succession, all hitting the target within inches of each other. Then she would make another pass, sitting backward on her saddle, and do the same thing. She could even stand on the horse and shoot accurately.

Aella didn't talk much and mostly stuck close Kydoime, scrutinizing anyone who ventured close. She had two bows and one was always strung and ready. At one point, Kydomine introduced her to Emily.

"I am honored to meet you," Emily said. "I am amazed by your skill with horse and bow."

Aella nodded, regarding Emily with wariness.

"They say you are a forest spirit," she said in Greek.

"The forest is my element, I suppose," Emily answered.

"Why do you ride with the Wolves?"

"I want to be a warrior."

Aella nodded and said nothing more.

The hemp tent was set up and music played. Emily got drunk and stoned. She put on her Greek tunic and helmet and marched around like a miniature hoplite, doing exaggerated about-faces and mimicking Agathon's constricted fighting style. The performance drew howls of laughter and many jeers. Afterward Kaplea sat next to her.

"We laugh at the Greek ways but I have seen a phalanx," she said. "Do not tell anybody I said this, but I would hate to have to fight against one."

"They are formidable," Emily said. "But there are ways of undoing them."

"You know these ways?"

"I have some ideas."

Before she could go on, Taval came over and took Emily's hand.

"Come, my little hoplite. It is time for bed."

~

The river crossing was an arduous affair, taking much of the day. The waters were still swollen from the spring rains. They had to unload the wagons and carry the supplies across by hand or by mule. They camped that night along its banks.

They did not break camp the next day. Taval and Kaplea decided it would be a good place to conduct training maneuvers with their respective arims. Taval had agreed to take in 20 young Lion warriors for the year. Kydoime wanted them to get experience with the traditional nomadic ways that the Wolf Tribe preserved.

Emily watched the exercises with interest, though disappointed she was still deemed too unskilled a rider to participate. A key drill was for a formation to gallop toward an imagined enemy then turn 90 degrees, shooting broadsides of arrows or hurling javelins as they went. They could turn again quickly, backward or forward as needed and repeat the process. It was an impressive display of mobile firepower. It would be devastating against lightly armored troops but not so effective against formations of heavily armored infantry.

Along with camp chores, Emily worked on her saddle with Chunya directing her efforts. It was a slow process.

That night Emily lay in bed, running her fingers over Taval's chest. They talked, mixing Greek and Lovta to make themselves understood.

"Does Kydoime want an alliance with the Wolves?" Emily asked.

"Yes," Taval said. "With the Wolves' help, she believes she could sweep the Persians from all Lovta lands."

"What does she offer?"

"Glory, gold and the right to trade directly with Artemios."

"Will the Wolves fight for her?"

"I do not know. Some bands might. I will present the offer to other war leaders."

"Do you want to fight for her?"

"Yes and no. I want to drive the Persians out but I fear our people will fall under Lion rule and become settled and soft."

"Does your heart want to fight for her?"

"Yes, my heart wants to."

Emily was amazed by how much she loved Taval. Two months ago, she wouldn't have thought it possible. In a way it was worrisome, another kind of drowning. She could see how she might become subsumed into his identity and become little more than a servant. But she sensed Taval didn't want a servant for a wife. He wanted a friend and an equal.

~

The Storm Wolves made leisurely progress northward. They typically stopped midafternoon. Taval and Kaplea thought their arims needed more training, probably for the benefit of the young Lions. One day they practiced unmounted fighting and Emily was gratified she could help, teaching the bow-legged horse warriors good footwork. Many of the non-warriors practiced, too, in case the camp was threatened directly.

The grasslands were undulating with patches of woods here and there where streams coursed through suitable soils. They came across the trail of a bison herd and decided to follow its track to the northeast. Two days later, scouts spotted the herd. The trail had descended into an area of low bluffs, some covered with larches. Taval said they were nearing a river called the Manyasin. Its meandering course led to a much larger river called the Tanasin that flowed from the north into Maeota Lake, which Emily knew to be the Sea of Azov. The Tanasin must be the Don River, she thought.

In the distant future, German armies would roll through these lands in a desperate bid to gain the Caucasian oil fields. It made her think of the world wars of the 20th century. From where she stood now, that future didn't seem like an improvement, nor did it seem desirable.

Hurlov stopped and grazed while she was in her reverie. She didn't notice and just stared to the west. She felt a hand on her shoulder. It was Zandra, riding his tall palomino.

"What do your eyes see, Tilkya?" The he-priestess asked.

"A future that is grim and horrible," she said.

"Must it be so?"

"We are small creatures and ignorant," Emily said. "What can we do to change the course the gods have plotted?"

"Come, we must not fall behind," Zandra said. "Perhaps the gods are plotting a new course."

Chapter 27 | Martial Art

THEY camped at the base of a wooded hill where a spring-fed brook trickled down to the prairie. Kaplea formed two hunting parties from her arim and they rode off toward the bison herd. Emily did her chores and worked on her saddle. The pieces were ready to be sewn together. She applied a reddish stain.

Three days later the stain was set. Emily sat in the afternoon sun, sewing the stirrups to her saddle using a thick bronze needle. Chunya was under a lean-to, working her loom. Zandra sat beside her, spinning thread. They chatted about mundane things. Emily's Lovta was improving but she couldn't keep up. The dull subject matter didn't help.

Kaplea had returned the day before, her mules packed with bison hides and meat. Taval went out with two hunting parties of his own.

Kaplea squatted beside Emily, scrutinizing the saddle. Emily thought it looked like a crude version of an English riding saddle with its upturned lips front and back. She had wanted a pommel but decided to keep it as simple as possible.

"This, you think, will make you a better rider," Kaplea said.

"I hope so," Emily said.

"It looks silly to me."

"Wait and see and judge when I am finished."

Kaplea rubbed her back.

"If you are lonely tonight without your husband, my tent will be open."

Before Emily could answer, they heard a galloping horse approaching from the south.

"A scout returns early," Kaplea said.

She strode toward the rider. Emily set her needle down and followed.

"Kaplea! Kaplea!" the scout shouted. "Riders approach. Many riders."

"How many, Mahalea?" Kaplea asked.

"One hundred fifty. Some of their horses have Persian crests," Mahalea said. The scout was a wiry woman with a weathered face and dark hair braided into a long tail.

Kaplea whistled the alarm, turning a lazy afternoon into hustling activity.

"How far out?" Kaplea asked.

"About ten miles. They are coming fast," Mahalea said.

"Damn the gods. I think we must flee."

"How many warriors are in camp?" Emily asked.

"About 70. My arim plus a few of Taval's warriors," Kaplea said.

"You do not think we can take them?"

"They have twice our number. We cannot risk our people."

"They will get our wagons and most of our goods."

"Sometimes it cannot be helped."

"We should get a better look at them. I have a device that will let us see them at a distance."

Kaplea frowned.

"Trust me," Emily said.

Emily put the old cloth saddle on Hurlov and mounted. She wished her new one was ready. She just needed to attach the second stirrup. She grabbed her satchel and, with Kaplea, galloped south toward the approaching enemy. Zandra found his mount and joined them. About three miles out they stopped at the crest of a low hillock. The approaching riders were just visible on the horizon.

Emily took out her binoculars and peered through them.

"What is this?" Zandra asked.

"A looking device. It makes far away things appear closer."

Through the lenses Emily saw a loose column riding at a trot. About a dozen of the riders wore plumed helmets and their horses had golden nose crests. The mass of riders appeared formidable. Could 70 Wolf warriors take them on? Emily began to turn ideas over in her mind. She gave the binoculars to Kaplea.

Kaplea handled them awkwardly and it took some time before she was able to see anything.

"Ah," she said then peered for a few moments. "It is clear they are following our trail. Some Persians, yes. The rest are Scyth mercenaries. I would say they have ridden for several days. They have few remounts.

Only some have bows. They do not have the look of a band that has fought long together."

"Do you think we could beat them?"

"We might have a chance. Still too risky. We need Taval's arim."

Kaplea handed the binoculars back to Emily and she passed them to Zandra.

"I have an idea," Emily said. "We send the remuda and a few warriors toward Taval. You take your arim and hide in the woods and we hide the wagons too. The Persians will chase the remuda. You follow out of sight and pinch them between your arim and Taval's."

"Ha!" Zandra exclaimed, just figuring out how to see through the binoculars. "Who can doubt that Tilkya was sent to us by the gods? Now we can see our enemies from far away."

"Your plan has merit," Kaplea said. "But I do not like exposing our non-warriors in the open."

"The plan is cunning, a fox's plan," Zandra said. "Our horses are fresh, the Persians' are tired. They will not catch the remuda before it reaches Taval. Then they will know the fury of the Storm Wolves."

"Your damned gods better be with us," Kaplea said.

Zandra cackled. "Oh, they are, they are."

~

Back at camp the non-warriors packed essentials onto mules. Kaplea ordered Mahalea to mount a fresh horse and ride quickly to Taval and tell him the plan. Soon the non-warriors and remaining warriors of Taval's arim were ready to go.

"Go Pakshakiz," Kaplea said to Emily. "Your place is with them."

"No," Emily said. "Let me be your eyes. I may not be much at fighting on horseback but Hurlov is a good mount and I can ride as fast as anybody with both hands on the reins. I will not hinder you."

Kaplea growled her acquiescence. The remuda moved out, heading northwest. Donya was in charge of the group.

Several warriors of Kaplea's arim pushed the wagons up the hill and into the woods out of sight. Emily put her new saddle on one of the wagons, hoping it would not be lost. Kaplea and her warriors led their horses into the woods and waited just over the crest of the hill.

Emily put on her leather girdle and green cloak. She found a patch of brush where she could hide and watch for the approaching force. A warrior named Javada was stationed behind her, ready to relay any important news to Kaplea.

They waited.

A pair of riders appeared on the horizon and stopped on a hillock perhaps 300 paces away. Scouts most likely. Emily trained her binoculars on them. They had ocher colored tunics and brown trousers. They were lightly armed with javelins and shields. Their attention was drawn to the northeast. They had spotted the remuda. One of the scouts turned back while the other maintained his position.

After what seemed more time than necessary, the main body of the Persian force appeared. A man on a gray horse wearing a golden helmet raised his arm and the riders stopped. He surveyed the scene for several minutes, talked with another rider, also wearing a polished helmet, then shouted orders. A dozen riders peeled off and rode toward what had been the Storm Wolves' camp. The main body cantered off to the northeast. One of the scouts remained on the hillock.

The riders coming toward the camp were led by a man with a bronze helmet and scale armor. His saddle and riding tack were trimmed with colorful finery. Emily backed away from her spot and whispered to Javada.

"Tell Kaplea the main body is pursuing the remuda. A dozen riders are milling about the camp and probably will find the wagons. A scout is maintaining overwatch on the hillock."

Emily crept back to her spot and wondered what Kaplea would do. She couldn't show her hand too early or the main body of Persians would return.

The commander of the riders at the camp looked alert and wary. Two of the riders had bows. The rest had javelins or spears. The commander pointed up the hill. Two riders dismounted and walked toward the wagons. Emily was crouched well off to the side so they weren't heading toward her. There was shouting. The men had found the wagons. Other men dismounted and ran up the slope. Soon there was hooting and merriment. They had discovered what to them would be a fortune. The commander was trying to call them back to their horses but was failing.

The scout on the hillock maintained his discipline, however, and he was the one Emily most worried about. When Kaplea's warriors showed themselves, he would be able to warn the main body.

The Scyth mercenaries remained at the wagons. They must be rooting through the goods, perhaps finding the wine. The commander remained mounted in the camp area, looking disgusted. One of the mercenaries appeared from the woods. His beard was salted with gray.

"We have the Wolves' bounty. We should take it and go," the man said in Greek.

"Mazdak wants the girl," the commander replied. "Once we have her we can come back for the loot. We have them on the run. We should press our advantage."

"The Lovta will be hard to catch and we should not go too far into their lands," the other man said.

"We have our orders. You should get the men back on their horses. I do not like this place."

Was she the girl, Emily wondered. Before she could give the question more thought, she heard a chorus of war cries from up the hill.

"Get back on your horses, quick!" the commander yelled.

She heard shouts and screaming coming from the woods. She loaded a bullet into her sling. A handful of mercenaries poured out from the woods, running for their horses. The commander wheeled around and waved at the scout on the hillock.

It was then Emily saw a lone rider racing toward the scout on a long-legged mare. It was Kaplea, head lowered, galloping hard, her red hair flowing. The commander saw her, too, and kicked his horse into motion. Emily stood, twirled her sling and flung the bullet, striking the horse in the flank. It bucked violently and threw the commander. She ducked down and loaded another bullet.

She could see the scout galloping to the northeast as Kaplea pursued. She had the angle and closed the distance. The scout managed to stay out in front but Kaplea was right behind him. She let go of her reins, drew her bow out of its gorytos and nocked an arrow while the mare continued at full speed. She aimed and loosed. The arrow struck the scout in the back and he fell from his saddle. Kaplea flew by the downed man, slowed her horse, wheeled around without using the reins, knocked another arrow and shot it into the man as she passed, continuing toward the camp.

Five of the mercenaries had found their mounts and were galloping off as several of Kaplea's warriors emerged from the woods on foot, wielding spears. The mercenaries headed toward Kaplea but she was soon joined by more riders from her arim, all shooting arrows. They made quick work of the mercenaries.

~

In the heat of the battle, one of the warriors had killed the Persian commander with an ax. Unfortunate, Emily thought, he would have had useful information. The warriors stripped the bodies of valuables, took what they wanted and loaded the rest into the wagons. They dragged the bodies into the woods to get them out of sight.

"What do we do now?" Emily asked Kaplea.

"We wait," she said. "It is too soon to pursue the main force."

Emily told her what she had heard the commander say.

"You are trouble, Pakshakiz."

"Who is Mazdak?" Emily asked.

"I have never heard of him."

"How long do we wait?"

"Until the sun nears the horizon. We will ride into the night. If Taval is where I think he is, we should put our enemies in a bind in the morning."

With the horses gathered, the warriors chatted about their various deeds during the fight. All agreed Kaplea's dash for the scout was a thing of beauty. Emily continued to work on her saddle, sewing on the second stirrup. She wanted to get it done before they left. She was just tying it off when Kaplea spoke.

"Gather up your gear. We leave soon."

Emily took her saddle to Hurlov. The cloth saddle would serve as a blanket. She threw on the leather one and cinched up its straps. Hurlov pranced and snorted at its unusual feel. The other warriors laughed. The turned-up lips of the seat and the dangling stirrups must look ridiculous to them. Kaplea watched her intently. Emily shouldered her satchel and grabbed her spear. She put her left foot in a stirrup and hoisted herself up. Her right foot instinctively found the other stirrup. Hurlov whinnied and reared up. The warriors laughed louder expecting her to fall. But she stayed mounted. Hurlov returned to all fours and she patted his neck.

"Easy boy, it's okay, trust me," she said in English.

Her feet had finally found the purchase they desired and she felt a sense of capability. She kicked Hurlov into a sprint. They jumped the brook. She wheeled Hurlov around at speed, holding her spear high, and raced back, yelling, "Yee haw," as they jumped the brook again.

She skirted a line of trees and threw her spear into one of them. It struck dead center with force and she did not waiver or struggle for balance in the saddle. She rode back into the midst of the warriors, reined Hurlov to a stop and reared him up a again, screaming her best war cry.

"I am Tilkya," she said in Lovta. "I ride with the Storm Wolves."

There was a momentary silence then Kaplea shouted her war cry and the others joined in. Emily's spear had penetrated the tree trunk so deeply she needed Javada's help to pull it out.

~

The arim rode northeast at a brisk trot. Javada, a small man, rode ahead about a quarter mile. He carried a signaling whistle that he could blow if he spotted eminent danger to the arim. Otherwise he was to keep a low profile in the hopes he would spot the Persian cavalry before they saw him. The terrain undulated with hillocks and mounds.

Emily rode behind the arim, tasked with guiding the captured Persian horses and keeping a rear watch. She was glad the new saddle was working out but she already saw ways to improve it. She also noticed spots where it was chafing Hurlov.

At twilight the arim stopped. Javada returned, reporting that he had not seen the Persians. With the coming of night, the arim set off again at a walking pace. A half-moon offered some light. Emily took the leather saddle off Hurlov and strapped it to one of the Persian horses. She walked and kept hold of its reins. Hurlov kept beside her without needing to be led. Kaplea rode over.

"You took off the saddle, I see," she said.

"It was chafing. I need to work on it some more," Emily said.

"You ride well with it but you are not a horse warrior yet. When it comes to fighting, you will have to stay out of the way. You need to learn the maneuvers and the signals before you can ride with the arim into battle."

"I understand. I will not hinder you."

"Good. I am glad we are clear."

~

They had walked about three hours when Javada returned again. He reported seeing the lights of campfires on the horizon. One of the warriors, a man named Kellvan, suggested making a night raid. Kellvan was the oldest of the warriors, late-thirties perhaps. He had a savage scar on his face that made him seem always to be sneering when he talked.

"We could kill many of them and scatter their horses," Kellvan said. Several teeth were missing from one side of his mouth.

"No," Kaplea said. "There are too many and they will be wary of a night raid. We will rest here and shadow our quarry in the morning."

Emily hobbled the Persian horse so it would not stray. Hurlov, she knew, would not go far. She wrapped herself in her cloak and tried to sleep.

~

It was still dark when she heard distant shouting. Kaplea was up and mounted.

"The Persians are moving out. We must stay on their trail without being seen," she said.

Javada returned from his post, looking bleary from his all-night vigil. The sun was just rising.

"They have moved off the crest," he said.

Kaplea ordered the arim forward and they trotted quickly to the base of the hillock where the Persians had camped.

"Tilkya, dismount and come with me."

Emily followed Kaplea up the hillock. They crawled on their bellies to the crest.

"Let me have your seeing device."

Kaplea peered through the binoculars for several minutes. Emily watched the Persians riding off in two columns side by side.

"I count 143 enemy. I have 58 warriors. Taval should have 67. It will be a good fight if we time it right."

When the Persian force was out of sight over another hillock, the arim moved forward again, riding at a fast canter. Once they reached the base of the next hillock, Emily and Kaplea went to the crest again. This time the Persian force was forming into battle lines -- three units of 40 warriors each. Each unit formed two rows, archers and javelin throwers in the front, spearmen in the back. A group of 20 or so lined up behind the three units.

"Their scouts must have spotted Taval's arim," Kaplea said. "He must be beyond the next hillock."

"What do we do now?" Emily asked.

"You stay here. When the Persians clear the next crest, clap twice as a signal. Clap once if you see something unexpected."

Kaplea went back down to her horse and issued orders. The warriors readied their weapons and put on their helmets. Through the binoculars Emily could see the Persian officers in a group, themselves receiving orders. She wondered what their plan was. The group of officers dispersed to their respective formations. The man she figured was the commander stayed back, surrounded by the twenty warriors. The commander shouted.

The three units moved forward, slowly gaining speed. They were galloping when they reached the crest and disappeared over the ridge. The group of 20 followed and soon it was out of sight. Emily clapped twice.

Kaplea's arim moved out in two columns, one led by her and the other by Kellvan. They thundered by Emily. She went down to Hurlov and strapped on the leather saddle. She grabbed her spear, put on her helmet and galloped after the arim. She was suddenly worried the battle could go badly for the Storm Wolves. What would happen to her then?

She slowed down when she passed the next crest, trying to make sense of what looked like pandemonium. She saw several riderless horses running away from the battle. There were shouts and cries of anguish. She veered right to circle around the south side of the battle to try to get a better view. A group of Scyth mercenaries had broken off and were fleeing south. She hoped that meant the Persians were losing.

Then she spotted Taval riding Skolov and swinging his sword. His arim had closed with the Persians and was engaged in close melee. She couldn't stand to watch -- a well-timed spear thrust or a swinging ax could mean death for her husband -- but she couldn't look away. Taval downed two warriors, one a Persian officer.

Another officer -- the commander, she thought, based on his plume -- broke away from the melee and fled south. Emily kicked Hurlov to full speed and went after him. The Persian had a shield in one hand and a sword in the other. Hurlov ran smoothly, Emily helping his motion by raising her rump off the saddle. She had picked a good line and would soon cut the Persian off. He saw her and realized his predicament.

"Tilkya! No! Let him go!" Taval shouted.

But the Persian commander had turned and was coming straight at her with his sword raised. Emily readied her spear. The distance closed rapidly. The moment before they would have collided, Emily pivoted her hips, feet firm in the stirrups, and threw the spear. She followed through with the motion, ducking her head and veering Hurlov off to the left. She heard a thud-clink and felt a sting at her side.

She was headed back toward the main battle when she realized she had no suitable weapon to use from horseback. She looked behind her. The Persian commander was on the ground, unmoving, impaled by her spear. She turned around to go retrieve it.

The spear had pierced the Persian's shield, went through his wrist, and penetrated his scale armor. His lifeless eyes were open, seeming to look at the sky. The spear's shaft held his arm and shield in front of him as if he was still trying to defend himself. Emily was stupefied by the fact that she had just killed a man.

~

She didn't know how long she stared at her victim before Taval reined up beside her. The fight was over and a grim stillness settled over the battlefield disturbed by the groans and bays of wounded warriors and horses.

"To kill a person changes you," Taval said. "There's no going back on it."

Several riders gathered around, murmuring at the spectacle of the skewered commander. Kaplea rode over, looked at the corpse for a moment then dismounted. She was splattered with blood but appeared uninjured herself. She walked over to the body, grabbed the spear and put her foot on the shield, pressing it to the dead man's chest. With a grunt she yanked the spear out. Blood dripped from the tip. It appeared undamaged. Kaplea handed the weapon to Emily.

"I believe this is yours, Tilkya," she said.

Emily took the spear. More murmurs from gathered warriors.

"There will be time enough to waggle our tongues," Kaplea said. "There is work to be done and wounded to care for."

Taval pointed to a bloodstain on Emily's tunic.

"You are hurt. We should tend to that now."

Chapter 28 | Respite at Lonely Hill

THE wound was not deep. Emily's thick leather girdle had done its job. They decided the cut didn't need stitching and would heal well enough on its own, though it would leave a scar. Others had not fared so well. Seven Wolves were dead including two of the young lions. Ten more were badly wounded. Zandra, Chunya and Taval were the most adept at treating wounds and they did their best for the injured. One man had to have his arm amputated, a procedure that often led to death. Emily helped as much as she could. She badgered them to sterilize the wounds and the tools they used.

Kaplea left with her arim to fetch the wagons and returned the next day. A mass grave was dug for the dead Wolves and Lions and their dead horses. They interred the bodies complete with armor, weapons, spindles and other implements of their lives. Zandra led an elaborate ritual to honor them.

They burned the bodies of the dead Persians and Scyth, 93 in all. Four Scyth had been taken prisoner. All the Persian officers were dead except one who had escaped along with about fifty mercenaries. The battle had been a slaughter, and a great victory for the Storm Wolves.

The prisoners talked freely and offered to swear oaths and join the Wolves. Kaplea wanted to kill them. Taval was undecided. The Scyth were kin to the Lovta and they had fought honorably enough. Kaplea thought that fighting for the Persians represented a betrayal of their noble ancestors and they deserved no mercy.

They learned from the prisoners that Mazdak was a general and an agent of Darius, King of Persia. Darius had sent Mazdak to consolidate and expand the empire's holdings along the northern shores of the Euxine Sea. They learned he was keen to capture a girl named Emily and sent the expedition to find her. The Persians had hoped to bargain for her. The prisoners did not know what the offer was.

In the end Taval sided with Kaplea. She and Kellvan dispatched the prisoners quickly with their war hammers.

"The Lions would make them slaves or sell them to Greek slave traders," Taval told Emily. "That is not our way. We kill our enemies or show them mercy. There is no in between."

"Why no mercy for these men?" Emily asked.

"I did not trust them," he said. "They had sworn oaths to the Persians and were too eager to betray those oaths. If we let them go, they would return to the Persians and fight for them again."

Emily wasn't convinced of Taval's reasoning, neither was she sure mercy was the right course. Her sense of morality was confused. The Wolves had a code of honor and unwritten laws but she was only beginning to grasp them. She was surprised at how readily she was adapting to the violence of this world. Did the violence contain a deeper truth, something that was missing from the modern world she once knew? The close presence of death certainly made her feel alive. Or was she rationalizing now that she had become a killer herself?

~

The Storm Wolves moved a few miles north to the banks of the Manyasin and continued upstream to a place where the river was fordable. They crossed and set up camp near a hill that offered a good view in all directions. They called it Lonely Hill and kept a constant vigil on its peak. Emily, when it wasn't her shift, lent the other lookouts her binoculars. She told them to be careful but there was no need. They treated the "seeing device" like a precious gift from the gods.

They were concerned about the possibility of a larger force of Persians following the one they had defeated. The river, Taval and Kaplea figured, would buy them time if a large force did appear. Feeling relatively secure, they prepared to celebrate their victory, rest for a few days, then decide their next course.

Emily had to sit through another tattooing. She was getting the spiral of a Storm Wolf warrior. Halaba was applying it to her belly opposite the fox. While he worked, Kaplea needled a "secret" tattoo on her back. She wouldn't say what it was. Perhaps it was a tiger, Emily thought, to mark the bond between them. Halaba shrugged.

"I do not know but Kaplea draws good animals," he said.

Halaba and Kaplea finished their tattoos, applying a balm to sooth the irritation and bandages to protect the skin while it healed.

~

The dead Persian commander's name was Kasran. His sword, armor and other possessions were Emily's. She didn't like the sword despite its gilded hilt and a polished blade. It felt heavy and awkward in her hand. Donya loved it, however, so they arranged a trade -- Donya's hammer for Emily's sword. The sword was much more valuable than the hammer so Donya threw in a blanket, a spindle whorl, a needle kit, and a skirt of thick leather flaps that served to protect the groin, hips and upper thighs.

The Persian commander had carried 500 silver drachmas and two ingots of gold. She also got his horse, a feisty gray mare. It was a good horse, Taval said, but might have a hard time surviving the winter. Emily named it Mazda.

Taval fixed the puncture in Kasran's scale armor and resized it to fit Emily. The Persian commander's helmet was too large but he found a smaller one from the head of a dead Scyth that fit about right. It was open faced and so better for horse fighting than the hoplite helmet. Taval attached the hoplite crest to the new helmet and repainted it with blue and orange stripes.

She tried on her new war gear, examining herself with a bronze mirror. She thought she looked like a cartoon character but the others seemed to approve.

~

Emily was immersed in cooking chores directed by a lean, weathered woman named Akkea who was in charge of the band's food supply. When it came to food, her word was law. Emily was chopping wild onions on a board on her lap, the afternoon sun casting long shadows, when she watched Taval stride up the hill, responding to shouts from a lookout. He peered through the binoculars, patted the lookout on the shoulder and came back down. He and a few warriors mounted their horses and rode away. He had sounded no alarm.

Perhaps a half an hour later, Taval returned. He dismounted and strode over to Akkea.

"Get more fires burning. We have company. An arim of Hawks will be here soon."

Kaplea was nearby cutting bison meat.

"Do not tell me Kraejik is with them," she said.

"I am afraid he is," Taval said.

The Hawks, Emily learned from Koia while the two gathered deadwood, were a large war band of the Wolf Tribe about 400 strong. Only one of its arims, about 60 warriors, would be visiting that night. Kraejik was the Hawks' principal war leader and was held in high esteem throughout the tribe.

"Why does Kaplea not like Kraejik?" Emily asked.

"He teases her and makes advances," Koia answered.

"She does not kill him?"

Koia shrugged. "He is a great war leader."

"Do you like him?"

"I would open my legs for him anytime."

~

At dusk horses rumbled into camp. Emily was in her tent taking the opportunity to wash up. The evening would be warm so she decided to forego trousers and just wear her blue tunic. Presently her hair was not braided. She pulled it back and fastened it with a simple leather barrette and a wooden pin. She felt an urge to look as good as possible. Part of her was annoyed by the urge. Nevertheless, she applied a touch of makeup, a dab of perfume and put on the songbird earrings. She winced when she put on the belt that held her puukko and Persian dagger because it pressed the bandages over her wound and fresh tattoos. She slid the belt down her hips a little further.

She emerged from the tent to see people greeting each other with handshakes and hugs. She could distinguish the Hawks by the feathers they sewed into their pointed caps.

"Tilkya, come," she heard Taval say.

He rarely issued commands to her but when he did her body seemed to respond before her will could catch up. That also annoyed her. She had no intention of disobeying an order but she wanted to at least decide to obey. That firm, resonant voice reached something deeper than her conscious mind. Taval had the knack of command and, she supposed, that was part of why she loved him. She hurried over and he introduced her to a handful of Hawk warriors including Kraejik.

"So this is your new wife," Kraejik said. He held Emily's chin with a large, powerful hand. "A bit small but excellent teeth."

She felt anger well up. She squinted and locked eyes with him. He was not as tall as Taval but tall nonetheless and barrel-chested. His beard and hair were mostly gray with streaks of brown. The sleeves of his tunic were cut short to show off his thickly muscled arms.

"Be careful, my dear Kraejik," a voice came from behind her. "Tilkya is more formidable than you might think and she walks with Samvi."

Kraejik looked up and released Emily.

"Zandra, you old charlatan," he said. "Are you still spinning tales for these gullible young Storm Wolves?"

"The tales I spin are the truth," Zandra said.

The two embraced and Kraejik kissed Zandra on the lips.

"You are a wretched flirt," Zandra said.

"Ha! Who would have thought I could have done that to my old war leader."

~

They feasted, set up the hemp tent, drank wine and told stories. Emily's understanding of Lovta was improving. The language actually incorporated many Greek words and she was able to get the gist of much of what people said, yet her ability to speak it lagged behind. The main topic was the Storm Wolves' defeat of the Persian force. They were calling it the Battle of Lonely Hill even though the actual battlefield was several miles away.

"That was a bold and clever plan, Kaplea," Kraejik said. "I salute you."

"It was Tilkya's plan, not mine," Kaplea replied.

All eyes went to Emily.

"That is correct," Zandra said. "I was there when Tilkya suggested it. Her name is no jest of the gods. She has the mind of a fox."

"And the heart of a lion" Halaba said. "I watched her slay the Persian commander in single combat. She took his charge and put her spear right through him."

"What say you, little one," Kraejik said. "Speak."

Emily wasn't sure what to say. Should she boast, affirm her great deeds? No, she thought. Maybe that's what they wanted but that wasn't who she was. She stood and straightened her tunic.

"I am a Wolf. I do what I can to help the tribe," she said. "It is the strength and courage of its people that move me."

There was a chorus of hoots and howling. Taval ordered the musicians to play and fetched Emily's spear.

"Dance for us, wife," he said.

She danced as ordered, entering into a kind of trance of movement, performing flourishes she hadn't known she could do. It was the dance of a warrior. She finished with her tongue-waggling war cry right in front of Kraejik.

"Ha! " He exclaimed. "Where did you find this creature, Taval?"

"I snatched her from the forest, my friend. She is niava."

~

Emily held her arms in the air, letting Taval change the bandages. She felt foggy-headed from the previous night's hemp and wine. She yearned for a cup a of coffee. She thought if it were in her power, she would mount an expedition to Africa just to find coffee beans. Taval chuckled when he removed the bandage from her back.

"You should not have let Kaplea give you a tattoo," he said.

"What did she do?"

"Best not to know, I think."

Emily found her makeup case. Even with the mirror she had to twist to see the tattoo. Despite the scabbing, the shape of it was clear -- a bushy-tailed squirrel holding an acorn.

"For shit's sake," she said in English then switched to Greek. "Now I am stuck with a squirrel on my back."

Taval shrugged. "It will look cute when it heals. Kaplea draws good animals."

"You are not angry she put that on your wife?"

Taval grasped her shoulders in his large hands.

"I believe you are a special woman, perhaps you will achieve great things, but the squirrel will keep you humble."

He kissed her neck and she soon forgot her irritation.

~

The leaders of the two bands met in council. They sat around a cooking fire, ate oatmeal and drank fermented milk. Present were Taval, Kaplea, Arlav, Zandra, Halaba, Kellvan, Kraejeck and two other warriors from his arim. Emily didn't expect to be part of it but Taval wanted her there. She sat between Taval and Kaplea.

"Thank you for the tattoo," Emily mumbled to Kaplea.

"You put a spell on me. I put one on you, Pakshakiz."

The group exchanged news. The Hawks had traveled north and raided the horse herds of the Sarma. The Sarma were a kindred people to the Lovta who inhabited lands between the northeastern mountains and a great river called the Goljasin. The Hawks stole many horses but the Sarma pursued them a long ways with a large force.

"The Sarma grow strong," Kraejik said. "The Lovta will have problems with them soon."

Zandra talked at length about the doings of the Storm Wolves over the past year, eventually getting to the attempt to kidnap Emily at Sinki that Kaplea thwarted.

"You are a warrior's warrior, Kaplea," Kraejik said. "If we were to marry, we would ride over the steppe like gods."

"Give it up, Kraejik," Kaplea said. "I will never marry you."

Zandra talked of Kydoime and how she seeks an alliance with the Wolves against the Persians.

"That skinny witch wants to be queen of all the Lovta," Kraejik said. "We should not come under her spell."

"She offers us direct trade with Artemios," Taval said. "And if we rid these lands of Persians, we could trade freely with all the Greek towns."

Zandra said the Persians were after Tilkya. They worried a large force might come to try again.

"Why do they want her?" Kraejik asked.

"She was brought here by the will of the gods from a distant land," Zandra said. "The Persians think she has knowledge that could help them with their wars."

"Do you have such knowledge?" Kraejik asked Emily.

Emily thought about her answer. Her Lovta wasn't good enough to say what she wanted to say. She spoke in Greek to Kaplea who translated.

"She says she knows some things that might be useful to the Persians but nothing so great as they imagine."

"What are the Storm Wolves' plans now?" Kraejeck asked.

"We told Kydoime we would raid the lands near Maeota Lake," Taval said.

Arlav spoke up. "We have just defeated a force of 150. That is more than she could have hoped. We have wounded to care for and valuable goods in tow. If we went to the coast, we risk getting trapped by Mazdak's army."

"This army of Mazdak, how large is it?" Kraejik asked.

"We do not know," Taval said. "One of the Scyth we captured said they left 300 horse warriors with Mazdak and more were coming. He is offering good terms to the Scyth, paying in silver coins."

"That is an expensive way to chase down one woman," Kraejik said.

"It's Artemios he wants," Emily said in Greek. Kaplea translated. "Mazdak probably thinks I would be a valuable hostage even if I do not have magic knowledge."

"Artemios is Huraslan's pet," Kraejik said. "The Lions have many warriors. Mazdak would have to build quite an army to take the city from them."

"But if Huraslan dies, everything is up in the air," Emily said. "Artemios becomes vulnerable. If Mazdak has a large force, it would be the time to strike."

Kraejik shrugged. "Why should we worry about one Greek town? It is the Lions' problem."

"The Wolves prosper from trade with the Lions," Arlav said. "Much of what we trade comes and goes through Artemios. If it falls, we would be forced to pay higher prices. If the strength of the Lions is broken, what happens to us? Caught between the Persians and the Sarma, we could get pushed back to the deep steppe, scraping a living from hard lands and fighting off the far-eastern tribes."

"This is an argument for another time," Taval said. "For now we should rest and care for our wounded. We can send scouts for news of Mazdak's army. Once we know more, we can decide our next move."

"My warriors and horses are weary. We will rest here with you," Kraejik said.

~

Kaplea suggested that Emily ride with her arim. Taval agreed, admitting he would worry too much if she rode with his, and so Emily embarked on her training as a horse warrior. Kaplea was a severe taskmaster and when she wasn't driving her hard, Kellvan was. Hot, wearying work, she trained mainly with the young Lions. They learned signals, maneuvers and formations and drilled until they became second nature.

Hurlov and Mazda grew accustomed to her saddle. She improved it by smoothing out edges and adding padding to minimize chafing. Her knees ached from all the riding. She hoped she was young enough and flexible enough that it wouldn't become a chronic problem.

Her saddle aroused curiosity, often in the form of jokes. Several people tried it. Most didn't like the stirrups -- they felt unnatural -- but some of the younger riders were interested. One of the Lions, a thick-chested man named Shavaris, was enthusiastic. He found he could wield his ax from Emily's saddle with much more power. She agreed to help him make his own saddle.

All the Lions spoke decent Greek and she liked training with them. They bonded as a unit and began to perform well in maneuvers. Emily worked hard and asked many questions of Kaplea or Kellvan, questions others were too shy to ask. The Lions came to look to her as a leader.

Kaplea instructed her in the use of her new hammer, called a sagaris. The head weighed less than a typical framing hammer. Its long shaft could be used with two hands which added power and made it easier to return to a ready position, yet it was light enough to use one-handed from horseback. It could be used to hook shields, weapons and body parts. Its spike was lethal but Kaplea advised using the hammer side most of the time. The spike could get stuck in whatever it hit. Emily couldn't hope to match Kaplea's skill any time soon. She strove just to be competent. Her spear would be her primary weapon; the hammer would serve as a backup.

The Storm Wolves had captured several high-quality bows from the Scyth mercenaries. Taval offered her one but she declined, saying others in the band had been waiting longer. She didn't want to add archery to the retinue of new skills she was learning. Not yet.

~

Emily stood on the peak of Lonely Hill under a canopy erected as shade for the lookouts. Other than patches of trees here and there near the meandering river, horizon to horizon, the terrain was flat grassland. She was on the great Eurasian steppe. Eastward, she knew, it must stretch for two thousand miles or more.

Koia sat beside her, repairing the leather wrapping of her newly acquired bow. She was delighted with it.

"It has some age but it still draws smoothly," she said.

"I thought Taval was having one made for you," Emily said.

"He is. When I get that one, I will give this one away. Perhaps to you. Its draw is not too strong for someone your size."

"Thank you," Emily said.

"Were you really sent to us by the gods like Zandra says?" Koia asked.

"I cannot say. It does not feel like that. It is not like I hear their voices in my head. Some kind of force or forces brought me here. Are the gods behind them? I do not know. To be honest, it feels more like a mistake than a plan."

"You seem older than your years, even older than Taval."

"Do I seem like a woman to you?" Emily asked.

"I do not understand. Of course you are a woman."

"Do I seem feminine?"

"You are not so girly as some but you seem like a woman at heart to me."

"I ask because I believe I was a man in a past life."

Koia giggled and slapped Emily on the rump. "You must have been a good man. The gods have rewarded you."

Emily giggled, too. It occurred to her the distinctions between masculine and feminine, so pronounced among the Greeks and even in the modern world, were not so stark among the Lovta. Being a woman wasn't a diminishment. It was part of the reason she felt so comfortable with the Wolves, even though, when she looked out at the vast, featureless steppe, she missed the forest, the hills and the city.

She turned her binoculars to the southwest where there were no mountains, no sea, no Artemios, just prairie, and two riders, obscured by shimmering heat waves.

"Our scouts return," Emily said.

~

Emily and Taval sat in their tent drinking wine. The smoke hole was open and the flap only two-thirds closed to let air circulate. Kaplea sat with them, in part, Emily thought, to escape Kraejik's advances. They talked about the plans they had discussed with other leaders.

Halaba, one of the scouts, had traveled several days and didn't see any signs of Persians until he approached the isthmus of the Phanagorian peninsula where it became thick with patrols. Shepherds complained they had been pushed off their pasture lands to make way for a huge remuda Mazdak was gathering for his army.

"We went as far as we dared but did not see the remuda," Halaba had said. "The Persians are being very wary."

"That settles it," Kraejeck had said to Taval. "They aren't coming after you and your bride. The Storm Wolves might as well join the Hawks. We can ride north and teach the uppity Sarma a lesson."

"Perhaps we will do that," Taval had told him. "The scouts that went down river have not returned. We will wait for their news."

In the tent, Taval put a bud of hemp on the brazier. He liked to inhale the fumes. He said it helped him think when making big decisions.

"We should strike," Kaplea said. "We can roll up their patrols and scatter their remuda. If they give chase, we can lead them onto the steppe as far as they choose to follow."

"It could be a trap," Taval said. "Perhaps they want to lure us in. Mazdak may think our victory will make us reckless."

Emily took a whiff of the hemp smoke. She thought she ought to invent a pipe.

"Kraejik is probably right," Emily said. "Mazdak likely figures he missed his chance. He certainly knows now his Scyth mercenaries need more work together to become good fighting units."

"Which is why we should hit them hard now, while they are still raw and disorganized," Kaplea said. "Show them the Wolves are not to be trifled with."

"We should keep in mind that Mazdak's primary goal is Artemios," Emily said. "He's not building an army to chase me around the steppe. He wants to break the power of the Lions and take the city. That is what will solidify the Persian hold on the region. I think Kaplea is right. We should raid their remuda. That would at least slow them down and keep them worried about their eastern flank."

"It is clear they are watching for us," Taval said.

"Then we should wait awhile," Emily said. "Let the summer heat wilt their vigilance."

"If you don't want to listen to me, perhaps you will listen to your wife," Kaplea said.

Taval grunted. He took another breath of hemp smoke and leaned back on a pillow with his arms behind his head.

"Leave me," he said. "Both of you. I need to think this through alone."

Emily was perplexed. This was her tent, too. Was she supposed to sleep outside? But before she could protest, Kaplea grabbed her arm.

"Come, Pakshakiz," Kaplea said. "You will sleep in my tent tonight."

~

In the relative cool of the morning, Emily continued training with the young Lions. Kellvan emphasized spear work. It was tricky because if you came in too hard, you could easily unhorse yourself. Emily's stirrups helped but she lacked the arm strength to hit the dangling target shield at full gallop and still hang on to the spear. Kellvan taught them to slow down before striking the target then gallop away.

Emily spoke to Shavaris, the stout young warrior: "If you had stirrups and something to support your rump, you could strike the target at full gallop."

She let Shavaris mount Mazda and he took up a long, broad-bladed spear. He charged the target. Kellvan yelled for him to rein up but he didn't. The spear struck the shield which splintered apart and the scaffold holding it tumbled down. Kellvan scolded him for his lack of discipline but he clearly was impressed, along with everyone else.

That evening, Emily helped Shavaris work on his own saddle. It would be a simpler version than hers -- a broad strip of bison hide sewn onto a cloth saddle with stirrups attached. Shavaris was eager to get it done quickly. Emily advised taking the time to do it right.

~

The second party of scouts returned the next day. They had little news to report except that river villagers talked of many Scyth warriors who were crossing the Tanasin including a band led by a man named Bolinthos. Wolf leaders discussed the news around the fire after supper.

"Bolinthos is a a Thracian word," Chunya said. "It means wild bull."

Emily thought Byon might know who Bolinthos was. It pained her a little to think of Byon. Marrying Taval felt like a betrayal. Her fears back then of being with a man seemed so stupid. But the gods had dealt their hand and she loved Taval now.

"I have made a decision," Taval said. "Here is what I propose ..."

The Storm Wolves' wagons were too laden with goods to accompany a deep raid and too valuable to remain out in the open without protection. He said the band would wait twelve days, then 20 warriors would escort the wagons and most of the non-warriors to Gipatsha, a semi-permanent Lovta settlement along the banks of the Goljasin. Taval and Kaplea would lead the other warriors west, lean and fast, in the hopes of being able to raid the remuda of Mazdak's army.

Kraejik was disappointed. He was the senior war leader but in this context he had no authority over Taval or Kaplea.

"Well, my friend," Kraejik said to Taval. "I see your mind is set. I think the risk is great and the prospects of plunder are low. Why are you so bent on this Mazdak and his army?"

"Mazdak tried to steel my wife," Taval said. "I need no more reason than that. I also promised Kydoime I would raid Persian lands. Our raid will show the Wolves are a threat that cannot be ignored."

Emily put another patty of dried bison manure on the fire. Kraejik twisted a piece of wool onto the thread dangling from his spindle whorl and spun the weighted disk.

"And you, Kaplea," Kraejik said. "Do you agree? You have your own arim and need not do Taval's bidding."

"Taval and I are agreed on this," she said. She was sewing a hem on a pair of trousers. How she did it with such little light, Emily didn't know.

"I have chosen Taval as my war leader," she continued. "His will is the will of Tavapa and Kurapa. Where he goes, I follow."

"You are the redheaded pride of the Wolf Tribe, Kaplea," Kraejik said, "You should lead your own war band -- the Tigers, eh?"

"That will happen when the gods decide it is time," she said.

Kraejik disengaged the thread from the spindle, wound it into a ball and put it into Chunya's crate. He stood up.

"I and my personal arim will raid with you," he said. "We cannot let the Storm Wolves get all the glory. The rest of the Hawks will escort your train to Gipatsha along with our remuda."

Kraejik walked away toward his tent.

~

Emily and Taval decided to sleep outside. They took their bedding to a flat spot on the slope of Lonely Hill. It was a moonless night and the stars shined brightly. The red spot of Mars was unmistakable. They took turns with the binoculars. Through them, the colors of stars could be discerned.

"Do your people fly to the stars?" Taval asked.

"My people are the Lovta now," Emily said. "But, no, the people where I come from cannot fly to the stars. They are too far away."

"They must be a hundred miles up in the sky."

"Much further than that, further than I have words to explain. If the fastest bird flew toward them for a hundred lifetimes, it would not even get close."

"Hmm, I am a large man but what you say makes me feel small."

Emily entwined her fingers with his.

"Is that so bad?" She asked.

"No, not so bad," Taval said. "If I want to feel big all I need do is stand next to you."

Emily slugged him in the chest and he laughed. They continued gazing at the stars. A friendly breeze kept the flies from being bothersome.

"Could Kaplea really start her own war band?" Emily asked.

"Yes, she is not bound to me except by her own choosing. She is a great warrior. Many would be happy to join her."

"Is she a greater warrior than you?"

"You have seen her shoot a bow and wield a sagaris," Taval said. "I cannot match her skill. Neither can Kraejik."

Emily rolled over and laid her head on his chest. He stroked her hair, tugging gently at her braid.

Chapter 29 | The Raid

EMILY and Kaplea rode southeast along the winding Manyasin River. The day was cloudy which brought some relief from the heat but that was offset by the humidity. Kaplea was teaching Emily the rudiments of scouting -- how to read the land, look for tracks in the grass, distinguish between horses and bison, estimate their numbers. Mahalea or Halaba were more practiced scouts than Kaplea but Emily guessed she wanted to get away from camp for a while.

They mostly kept silent as they rode, which is what good scouts do -- stay alert and keep your eyes moving. At a distance the landscape appeared flat but up close there were undulations and hillocks. Kaplea would stop on a hillock at the point where she could just see over the crest while most of her horse remained hidden from view. The idea was to see without being seen.

At midafternoon they came to an area of freshly grazed grass. Kaplea stopped and dismounted. She felt the grass stubble and looked at the hoof marks.

"Sheep," she said. "Shepherds were here with their flock. Two days ago, I would say. We will catch up with them soon."

"Are we returning to camp today?" Emily asked.

"Yes, I think so, but we will ride part of the way at night. We should quicken our pace."

Trotting for a half hour or so, they approached another hillock. Emily did the honors, slowing Hurlov and stopping just as she could see over the crest. She was surprised by the sight of a very large and long lake, its waters gray to match the sky. It was perhaps a mile across but she could not see its far end.

"Manota Lake," Kaplea said as she edged up beside Emily on a white gelding named Kydon. "And there are our shepherds."

Several hundred sheep were spread out along the lake's near shore. Emily saw three riders tending to them.

"Are they Lovta?" Emily asked.

"Yes, and members of the Wolf Tribe. Most of our people are herders and do not ride with war bands unless the tribe is threatened."

Kaplea hailed the shepherds who wore plain flax tunics, trousers and the blue felt hats of the Wolf Tribe. Two had bows, the other carried a spear. The two with bows rode toward Emily and Kaplea on small but sturdy horses. Both were men and had gray patches in their beards.

"Kaplea, we are pleased and honored to see you," one of the men said. "What news do you bring?"

Kaplea recognized the man whose name was Molav. She introduced Emily as Tilkya, wife of Taval. Kaplea told him of the battle with the Persians and Scyth mercenaries. The shepherd with the spear rode over. He was a young man and seemed tongue-tied at the sight of Kaplea.

"We will be lighting our cooking fire soon," Molav said. "You are welcome to eat with us and camp here."

"No, we need to get back," Kaplea said. She told them the Storm Wolves were camped at Lonely Hill with the Hawks. She said the supply wagons would be heading out for Gipatsha in two days and the Storm Wolves had plenty of goods to trade. She arranged a rendezvous between the shepherd's band and the wagon train.

"Arlav will treat you well," she said.

Molav turned to Emily. "We have heard of you, Tilkya. You are the niava Taval took for a bride. We welcome your spirit to the Wolves. We hope Samvi is pleased with the marriage."

"I am pleased with the marriage and proud to be a Wolf. I believe it is the desire of Samvi."

"Farewell, Tilkya," Molav said. "And farewell, noble Kaplea. You are the beating heart of the Lovta."

~

Kaplea and Emily rode fast now, wanting to cover as much distance as possible before dark. When night came they slowed to a walk to protect their horses' legs. With the cloud cover, they could hardly see beyond a few paces. Kaplea knew instinctively where to go. Emily was disoriented but strove to keep her senses open and feel the landscape as it rolled by. A windless silence prevailed and the only sounds were the hoof beats of Hurlov and Kydon and the rustling of the saddles.

Emily thought she heard another rustling but couldn't place it. She dismissed it as nothing until she heard it again, to her left, it seemed. She grabbed Kaplea's arm and reined up. Emily put her finger to her lips and listened. She heard rustling sounds from more than one location. Then Kydon snorted and stamped.

"Wolves," Kaplea whispered. She took her bow from its gorytos and nocked an arrow.

Emily laid her spear across her lap and got the flashlight from her satchel. When she heard another rustle, she pressed the button. She caught a large, gray wolf in its beam. The residual light exposed the shadowy profiles of three other wolves. They were startled and froze in place. Kaplea drew back her bow.

"No," Emily said. "They are just curious, I think."

She kicked Hurlov into motion and charged the pack, yelling, "Ya! Ya!" and keeping the beam on the large one. The wolves bolted and were quickly out of sight. Emily stopped and Kaplea was soon beside her.

"You are a niava of Samvi, protector of animals," Kaplea said, a tone of wonder in her voice.

"Perhaps I am," Emily said.

"And you wield a scepter of light."

"It is just a device of my former people," Emily said and handed the flashlight to Kaplea.

Kaplea handled it with reverence at first but soon was playing with the beam, shining it everywhere and switching it on and off. She put the light on Emily and, to Emily's astonishment, giggled. Kaplea dismounted.

"We will rest here a while," she said.

Kaplea kept the beam on Emily. "You are a strange creature, Tilkya Niava. I do not know why I love you but I do. Undress for me and I will undress for you."

Emily did so slowly and Kaplea watched with fascination. She handed Emily the flashlight and began to undress. She took everything off except the Tiger Stone which lay snugly in her ample cleavage. Her magnificently muscled rump and thighs were a wonder to behold. She primped and strutted in the light of the beam like she was the most potent being on earth. Perhaps she was, Emily thought. Kaplea unfurled a blanket and the two made love on the grass.

Sweating and breathing hard, they held each other in their arms. The wolves of the nearby pack howled. Kaplea and Emily howled in response. The horses snorted and whinnied their disapproval.

~

Through her binoculars Emily saw the dim and dying glow of a campfire about 600 paces away. It was the fire of a Scyth patrol. She could discern no activity. Koia lay beside her as they looked out over the crest of a coulee. Behind them a score of warriors and their horses rested. No one talked. Surprise was essential. Koia patted Emily on the back. The time was near. Soon the sky would glow with the twilight of the coming dawn and the warriors would attack. Emily would lead them.

Taval and Kaplea had put her in charge of the young Lion warriors. A few warriors from Taval's and Kaplea's arims filled out their ranks including Koia and Donya who Emily was supposed to rely on for guidance and experience. If any of the veteran Storm Wolves resented Emily's leadership, none showed it.

Emily put on her helmet and mounted Mazda. Her spear had an orange guidon tied to it for use as a signal. They had set out three days prior from Lonely Hill, riding fast. Halaba's expert scouting had led them to this spot undetected, or so they hoped. Taval's arim was on the right flank a quarter mile away and Kaplea's was on the other side. When Emily started her attack on the patrol, the arims would ride west hard and fast in the hopes of catching Mazdak's army by surprise and scatter its remuda.

Emily's job -- once her troop, dubbed the Storm Rats by Kaplea, wiped out the patrol -- was to hang back and protect the spare horses, a small remuda about a mile back tended by teenage warriors-to-be. The Storm Rats would also act as cover for the inevitable retreat of the main arims and a communication point with Kraejik's arim. Taval and Kaplea were counting on her tactical sense to make good decisions if things got dicey.

Kraejik's arim, reinforced with warriors from the Hawks' other arims, numbered about 100 and had set out a day before the Storm Wolves.

The arim rode northwest along the river toward Maeota Lake. The Hawks would attack or plunder targets of opportunity along the way to divert attention from the Storm Wolves. This night they were supposed to be riding south in the hope of meeting Taval and Kaplea at the encampments of Mazdak's army.

The plan was risky. They relied on mobility and surprise to keep the enemy off balance and avoid getting ensnared by a larger force.

Koia mounted her long-legged mare, a speedster named Chupla. Her job, along with three other fast riders, was to circle around the patrol's camp and cut off any enemy that tried to flee. Koia was eager to use her newly acquired bow in battle.

At the first inklings of twilight, Emily raised her spear and the Storm Rats rode out of the coulee at a walking pace. They wanted to close the distance as much as possible without being seen or heard. Strapped to her saddle on the right was a quiver that held three short javelins. Strapped to the left was her shield. From her belt hung her sagaris, dagger and puukko.

They had advanced about 100 paces when she saw someone stirring in the camp and heard voices. Emily lowered her spear and the warriors kicked their horses to full gallop. Shavaris was at her right, seated in his new saddle, wielding a long spear and a wooden shield. He leaned forward, his feet firmly in the stirrups. Donya was at her left, bow out and arrow nocked.

Shouts came from the camp and men scrambled to unhobble their horses. Most were too late. When the Storm Rats got within shooting range, four archers loosed their arrows. Emily gripped her spear and reins in one hand and readied a javelin with the other. When they got close, she hurled it and struck a man in the hip who was trying to mount his horse.

The archers reined up and let the others crash the camp with their spears. Emily didn't get the opportunity to use hers as she passed through the camp. But she knew it was a slaughter. One rider got away but Koia pursued. The Scyth scout was trying to string his bow as he galloped. Koia closed and shot three arrows. One missed but two hit and the rider went down.

Emily wheeled around. Mazda was not as quick in the turns as Hurlov but she was faster. One of the Scyth was trying to run away on foot.

Shavaris was about to skewer him when Emily shouted, "Hold! Sharvaris. Do not kill him." Shavaris complied and settled for knocking the man off his feet with the butt end of his spear.

There was enough light now that Emily could see the arims of Taval and Kaplea racing to the west. The raid was on.

~

The prisoner squatted on the ground with bound hands. The other Scyth mercenaries were killed in the assault. The prisoner was a wiry man with his bottom front teeth missing. He spoke freely when Emily questioned him in Greek. He said they hadn't expected an attack by the Wolves here.

He had heard of a raiding party to the north and knew that a large squadron was dispatched to intercept it. The encampment of the main army was due west only a few miles away. They were more worried about Kydoime's Lions raiding across the Jumasin.

"How large is Mazdak's army," Emily asked.

"Large. I do not have a head for numbers."

"Guess," she ordered.

"Five hundred horsemen, a thousand foot soldiers."

"All of them Scyth?"

"The horse warriors, yes. Mazdak is paying well. The footmen are Persian. More are coming, too, brought on ships."

"How large was the squadron dispatched north?"

The prisoner shook his head. "I was not there to see it. Bolinthos leads it. I know that."

Emily tried to visualize the situation in her head. Taval and Kaplea were headed toward an army larger than expected. The infantry was not a worry -- the Storm Wolves would not engage them -- but 500 horse warriors were a worry. Some were dispatched to chase Kraejik. How many? A lot, she thought, if Mazdak had learned anything from the defeat of his force at Lonely Hill. She guessed 250 to 300. Kraejik could be in trouble.

Emily's Storm Rats were divvying up coins and weapons found on the dead Scyth. There were three good bows. Donya offered one to Emily but she declined, thinking it better that someone who knew how to use it should have it. The additional bows did increase her unit's firepower.

"What should we do with him?" Shavaris asked, pointing to the prisoner.

"Let him be. He is no threat to us now," Emily said.

"Kaplea would kill him," Donya said.

"Perhaps, but I am not Kaplea."

Emily put her spear to the man's throat.

"If you survive and get back to your people, tell them Tilkya Niava, slayer of Kasran, spared your life."

The prisoner nodded.

"Mount!" Emily shouted. "We need to be alert and ready to ride at a moment's notice."

~

Emily scanned the horizon with her binoculars. If Mazdak's encampment was only a few miles away, Taval and Kaplea would be there now. She suppressed her sense of dread and worry. This was a warrior's life, she reminded herself. Warriors died and to do so in battle was a high honor. Still, she couldn't help but think of lying with Taval under the stars. She hoped she would have the chance to do it again.

Her thought was broken by the sight of a rider approaching from the northwest at full gallop. Adjusting the focus, she could make out a feathered cap.

"One of Kraejik's warriors," Emily shouted. "Come! We ride to him."

The eager Storm Rats followed Emily and reined up when they drew close to the Hawk warrior.

"What news?" Emily asked.

"Kraejik is beset," the warrior said. "He may be surrounded. He is trying to fight his way out of a trap."

The warrior explained that Kraejik had attacked a small force as he was headed south. When Kraejik's arim was engaged, two enemy arims closed in from the sides. Kraejik disengaged and was trying to slip the noose and head this way.

"He needs help. His retreat north is blocked and the east door is closing," the warrior said.

"How many of the enemy?" Emily asked.

"Two hundred. Maybe more. They were quite spread out when I left."

"I fear we have too few to be of much help," Donya said.

"We must try," Emily said.

She called over a Lion warrior named Thoeke. She was the fastest rider who didn't own a bow.

"Thoeke, ride west and find Taval or Kaplea," Emily said. "Tell them what is happening and that the Storm Rats are riding to help Kraejik."

"Yes, Tilkya," Thoeke said and sprinted away.

Emily ordered a young man named Pakeus to ride to the remuda in the rear and bring it up to this point.

"We will need fresh horses before this is over," she said.

"I want to fight," Pakeus objected.

"I wager you will get your chance. Now go."

To the Hawk warrior, she said: "Mount a captured horse and follow Thoeke. Taval or Kaplea will want your guidance."

Emily raised her spear and lowered it. The Storm Rats galloped northwest toward Kraejik's arim where, Emily thought, death may very well await them.

~

Emily strained to see what was going on as they approached a mass of riders headed mostly east but also a little north. Her troop rode at a cruising gallop rather than a sprint to conserve energy. Her binoculars were useless at that speed, however. When she judged they were close enough, she signaled a halt and put the lenses to her eyes.

Kraejik's arim was in a running fight with two flanking forces. The north and furthest force was the larger of the two. The Hawks were trying to veer away from it and head southeast but the flanking force to the south, perhaps 50 riders, was trying to push them northward. If the Hawks turned on the south force, they would be enveloped by the north force and wiped out. Emily saw what she needed to do. She put away her binoculars, unhitched her shield and slid her left arm through the straps.

"Bows nocked, spears ready," she ordered. "Ride fast but stay in formation. Do not shoot until I give the signal. Go!"

Nineteen riders of the Storm Rats including Emily -- eight bows and eleven spears -- galloped toward the enemy. The morning sun, just above the horizon, was behind them. The south force was exchanging shots with Kraejik's warriors. Both groups moved at a slow gallop, their horses tiring after a long chase. The large force on Kraejik's north flank had gained an angle and were closing the distance.

The Storm Rats got to within 100 paces of the south force which appeared unaware that a new set of riders was approaching them.

"Loose!" Emily shouted.

The eight archers released their arrows. One Scyth was struck and fell off his horse. Others looked around in confusion. Another volley and two more went down.

"Archers hold! Spears forward!"

Emily kicked Mazda to a sprint. Shavaris galloped beside her, both shouting war cries. The enemy riders were confused, many scrambling to switch to melee weapons, a few panicked and turned away, colliding with and disrupting those coming up from behind. Then the spears of the Storm Rats were upon them.

Emily hardly knew what was happening between the shouts, screaming and jostling horses. She could see Shavaris knocking riders off their mounts with his long spear, using the leverage provided by his stirrups and saddle. Emily jabbed at any target she could find. Bumping an enemy horse, Mazda stopped her gallop and reared up. Emily kept her saddle and caught a glimpse of what was happening. The Storm Rats were diffused within a confusion of riders.

"Break off!" She shouted. "Break off! Ride south!"

She wheeled Mazda to her left and urged her into a gallop. Mazda needed little encouragement to run away. Getting clear of the fray, she looked around -- ten spears counting herself. Someone must have fallen. A few Scyth pursued, shooting arrows, but Donya, Koia and the other archers covered their retreat with their bows.

The Scyth arim now had worse problems than the Storm Rats. Kraejik's Hawks had seized the opportunity and turned southeast. They were passing close to the disrupted Scyth warriors, raking them with arrows. Several fell. Most fled in disarray.

But the Hawks and the Storm Rats were still in trouble. From the north, about 100 Scyth warriors continued their pursuit as well as a trailing force coming up from the west. Emily signaled the Storm Rats to rally around her. She saw that Koia had an arrow sticking in her shoulder. Grimacing, Koia pulled it out and threw it to the ground. The Storm Rats galloped off to link up with the Hawks.

Emily saw Kraejik working his way toward her. She looked behind her. The Scyth bands were linking up and the scattered warriors were rallying. She could see another group of riders on the horizon riding up from the southwest.

"Where is Taval and Kaplea?" Kraejik asked.

"They should be coming. I sent word to them," Emily said.

"We cannot keep this pace much longer," he said. "Our horses are flagging."

"Keep riding southeast," she said. "I had our remuda brought this way so there will be fresh horses."

"Good girl."

~

The distant tall figure on a long-legged mare let Emily know the band coming from the southwest was Taval's arim. He veered due east and was riding hard to link up with Emily who was veering toward him. Beyond Taval's arim, Emily could see hundreds of riderless horses galloping east. By the time she reached Taval, she could make out Kaplea's red hair. Her arim was driving the herd forward.

"The Hawks were nearly trapped," Emily said. "Their horses are exhausted. I told Kraejik his people could mount fresh horses from our remuda."

"We will need to cover them when they remount," Taval said.

He sent a rider to Kaplea to let her know the situation. When they reached the remuda, the Hawks halted and the Storm Wolves assembled in a line to fire at the oncoming enemy. The Scyth were not riding fast, their horses as tired as the Hawks', but they were closing. Emily saw a Hawk warrior put his saddle on Hurlov. She had hoped to use him for the getaway because of his greater endurance. She patted Mazda's neck.

"Hang in there, girl. We have some riding yet to do."

The approaching Scyth were now massed as one army, 250 strong, Emily estimated. There were close to 200 Between the Hawks and the Storm Wolves. If the two sides closed, she thought, it would be a bloody affair with no telling who would prevail. She looked at Kaplea, whose arim had fallen into the line. Her eyes were fierce and eager for battle. Kydon snorted and stamped. Kaplea had to be worth at least 50 warriors, Emily thought, so the odds were about even.

Shavaris was beside Emily again and she put a hand on his shoulder. "You fought well," she said. "None could stand before your spear." "Thanks to you, Tilkya," he said. "Point the way and I will go."

When the enemy got to within 500 paces, Taval pulled back an arrow, aimed high and loosed. His powerful bow and extra-long draw imparted tremendous energy to the arrow and it hissed through the air. But no one could hope to shoot that far -- seconds passed then a Scyth warrior fell from his horse -- except Taval.

The Storm Wolves cheered. Kaplea let out her war cry. The pace of the enemy approach slowed and then stopped. Apparently they weren't yet ready to go toe-to-toe with the Wolves, terrors of the steppe.

~

When Kraejik's Hawk's had remounted, the whole force of Wolves galloped away to the east. The Scyth force did not pursue them though scouts followed. Taval slowed the arims to a trot then to a walk by late morning. The day grew hot. Emily took off her helmet and shoved it into a saddle bag.

The raid had gone well. The Storm Wolves bagged more than 300 horses, a significant blow to Mazdak's army. Kaplea and Taval had encountered little resistance. Most of Mazdak's cavalry had pursued Kraejik and what was left retreated behind entrenchments guarded by ranks of spearmen. The unused horses of the Persian remuda were left for the taking though it was too large for Kaplea to take them all.

Kraejik's arim had plundered a trade caravan but only relieved its frightened members of their coins and jewelry and left them their bulk goods.

Success had a price and the Hawks bore the brunt of it -- eleven warriors killed and fourteen wounded. Emily had lost a Lion spearman during her charge and Koia was wounded.

Emily saw Koia slumped in her saddle. She pointed this out to Kaplea and the two of them rode over to her.

"The arrow was poisoned," Koia said. She sweated profusely and her face was blanched.

"The vermin," Kaplea hissed.

She rode close beside Koia and helped her out of her armor. She cut away the tunic. The wound was swollen and purple. Kaplea washed it with water and applied some leaves from her pouch.

The use of poison arrows was fairly common among the Scyth and the Lovta. Kaplea and Taval didn't like poison because it offered no real battlefield advantage except that a wounded enemy was less likely to fight again. The poison was expensive -- extracted from vipers and mixed in a special paste -- and dangerous to handle. Warriors who used poison kept it in bronze containers on their belts and dipped their arrows in it before shooting.

When the sun was setting and the air cooled, Taval ordered the pace quickened. They trotted until dark then slowed to a walk. Koia now rode with Donya who held her up. After two hours of walking, Taval ordered a stop. They would rest until morning. The Hawks were spared watch duty. Taval and Emily stayed up for the first watch though they had hardly slept the last two days. They rode out a ways from camp.

"Donya tells me you fought bravely and led well," Taval said. "You saved Kraejik's ass."

"I did what I thought needed doing," Emily said.

Taval held her hand. "We should stay quiet and listen for approaching enemies."

~

Koia died during the night. The wound was not deep but the poison had spread through her body. Perhaps the arrow had punctured a vein or an artery, Emily thought. Donya tearfully wrapped Koia's body in a blanket and Taval helped lift it onto Chupla, Koia's horse. Emily fought back her own tears.

The band moved on. There was no time to mourn the dead. They had to get well away before their enemies could recoup their strength. The Storm Wolves and the Hawks galloped in the cool of the morning, walked in the heat of the day then moved fast again as evening approached. It was a grueling pace but it kept them unmolested.

On the third day, they encountered a bison heard which was being tailed by a hunting party of the Lion Tribe. They exchanged news with the Lions, traded a couple of horses for bison meat and moved on.

On the seventh day, they arrived back at Lonely Hill along the Munyasin. There was a sense of relief when they forded the river. Taval decided the Storm Wolves would rest for a few days.

They buried Koia at the top of Lonely Hill. Donya and Kaplea carefully put Koia's armor on her corpse. In the grave they placed her weapons, spindle whorl and other personal items, except the bow. It was too valuable and one of Taval's warriors received it. Emily thought it too bad that Zandra wasn't there to give the eulogy.

That evening they celebrated the success of their raid. After a trip to the hemp tent, Emily was obliged to tell of her part in the battle. She deemphasized her role and heaped praise on members of the Storm Rats for their skill and discipline. Kraejik then spoke.

"It was like Tilkya descended from the sky," he said. "They did not see her until she was upon them. The poor Scyth thought they were attacked by griffins."

Soon the warriors were shouting for Emily to dance. They never seemed to tire of her clever spear flourishes. That night she enjoyed a blissful sleep under the stars in Taval's arms.

Chapter 30 | The Wide World

THE Storm Wolves rested one more day then set out for Gipatsha. The Hawks continued to ride with them. Kraejik did not want to miss the glory as they approached with a remuda enlarged by 300 horses stolen from the great Persian captain.

The days were long and marked by brain-wearying heat. The nights were long, too. Packs of wolves tailed the band and everyone pulled shifts to keep them away from the remuda. Occasionally an antelope or bison carcass would be left behind with much of its meat to keep the wolves' occupied. At night, when minding the remuda, Emily practiced with Taval's lariat. After what seemed a hundred tries, she finally got the loop around a horse's neck.

~

The tedium of horizon-to-horizon prairie, where no hills or trees could be seen, took on a different aspect by the fifth day. The hugeness of the world sunk into Emily's bones. She was serving a stint as flank scout and no one else was around. With little specific for her senses to lock onto, her mind went into a kind of thoughtless expansiveness. It felt not so much like she was a part of the world but, rather, the world was a part of her.

Hurlov broke her meditation with a snort. A jackal trotted across her field of vision. It stopped and looked at her and Hurlov, its mouth open in a canine smile. I am the world as much as you are, it seemed to say. Emily cackled at her own hubris punctured by the laughing look of a lowly jackal.

~

Fifteen days out from Lonely Hill, they made Gipatsha. Emily guessed they had traveled nearly 300 miles. As they approached, they encountered herds of horses, sheep and some cattle. The Storm Wolves and the Hawks had to work to keep their horses separated from other remudas. Scouts went ahead to alert the city of their arrival.

The city was a collection of hundreds of tents situated on a plateau rising from the steppe. Many of the tents were quite large and supported by internal frames. Yurts, Emily thought. Before reaching the plateau, a group of warriors greeted them. It was a friendly encounter and most of the people knew each other. Emily and her stirrups drew curious glances. The warriors told Taval and Kaplea where the other Storm Wolves were camped and where they could take the remuda to graze.

The meeting with the non-warriors was joyful. Zandra cried. Arlav was vexed by the large number of new horses to be cared for and immediately went to work organizing them. Taval and Kaplea had agreed to give Kraejik half the captured horses.

Emily embraced Chunya.

"The raid went well, I see," Chunya said.

"Yes, but we lost Koia, killed by a poisoned arrow."

"That is sad. Donya must be heartbroken."

Chunya talked of people Emily needed to see. Apparently there were several Greeks living in Gipatsha. One couple in particular wanted to meet Emily and were interested in her saddle.

"You will like them, I think," Chunya said. "But first you will meet the tribal elders."

~

The sun had not risen far above the horizon when Emily, Taval and Kaplea rode their horses up to the Gipatsha plateau. The settlement bustled with people, horses, goats, donkeys, dogs and chickens. Smoke rose from many earthen furnaces. The stringent odor of metal working often caught Emily's nose when the wind was right. Tent neighborhoods were formed in sections, defining causeways that radiated from the center in spokes and circles.

Taval led them on a detour that skirted the rim of the plateau. On the eastern side, they could see the great Goljasin River. Its many channels coursed through thick marshes and woods, the first trees Emily had seen in days. Taval said the river flowed south into the Ocean of Hyrca.

That ocean must be the Caspian Sea, Emily thought, and the Goljasin was the Volga River. The city that would be known as Stalingrad would rise up somewhere around here, she thought, further north probably. There the battle of all battles would be fought. She wondered if that horror would play out again in two and a half thousand years.

They turned their horses back toward the town center. Emily wore striped trousers, a blue tunic and her felt cap. Her Persian dagger hung from her belt.

At the center of the city was a large round yurt. A blue banner with a golden wolf's head waved from a pole. A handful of Hawk warriors loitered outside. Kraejik was inside. Soon Taval and Kaplea were invited in. Emily waited outside, talking amiably with the Hawks, feeling like a fellow warrior.

Eventually she was summoned. Inside a dozen elders sat in a semicircle. Most wore richly dyed robes with intricate patterns. Many were hefty and bordered on being fat. Four of the elders were women. One of the elder women stood up.

"You are the one called Tilkya, Taval's new bride?" The woman asked. She had gray hair braided into two long tails. She was portly and her mouth was wrinkled.

"Yes," Emily answered.

"Come. Let me have a look at you."

Emily approached the woman who then fondled Emily's arms and legs, gripped her chin and looked at her teeth.

"They say you are niava, a nymph of Samvi. Is this so?"

"I believe Samvi guides my steps but I am a woman, not a spirit."

"Zandra tells us you fell from the sky and were not born in this world."

"I did fall from the sky but I was born on this earth, though very far away and in a different time," Emily said.

The woman grunted, gripped Emily's hand in both of hers and looked into her eyes. "Your husband says you are a skilled hunter, that you killed a Persian chief in single combat and led warriors into battle against great odds."

"Yes."

The woman released Emily and returned to her seat.

"You may go," she said.

Outside Emily was challenged to a slapping game by a young Hawk warrior. He was thin, wiry and quick. They were well matched but Emily won more often than not. Her reflexes were becoming well-honed and she was reading the eyes and movements of her opponents with better speed and accuracy.

Taval and Kaplea finally emerged from the yurt. Taval put Emily in a headlock and rapped her head with his knuckles.

"Cut it out," Emily reflexively said in English.

Taval laughed. "The elders like you."

"What did they say?"

"Not much, but I could tell."

"What is the Wolf Tribe coming to when we let squirrely girls into the fold?" Kaplea asked.

~

That night there was a feast on the plateau to celebrate the victories of the Storm Wolves and the Hawks. Many fires burned and many hemp tents seeped their intoxicating smoke. Wine and beer flowed freely. A bull was sacrificed and Emily and Taval stripped to their trousers and painted themselves in blood as did Kaplea and many others. Donya sang while musicians played. She sang the praises of her lost Koia and her honorable passage to the next world as a warrior who died in battle.

Kaplea recreated the dance she performed on Emily's wedding night and Emily responded with hers, ending with her trademark tongue waggle. Taval performed his storm dance with sword and shield which Emily had not seen. It began precise and elegant, much like Pantheras' technique then exploded into a whirling fury, the bright steel of his long sword flashing like lightning.

Later, after much wine, Taval picked up Emily like a sack of beans.

"Where is Zandra?" He bellowed. "We have business."

He found the he-priestess sitting near a hemp tent, swaying back and forth in a kind of ecstatic trance.

"Zandra, you drunken goat," Taval said, putting Emily down in front of him. "I will be married to none other than an equal. Make it so!"

Zandra snapped out of his trance and stood. He looked at Taval and touched his face with his hand.

"My poor Taval," he said. "I do not have the power to make you her equal. You must live as you are and be content."

Taval laughed so hard, he staggered and fell to the ground. Emily looked around, found Kaplea and waved her over. Together they helped Taval to his feet.

"Husband, you are drunk," Emily said. "It is time to return to our tent."

"Yes, my wife."

~

Emily sat at a table under a canopy that shaded the morning sun. With her were Chunya, Shavaris, and a Greek couple -- Akakios and Zenobia. Three children chased each other around the yard. Nearby was a yurt, a stone forge and a large, open tent. Akakios was a metal smith and Zenobia a leather craftswoman. They ate cakes and drank fermented milk. On the table were two saddles -- Emily's and Shavaris'.

"Your leather work is wanting," Zenobia said. She was a hefty woman with dark hair. "But these footholds are ingenious. Stirrups, you call them?"

"Yes," Emily said.

Shavaris, the stocky Lion warrior, talked about how useful the stirrups were and the supporting lips of the saddles, how he could use his spear with much greater leverage. He boasted about the warriors he had unhorsed during the brief battle with the Scyth mercenaries.

"The lips should be built up more," Emily said. "To better secure the rider."

"Yes, that makes sense," Zenobia said.

"Shavaris and I have talked much about this. If a formation of warriors could be equipped with these saddles, and horses well armored, and the warriors carried thick shields and heavy spears, it would be a potent weapon," Emily said.

"I am not sure I see what you mean," Akakios said. A smallish man with a trim beard, he had a narrow frame but thick arms.

"Warriors so equipped could charge their enemies at speed, using weight and momentum to scatter them," Emily said.

"I suppose that would be true," Akakios said.

"What would it take to equip such a formation?" Emily asked.

"How many warriors?" Akakios returned.

"Thirty or forty to start with."

"By when?"

"Next spring."

"It could be done. I would need to hire help."

"What would it cost?"

"A pretty sum. I would need to do some figuring."

"I will speak with my husband and Kaplea."

They talked more about the design of the saddles. Zenobia had many ideas. For horse armor, Emily suggested wedge-shaped bronze plates for the front and scales for the sides. Eventually the conversation turned to other things.

"Why do you choose to live with the Wolf Tribe?" Emily asked the couple.

"We came to Novorosa from Miletus, looking for a fresh start," Zenobia said. "But life was too constricting for me. I do not want to spend my days confined to the gynaeceum spinning yarn and gossip. So we took up with a caravan of Lovta traders and eventually came here. We like the way men and women mingle freely and do what they want to do."

"So do I," Emily said.

~

That night Emily pleasured Taval as energetically as she could. When he had spent himself, she lay in his arms.

"Husband," she said. "I have a favor to ask."

"Anything you like, Vashakiz."

Emily looked into his eyes and smiled.

~

Arlav, Kaplea, Taval, and Emily stood outside Arlav's tent. Emily scraped lines in the dirt with a stick which kicked up little streams of dust carried away by the relentless steppe wind.

"A force so equipped would give us an advantage. It would not replace archers or javelineers but support them, give us options we would not otherwise have,"

"They would slow us down," Kaplea said. "Our strength is swiftness. We must preserve our speed."

"The equipment could be stowed in wagons or on mules and used only in need. It would not slow us down any more than the rest of our gear. Think of it. The force could charge even a phalanx, break up the formation, and leave it vulnerable to our arrows and javelins."

"Do we really need it?" Taval asked. "We have proven ourselves masters of the steppe."

"We are masters today," Arlav said. "What about tomorrow? The Sarma press us from the north, the Persians from the west and the south. The Greeks are fickle people. They could turn against us and they breed like rodents. We are not so numerous as we once were. I think it wise to take what advantage we can. Perhaps this is why the gods saw fit to bring Tilkya to us."

Emily suppressed a smile. She knew she would have her way. Arlav was on her side.

"Can we afford it?" Taval asked.

"Taval and Kaplea," Arlav answered. "Your exploits have made us rich in goods, silver and gold. We have more than I know what to do with. Yes, we can afford it."

~

The Storm Wolves needed to move on, otherwise their large remuda would overgraze the grasslands surrounding Gipatsha. The band now had more than 200 Persian-bred horses. They would struggle to survive the hard winter of the steppe. Arlav recommended taking them south and trading them off. Taval and Kaplea agreed.

They lingered in Gipatsha a few more days. Arlav was negotiating several agreements with Akakios and Zenobia plus suppliers and labor for Emily's heavy cavalry. Shavaris and two of his Lion friends would stay in Gipatsha, as well as Kellvan, to oversee the project and recruit suitable warriors.

Many young warriors, attracted by the successes and bounty of the Storm Wolves, wanted to join the band. They took in twenty. Arlav didn't want to provision for more and didn't want to stretch the capacity of their wintering grounds. Most of the recruits were relegated to the Storm Rats and they spent a couple of hot days training in formation riding. While raw and inexperienced, the Storm Rats were becoming a genuine arim and Emily was proud to be its commander. Donya rode with them as Emily's second. All told, the Storm Wolves ranks had swollen to 150 warriors.

Kraejik's Hawks departed Gipatsha to go trade with the Eagles, a Lovta tribe that roamed the steppe east of the Goljasin. Before the Hawks left, Arlav bought their Persian horses and added them to the Storm Wolves remuda.

~

One evening, Unkati, one of the tribal elders, invited Emily into her large yurt. Several candles illuminated an interior of exotic rugs, hanging beads and many ornaments, including a fine Greek vase depicting a scene of Scythians battling griffins.

"Sit," Unkati ordered. "And remove your tunic."

Emily obeyed and Unkati produced a bowl of ink and a tattooing needle.

"From all I hear, you have proven yourself a hard worker, a brave warrior and a leader, seemingly wise beyond your years. Even fierce Kaplea respects you and that is something. Perhaps Zandra is correct; you are touched by Apma."

Unkati rubbed a balm on Emily's left shoulder, dipped the needle into the ink and started poking her. Emily winced.

"Our tribe needs people like you," the old woman continued. "I hope you bear Taval many children."

Emily flushed, still apprehensive about getting pregnant. She didn't reply.

"Wherever you came from, it is clear you are of noble stock. Zandra saw this and gave you a noble name. I see it and mark you with a noble stag."

"Thank you," Emily said.

"I hear you had council with Kydoime, just the two of you, in the field between the Lions and the Wolves."

"Yes."

"Do you consider her a friend?"

"I suppose. She, in a way, protects my friends in Artemios."

"If she called for aid, would you go to her?"

"It would not be for me to decide. I would not abandon Taval or Kaplea if that is what you mean. But I favor aiding Kydoime. The Lions and Artemios are bastions against the Persians. If they succumbed would the Wolves be far behind?"

"I am glad to know where you stand. Soon the Wolves will have to decide. Some favor Kydoime, others favor Takahal, Huraslan's nephew. Takahal would give up Artemios to the Persians in exchange for great wealth and generous trading terms."

"Who do you favor, esteemed Unkati?" Emily asked.

"Kydoime. She shines with the spirit of the Lovta and is not seduced by Persian riches. But others, like Kraejik, favor Takahal. They fought together against the Persians many years ago. Your Taval, still a teenager, fought in Kraejik's arim. Kraejik was his mentor."

Emily realized Unkati was worried which way Taval would fall on the issue. Would his loyalty to his old war leader trump other considerations? Emily didn't think so but remained uncertain about the bonds these people had with each other. Unkati was looking to Emily to be an ally when it came time to decide.

~

The Storm Wolves moved on, following the Goljasin to the estuary that emptied into the Hyrca Ocean, the Caspian Sea. There they camped near a fishing village. Its inhabitants were experts at catching the sturgeon that grazed the brackish shallows of the vast delta. For the first time in Emily's life, she ate caviar and enjoyed its delicious saltiness.

The band followed the shores of the Hyrca for a day but the land was desolate, very hot and offered poor grazing. The Caspian Sea, Emily recalled, was below sea level. It was a lonely ocean, cut off from its brethren.

The band turned inland in search of higher ground, better grass and better water. Heading southwest they skirted an area of low but rugged escarpments then turned due south, spending two days on a barren plain that offered little water and poor grazing.

From time to time, they would see ponds of thick oil that seeped up from the ground. The Caucasian oil fields, Emily thought. The oil was of limited use in this time but so much prized in the distant future. Hitler had sent an army to take it. Emily just wanted to get away from its noxious smell.

Eventually the grass grew richer and the streams less alkaline. They made it to a river the Lovta called the Unyasin. It flowed from the mountains to the Hyrca. They rested there for two days to let the horses graze and refresh. Emily went on her first bison hunt. Being a beginner she was mostly just in the way. Nevertheless the chase was exhilarating. She also saw lions up close. Wolves no longer trailed the remuda but now they had to worry about the big cats. The band forded the river and continued south.

In this land of rolling hillocks thick with grass, the Storm Wolves kept themselves on war alert. Roving bandits were not unknown and an incursion of Persian cavalry was possible. The Persians controlled the fortress city of Darband many miles to the southeast that guarded the gap between the Kaukasos Mountains and the Hyrca. It was the gateway to the heart of the Persian empire.

At least one arim always stayed ready for battle. Emily's Storm Rats pulled the night shift most of the time. She got little sleep and it made for weary days in the saddle. One night a lioness got one of the horses that had strayed too far from the remuda. Emily heard the struggle and galloped toward it. The lioness sprinted off into the darkness. Emily hurled a javelin but only struck the ground. The horse was mortally wounded and shrieking. She put it out of its misery with the spike of her sagaris.

The death cries and the blood would attract hyenas and probably more lions. Her Storm Rats rallied around her. Using several ropes, they dragged the carcass about a half mile from camp. Shadowy dog shapes circled around and yelped as they untied the ropes. The horses were jittery and they hurried back to camp. She could hear snarls and yapping as the hyenas and lions played out their drama over the spoils.

The whole camp was awake and before the sun rose, they moved out.

~

Late the next day, bone weary from the night's excitement, Emily could hardly keep her eyes open in the saddle. Taval rode beside her.

"Look up my lazy wife," he said.

She did and was refreshed to see the purple ridges and peaks of mountains. She had come to wonder if they ever existed. There was something more to the world than endless steppe.

A day later they came to another river, the Garusin. They were in the foothills now and trees became more abundant. They followed the river upstream west and then south toward the mountains. After a day of this they came to a walled settlement nestled at the feet of two large hills.

The town was called Shketa and the people there were known as the Moshi. Taval said they had lived in these hills and mountains for centuries. The walls were earthen works topped with wooden ramparts. The gates opened and emissaries dressed in colorful tunics and trousers rode out to greet them. Taval said the Storm Wolves were here to trade horses. The emissaries informed him where they could camp and said they were free to enjoy what the town had to offer.

The next day Taval, Kaplea, Arlav and Halaba, who spoke the Moshi language, went into the city to find buyers for the Persian mounts. Emily was left in charge of the camp which was set up near a small tributary stream. She sent out the usual scouts and assigned shifts of horse herders. Her directions weren't really necessary; the activities were a matter of routine. Arlav had distributed shares of coin and gold and warriors and non-warriors alike went in shifts into the city to ply its market and enjoy its entertainments.

Taval returned after dark while Emily was getting ready for bed. The tent was comfortable, the late summer air cooler in the hills.

"We should get good prices for our stock," he said. "The Persians, they say, are greedy for all the horses they can acquire."

344

"We steal Persian horses at one place and sell them back at another," Emily said.

"It is no sorrow to me, wife, that one end of the empire doesn't know what happens at the other."

Taval crawled into bed and they made love for the first time in many days.

~

Emily and Kaplea stood just inside the entrance of a large tent erected on the edge of Shketa's market square. They looked on at the other women of the Storm Wolves who had come to town with them. They were ogling at the array of fabrics and ready-made garments on display. Chunya was there as well as Akkea, the chief cook, Mahalea, the wiry scout, and Thoeke, the young Lion warrior in Emily's arim.

Thoeke was tall, lean and shapely with thick locks of black hair. She reminded Emily of Kydoime, a young version with no battle scars. The other women delighted in adorning Thoeke with fancy gowns because she wore them so well. Emily was amused by it for a bit. She wondered if Taval would like it if she wore such feminine finery. Soon she became bored and so did Kaplea.

"They make good honey mead here," she said. "Let us go find a bowl."

Emily told Chunya they would meet them back at camp and asked her to pick out something Taval might like.

Emily and Kaplea walked through the market toward an open pavilion where food and beverages were served. The town was comprised mostly of wooden buildings on earthen foundations. The people wore colorful long robes and head covers. Women appeared to mingle freely. The men mostly went about unarmed except perhaps for daggers at their belts. The only soldiers she saw were on the ramparts. They carried spears and bows and wore leather cuirasses and helmets.

Emily wore her blue cap and a tunic without trousers. When not riding she found it more comfortable in warm weather. Her sagaris and dagger hung from her belt. Kaplea had on a burnt-orange tunic with a paisley-like pattern of reds and blues. She carried a hammer and knife as well but, as usual, wore no head cover. People would gawk at her red hair and respectfully step aside as she walked through the crowd. She was known here and feared.

The pavilion covered several long tables with benches and a long serving counter. Emily and Kaplea ordered mead and sat at the end of one of the tables. There were a few rough-looking men at the other end -- long beards, hide tunics and axes on their belts. Mountain people, Emily thought, coming down to trade in the settlement. They looked like the types that might pick a fight but they mostly kept their eyes and their talk to themselves.

Emily and Kaplea sat side by side and watched people mill about the market square and come and go from the pavilion. Two men approached them carrying mead bowls.

"Pardon us, ladies, but do you mind if we sit here? It is getting crowded," the younger and smaller of the two said in Greek.

"Be our guests," Kaplea said in an uninviting tone.

"Um, well, thank you then," the young one said.

The older one nodded and they sat down, the young one opposite Kaplea. He was thin, not very tall and had a thick mop of dark brown hair and a beard trimmed in Greek fashion. The older man was taller, stouter, had gray hair and a beard that was not so well trimmed.

"My name is Diodis and this is my uncle, Gaios," the young one said. "We are travelers from Ephesos. May I ask your names?"

Emily waited for Kaplea to respond but she just glared at the young man who fidgeted under her gaze.

"My name is Tilkya and this is my war leader, Kaplea," Emily said to break the silence. She reached out and shook the men's hands.

"War leader? That is fantastic," the young one said. "You are Scythian warriors, no? We were told we might see female warriors if we came here and now we meet them face to face."

"We are Lovta, not Scythian." Kaplea growled.

"Um, yes, my apologies. I meant no offense. Quite the opposite. You are wondrous to behold," the young one, Diodis, said.

"There are people called the Scyth that inhabit lands east of Thrace and north of the Euxine," Emily said. "The Lovta are a kindred people."

"That is excellent," Diodis said. "Just the kind of knowledge we seek. Tell me, is it true you drink the blood of your enemies?"

"Only those who pester us with questions," Kaplea said.

Diodis was taken aback by Kaplea's menacing tone. Gaios, the older one, chuckled.

"You must excuse my nephew," Gaios said. "He is boundlessly curious."

"Ephesos," Emily said. "I have heard of the city but do not know where it is."

"It is in the land of Ionia some distance north of Miletus," Gaios answered. "It is near the great Temple of Artemis."

Emily wondered if Kallisto had ever visited that temple. She was Lydian so likely would have. Emily was going to ask if the men knew who Kallisto was but thought better of it.

"Artemis is a goddess we honor," Emily said, "though we know her as Samvi."

"Samvi? I had not heard her called that before," Diodis said. "What other gods do you honor?"

To Emily's surprise, Kaplea answered and talked at some length about the Lovta gods. Diodis paid rapt attention and seemed unable to take his eyes off her. The conversation continued past noon and they ate bowls of soup and bread for lunch.

In their travels Gaios and Diodis had been as far south as Egypt and as far east as Persepolis. They had decided to take the Darial Pass over the mountains in the hopes of seeing the women warriors of Scythia. Gaios was a poet and storyteller like Kallisto's husband, Nikanor. Diodis aspired to be a philosopher and wanted to write a great compendium of the peoples of the world and their histories.

"Where will your band, the Storm Wolves as you say, go from here?" Diodis asked.

"West a ways to find good wintering grounds," Kaplea said.

"There is a caravan leaving here in a few days to take the pass to Armenia. We had planned to travel with it but perhaps we could travel with the Storm Wolves for a time. There is so much to learn and it seems we have only scratched the surface."

"Diodis," Gaios said. "Your forwardness astounds even me."

"Think of the knowledge we would gain and the stories you could tell. The salons of Miletus would beg for our attendance."

"Winter is not so pleasant in this part of the world," Kaplea said. "You would find it hard to endure."

"We have endured much in our travels," Diodis said. "We can provision ourselves and even wear trousers if we must. What do you say, mighty Kaplea? We would not be a burden to you."

Diodis put his hand on Kaplea's. She did not withdraw it.

"Can you ride a horse?"

"I have a few times," Diodis said. "Gaios is, well, better on his feet. We have a sturdy cart and mules. We could keep up with your wagon train."

"I do not think so," Kaplea said. "We have too many mouths to feed as it is."

"We can bring our own food. We would lend a hand in any way that we could."

Kaplea stood. "We should get back to camp, Tilkya."

"Say you will think about it," Diodis pleaded.

"We will mention it to our other leaders," Emily said. "I would not be too hopeful."

~

Emily and Kaplea left the pavilion and walked toward the city gate.

"Those two are peculiar," Kaplea said. "Greeks are a funny lot."

"You like him," Emily said.

"Like who?"

"Diodis, the small one."

"He is pleasing to look at."

"Ha! Taval may like squirrelly girls but you like squirrelly men."

"Say a word of this to anybody and I will feed you to the lions and be glad of it."

~

That evening Emily told Taval about Gaios and Diodis.

"They asked if they could spend the winter with us," she said.

Taval mulled the idea for a moment.

"Winter can get very dull," he said. "A Greek poet and a philosopher would help pass the time. I'll talk to Arlav. I say why not if Kaplea is willing."

"I think she will be."

Chapter 31 | Winter

THE Storm Wolves followed a course west by northwest over rolling foothills. Gaios and Diodis traveled with the wagon train. They had two mules, one pulled a cart, the other walked beside them. The pair preferred walking. Both used staves and on their belts wore pouches and utility knives. They were the Wolves' pet Greeks, Emily thought, or perhaps the Wolves were their pet Scythians.

Before they left Shketa, the traders came for the Persian horses. Emily gave up Mazda though it saddened her to do so. She was a good horse. As compensation Arlav let her pick a mount from the communal stock. She chose a lively sorrel mare with a flowing dark mane and tail. Not as long-legged as some but she had good agility, acceleration and stamina. She resembled the plastic horse she had given Taval on their wedding night. She named her Polly.

Polly didn't like Emily's saddle at first and bucked her off. Emily stayed mounted on the second effort and Polly acquiesced. She was a willful horse that needed firm handling but she was eager to run. There was broad agreement among the tribe that Polly was a funny name for a horse.

~

Three days out of Shketa, Emily rode with Taval in a scouting party of twenty warriors. Traversing a low section of a ridge, they came to a long valley with a small river coursing through it. The valley was flanked by grassy ridges dotted with a few bushy junipers. At the south end of the valley was the edge of an oak forest.

"This will be our winter home," Taval said.

The party rode down into the valley and followed the river upstream. The rich grass had not seen much grazing. As they neared the forest, they saw an encampment. A dozen or so men scurried about, having seen the Storm Wolves coming. Emily counted two horses and three mules. The men, wearing hide tunics and tattered cloaks, grabbed their spears and axes. Two had simple wooden bows. The Storm Wolves readied their bows in response. Taval signaled them to hold fire and halted the party about 30 paces out.

"Ho there," he bellowed in Greek. "I am Taval, leader of the Storm Wolves. This is our wintering ground. You will have to leave."

The men murmured among themselves. None wore armor. They would be no match for even the scouting party. One of the men stepped forward.

"Who are you to say we cannot stay?" He shouted.

"I told you who I am. My war band will be here before the sun sets. If you are still here, there will be no parley. We will kill you. That is all I am going to say."

At that point the scouting party turned and rode away. Taval stationed two lookouts on a ridge. Back at the main column, Taval told Kaplea about the men.

"Bandits, no doubt," she said. "You should have killed them. They might be trouble later."

"I do not think so," Taval said. "If they become a problem, we will kill them then."

When the column arrived at the valley, the men were gone.

~

The Storm Wolves set up camp in the usual manner but the next day Arlav assigned work details to build three large yurts on earthen foundations that already existed from previous winters. In need, if the weather became very cold, all members of the band could sleep in them, drawing warmth from each other and the fire pits within.

Shortly after their arrival, people started coming down with colds. Emily figured they must have picked up the bug in Shketa. A few people became feverish, otherwise the symptoms were not severe. Taval caught it but Emily did not.

One day it rained and Kaplea decided it was a good day to practice slinging from horseback. Bows did not work well if their strings became wet. Slinging from a horse was tricky and required an overhead twirl. One had to be careful not to hit the horse in the head. No one was very accurate with the technique but when bullets were hurled in mass volleys, they could be effective against enemy formations. It was a particularly miserable drill for those who had colds, including Taval who did not shirk the exercise.

Emily obtained a few mint leaves from Akkea and brewed a tea which Taval appreciated. She gave him aspirin which he appreciated more. She lay in his arms and didn't get much sleep as he snored through the night.

~

The Wolves sent out two hunting parties to scout for bison and antelope. They also sent sections of the remuda onto the prairie to graze in order to conserve the grass in the valley for winter.

Taval stayed at the camp and helped with the yurts. He wanted to get over his cold before he went hunting. Emily mostly worked with Chunya on clothing. As part of the deal for the Persian horses, Arlav had purchased a stock of furs. Chunya, Emily and others sewed them into cloaks and caps.

The afternoons were leisurely. They had come to the wintering grounds early and there was no particular hurry. Emily often practiced with her weapons. While slinging at a tree stump, Diodis joined her. He was good with a sling and knew a variety of techniques.

"We found it best when traveling to appear as non-threatening as possible so we do not carry swords or bows. But we do want to be able to defend ourselves if necessary," he said.

"A sling is an excellent weapon," Emily said. "But not so good in close quarters."

"That is why we have our staves," Diodis said. "They are good weapons. The Egyptians fight wonderfully with them."

"Shall we spar? You can show me."

"My pleasure."

Diodis was good, very nearly her match. In fact, his technique was better but he didn't quite have her reflexes and instincts.

"I have not seen a woman fight so well," Diodis said. "Gaios might give you a tougher time than me."

"There are women in camp more skilled than myself," Emily said.

She told him of the time Kaplea killed four men with her hammer.

"Incredible," he said. "She bestrides the world like a war goddess. Do you truly believe no man could best her, not even your giant of a husband?"

"Who can say for sure? Taval has a long reach and is strong as a bear but he does not have Kaplea's skill or quickness. I do know a man, Byon, a Thracian warrior, who taught me the basics. He could get into a fighting trance. In that state, he would be very hard to defeat. Even so, I am not sure he could stand up to Kaplea's ferocity."

"A Thracian warrior? Where did you meet him?"

"In Artemios, a Greek colony on the Euxine. I lived there for a time."

"I have heard of Artemios, a new project of the Phocasian and Ampeliosian clans. Why were you there? Were you not born Lovta?"

"No. I am a newcomer to the tribe."

"Where are you from?"

"It is a long story."

~

Taval thought it time that Emily learn to shoot a bow. Using a three-fingered loose and setting the arrow on the left side of the bow, she could shoot fairly well. But the Lovta technique was to shoot from the right side using a thumb release. A ring was used to protect the thumb. In skilled hands, the technique allowed for very rapid shooting. Emily was not so skilled. Her first shots were wild and she struggled to achieve meaningful accuracy.

"You will never challenge Aella but you will improve with time," Taval reassured her.

She had to borrow bows to practice. She liked Mahalea's the best because its draw was manageable. Donya's was just at the limit of her strength. Kaplea's and the men's bows were too strong. Taval's was impossible.

She learned how to care for a bow and keep the string in good condition as well as how to fletch arrows and mount heads. They employed two basic types -- leaf-shaped broadheads for hunting, and narrow warheads made for penetrating armor.

~

Gaios and Zandra became friends and spent much time together. The Greek guests were at first put off by this strange man who dressed and acted like a woman but Zandra won them over with the earnestness with which he talked about the Lovta gods and people.

Emily noticed that Donya was attracted to Gaios and sat by him whenever she could at the fires. Gaios taught her Greek songs which she sang beautifully. Emily sometimes joined in.

Kaplea returned from a hunting trip with a wagon full of bison and antelope hides. Taval was over his cold so went out with his own hunting party. Emily chose to stay behind and hunt in the forest instead, mostly bagging small game with her sling.

With Kaplea back at camp, Diodis tailed her and peppered her with questions. She often expressed her annoyance and threatened to dismember him, feed him to the lions or drink his blood, but she never really shooed him away.

One evening around the fire, while people spun hemp into a yarn that would be used to make cordage, Kaplea told the story of the Battle of Lonely Hill. Folks were astonished when Diodis retrieved a sheet of papyrus, an inkwell and a feather and began to write. Emily figured he must be taking notes.

"Do not be alarmed," Gaios said. "Diodis likes to scribble on his sheets. He believes knowledge can be confined within marks on paper. He does not understand that written knowledge is false wisdom. True wisdom can only be conveyed through speech."

"Gaios, you are old and senile," Diodis said. "Writing will surely elevate mankind to great heights as generations of knowledge accumulate and are preserved."

Kaplea put a hand on Diodis' back. "Are you writing what I said?"

"Not as such. I am writing a poem about you."

"To compose with a pen and in silence. It is an insult to the muses," Gaios said. "But perhaps you could share it with us."

"It is only one verse," Diodis said then read the poem:

Kaplea races the wind on her golden mare
The gods envy her flaming red hair

354

Her enemies flee in panic and terror
But her arrows find them without error
Four men with staves cannot compete
Her hammer lays them dead at her feet
She is the tiger that hunts with wolves

Emily was about to laugh but saw others nodding their approval. Kaplea was blushing.

"Not bad, young man," Gaios said. "But I recommend you stick to philosophy."

Diodis waved the sheet in the air to dry the ink then handed it to Kaplea.

"You may have it, noble Kaplea," he said. "Though it is not much."

Kaplea handled the sheet reverently, staring at the letters. Emily knew she couldn't read them. The Lovta did have a simple system of writing, pictograms that conveyed basic information -- direction, location, good hunting, enemies near and so forth. Messages could be carved on pieces of wood or left on poles for others to find. But they had nothing like Greek writing.

Kaplea whispered something in Diodis' ear then went to her tent.

"Do not fold it or roll it until the ink is set," Diodis said.

Emily thought it best not to visit Kaplea that night. She likely would not be alone.

~

The temperature cooled as autumn deepened. The yurts were complete. Kavad, the band's multi-skilled craftsman, made a furnace of stones and earth. With it he could repair bronze tools, armor scales and helmets. Several trees were cut down to lay in a store of wood for the winter fires and to make charcoal.

Emily continued to hunt in the forest and Mahalea became her frequent companion. Not much of a talker, she was a good tracker and could be nearly as stealthy as Emily. They contented themselves with small game at first. Mahalea was deadly accurate with her bow. They did notice plenty of deer sign -- antler rubs, scat and tracks -- and occasionally spotted one. The rut was near and it would be a good time to bag a buck. The deer here were large, had red coats and could have enormous racks.

Signs pointed to an area of reeds where a deer was bedding and the tracks suggested it was large. The next day Mahalea set up in ambush along a game trail and Emily circled wide behind the bedding area hoping to drive the animal back toward Mahalea. The plan worked and Mahalea downed a 12-pointer. She was proud as could be. They boiled the flesh off the stag's head and mounted it above the entrance of one of the yurts.

~

Gaios and Diodis asked Emily to take them hunting and one morning, while Mahalea was out scouting, she obliged. The Greeks brought their walking sticks and their slings but were entirely too noisy and talked too much to do any real hunting. She decided to consider the outing a pleasant walk and a chance to explore. They followed the river into the forest a ways then up a feeder stream trickling down from a ridge. They crossed over its crest and descended into stands of tall beeches.

"Why are we going this way?" Diodis asked.

"I had not gone beyond this ridge yet. I thought I would see what is down here," she said.

She walked with her spear and kept its wicker cover on.

"I find it interesting that you have been with the Wolf Tribe only a short time yet you are a leader among them," Diodis said.

"They believe she is touched by Apma, the great earth goddess," Gaios said.

"Is that so, Tilkya?" Diodis asked.

They came to a deadfall. Emily set her spear against the log and sat down, taking a swig from her water skin. The two men joined her.

"That I am touched by the gods may be as good an explanation as any," she said. "I was touched by something well beyond my comprehension. That I know."

"Tell us."

Emily thought for a moment. "Imagine you were a man, a warrior, seasoned by many campaigns, and one day you woke up in the body of a woman."

"It would be like a curse of an angry god," Diodis said.

"Among the Greeks you might see it that way. You would no longer be able to follow your nature as a warrior," Emily said.

"You would be compelled to spend your days with women and do women's work," Diodis said.

"Precisely."

"Do you believe this really happened to you?" Diodis asked. "That you were born a man and now live as a woman?"

"I thought so but now I am not sure. It is like I was born both."

"Do you think of yourself as a man or a woman?"

"A woman. The man is just a memory."

"Fantastic," Diodis said. "Impossible, of course, but fantastic."

"Diodis does not comprehend poetic truths, only literal ones," Gaios said. "What you say does fit your character, Tilkya. You have a presence beyond your size and sex."

"Does sex really have that much to do with it?" Emily asked. "Have you ever met a man with a presence more forceful than Kaplea's? And you have not met Kydoime, a noblewoman of the Lion Tribe who commands many arims."

"True, true," Gaios said. "Much food for thought. I am glad to be able to spend time with the Lovta, such a different kind of people yet people all the same."

Dioids shook his head. "Living with the Lovta makes me think 'man' and 'woman' are false distinctions."

"The distinctions are not false," Emily said. "But it is false to think of them as opposites."

~

Taval returned from his hunting excursion with more hides and meat. The take included a large lion that Taval killed with his bow. The lion's hide was draped over a mule and its head bobbed to the mule's trot. It invoked a sense of dread in Emily.

She went to her tent early that evening and put on the gown Chunya had bought for her at Shketa. It was white, made from fine linen and styled like a Greek chiton. Narrow shoulder straps widened to her breasts and a strophion pushed them up. The skirt portion hung to her ankles and it was hemmed with gold. Chunya had bought a gold belt to wear with it and a gold chain for a necklace that went well with her songbird earrings. She put on a little eye shadow, lipstick and perfume. She thought the dress might look silly given her face and arms were so ruddy with sun and the rest of her skin was white. She hoped Taval would like it. She had been eager for him to return.

When Taval stepped in and looked at her, a smirk crossed his face and his silver eyes had that mischievous gleam. Emily drank in the reaction.

"You like it?" Emily turned around for him.

"Mmm"

"That figures," she said. "What you really want is a delicate little Greek girl."

"That is true, but you will suffice."

Emily slugged him then poured him a bowl of wine.

"Did that lion attack the horses?" She asked.

"No. I had an opportunity and I took the shot. One of my best, I pierced its lungs at a hundred paces. I wish you could have seen it."

"It worries me," Emily said. "There are people where I come from who think it is bad luck to kill a large predator like a lion or a tiger."

"You are a nymph of Samvi. I should bear that in mind. We will sacrifice a horse to appease the goddess and all will be well."

Taval leaned over and kissed her. Soon she forgot her misgivings.

~

The days grew colder and rain came frequently. When not serving stints tending horses or patrolling with her Storm Rats, Emily hunted, worked on clothing and practiced weapons skills.

When it was raining, people spent most of their time in the yurts, working on various crafts and kibitzing. Gaios entertained people with stories, songs and poems while he whittled away at odd bits of wood, making little figurines. He made for Emily a fox's head which she mounted on the bronze clasp that held her green cloak. Mostly he gave them out as toys for the children. Diodis continued his endless questioning. He currently was milking Zandra of all the Lovta lore he could get.

One day a patrol returned escorting a party of Lions. The party's leader was Uratan, Kydoime's husband. Emily remembered seeing him the previous year in Artemios. He and Taval greeted each other outside the main yurt.

"Uratan, it is good to see you," Taval said. "I hope you do not plan to steal our horses."

"Some other time, noble Taval. I am here to counsel and exchange news." Uratan looked at Emily. "This is your wife, Tilkya?"

Taval introduced them and they shook hands.

"You appear to be thriving among the Wolves, Tilkya," Uratan said. "You are much on people's minds these days."

"She bears the stag of nobility given to her by Unkati at Gipatsha," Taval said.

"Which is as it should be," Uratan said.

The Storm Wolves feasted that night with their Lion guests. Uratan was greatly amused by the presence of Gaios and Diodis. Diodis, of course, asked him many questions.

~

The sun was out the next day and the band's leaders rode to the crest of the west ridge to counsel with Uratan. The view was marked by forested hills to the west backed by high, snow-capped mountains. Their cloaks flapped in the chilly morning breeze.

"Huraslan is near death," Uratan said. "It is unlikely he will survive the winter."

"When he goes, will Kydoime become queen?" Kaplea asked.

"That is Huraslan's desire and she has the support of the elders," Uratan said. "But Takahal is strong and tries to make a case to the people that he would be the better ruler. He favors peace with the Persians. He would give Artemios to them in exchange for preferred trading privileges with the empire."

"Will Takahal make war on Kydoime if she is made queen?" Taval asked.

"We think so, yes."

"Does Kydoime have the strength to defeat him?"

"Yes, as it stands now," Uratan said. "But many Lion warriors like the idea of an alliance with the Persians. They would have the opportunity to earn glory and riches by fighting in the empire's wars."

"Will Takahal have Mazdak's help to gain the kingship?" Emily asked.

"We believe he will."

"Kydoime wants an alliance with the Wolves," Taval said.

"Yes, to preserve the independence of the Lovta," Uratan said.

"When spring comes, we will return to Gipatsha," Taval said. "I am inclined to fight for Kydoime and will encourage other Wolves to do so."

"I am glad to hear you say it, Taval," Uratan said. "I can ask for no more."

"Does Kydoime's offer of free access to Artemios still stand?" Arlav asked.

"It does, Arlav, my friend. I cannot overstate what it would mean for Taval and Kaplea to fight with us. Their names are known throughout the kingdom. The raid on Mazdak's encampment was a marvel and the slaughter at Lonely Hill has put the Scyth in fear of the Wolves. The Greeks call you the Wild Scythians."

"Tilkya also played a part in those victories," Taval said.

"So I have heard," Uratan said. "Many say she is a sorceress."

"I'm no sorceress." Emily said. "I toss a javelin with my hands like everyone else."

"Regardless, Kydoime would be pleased if you fought with us."

"I have friends in Artemios. Do you have word of them?" Emily asked.

"They are safe for the time being," Uratan said. "We know the Persians have become keenly interested in you and your friends. Who knows what steps they will take? Agathon smells war coming and is determined to fight and so is the new oikist, Pantheras. I will bring them news of you if you would like."

"Yes, please do."

They talked on for a while longer, then Uratan and Taval rode off together to chase a group of antelope they spotted on the plain to the north. Emily and the others returned to camp.

~

It was a cold night but not so cold that Emily and Taval needed to sleep in the warmth of the yurt. They lay under several blankets, gaining warmth from each other.

"Do you believe Kydoime has the strength to hold off Takahal and the Persians?" Emily asked.

"I fear not. Uratan talked of plans for retreat if the need arises."

"That does not bode well."

"You want to help your friends in Artemios."

"Yes, but I am married to you and bear the marks of the Wolves."

"We could ride to Artemios now, offer our arims to Agathon."

"No. Agathon would welcome us but our numbers are too few to make much difference. We would lose our advantage of mobility and surprise. Uratan and Kydoime are right to plan for retreat. Bend to the initial onslaught, let the enemy become overconfident then choose the moment to strike back."

"Artemios may fall in the meantime."

"Perhaps, but it will not go easily. My friend, Alex, will be helping Agathon. He is much better at making things than I."

"What do you mean?"

"The Persians may find nasty surprises waiting for them."

~

Uratan and his party departed and the band settled into a winter routine. Snow came eventually and bitter cold. People huddled in yurts when not out doing necessary chores. Emily convinced Gaios to whittle checkers pieces and Chunya painted boards on scraps of cloth. The game was a hit and helped pass the time. Emily was the best player at first but Diodis quickly rose to her skill level.

One evening, Diodis used the checkers pieces to explain how the sun and the planets revolved around the earth.

"There are times when the planets seem to go backwards," he lectured. "This is often seen with the red planet, Aris. But it is explained when you realize that Aris makes smaller circles in its circle around the earth."

Onlookers nodded, seeing how it made sense when Diodis showed them with the game pieces. Emily chuckled.

"You do not believe it, noble Tilkya?" Diodis asked.

"I believe the earth goes around the sun as do the planets," she said. She arranged the checkers to show her idea.

"You see, the earth rotates as it revolves around the sun. The planets revolve at different speeds and distances from the sun. That is why you get apparent backwards motion."

"But the earth is stationary."

"It only seems that way when you are standing on it. It is a matter of perspective."

Diodis stood perplexed over Emily's alternative model of the heavens.

"What do you say to that, smart boy?" Gaios asked.

For the first time since Emily had met him, Diodis was tongue-tied.

~

Outbreaks of bickering happened from time to time and once two Lion warriors started fighting, presumably over the affections of Thoeke. Taval let the fight go on for a while before breaking it up. Yet Emily was impressed that, by and large, the Storm Wolves remained amiable even when cooped up.

They rode their horses only when necessary, conserving their energy so they could better endure the winter. Lions occasionally were a problem and keeping them away from the remuda was an ongoing challenge. Inevitably some horses were lost.

They had a large store of oats, obtained at Shketa, to be used in the event the snow became too deep for the horses to graze. The oats wouldn't last long but would help the animals survive until spring.

When the weather was not too cold, the warriors practiced fighting on foot. They shot arrows in formation, hurled sling stones, and occasionally fought mock melees with shields and sticks. The men had the clear advantage in the melees. The large women, like Kaplea and Donya, did fine but the smaller women, like Emily and Mahalea, got knocked around easily. She would make a poor hoplite, Emily thought.

Wrestling was a popular activity inside the yurts. Emily was particularly bad at it. Even Mahalea, who was about the same size, beat her regularly. She was determined to learn the basics, however, and didn't shirk from participating. She was squirmy and could wiggle out of holds with her flexibility but against the men she was too easily manhandled.

Once, wrestling against Javada, she had somehow maneuvered behind him and almost had a good headlock going, but Javada was able to power out of it and slam her to the mat. Afterward, she gloomily nursed a sore shoulder. Taval rubbed her back.

"Do not worry yourself, Vashakiz," he said. "You are a fighter, not a wrestler. Everything is different when death is in the balance and there are no rules."

Gaios was nearby and asked Emily what Taval had said. She translated.

"Ah, Taval reminds me of a general I knew who complained that top athletes were no good in battle. They are too bound to the rules of their contests."

"True," Taval said in Greek. "Look at the way Pakeus straddles Kavad. Pakeus will win the bout but if it were a real fight, Kavad could attack his eyes or his groin. If he had a knife or a stone, he could kill Pakeus with his free arm."

Emily remembered the encounter with Hydakoles that seemed so long ago. She had been scrappy then but now she was stronger and much more capable. She was a warrior, someone to be feared.

~

As it turned out, the winter, by and large, was a dry one. The horses fared well. When the snow began to melt, the oats were fed to the horses to strengthen them. The Storm Wolves would be leaving early for Gipatsha.

Chapter 32 | All That Lives

WHEN the Storm Wolves left their winter camp, they headed for Shketa to trade their surplus hides before moving on to Gipatsha. Kaplea rode ahead with the scouting party. Not on duty, Emily walked with Gaios and Diodis. The pair would part ways with the band at Shketa. A chilly mist hung in the air and Emily kept the hood of her cloak up.

"I will miss Kaplea," Diodis said. "I doubt I will ever meet her like again."

Emily imagined the wonder in people's eyes when Diodis told them of his liaison with a warrior woman of Scythia. She wondered what influence it would have on his Greek friends. Would they rethink their attitudes toward women? Probably not.

"I will miss all of the Storm Wolves," Gaios said. "We could not have asked for more generous or interesting hosts."

"Where will you go now?" Emily asked.

"We will take the pass over the mountains and head for home," Gaios said. "I long to see Ephesos again and the warm shores of the sea."

"I would be careful," Emily said. "Trouble brews between the Greeks and the Persians. There will be war."

"How do you know this?" Diodis asked.

"Zandra tells me Tilkya knows the future," Gaios said. "She is a seer."

"I know a future. How things will turn out now, I am not sure."

"You are a strange one, Tilkya," Diodis said. "I will miss you, too. I would love to take you to Miletus to see the philosophers and watch you tie their ideas into knots."

"Maybe you can do that for me," Emily said.

"You should be careful as well," Gaios said. "It sounds like war is brewing in these lands. I hope Kydoime prevails and Artemios remains free of Persian rule. Send us news if you can."

"Perhaps some day after the battles are fought, you and Taval, and Kaplea, too, could visit Ephesos," Diodis said. "You would be treated as honored guests."

"I do not think Taval and Kaplea would fit in well in the cities to the south," Emily said.

"They would terrify everyone. It would be wonderful," Diodis said.

Emily suddenly had a vision of riding into one of the great Greek cities, Miletus maybe, or Athens. Kaplea was at her side, an army marched behind her and people trembled in awe. What vainglorious nonsense, she thought.

~

Emily rode with her arim perhaps two miles ahead of the main column, serving as the forward patrol. They were following a well-trodden path that wound its way east through rolling hills and eventually to the Hyrca Ocean. The Storm Wolves were taking an easterly course before they turned northward. The normally parched lands would have good grazing this time of year and dry stream beds would be swollen.

Emily spotted a riderless horse ahead, Mahalea's mount. She looked around and saw the scout waving from near the crest of a low ridge. She halted the arim, dismounted, climbed the ridge and lay beside Mahalea at the crest.

"There," Mahalea said. "Persians."

Emily put the binoculars to her eyes and saw a group of riders heading southeast. There were lightly armed with javelins and wore no armor that she could see.

"Scouts, I suppose. What are they doing out here?"

"Hard to say. Maybe clearing the way for a caravan," Mahalea said.

"Have they spotted us?"

"Possibly."

Emily and Mahalea went down the slope and rode back to the main column.

"Persian scouts. They may have seen us," Emily reported to Taval and Kaplea.

"Hmm, probably not worth worrying about," Taval said.

"We should turn north now and get out of these hills," Kaplea said.

"Yes, I suppose you are right."

~

The Storm Wolves turned north and within a day were out on the steppe. The journey was easier than when they had come to Shketa. The temperature was milder and their remuda was smaller. Crossing the Unyasin River, however, was an ordeal that required ropes and rafts.

After eighteen days the band arrived at Gipatsha. The latest news was that Huraslan, king of the Lion Tribe, still lived.

"He's a tough old cur," Kaplea said.

~

Emily looked over the array of saddles that Zenobia, the hefty craftswoman, had made and was amazed. Wooden inserts provided generous support for the rider front and back. The seat portion was covered with fleece for comfort. Generous flaps hung on each side, tanned smooth to prevent chafing the thighs. The adjustable straps of the stirrups were attached so they wouldn't chafe the horse's flanks. The saddles were unadorned except for one.

"Taval requested a special one for you," Zenobia said. "What do you think?"

"It is beautiful," Emily said.

Gold rhinestones edged the contours of the saddle. On one flap was embossed the figure of a gnarled oak tree, on the other a running fox.

"A saddle fit for a queen, no?" Taval said.

"They still look funny to me," Kaplea said. "You won't catch me using one."

Twenty-five were completed and six more were nearly done. Also impressive was the horse armor that Akakios created. Narrow, wedge-shaped bronze plates fronted skirts of iron scales. Narrow plates would protect the horses' snouts.

The equipment was stored in a yurt out on the plain and around it was a corral where the chargers were kept, thirty of the largest mounts Kellvan and Shavaris could find. The pair had recruited twelve warriors so far, men Kellvan knew and trusted, but many others were eager to join. He wanted Taval and Kaplea to vet them. All the warriors were built like Kellvan and Shavaris, large and muscular.

For mobility, Kellvan said, the warriors should ride separate horses. The armor could be rolled up and stowed on the heavy mounts. Each warrior should have an attendant to help him prepare for battle when the time came.

Attendant? A squire, Emily thought. They were creating the world's first knights.

Shavaris put armor on one of the horses and demonstrated. He sat tall and firm in the saddle which allowed him to take full advantage of his upper body strength. It occurred to Emily that the saddles were negating the advantage women had on horseback where their lower centers of gravity made them more stable than the large men.

They decided Kellvan would lead the new force of heavy cavalry and Shavaris would be his second. Emily knew she was too small for the role but would help with training and tactics.

"They will need support from light cavalry," she said. "We will have to figure that out. We should set up dummies. The horses will need to get used to charging groups of spearmen."

"What shall we call this arim of heavy cavalry?" Taval asked.

"Tekepa," Kaplea sneered.

"Ha! So be it," Taval said.

This most advanced force of armored horse warriors, Emily mused, would be known as the Billy Goats.

~

Emily spent most of her time working with the armored cavalry. Taval and Kaplea vetted several more warriors and the Billy Goats now had a full complement of 30, all men. Several more warriors were allowed to join the Storm Wolves. They sensed war was coming and Taval and Kaplea were the rising stars of the Wolf Tribe. Tilkya was their lucky charm.

Shepherds bringing in their flocks relayed news that Huraslan still lived. The danger of immediate strife in the Lion Tribe seemed averted for now.

Emily was amazed when she learned how much the community had pitched in to help with the making of the saddles and horse armor. Some scoffed but many were curious and the practice field always had onlookers. There were teething pains, however. The saddles were easy enough to get used to but it was a struggle to get the horses accustomed to the armor. Akakios stayed busy making adjustments.

The biggest problem was getting the horses to charge the phalanx of dummy spearmen. Emily, remembering what she knew of medieval knights, suggested using blinders. That seemed to help.

Emily's Storm Rats trained with them as they worked on ways to provide cover for the armored cavalry. All the warriors selected for the Billy Goats possessed good armor and substantial helmets. They wore greaves to protect their legs and made heavy shields out of wood and metal. On them they painted colorful horned monsters.

There were days when Emily would grow sick of the men and go spend time with Chunya to help work on clothing. At times she missed the pleasant evenings in the gynaeceum at Agathon's farmhouse.

~

One day Kraejik's Hawks returned from their wintering grounds to the east. Kraejik, upon hearing Huraslan still lived, was eager to go raid the Sarma.

"We need to teach them a lesson," he said.

That night, in their tent, Taval told Emily he planned to take his arim north with Kraejik.

"I owe him," he said.

"What if war breaks out with the Lions and Persians?" Emily said. "We will need to act fast."

"If Huraslan survived the winter, he will probably live through the summer. I will not be gone long, thirty days at most."

"We should all go," Emily said.

"No, you have business here and so does Arlav. It will be a quick raid. Steal a few horses and come back."

Emily stood up and removed her tunic.

"I will miss you," she said.

Taval pulled her close and slid his hand down her trousers.

369

"I will miss you, too, Vashakiz."

~

While Taval rode north with the Hawks, Kaplea rode west with her arim. Her purpose was not to raid but gather news of the Lions and Persians.

Emily continued to work with the Billy Goats and the Storm Rats. After ten days they were ready to mount their first charge in formation at the dummy phalanx. The Storm Rats led the attack, hurling javelins as they closed then wheeled ninety degrees to make way for the charge. The Billy Goats smashed into the phalanx and obliterated the dummy spearmen. Onlookers cheered. The Billy Goats howled their war cries. Kellvan remained somber.

"If a real phalanx holds its ground, many of us will die," he said to Emily and Shavaris.

"But will they hold their ground against the charge?" Shavaris asked.

"Aye, perhaps fear is our best weapon."

~

Three days later Kaplea returned and she and Emily spent the night together. Kaplea learned that Mazdak's army of Scyth mercenaries had swelled to more than a thousand. She heard talk of large formations of Greek hoplites drilling near the cities of Novorosa and Phanagoria. Four triremes were stationed at Novorosa's harbor -- Novorosa's own ship, one from Phanagoria and two from the Bosporan Kingdom.

"They plan to attack. They may not wait for Huraslan to die," Emily said.

"The Lions will stop them," Kaplea said.

"If their target is Artemios, they may go by sea and storm the city before the Lions can help."

"We met a party of Lion scouts," Kaplea said. "They served Takahal. They say Kydoime grows impatient and plans to murder Huraslan."

"Ridiculous," Emily said.

"It is a scheme of Takahal and the Persians. They sow dissent against her."

"We must move soon if we are to help Kydoime," Emily said.

"When Taval returns we will put the matter to the tribe."

"And if we do not get the support of the other leaders?"

"Then we convince Taval to ride out with just the Storm Wolves," Kaplea said. "Many would join us, I think."

Emily embraced Kaplea, a long, squeezing hug.

"My bleeding is late," Emily said.

"Yours comes at the same time as mine. It should have happened days ago," Kaplea said.

"I know."

"You should not be surprised the way you and Taval go at it."

Emily couldn't fathom being pregnant, just couldn't wrap her mind around the idea. She tried to forget about it by losing herself in Kaplea's caresses.

~

Emily sat with Kaplea, Chunya and a few other women in Zenobia's yard. Chunya worked her loom, Kaplea painted the face of a fox on Emily's shield. Emily polished her armor.

"The Hawks have returned!" Someone shouted.

Emily sprang to her feet and mounted Hurlov. Kaplea followed her. They rode to the north edge of the plateau and saw a long column of riders, mules and wagons. The remuda looked small. They must not have stolen many horses, Emily thought. She reached for her binoculars. She could make out many wounded riding in the wagons. Where was Taval? He was always easy to spot. Where was his arim? She saw a few Storm Wolves. Halaba, the scout and Taval's close friend, was among them.

"I do not see Taval. Something has happened," she said. She handed the binoculars to Kaplea.

"They got into a bad fight," Kaplea said. "Damn that Kraejik. Damn him."

The two galloped out to meet the returning war party. Kraejik was leading the column. He ordered a halt.

"Kaplea, Tilkya," he said.

Emily could tell by his tone something had happened. A knot formed in her stomach. Bile welled in her throat. She couldn't speak.

"What happened? Where is Taval?" Kaplea asked.

Kraejik shook his head. "Taval and his arim were caught in a tight spot. He did not make it. We arrived in time to drive the Sarma off but I could not save Taval. I am sorry. He fought like a demon. He must have felled a dozen or more before he perished."

"No!" Emily yelped.

"Where is his body?" Kaplea asked in a low tone.

Kraejik inclined his head. "In the first wagon."

Kaplea rode to the wagon and Emily followed. Taval's body lay wrapped in a blanket. Kaplea pulled the cloth back from his head. His helmet was still on. It had been pierced with a sagaris spike. His neck showed wounds on either side, apparently pierced by an arrow. His sword and gorytos lay beside him. The bow was broken. Emily dismounted, put her hand on Taval's soft, wonderful beard and sobbed.

Halaba rode over. He and Kaplea put their arms on each other's shoulders.

"What happened?" Kaplea asked.

"I do not want to speak about it now," Halaba said.

Emily stood, wiped the tears from her face and mounted Hurlov. Kraejik rode over and put a hand on her shoulder.

"He was a great warrior. His death is a great loss for the tribe," Kraejik said. "I will help you in any way that I can."

"Thank you," Emily said.

Kaplea and Halaba said nothing.

~

The Storm Wolves had lost seventeen dead and twelve wounded in the debacle. That night in Emily's tent, Halaba explained what he knew to her and Kaplea.

The raiding party was fourteen days north when Hawk scouts reported seeing a large remuda. The terrain was hilly with scattered woods and coulees. Kraejik's plan was for the Hawks to approach frontally while Taval's arim swung around to attack the Sarma's flank.

"It seemed like a good plan," Halaba said. "I scouted the left flank to make sure we wouldn't be surprised from that direction. The Hawks were supposed to screen our right flank so no one could slip through the noose."

Halaba said he heard shouting and learned later that the arim had run into an ambush. Taval immediately ordered a retreat but they were cut off by a Sarma arim that somehow got through the screen.

"I rode as fast as I could back to them. When I got to the crest of a hill, I saw our arim was surrounded and battling for its life."

"Where was Kraejik?" Kaplea asked. "He should have smelled trouble and come to Taval's aid."

"That is just it. I think he was close by, waiting," Halaba said. "I saw a Hawk scout on a far crest. I signaled her with my spear. I know she saw me and I know she could see that Taval was in trouble. She signaled to someone on the other side of the hill she was on. Soon two Hawk arims appeared and charged the Sarma force. When the Sarma saw the Hawks coming, they retreated."

"Were the Sarma outnumbered at that point?" Kaplea asked.

"No, the Sarma still had numbers."

"Yet they retreated?"

"Yes. It seemed odd to me."

"Who was the scout you saw?"

"I am sure it was Belnya."

"That is Kraejik's woman."

"Would Kraejik really do that?" Emily asked. "He can be an ass but would he really set Taval up to be killed? He is a Wolf. He is Lovta."

"Taval was starting to outshine him as a war leader," Halaba said.

"I do not know," Kaplea said. "We must keep this quiet. I will talk to Chunya. She has a way of finding things out and won't arouse suspicion."

~

The next morning Emily had little chance to mourn or reflect because she received a steady stream of visitors to her tent offering condolences. The visitors included Taval's aunt and members of her family who Taval supported. Emily told them she would continue the support as best she could.

Arlav was among the visitors. He gave a rough accounting of what Taval owned. He was a wealthy man by Lovta standards and his wealth was now hers. Taval's aunt or her children might make claims to the wealth, he said.

"I want to be generous with them to forestall any bad blood," Emily said.

"A wise choice," Arlav said. "I think I can appease them adequately."

"What will happen to the Storm Wolves now that Taval is dead?" Emily asked.

"We will have to decide," he said. "I think everyone will support Kaplea as our leader."

Emily was also visited by Unkati, the tribal elder who had given her the tattoo of nobility.

"Taval's loss is a grievous blow," Unkati said. "It is too bad you have not born him a child."

Emily considered telling her that she had missed her period but decided against it. She wasn't sure yet she was pregnant.

"Kaplea and I want to help Kydoime when the time comes," Emily said.

"Without Taval it will be difficult to rally the tribe to your cause," Unkati said. "Kraejik is our most prominent war leader and favors Takahal. But we shall see."

Unkati explained that in two days' time, a funeral party would ride out to bury Taval and the other slain warriors on the steppe. Emily needed to decide what goods would go into Taval's burial mound, a task she dreaded.

~

That afternoon Emily had time to herself and went through Taval's things. She found a box filled with ornaments and jewelry. She didn't know what they meant or what they were for. Possibly they had belonged to his first wife.

Tucked in the bottom of a crate, she found a long object wrapped in oiled cloth. She unfolded it and saw that it was the Corinthian dagger

Byon had given her. Taval, you bastard, you stole it from me, she thought, remembering that day a year ago when he had kidnapped her. It occurred to her that the dagger had been for Taval a secret totem he kept in order to bind her to him. Tears streamed down her cheeks.

"Goddammit, Taval, what the fuck am I going to do without you?"

~

Hundreds attended the funeral. Zandra led the ceremonies and they sacrificed several aging horses. A large grave was dug for the dead warriors, their gear and the horses. Emily, Kaplea, Halaba and Donya lowered Taval's body into the pit. With him went his armor, shield, best tunic and trousers, his sword, his gorytos, bow and arrows, lariat, spindle whorl, and sewing kit. Emily had put the Corinthian dagger on his belt and the plastic horse in his pouch. She chuckled inwardly at the thought of future archaeologists digging up the grave, finding the plastic horse and seeing the inscription on its belly: "Made in Portugal."

The funeral procession rode back to the settlement under the deep orange glow of the sun setting on the steppe.

Chapter 33 | Reckoning

THE whole of the Storm Wolves met out on the plain. Heavy clouds rolled overhead and the afternoon air was chilly. Emily and Kaplea walked toward the group. They were the last to arrive. Kaplea was dressed in her finest clothes, an indigo tunic trimmed with gold and orange trousers crisscrossed with red lines. She even consented to letting Emily apply a touch of makeup. She looked glorious but Emily knew she was nervous.

"I do not see ahead like Taval could, or you can," Kaplea had confided.

"You will know what needs to be done," Emily reassured.

The band's members made way for the pair and they took their place at the center of the gathering. Zandra spoke.

"Taval was one of the great warriors of the Lovta," he said. "He rides now with the gods. Taval led us well and we have grown rich because of him. Yet even he acknowledged he was not the greatest warrior among us. That warrior, we all know, is Kaplea. Ride for a month in any direction and she will be known and feared. It is sad that her time comes on the heels of tragedy but it is her time now. I raise my hand for her. Who else will join me?

All hands went up with a cacophony of cheering -- "Kaplea! Kaplea! Kaplea!" -- that took some time to subside. Then they got onto other business. Kaplea would continue to lead her personal arim and Halaba would take over Taval's. Kellvan would lead the Billy Goats and Emily the Storm Rats.

"Like Taval did with me, I will consider Tilkya my co-leader," Kaplea said. "Her commands are my commands."

"Yes," Zandra said. "We will need the fox's cunning and foresight."

The Storm Wolves feasted, drank, smoked and danced well into the night.

~

Emily and Kellvan took the Storm Rats and the Billy Goats out on an overnight excursion. The Billy Goat warriors rode lighter steeds while attendants led the heavy mounts carrying the horse armor. At a random point in the day, Emily whistled the alert and Kellvan ordered the men to prepare for battle. As quickly as they could, they saddled the chargers, put the armor on and equipped themselves. Emily had counted to 536 when all the warriors were ready to go. Not bad, she thought, but it could be faster.

They practiced more, then camped for the night. The men, she noticed, were very friendly toward her and often made eyes in her direction. She supposed, as Taval's widow, she would be a good catch. She maintained a cold countenance to discourage them.

Back in Gipatsha, Arlav had something for her. The bow Taval was having made for Koia was ready. It was Emily's now. It had sinuous curves and beautiful red leather wraps on its limbs with black lacing. Its draw was stiff. Koia had been a strong woman. It came with a gorytos that was not yet decorated. Emily offered it to Donya for her son but she declined, saying he needed to earn his own bow. Emily decided to loan it to Thoeke who was a considerably better archer. Might as well put it to good use, Emily thought. Thoeke was thrilled and thanked her profusely.

~

That night Kaplea summoned Emily and Halaba to her tent. She was grim-faced and brooding.

"Chunya and I have learned things," she said.

The summer before last, Kraejik had visited Takahal and they spent many days hunting together. Last fall, when the Hawks headed east to their wintering grounds, Kraejik took a small hunting party north and was gone more than twenty days. They did not return with much game. Belnya, Kraejik's woman, was with them.

"So you think he arranged a deal with Takahal?" Emily asked.

"Yes, and when Taval became a threat to the plan, Kraejick decided he needed to get him out of the way."

"What was the point of the trip north?"

"To meet with the Sarma and arrange an ambush," Halaba said.

"But the Sarma are enemies."

"Raids and counter-raids, yes, but we are not really at war," Halaba said. "If Kraejik wanted to negotiate something with them, he could do it."

"Why would the Sarma want to help Kraejik?"

"Killing Taval and a victory over his arim would enhance the reputation of any Sarma war leader," Kaplea said.

"Kraejik has wealth to offer, too, and maybe promised Persian gold. Who knows?" Halaba said.

"This is all possible, I suppose," Emily said. "But it seems like a stretch. There is no proof."

"Chunya has spoken with the wives of several Hawk warriors," Kaplea said. "Many think Kraejik waited too long to order the attack. They think if the Hawks would have attacked sooner, they could have saved Taval."

"Suspicious, yes, but not proof."

"You do not wish to avenge your husband?" Kaplea asked.

"If I knew for sure, I would kill Kraejik myself or die trying."

"What do we do now?" Halaba asked.

"Bide our time. Wait for the right moment and pray to the gods for justice," Kaplea said.

~

A large band of Lovta riders arrived from the east. They were from the Eagle Tribe, rugged warriors of the deep steppe. They had raided a caravan the previous season and brought booty to trade including many rolls of silk cloth. The Wolves feasted and celebrated with their Eagle cousins.

Two days later a messenger arrived from Aslatsha, the Lion Tribe's capital settlement. Huraslan was dead and Kydoime asked for aid to secure her queenship.

~

A late spring storm rumbled in the west but the night sky above Gipatsha was clear. Torches ringed an area in the center of the plateau; the flames danced in the gusty breeze. The leaders, priests and priestesses of the Wolf Tribe assembled, the Storm Wolves represented by Kaplea, Halaba, Arlav, Zandra, Kellvan and Emily.

Kydoime's messenger, Theroba, stood in the center of the gathering and spoke. He was tall and lean, had dark brown hair and a close-cropped beard worn like the Greeks. His voice was clear and loud.

"Noble leaders of the Wolf Tribe, our Lovta sisters and brothers, I bring you the sad news of King Huraslan's death. He was a great ruler much loved by the people of the Lion Tribe who prospered by him. Kydoime has taken his place as queen by the will of the Lion elders and people. Kydoime is wise and strong and will lead the Lion Tribe well.

"But her rightful place as queen is challenged by the traitor, Takahal. He likely rides against her as we speak."

"Takahal is no traitor," Kraejik bellowed. "He is a noble Lovta warrior and has the right to be king. Kydoime is the usurper."

"Let the messenger speak," a Wolf elder shouted.

"Takahal is a traitor not because he challenges Kydoime," Theroba continued. "He is a traitor because he challenges the will of the elders. He lacks the strength within the tribe to defeat Kydoime. If he had such strength, the elders would make him king. Instead of recognizing Kydoime's right to be queen and honorably serving her, he allies himself with Mazdak, the agent of the Great King Darius of Persia. Mazdak prepares an army to march against the Lions and Takahal joins him. Takahal has become a Persian servant. It is a fate that may await all Lovta people if Kydoime does not prevail."

"Lies," Kraejik rumbled. "Takahal fights for what is rightfully his. The Wolves have no cause to interfere. We would not want the Lions to meddle in our disputes. We should not meddle in theirs."

"Kydoime does seek the aid of the Wolves," Theroba said. "But she would not if it were simply a test of strength between her and Takahal. She would gladly meet that challenge without assistance. Who she really fights, however, is Mazdak. Takahal is now little more than another commander in the Persian army. Mazdak and his master, Darius, wage war on all the Lovta. That is why we seek your aid so we can unite in strength instead of being defeated piecemeal.

"If the Wolves decide to fight, Kydoime offers perpetual access to trade with Artemios without tariffs. I have confidence the Wolves will choose a just course."

Theroba left the center and joined his warrior escort. Kraejik stepped forward.

"This is just a scheme of Kydoime's to make the Wolves her subjects just as Huraslan tried to do long ago," Kraejik said. "We should not aid her. Takahal will bring peace with the Persians and our trade will become richer because of it. The Persians are no threat to us out here. They fear the Wolves and will not make war against us. It is the Sarma who are our real enemies. We must direct our attention toward them. The Lions can take care of themselves."

As she listened to Kraejik speak, a rage swelled in Emily. There was something in the way he argued, something in his strut, something in the sweep of his cloak, in the way he gestured. He acted as if he had no peer among the Wolves. He acted like a king. At that moment she knew in her heart, whether by stratagem or opportunity, Kraejik had a hand in Taval's death.

"If the Sarma are our enemies, why did you let them kill Taval? Emily asked, her voice cracking.

"Quiet, little Tilkya," Kraejik said. "You have no voice here. I know you are distraught and your mind is addled so I will forgive your insult this once."

Emily was so enraged she couldn't speak. Blood rushed to her cheeks. She put a hand on her Persian dagger but Kaplea held her back. Halaba stepped forward.

"Noble Tilkya asks a fair question," Halaba said. His voice quavered. Emily knew he was putting his life on the line. "I was there. I saw what happened from the ridge top. I know the Hawks could have attacked the Sarma sooner than they did. The Hawks were supposed to screen Taval's flank yet the Sarma got through."

Emily could see the fury rising in Kraejik as he stared Halaba down. Murmuring and talk spread through the gathered leaders.

"Quiet!" Unkati, the village elder, shouted. "What do you say, Kraejik? Halaba is a good scout with keen eyes who knows what he sees."

The murmuring died down and Kraejik took a moment to compose himself and regain his regal bearing.

"Even the best scouts make mistakes and eyes can deceive in the heat of the moment," he said. "Yes, our scouts were late in spotting the Sarma arim but when they did, I rushed to the scene as quickly as I could. We paused briefly behind a ridge to assess the situation, to make sure we would not be surrounded ourselves. Then we attacked and drove the Sarma back."

Kaplea stepped forward.

"Halaba's eyes did not deceive him." Kaplea spoke slowly, her voice gritty. "You waited until Taval was dead then attacked. Yet the Sarma retreated when they still had numbers. Why? You wanted Taval dead because his reputation surpassed your own and he favored fighting for Kydoime. What kind of deals did you make with Takahal and the Sarma?"

"Baseless lies from Kydoime's pet." Kraejik snarled. His eyes narrowed and his face reddened. "Taval died because he blundered into a trap."

"He died because he trusted you," Kaplea said.

"I can take no more of these insults." Kraejik drew his sword and advanced toward Kaplea. "Withdraw your words or I will strike you down."

In hardly a blink of an eye, Kaplea's sagaris was in her hands. She sidestepped into the open area, hissing through curled lips. With her war hammer out, Kraejik became wary. The two circled each other.

"Do you seek war within the tribe?" Kraejik asked. "Your Storm Wolves cannot defeat the Hawks."

"I seek justice," Kaplea said.

The gathering watched silently. No one ventured to interfere.

"You are no match for me, woman," Kraejik roared. "Stand down and I will spare your life."

Confident words spoken with certitude, Emily thought, but his eyes betrayed fear. He knew he was the one who was outmatched.

Emily was aware that in a duel such as this, each of the fighters has a killing radius around them determined by the reach of their weapons. To advance into the radius was dangerous and often it would be the defender who had the advantage if he or she could evade the attack and counterstrike.

Kraejik had put himself in a position where he had to attack. He would lose face if he didn't carry through with his threat. Kaplea knew this and waited for him to advance.

Kraejik feinted a thrust but Kaplea didn't react. His feet and body hadn't moved close enough to allow his sword to reach Kaplea. The circling continued. Kaplea wielded her hammer with two hands, holding it in front of her, bobbing it and keeping it in motion. No fancy flourishes or twirls, just ready to strike when the moment came.

Emily could tell Kreajik was frustrated and unsure what to do. Finally he gave a great war cry and bull rushed Kaplea, his sword cocked to swing and left arm forward to act as a shield against her hammer blow. It was a desperate move but possibly his only choice. If Kaplea lashed out with her sagaris, he could sacrifice his left arm to block it and slash her with his sword. If she tried to block his attack, he would be on her and the fight would become a grappling match where his size and strength would give him the advantage.

Kaplea didn't oblige either scenario. Instead of immediately striking with her hammer, she sidestepped to her right and forward, ducking as she did so. Kraejik's slashing stroke missed and, with a low, backhanded stroke with her left hand, Kaplea hooked Kreajik's leg with her sagaris and sent him sprawling to the ground.

Then she pounced. Kraejik couldn't gain his feet and vainly tried to ward off the rapid succession of hammer blows with his arm and sword. Soon he was helpless and groaning. Kaplea turned the head of her sagaris so the spike was forward and buried it in his skull.

~

Kaplea yanked the sagaris from her victim's head, the spike dripping with blood. She was still in a fighting stance and slowly turned around, her eyes on the people around her, waiting, it seemed, for someone to try to avenge Kraejik's death. A tall, long-haired man stepped toward her. Emily recognized him, a Hawk war leader named Gugama. He approached within striking distance of Kaplea's terrible hammer but he did not draw his sword. The blood fury remained in Kaplea's eyes.

"Halaba is correct," Gugama said. He had a short-cropped beard but a long, braided mustache. "The Hawks should have attacked sooner. It has nagged me ever since. Taval was a good friend. I did not know why Kraejik waited. Like Taval I trusted him and thought he had good reason. Now I see things clearly. Kraejik brought dishonor to the Hawks. Through you, Kaplea, Pava has delivered justice. Tavapa rumbles in the west, calling us to Queen Kydoime and our Lovta kin."

Gugama drew his sword. Kaplea readied her hammer but Gugama did not strike.

"I offer you my sword and my arim," he said. "I will go where you lead."

Gugama extended his hand. Slowly Kaplea seemed to emerge from her battle trance. She shook his hand but did not say anything. She appeared beyond words. She slipped her sagaris into its belt loop, walked over to Emily and embraced her, kissed her forehead, then walked from the gathering to Kydon, mounted and rode away.

"Where is she going?" Emily asked Halaba.

"To compose herself," he said. "Such a fight is not easy to shake off. She did not like Kraejik but she had known him all her life."

Emily saw Belnya, Kraejik's concubine, kneeling over the corpse. It was a tragedy to lose a war leader of such stature and the Wolves had lost two in short order. Emily's anger turned to doubt. Had Kraejik really committed the crimes he was accused of? Perhaps his only crime was being nervous and uncertain at a critical moment. She likely would never know for sure. With Kaplea gone, she would have to speak for the Storm Wolves. She stepped forward.

"The Storm Wolves favor aiding Kydoime," she said. "We plan to ride as early as possible."

Belnya gave her a hard look. Emily thought she might attack and then she would be locked in her own death struggle. But Belnya just stood and returned to her place in the circle. It was hard to read the grim expressions as people looked on at Emily. She stepped back beside Halaba.

One by one the other arim leaders voiced their desire to aid Kydoime. No one dissented. Only a few remained silent. The elders conferred among themselves then Unkati spoke.

"We will give aid to Kydome. We meet in war council at sunrise."

~

Emily was relieved to see Kydon grazing near Kaplea's tent in the morning twilight. Kaplea had not come back by the time Emily had turned in. Where had she gone, Emily wondered. Perhaps she had sought answers on the prairie from the stars and the wind.

Emily stood outside the tent. "Kaplea, the war council is soon. The tribe has agreed to help Kydoime."

"You go," Kaplea said from inside. "You speak for me. You have a good mind for these things."

"But we need you, Kaplea."

Halaba was nearby. He walked over and put a hand on Emily's shoulder.

"She will come when she is ready," he said.

~

The elders were unwilling to muster the full strength of the Wolf Tribe. The Sarma were a threat and Gipatsha must be protected. They decided the Storm Wolves should lead the contingent and Kaplea would be the principal war leader though she was not yet present to accept the honor. Gugama would add his arim and several others would also join. The force would amount to about 800 warriors, enough, the elders were confident, to tip the balance in Kydoime's favor.

Emily thought they should commit more strength but didn't argue. She wished Kaplea were here. Theroba, Kydoime's messenger, said he had hoped for more warriors but was pleased with whatever they could send.

The visiting Eagles from the east had little interest in helping the Lions but Emily suspected they would be interested in plunder. She suggested they could raid the Euxine coast near Novorosa and Phanagoria. With the Persians committed elsewhere, it would be easy pickings. To that they readily agreed. Emily hoped their raids might force Mazdak to send valuable troops to deal with the Eagles, who, she figured, were probably wilier and scrappier than even the Wolves and almost certainly more ruthless.

"It is a long way to Aslatsha," Emily said to the messenger. "Will we arrive soon enough?"

"It will take time for Mazdak to gather his infantry and bring them to bear," Theroba said. "There is a good chance Aslatsha will still stand. If not, Kydoime will retreat to the forests. There is a hidden valley that once was home to a Cimmerian settlement. It can support many horses for some time."

"Is it about three days walk southeast of Artemios?" Emily asked.

"Yes, you know of it?"

"I have been there."

"Excellent. We will send word if the queen retreats."

The war council continued to make plans, mainly on the route. They agreed that many scouts should be employed. The war party would need information and must not be taken by surprise.

They all turned at the sound of an approaching rider whose red hair was unmistakable. A train of townsfolk and children followed in her wake. The beating heart of the Lovta, Emily thought.

Kaplea approached the assembled war leaders and reined Kydon to a stop. All stood in silent attention.

"I hope the plans are set," she said. "Now it is time to ready your arims. We ride at noon."

Chapter 34 | The Tiger

THE Wolf army made barely ten miles the first day before making camp on the plain. Half of Gipatsha, it seemed, followed them. Arlav had been beside himself trying to ready the supplies needed. His priority was packing wagons with oats to help keep the horses strong for the long journey.

The messenger, Theroba, and his escort, supplied with fresh horses, set out immediately after the war council. Kaplea sent Mahalea with him. She was to return to the Wolf army as soon as she had word of Kydoime and the whereabouts of her forces.

The mood was festive that evening. Several goats and lambs were sacrificed to the war god, Kurapa. Kaplea dutifully participated in the ceremonies but went to her tent early. Emily soon followed and found Kaplea fingering the Tiger Stone and looking at the papyrus sheet that bore Diodis' poem.

"I do not know if I am ready for this, Tilkya," Kaplea said. "So much at stake and so many people to be responsible for. I wish Taval was here."

Emily poured wine into bowls and they drank.

"You are the finest warrior on the steppe," Emily said. "Taval looked up to you. People revere you. You are their queen, if not in name then in spirit. It is a burden I cannot fathom but if anyone can bear it, you can."

"I do not want to be queen. I want to be a warrior."

"Your problem is that you are too good a warrior, so good you became queen. Feeling doubt is a good sign, I think."

"I hope you are right. I hope you will help me."

"I will help you, Kaplea, with all my energy to my dying breath."

Kaplea pulled Emily close and hugged her tight.

~

Kaplea set a brisk pace the following morning and left a cheering crowd behind. The Wolf army was really little more than a battalion, Emily thought, but the sight of the column was impressive -- 800 warriors with three times as many horses and about 100 mules. Non-warriors were kept to a minimum -- herders to mind the remuda, wagon drivers and a few others including Arlav, Zandra, Chunya, and Kavad the craftsman.

For each of the first few days they averaged about twenty miles. When they stopped to make camp, Kaplea would order a few arims to practice maneuvers. She wanted everyone to be using the same signals given with shouts, whistles, horns and guidons. At night the war leaders would discuss tactics and the kinds of things they might do.

Gugama proved a capable leader with a head for tactics and a forceful presence so Kaplea designated him second in command. Emily's formal position was leader of the Storm Rats but her closeness to Kaplea was known and her commands and suggestions were respected by all.

The strategy at the moment was simple -- steer a course straight for Aslatsha and learn what they could as they went. Scouting parties screened the column's front, rear and flanks. Individual scouts ranged farther afield. Most often the lead scouting party was Emily's arim. After a few exchanges of warriors with other arims and some horse trading, the Storm Rats, now 40 strong, were made up of fast riders and mounts. Emily drilled them to be nimble and quick in attack and retreat.

On the eighth morning, Kaplea ordered the traveling pace quickened. It was also a morning that Emily threw up her breakfast. Chunya saw her.

"You are pregnant," Chunya said. "You should have stayed in Gipatsha."

"This is where the gods want me," Emily said. "The child will have to endure it. Please, I ask that you not speak of it with anyone else."

"If you wish. Does Kaplea know?"

"She does."

"I will have to think about clothing for the child. Kavad can build a crib."

"It is months off yet."

"Which will come sooner than you think."

~

On the 15th day out, Emily and the Storm Rats were patrolling ahead of the main column. The sky was cloudy and produced light rain in spurts. Emily estimated the Wolf army was making close to 30 miles a day now. The horses appeared in good shape. The solstice was some days away. The full heat of summer had not yet arrived.

Donya and Thoeke rode at her side. Because of her intelligence and charisma, Thoeke was third in command of the Storm Rats after Donya. Emily was not surprised when Thoeke confided that she was Kydoime's niece.

In the distance through the drizzle, Emily saw a rider approaching. She raised her spear and the Storm Rats immediately tightened their ranks. She looked through her binoculars and saw the telltale blue cap with an orange stripe and she recognized the highly decorated gorytos at the rider's hip. Mahalea had returned.

"Take over, Thoeke. Donya and I will ride with Mahalea to the column. Let us hope the news is good."

~

Rain poured on the camp that night. The war leaders and Mahalea crowded into Kaplea's tent to discuss the news. Mahalea had met a scouting party of Lions loyal to Kydoime. The queen had retreated to the forest. Takahal, with Mazdak's help, had taken Aslatsha and declared himself king of the Lion Tribe.

"What are the numbers?" Gugama asked. "Kydoime would not retreat unless the odds were stacked against her."

"She had gathered 2,000 warriors by the time Takahal made his move," Mahalea said. "Takahal raised 1,500 but he was joined by Mazdak's army -- 1,500 Scyth and 2,000 Persian infantry. She could not hope to defend Aslatsha against them. The town has no walls."

"Our numbers would not tip the balance against such a force," Gugama said.

"Our numbers would give Kydoime a chance against enemy horse warriors if we could draw them away from the infantry," Emily said.

"The scouts told us a force of Greek hoplites from Phanagoria and Novorosa march toward Artemios," Mahalea said.

Emily felt anxious. Could Artemios stand against them? What would happen to Nancy and Alex if the city fell?

"What can Kydoime gain by hiding in the forest?" Gugama asked. "The war looks lost before it has begun."

"Perhaps she plans to raid from the hills and keep Takahal off balance until the situation becomes favorable," Emily said.

"We do not know what Kydoime intends," Kaplea said. "We must go to her and find out. If she believes the war is lost, we shall go home. If she wants to fight, we will fight."

"Make no mistake, Kaplea," Gugama said. "I will follow you to certain death but how now do we find Kydoime?"

"Theroba said she would go to a hidden valley in the hills," Kaplea said. "Tilkya has been there before."

"Yes, I have been there," Emily said. "Halaba, do you know the place where Taval saw me kill the warthog? From there I know the way."

"Yes, I know the place," Halaba said. "You do not know it but Taval and I watched you gut the beast while we hid in the grass on the hill."

"I could have used your help," Emily said.

"We decided to let you do the work then we would take the pig and you for ourselves," Halaba said, smiling.

"Men," Kaplea grunted. "Halaba, how many days to that spot?"

"Five days will get us there," he said.

"We will get there in four," Kaplea said.

~

Three days later the hills and mountains of the Kaukasos loomed in the distance. The Wolf army steered a more southerly course, skirting the edge of Lion territory though there was no defined boundary. Emily rode beside Kaplea at the head of the main column along with Zandra. A scout who was probing the western flank of the column returned with news of a large party of riders, about 200 strong, riding east.

"Kydoime's warriors?" Kaplea asked.

"Takahal's by the look of them," the scout said. "They wear golden caps and have yellow guidons."

"Will they spot us?"

"Perhaps. They will certainly cross our trail."

"We must deal with them," Kaplea said.

Kaplea gave the order and horns sounded. The Wolves prepared for battle.

"What is your plan, Kaplea," Emily asked.

"Meet them head on in force," Kaplea said.

"They will see our numbers and flee."

"Most likely, yes."

"Should we not try to destroy them?" Emily asked. "Two hundred fewer warriors could make a difference in battles to come. I could lead the Rats, the Goats and a couple of other arims, circle around and cut off their retreat."

Kaplea mulled the idea, frowning. Zandra spoke up.

"A good plan, Tilkya." he said. "But I do not think we should start bloodshed just yet."

"Zandra is right," Kaplea said. "If they were Persians or Scyth, I would not hesitate to slaughter them, but they are Lions."

"Kaplea worries if we kill Lions on our own, Takahal can claim the Wolves make war against them and use that to persuade the whole of the tribe to accept his leadership," Zandra said.

Emily hadn't considered the political angle but it made sense. If they were going to fight Takahal's Lions, they needed to do it under Kydoime's leadership, otherwise the Wolves look like enemies of the Lion Tribe. Kaplea and Gugama rode out with 500 warriors. Emily stayed behind with Halaba to keep the rest of the column moving.

That evening while making camp, Kaplea and Gugama returned.

"You chased them off, I gather," Emily said.

"Yes," Kaplea said. "We advanced toward them at a trot and they retreated. We pursued them a few miles then turned back."

"Takahal will know the Wolves knock at his door."

"Yes."

"And that the tiger woman leads them."

~

The next afternoon they arrived at the edge of the forest. Emily recognized the spot where she had killed the warthog while Taval looked on. She missed him and his enveloping, muscular embrace. She would never feel it again. She and Kaplea stood on the small hill looking down. Halaba and Gugama stood with them.

"You know the way from here, Tilkya?" Kaplea asked.

"Yes, but the way is through the forest," Emily said. "It will be difficult with so many horses."

"How far?"

"Five days. Maybe six. And there is some craggy terrain that will be hard on the horse's hooves."

"We should skirt the forest until we are closer," Gugama suggested.

"Takahal may come for us with numbers. We do not want to risk getting trapped," Halaba said.

"If we skirt the forest for a day, will we get passed the crags?" Kaplea asked.

"Yes, I think so," Emily said. "If we ride hard tomorrow we should come to a sizable valley. If we go over its western ridge, we will come to a smaller valley. From there it will be all forest."

"We will do that," Kaplea said. "I do not think Takahal will be able to reach us tomorrow. There is still daylight left. Let us get some more miles in before we camp."

~

The following day they made northwesterly arc, riding as fast as the mules could pull the wagons. They reached the valley by midafternoon where they found a large herd of bison with attending lions and hyenas. Riding into the midst of the herd, it took nearly every Wolf rider to keep the remuda together and ward off predators. Kaplea ordered no hunting.

"Of all the times to meet such a herd," Halaba said. "We cannot take advantage of it and it slows us down."

"No, Halaba, it is a gift from Samvi," Kaplea said. "The herd moves southeast. It will obscure our trail and confuse Takahal's scouts."

The Billy Goats led the way, using the butt ends of their heavy spears to clear a path for the column, now densely packed. Emily could see the rocky prominence of the ridge that she and Hank climbed nearly two years ago. It was late afternoon by the time they reached the base of the ridge. Kaplea ordered the wagons to be dismantled and hidden in the trees. Essential gear would be packed on mules or horses.

Emily, mounted on Hurlov, stared up the ridge. Zandra trotted up beside her.

"What do your eyes see?" Zandra asked.

"Only trees," Emily said. "It is what your eyes will see that I am thinking about."

"What will they see?"

"The place where I entered this world."

"It is a sacred place then. We shall honor it."

~

Kaplea sent scouts over the ridge who returned bewildered by what they saw but reported no other people were there. Kaplea led the column up and over the ridge and into the bowl-shaped valley containing the wreckage of Flight 7075.

"Set up camp," Kaplea ordered. "Do not disturb the ruins."

The Wolf warriors filed into the valley and began their work with little talk. Emily wondered what they felt. A kind of awe, she supposed, at seeing something they could not have imagined. It was a good moment for Zandra, she thought. The wreckage added realness to the stories he had told. Kaplea maintained her command presence, clearly working hard not to display any wonderment, but sometimes she stopped what she was doing and stared.

"This is what remains of your air-ship?" Kaplea asked.

"Yes."

A ring of torches was lit that night and a horse, wounded by a bison's horn, was led out to the middle of the ring. All the Wolves looked on. Emily and Kaplea stood beside Zandra as he spoke.

"We make this offering to Tavapa who opened the sky and delivered Tilkya to us on the air-ship. There is great purpose in this and the Wolf Tribe is bound to it, indeed all Lovta are bound to it, perhaps even all people. It is here the gods began to reshape our destiny. May we find the wisdom and the courage to live as we should and face death with honor."

A large warrior swung an ax and with one blow felled the horse. Silence endured for a time while the horse twitched in its death throes. Emily felt the eyes of the tribe upon her. She tried to think of something to say. She did not want to be a messiah.

"I cannot say that I am an agent of the gods," she said. "I can say I am proud to be a Lovta warrior. I do not wish to be anything else. I do wish to fight and face death with my Wolf brothers and sisters. I can think of no higher honor."

There were no rousing cheers, just nods and murmuring. The gathering broke up. It was late and people were tired and wanted rest. There was hard traveling ahead. Emily ordered the detail assigned to disposing of the dead horse to place the carcass at the base of the north ridge inside the trees a ways. An offering to her own god, she thought.

∼

Emily woke before dawn. Kaplea snored beside her. She nudged Kaplea who grunted.

"What do you want, Pakshakiz?"

"Get your cloak and come with me," Emily said.

"What for?"

"Trust me."

Kaplea put on her cloak, cinched up her belt and slid her sagaris into the loop. Emily did the same and grabbed her spear. Emily led Kaplea toward the north ridge and on the way met a sentry.

"All is well, Kaplea," the sentry said.

"We are going into the forest," Emily said. "We will be back shortly."

The sentry looked at Emily like she had lost her mind.

"Samvi calls us," she said.

"Tell Gugama I want everyone ready to march by dawn," Kaplea said.

A few yards into the forest and darkness was nearly complete. Emily clicked on the flashlight, keeping the beam close to the ground. The horse's carcass was not where the men had left it but the trail of blood was clear enough.

"What could drag a horse like that? A bear?" Kaplea whispered.

Emily put her finger to her lips and shook her head. She pointed the beam to a paw print on the ground the size of a dinner plate. Emily couldn't see Kaplea's expression but her hammer was out. Emily started up the slope but Kaplea shook her head. Emily nodded and pulled Kaplea's arm. They advanced slowly.

They found the carcass about 50 paces up. Chunks of flesh had been torn from it. Predawn light was barely detectable in the trees. They could hear the camp stirring below. Emily heard something else, too, a faint rustling. She halted and put her hand on Kaplea's shoulder. They waited and Emily strained to listen. A slight breeze whispered through the leaves. A smell hit her nose and it was like a slap in the face. She knew the smell and it came from behind them.

She turned around and scanned the trees with her flashlight. There it was, hugging the ground in a crouch, orange and black fur reflecting the light. The tiger was startled by the beam. It rose to its feet and roared, deafening, terrifying, it seemed to vibrate the ground. Kaplea let go a war cry and raised her hammer. The tiger and Kaplea stared at each other for a moment then the tiger turned and bolted down the slope.

Soon they could hear the panicked baying of horses and people shouting. Kaplea and Emily ran toward the camp. They reached the clearing just in time to see the tiger disappear back into the forest to their left. Warriors hurried to ready their javelins or string their bows.

"Do not worry," Emily shouted. "The tiger will not attack. It has met its kindred spirit, Kaplea, our leader."

Kaplea strode through the crowd of warriors and Emily padded behind her.

"Stop gawking and get ready," Kaplea ordered. "We move when the sun is up."

~

Emily led the way. It was slow going for the long column of warriors, horses and mules picking their way through the trees. Emily felt she was in her element but she knew the others were not accustomed to so much walking.

When she found the little stone hut with a tiger's face painted on it, the going got easier with a trail to follow. She then was able to scout out ahead a hundred paces or so, keeping an eye out for potential enemies. It occurred to her that even a small force of light infantry could do real damage. Fortunately they encountered no one.

Late in the afternoon of the third day in the forest, the column was rounding Willow Bog. Flies and mosquitoes swarmed and some of the horses threatened to bolt. As the vanguard wearily climbed out of the swampy area, Emily waited for Kaplea.

"This is a hard road for horse people, Pakshakiz," Kaplea said, slapping a fly on her neck.

"We are almost there," Emily said. "I imagine we will encounter sentries soon. How do you want to handle it?"

"You and Mahalea mount up and ride ahead. Javada will follow. Put on your orange tunic and blue cap and don't get yourself shot."

Emily saddled the sure-footed Hurlov and rode up the slope with Mahalea, Javada about 50 paces behind. They rounded a bend and surprised a half dozen warriors on foot, straddling the trail in a picket line. Emily was relieved to see they wore red caps. The warriors quickly nocked arrows and drew them back.

"Halt!" A man shouted.

Emily and Mahalea complied. "Do not shoot," Emily yelled. "We are friendly."

"Who are you?"

"Tilkya and Mahalea of the Wolf Tribe. We come with Kaplea to aid Kydoime."

The man spoke to the others at his side. One warrior hurried off. The man approached.

"You look like Lovta but your accent is strange," he said. He was short and stocky. He wore no armor but carried a sword at his hip.

"We are Lovta," Mahalea assured him.

"I suppose it is so," the man said. "And thank the gods. We need all the help we can get. We will have to wait here until someone comes to confirm you are who you say you are. Takahal is not above dirty tricks."

"We will wait," Emily said.

The man remained wary and they waited in silence. Some minutes later they heard the galloping of horses coming down the slope. They stopped at the picket, about a dozen of them. One rider approached. It was Uratan, Kydoime's husband.

~

The once bucolic valley was now crowded with thousands of people and horses, hundreds of tents and fire pits. The grass was lush and green. There was plenty of grazing but Emily wondered how long it could last with so many horses and the Wolf remuda adding to their numbers. Whatever Kydoime was going to do with this army, she would have to do it soon.

Kaplea led the Wolf column into the valley, Uratan beside her, Emily and Gugama close behind. Kydoime met them on a tall black stallion. Reining up beside Kaplea, the two embraced from their saddles.

"Well met, sister," Kydoime said. "I was confident you would come."

"I regret I only bring 800 warriors but they are the best of the Wolf Tribe," Kaplea said.

"Eight hundred will serve. We are now a match for Takahal and Mazdak's cavalry," Kydoime said. "Uratan will show you where to camp and where your remuda can graze. Come to my pavilion when you are ready. We will eat and talk. We have bad news from Artemios and must decide what to do."

"What news from Artemios?" Emily asked.

"Ah, Tikya, I am glad you are here. I am saddened to hear of Taval's death, a great loss for all the Lovta. Just today a messenger arrived to the say the city is attacked. We do not know if it is taken or not."

"Do you plan to aid Agathon?"

"We will discuss it tonight"

~

The Wolves set up camp a considerable distance from Kydoime's tent and pavilion. Emily helped dig a latrine pit. The tired horses and mules were eager to graze. There had been little for them to eat since entering the forest. The mood became festive and several Lions helped out. The young Lions who had joined the Wolves the previous year, like Shavaris, Thoeke and Pakeus, were happy to be among their fellow tribemates again. They chattered on about their adventures with the Wolves.

It was dusk when Kaplea, Halaba, Gugama and Emily approached Kydoime's pavilion. Many fires burned and the smell of roasting meat filled the air. Emily saw a dark brown gelding with a white stripe on its snout and one white hoof. Looking around she saw a brown-haired man wearing a gray cloak fringed with a red Greek-key pattern. She startled the man by putting a hand on his shoulder.

"Hello, Byon," she said.

He turned and stood abruptly. "Emily!"

They looked each other over for a moment then embraced.

"I did not think I would see you again," Byon said.

Kaplea stood close, giving him a narrow-eyed look.

"This is Byon," Emily said. "The friend I talked about. Byon, this is Kaplea, our war leader."

Byon and Kaplea clasped each other's arms firmly.

"You are the man who taught Tilkya her clever spear tricks." Kaplea said.

"Yes. She was a good student."

"Come, let us eat," Kydoime said in Greek. "We can get reacquainted later. We have business to discuss. Noble Byon, give us your news."

They ate bison meat with greens and nuts and watery wine. Emily was famished. She craved the dried apple slices Phoibe would serve her but the food before her would have to do. Byon recounted events so far as he knew them.

Several days prior Agathon's Thracian cavalry, led by Callias and Byon, spotted an army of enemy hoplites marching down the coast road toward Artemios, about 2,500 strong with additional light troops. Agathon decided to meet them head on and raised Artemios' full muster which amounted to 1,500 hoplites plus a few hundred peltasts and archers. He marched out of the city with a thousand and set up a defensive line where the road passes through a narrow area between the sea and high cliffs. After two days of inconclusive fighting, Agathon still held his ground but had been wounded by an arrow.

Screening the other approaches to Artemios, Callias' cavalry spotted a force of Scyth riders and Persian infantry heading down the road from Aslatsha. The force threatened Agathon's retreat. Pantheras, who commanded the troops still in the city, ordered the remaining hoplites to march out and block the Persian's advance in the hopes of giving Agathon a chance to get back to the city. It was clear that Artemios would come under siege. Pantheras sent Byon and 40 peltasts to find Kydoime and seek aid.

"I do not know what happened," Byon said. "We hope Agathon got his troops back safely."

"How bad is Agathon's wound?" Emily asked.

"Bad, I heard. He may not live."

"How many Scyth and Persians were approaching?" Uratan asked.

"We do not know. Mazdak is with them. We think a large force," Byon said.

"This is our opportunity," Uratan said. "Mazdak has weakened his defense of Aslatsha. We may be able to retake it."

"Indeed, we have a chance," Kydoime said.

"What of Artemios?" Emily asked.

The Lion war leaders around the circle looked at her curiously.

"Artemios may already be taken," Uratan said. "This is our moment to seize Aslatsha and defeat Takahal."

Emily took a drink of wine from her bowl and wiped her mouth with a cloth.

"I do not believe Artemios will fall so easily," she said. "But it cannot hold out forever. I know Takahal is a usurper and a traitor but Mazdak is our real enemy. He wants the Lions to make war on each other. This will give him the time he needs to reduce Artemios. Even if you defeat Takahal and retake Aslatsha, the victory will be a hollow one. The Persians will control all the trade with the Greeks."

"We know Persian infantry garrison Aslatsha," Kydoime said. "They will be difficult enough to dislodge. Greek hoplites with their heavy shields and armor are a different matter. There is little room to maneuver around Artemios. It would be difficult to outflank the phalanxes."

"If we move quickly, we should have surprise on our side," Emily said. "Also, the Wolves have an arim of heavily armored warriors with special saddles and long spears. It should be able to break up a phalanx. We have trained for this all spring."

Kydoime looked to Kaplea. "Is this so?"

Kaplea nodded.

"Agathon, or Pantheras, will march out to join the battle, so we may even have numbers," Emily went on.

"Zandra chose your name well, Tilkya," Kydoime said. "Excuse me while I discuss the matter with my people."

The Lion warriors walked off to huddle, speaking to each other with animated gestures. After several minutes, Uratan and the other leaders returned to the circle while Kydoime walked away into the darkness.

"The queen is making up her mind," Uratan said.

They finished their meals, drank wine and talked of small things. One of the Lion warriors estimated that with 8,000 horses in the valley, good grazing would only last a few days. Maybe a half hour passed when Kydoime returned. She stood in the center of the circle. Still in the depth of thought, she idly fingered the scar on her face.

"I am inclined to help Artemios," she finally said. "I pledged to protect the city and now is her time of need. Yet I do not want to waste the effort if the city is already taken. We must find out and learn the disposition of our enemies."

"I will scout the enemy," Emily said. "I know the woods and hills around Artemios."

"You?" Kydoime asked.

"Tilkya is niava, a forest spirit," Kaplea said.

"I have hunted with her," Byon said. "She moves silently in the forest and is all but invisible. I will go with her. I command 40 Thracians, all skilled woods fighters."

"Very well," Kydoime said. "Let Tilkya Niava be our eyes."

They continued to iron out plans. Emily and Byon would set out in the morning. The main force would follow the next day. The hope was that the way would be clear to the villages of the hill people. They would rendezvous there and make final plans for the attack. If Artemios was taken, they would head for the plains and make their war on Takahal.

Chapter 35 | Niava

EMILY walked beside Byon along the trail that led to Bloody Meadow. Behind them Mahalea, Thoeke and Pakeus led fresh horses provided by Kydoime. Thirty-five peltasts followed. The other five scouted ahead a few hundred paces. A stiff wind swayed the branches above but it was little more than a breeze on the forest floor. Emily talked of her time with the Wolf Tribe.

"You are a leader among them. I see it in their eyes," Byon said. "I am sorry Taval died. I would have liked to meet him."

"You would have been friends, I think," Emily said.

"I regret I did not win your heart."

"I am sorry. I was not ready back then."

"You were ready for Taval."

"Not entirely. He pushed me over the edge, forced me to decide."

"Perhaps I should have kidnapped you and taken you to Thrace."

"Perhaps you should have. I think you would have won me over eventually. I have thought of you often. Tell me, do you know what happened to Pantheras and Dokaris after I left them?"

"Yes, Dokaris is dead. He put up a fierce fight against the Persians but caught an arrow."

"And Coystus?"

"He lives. He took two arrows and an ax blow to the head and yet survived."

"I am sorry about Dokaris. I know he was your cousin. I am glad Coystus lived. We had become friends."

"Like a dog is friends with his master. He worships you still."

"Acasius and Pantheras were taken prisoner?"

"Yes, but Agathon learned of the Persian expedition and sent Callias and me down the coast to intercept them. We found their beached ship but its crew put it to sea before we got to it. So we waited and ambushed the Persians when they arrived at the coast. After a short battle, the

Persians called for parley. In exchange for Pantheras, Acasius, Coystus and two slaves, we let them sail away."

"Sensible," Emily said. "But the Persians must know now that Alex, Nancy and I are from the future."

"Yes, it has caused a stir. I think we would be in deeper trouble except the Greeks of Miletus, Ephesos and other cities have rebelled. We might be feeling King Darius' full weight otherwise. Word is he knows of you."

"That is why Mazdak was eager to capture me."

"We heard about events at Sinki and the Battle of Lonely Hill. Your raid on Mazdak's horse herd has become legend. Everyone fears the wild Scythians of the Wolf Tribe. I wish I could have been with you."

They came to where the trail merged with the cart track and found the forward peltasts waiting for them. Emily ordered Thoeke and Pakeus to ride up the road a few miles to scout that approach while the rest went down the road toward Bloody Meadow.

"How is Nancy?" Emily asked.

"She is well. She has become quite popular among the ladies of Artemios. She and Bereneke visit each other often," Byon said.

"What of Alex?"

"He has been busy with many projects. I do not know what all. He has built several engines that can hurl stones great distances. I hear he has been able to produce a liquid that catches fire easily. Many smiths and carpenters work for him now."

"And Pantheras?"

"So far he seems an able leader."

"Is Acasius still with him?"

"No. Acasius returned to Miletus last autumn."

"Phoibe?"

"The house slave?"

"Yes."

"She is fine, I think. She is at Nancy's side most of the time."

A peltast from the forward group returned to say the meadow ahead was clear. The company made camp on the grass and lit three cooking fires. Thoeke and Pakeus returned with nothing to report. They ate supper and chatted afterward. Mahalea told the story of the Battle of Lonely Hill. Her gravelly voice and rough-hewn looks added gravity to the tale. She talked about Emily's stirrups and how she killed the Persian commander, Kasran.

"You became a warrior that day," Byon said to Emily.

He put his arm around her and she rested her head on his chest. Those who were not on watch went to their bedrolls. Emily continued to sit with Byon, watching the dying fire. She felt tears coming but wasn't sure why.

~

Emily crouched on an outcropping that overlooked the long valley containing the villages of the hill people. Byon and Mahalea were beside her.

"I do not see any sign of Persians," Emily said. "This should make a good staging area for our attack."

They assembled the peltasts into a column and marched into the valley. Emily told Thoeke and Pakeus to stay behind in case of trouble. They passed through the battlefield where Hydakoles' bandits had been routed and approached the near village. Men shouted their arrival and the old man with the leopard-skinned tunic came out to greet them. He shook hands with Byon.

"Hello, venerable Bartai," Byon said. "What news do you have?"

"Bad news," the old man said in rough Greek. "Artemios surrounded."

"Is the city taken?" Emily asked.

The old man looked her over. "I know you. The woman who carries a spear and travels with warriors."

"Yes, I am called Tilkya now," she said.

Bartai put a hand on her shoulder. "There was a great battle three days ago. The walls held. Come, we get you food and talk more."

Emily ordered a peltast to fetch Pakeus and Thoeke. The rest made camp. The villagers served soup, jerked pork, barley and greens. The old man and a couple of others ate with them.

"The Persians have not bothered you?" Byon asked.

"No," the old man said. "Patrols ride up to the river but go no further."

"Do you know of Kydoime?" Emily asked.

"The queen of the Lion Tribe, yes," Bartai said.

"She will be here soon, probably tomorrow, with many warriors," Emily said. "It is important they are not seen by the Persians."

"If they stay at this end of the valley, they will not be seen."

"We need to scout Artemios. Is there a way other than the road?"

"Other trails, yes. A hunter will show you."

They were served beer. Emily limited herself to one bowl and recommended the others do the same. They needed to be sharp for tomorrow's scout. Nevertheless, the beer brightened the mood and squelched Emily's anxiety about the coming days. Some of the peltasts flirted with Mahalea and Thoeke, particularly Thoeke. Emily set up her nylon tent. Byon ordered the others to their bedrolls.

"Get some sleep," he said. "It may be the last you get for a while. We move out before dawn."

Emily watched Byon spread his bedroll. He looked good. Every movement of his sinewy body was relaxed and assured. She felt a tingle in her nethers. That damned beer, she thought. Her body swayed to some inner melody. She stood and walked toward him. She breathed heavily, her nostrils flared.

"Is something wrong?" Byon asked.

She took his right hand with both of hers, raised it to her mouth and licked his palm. She pressed herself against him. His eyes went from perplexity to fierceness, that same look he had that day when they fought with sticks and he bruised her ribs. He clutched her head with his hands and they kissed. She felt him grow hard. When their lips parted, she led him by the hand into her tent.

~

It took an effort of will to get up and release herself from Byon's arms. She sorely wanted to make love to him again but there was work to be done. Outside, a village hunter waited for them. Emily ordered Thoeke and Pakeus to return to Kydoime and let her know the way to the village was clear.

"With luck, we will be back here tonight," she said.

Emily, Byon, Mahalea and the peltasts followed the hunter on foot across the starlit valley. Emily traveled light, wearing her brown tunic and green cloak, carrying her satchel, sling, puukko, dagger and spear. Near the second village they diverged from the road, waded across the river and headed up a narrow trail at a jog. Despite the quick pace, and the fact that there were 44 of them, they moved quietly. When the sun was up, they paused briefly to catch their breaths.

"You are a creature of the forest," Byon whispered to Emily. "You should come with me to Thrace. It is a land of forests."

Emily rubbed his back. "I am bound to the Lovta. The Wolves are my kin now. I should think they would welcome a good horse warrior such as yourself."

Byon smiled and shook his head.

~

When the sun neared its morning apex, they stopped at a small clearing. A breeze blowing in from the sea waved the tree limbs above. The hunter pointed in a northwesterly direction.

"Over that ridge, next hill is temple," he said. "I wait here."

The rest of the party continued on and climbed the near ridge. They crept up slowly to the crest, fearful of possible patrols. Emily found a spot where she could see through the trees. Using her binoculars, she looked at the peak of the temple hill. It would be the perfect place to get a view of the city. Before long, however, she noticed men moving on the peak. Persian lookouts, she figured.

"Damn," Emily muttered in English, though there was little reason to hope the peak would be unoccupied.

"We could kill the lookouts and be gone before anybody could reach us," Byon suggested.

"No," Emily said. "We do not want to reveal ourselves if we can help it. There are other places to get a view. I can find one without being detected."

"I will go with you," he said.

"I should go alone. It is our best chance. You cannot move as quietly as me."

Byon nodded. "Be careful and retreat at any sign of trouble."

"I will be back before the sun is two hands above the western horizon," she said.

She put up her hood and slipped silently into the trees.

~

Emily worked her way down the ridge using her spear as a prop to ease her descent. There was a flat area at the base of the ridge before reaching the slope of the temple hill. She picked her way slowly through accumulated deadwood and stopped at the base of a large oak. She heard something to her left. A pig foraging, perhaps, she didn't know. She pulled the wicker cover off her spear and moved in a crouch, very slowly, toward the sound.

From behind a tree she saw an open area illuminated in patches by the noon sun. There was a woman at the other end, hunched over, using a small spade to dig roots. She wore a rough brown robe and a felt hat covering dark, braided hair. The angular body seemed familiar.

Abruptly the woman stood and looked in Emily's direction. Emily made no move. She was in shadow. The woman looked around, stuffed the freshly dug root into her bag and slowly walked toward Emily. A spot of sun caught the woman's face and Emily recognized her.

"Kallisto," Emily whispered.

Kallisto stopped. "Who's there?" She asked in a low tone.

Emily stepped forward and pulled back her hood. Kallisto's arms fell to her side. The spade dropped from her hand.

"Emily," she said. "This cannot be."

Emily went to Kallisto and embraced her.

"Oh, my child, why are you here? How?" The priestess asked.

"I have returned," Emily said.

"But Artemios is surrounded. I fear it will succumb soon. There's nothing that can be done. You must go back to your Scythians. You will be safe with them."

"I came with my Scythians. Kydoime leads an army to relieve Artemios. My tribe has joined her. I am here to get a look at Mazdak's army so we can plan our attack."

Kallisto was dumbstruck for a moment. With a deep breath, she regained her composure.

"Something told me you would come but I could not let myself believe it," she said. "They call you Tilkya Niava. True?"

Emily nodded. "That is my name now, yes."

Kallisto looked Emily over, touched her belly, sliding her hand up to one of her breasts which had swollen somewhat of late.

"You are pregnant," Kallisto said. "The man who became a woman is going to be a mother."

"I try not to think about it."

"Soon you will think of little else," Kallisoto said.

"I would love to catch up but I have urgent work to do," Emily said. "Byon and his men are waiting on the next ridge. Is there a place I can get a view of the city and not be seen?"

Kallisto thought for a moment. "Yes, you can see the city from the temple."

"No Persians are there?"

"No. They leave it alone, and me for the most part. A patrol comes through twice a day. The morning patrol has already come. The afternoon patrol will not be here for some time. Come with me. I have an idea."

~

The two climbed the temple hill toward Kallisto's home. Emily lagged behind about 30 paces in case they encountered someone. They stopped at the point where the trees opened to the homestead's clearing. Emily could see Mucha, Kallisto's helper, tending the garden. She wore a flax robe and a felt hat with a wide brim.

"Wait here," Kallisto said.

The priestess went to Mucha, spoke a few words and ushered her into the house. Kallisto returned with Mucha's robe and hat in her arms along with a basket.

"Here, put this on over your clothes," Kallisto said. "From a distance you will look like Mucha."

Emily donned the robe and hat then hid her spear in a bush. Otus, the dog, ran over and greeted them with a bark.

"Shh," Kallisto said. "You know Emily. Nothing to be worried about."

She and Emily walked toward the temple.

"The old man at the village said there was a battle a few days ago. Do you know what happened?" Emily asked.

"Yes," Kallisto said. "I watched from up here. I was terrified. Nikanor is trapped in the city. Four triremes, followed by smaller vessels, tried to force the harbor at the same time the Perisans and Novorosians attacked the walls. But Alex built machines that hurled pots of liquid that burst into flames when they struck the ships. It was horrible to see. I could hear the screams of burning men from up here."

"They were driven back?"

"Yes, two ships were fully engulfed in flames. The others retreated and landed at the south beach, out of range of the ... engines."

"Catapults."

"Yes, that is what Alex calls them. They spooked the Persians who stay well back from the walls."

Emily thought about the time she, Alex and Nancy talked about the possibility of changing history. There could be little doubt now.

They arrived at the temple and walked down the corridor of oaks that framed the walkway to the entrance. They reached the ledge where stone steps descended to the path that led to the city. Artemios was in full view. They sat in the shade and Kallisto laid out food while Emily peered through her binoculars.

She could see a trireme beached south of the town and nearby was an encampment of hoplites. She guessed the number to be about 500 with some Persian light infantry in the vicinity. She could see the other trireme in the water, apparently patrolling the harbor's entrance but staying out of range of the catapults.

On the farmlands east of the town were several camps of Persian infantry. She could see Agathon's farmstead which appeared to be a marshaling yard for Scyth horse warriors.

"Mazdak stays in the house," Kallisto said.

"Have you met him?"

"Yes. He is actually quite polite. He has offered to parley but Pantheras refuses to negotiate surrender. Or so I am told."

North of the city, along the shore, Emily could see several large encampments of hoplites. The main body, she thought, perhaps 2,000. She was unable to see up the road that led to the villages.

"What is up that way? Do you know?" She asked.

"They have dug a long trench to block the way. I hear them cutting down trees and building other things. I do not know what."

Siege equipment, Emily thought, possibly ladders, ramps, towers or battering rams.

A fair distance north of the city, the shore road branched, one heading inland toward Aslatsha, the other along the coast to Novorosa. She couldn't see what, if anything, was happening there. The walls of Artemios appeared in good shape and the outer trench was filled with water. Yet the walls were not that high. With enough ladders and ramps, the attackers could overwhelm the defenses. When would Mazdak attack? Perhaps he was content to just starve them out.

"How much food does Artemios have?"

"Plenty, I am told, enough to last months."

Mazdak wouldn't want to wait months, not with Kydoime's army still undefeated. Emily continued to scan the scene below, trying to commit details to memory.

"I understand you are married," Kallisto said. "I was surprised you took a husband. We are told his name is Taval. Is he a good man?"

"He was a good man," Emily said. "He died this spring during a raid."

"I am sorry," Kallisto said. "Did you love him?"

"More than I can say."

"You carry his child?"

"Yes."

"What was he like?"

"Brave, smart, strong. He could shoot an arrow beyond 500 paces. A good sense of humor. A natural leader. He was very tall."

"Like you were when you were a man."

That hadn't occurred to Emily. Did she love Taval because he reminded her of who she once was? A psychologist could have a field day with that one, she thought.

"I would like to hear how you two met," Kallisto said.

"It is quite a tale but I have no time to tell it. I think I have learned what I can. I need to get back."

"At least pay your respects to Artemis before you go."

They went to the altar. Kallisto filled a cup with water from the fountain, intoned a few words and handed it to Emily. She drank without reservation. She looked into the eyes of the painted figure of the goddess.

"I'm your pawn now, I suppose," she said in English. "I hope you know what you're doing."

"What did you say?" Kallisto asked.

"That is between me and Artemis."

Kallisto smiled. "You know you are already a person of mystery around here and beyond -- a nymph, a witch, a magical being. If Kydoime's army prevails and you are with her, your reputation will soar."

"I am not sure I can stop that," Emily said.

"No. But what you do with it is the question. People will want to follow you. I think the Thracians here would do your bidding even now."

Emily didn't respond, didn't know what to say.

"Do you still have the Tiger Stone?" Kallisto asked

"No, I gave it to Kaplea. I believe she is its true owner. Her name means tiger woman."

"'We have heard the name. A fierce warrior, they say?"

"Kaplea is the essence of fierce. She is the goddess of battle and she comes to Artemios."

~

They left the temple and returned to the homestead. At the edge of the forest, Emily removed Mucha's robe and hat and retrieved her spear. She embraced Kallisto.

"You fill me with hope, Tilkya Niava," Kallisto said. "If the gods are with anybody, they are with you."

"I will settle for a little luck. We are going to need it," Emily said.

She turned and entered the woods.

"Emily," Kallisto said

"Yes."

"If the gods offered to make you a man again, would you accept?"

Emily stopped and thought a moment. She put a hand on her belly.

"No, Kallisto, I do not want to be anybody other than who I am right now."

Kallisto's smile betrayed a hint of triumph.

"Good bye, Emily."

"See you soon, Kallisto."

~

Emily went down the slope still thinking about Kallisto's question. It occurred to her that she never really had been a man, that somehow her memories had been wiped clean and those of Fred Harper imprinted on her brain. Now that those memories had receded and new ones accumulated, it felt like she had always been a woman. Yet the sense of being Fred Harper was so strong early on. Her sense of "I" felt like a continuation of Fred's "I."

But was it really? Maybe a person's "I" was a kind of fiction, a product of memory. Maybe the event created a new person, neither Emily nor Fred. It created Tilkya, Tilkya Niava.

~

Tilkya's thoughts were broken by the sound of voices and movement in the forest. Was it Byon's peltasts? They were supposed to wait on the ridge. She stopped and crouched in shadow. The movement was coming from the west, up from the seashore. A patrol, she thought. Dammit. She could hear several of them and they were spread out. She was near the midpoint between the hill and the ridge. They would be upon her in moments.

It seemed too risky to hide. She moved quickly toward the ridge, resisting the urge to run. She was nearing the base of the ridge when her foot found a dry branch. She was moving too fast to prevent it from cracking. She heard a shout and the pace of the patrol quickened.

Goddammit. She took off at a run up the ridge. She could hear and feel the pursuit behind her. They were gaining.

"Stop or we kill you," a man shouted in strangely accented Greek.

Tilkya ignored him and kept running. A javelin grazed her shoulder and thudded into the ground. She ducked behind a tree, stopped, turned, stepped out and surprised the closest man behind her -- a young man with a trim beard, dark hair and brown skin. He wore a simple flax tunic, cloth cap and carried a wicker shield. He didn't react quickly enough. Tilkya thrust her spear into his chest just below his neck and yanked it back. The man staggered back gurgling blood. But the others were upon her. She stepped back behind the tree just as two javelins flew by. Another man appeared before her, larger, older, carrying a shield and a spear. Tilkya went into a low defensive posture and hissed. The man drew back his spear.

Suddenly and arrow appeared in the man's head and he dropped to the ground quivering. Then a shower of javelins rained down on her pursuers. Many found their marks. She saw Byon rushing toward her flanked by his men. Mahalea was behind him, an arrow nocked in her bow.

"Kill them all! Let none escape!" Byon shouted

The peltasts pursued the Persian warriors who were now greatly outnumbered. Byon stopped beside Tilkya who was panting.

"Are you well?" Byon asked.

"I am fine," Tilkya said. "Thank you. I was in a tough spot."

Byon pointed to her shoulder. "You are bleeding."

"Just a scratch. I am fine."

"We had better look at it."

Tilkya took off her cloak which now had a cut in it. The sleeve of her tunic was bloodstained and covered the wound.

"Take that off too so we can see what it looks like," Byon said.

Tilkya hesitated.

"Do not be a fool."

Tilkya undid her belt and pulled off the tunic. Byon examined the cut.

"Not bad. Only the skin is cut, I think," he said. "You could use a stitch but no time for that now."

Tilkya retrieved her first-aid kit, unwrapped an alcohol swab and told Byon to apply it to the wound. She unwrapped a bandage and got out the tape. Mahalea was securing the immediate perimeter. When she returned and got a look at Tilkya's back, she started laughing that gravelly cackle of hers.

"Is that a squirrel? Mahalea asked.

Byon, who was putting the bandage on, craned his head around.

"Why do you have a squirrel tattooed on your back?"

"It is Kaplea's joke," Tilkya said.

"Kaplea calls Tilkya, Pakshakiz," Mahalea said. "It means squirrel girl."

"Well, squirrel girl," Byon said. "Our situation has become trickier."

"Yes, the lookouts on the hill will have heard the commotion."

"Perhaps, but the wind above the trees is strong. They might not have heard anything."

"They will miss the patrol soon enough," Mahalea said.

"True," Byon said.

The Thracian warriors started returning from their pursuit. They seemed confident they had killed everyone in the patrol. They started picking up javelins and looting the bodies but there wasn't much to be had. Some sneaked glances at Tilkya's bare torso but mostly they averted their eyes. She remembered that to the Thracians of Artemios, she was a witch. She guessed Coystus had further enhanced her reputation among them.

"We should get going," she said.

"You and Mahalea go," Byon said. "The men and I will stay. We can keep the Persians busy and off your trail."

Tilkya nodded, realizing immediately that it was the right decision. The Thracians were woods fighters and would be hard to entrap. Also, the presence of a small band of Thracians wouldn't necessarily give away the imminent attack of Kydoime's army. The capture or killing of herself or Mahalea would. She put her clothes back on.

"When do you think Kydoime will attack?" Byon asked.

"I am not sure," Tilkya said. "Tomorrow at the earliest, three days at the latest. I have a plan brewing. If Kydoime agrees, expect the attack to come the day after tomorrow."

Byon nodded. Mahalea put a hand on her back.

"Come on, Pakshakiz," she said.

"*Pakshakiz*," Tilkya said to Byon. "Use that word to identify yourselves when you encounter Lions or Wolves."

"Weasel, fox, squirrel, wolf, which animal are you?" Byon asked.

"All of them. I am Niava."

~

In the depths of the forest, twilight comes early. Tilkya and Mahalea had to stop for a breather. The pace had been hard and Tilkya's legs burned. Mahalea rubbed her thighs, too, but the hunter did not appear tired. He drank from his skin and ate a doughy ball of something that had been wrapped in a leaf. Tilkya took out her last two energy bars and handed one to Mahalea who was puzzled. Tilkya had to unwrap it for her. She scrunched her nose at the taste but ate it anyway.

"It will give you strength for the last leg," Tilkya said.

She guessed it would be another three hours to the villages.

"Can you find the way at night?" She asked the hunter.

"I can find."

She asked him if there were a way to lead many warriors and horses to the coast south of the city, out of sight of the enemy camps. She had to explain herself using stones and a stick.

"There is a way," he said. "Slow for horses."

"A day?"

The hunter shrugged. "A day, some of next day."

The three continued on, Tikya and Mahalea staying close behind the hunter. Night brought with it clear skies and a nearly full moon. It was still quite dark on the forest floor yet the hunter stuck to the trail, by feel sometimes, it seemed. The hunter stopped when they reached the base of a slope. Tilkya remembered the trail turning abruptly upward somewhere near here. The hunter worked his way along slowly and seemed uncertain.

"Would a light help?" Tilkya asked.

"Yes. But no torches."

Tilkya produced her flashlight and turned it on. The hunter's face became one of near terror. He exclaimed in his native language.

"Fear not. It is just a light," Tilkya said.

"Kaplea said you had a scepter of light," Mahalea said. "She did not lie."

Tilkya shined the beam on the slope as they moved forward.

"Ah, here," the hunter said.

She kept the light on as they climbed the steep portion of the trail. When it leveled she turned the light off. They had to stop a moment to let their eyes adjust.

~

Tilkya guessed it was about midnight when they waded across the river near the far village. In the moonlight she could see the vast remuda and many tents. She wondered what the villagers thought of having a Scythian army at their doorstep. They were met by a patrol of riders with arrows nocked.

"It is Tilkya and Mahalea," she said.

The hunter went his own way and two of the scouts pulled Tilkya and Mahalea onto their mounts and carried them to Kydoime's tent. The queen had not yet gone to bed and was up talking with Kaplea. Tilkya stumbled on her sore legs when she dismounted.

"The forest spirit returns. What news?" Kydoime asked.

"Artemios stands," Tilkya said. "Mazdak will attack again soon. We must act quickly."

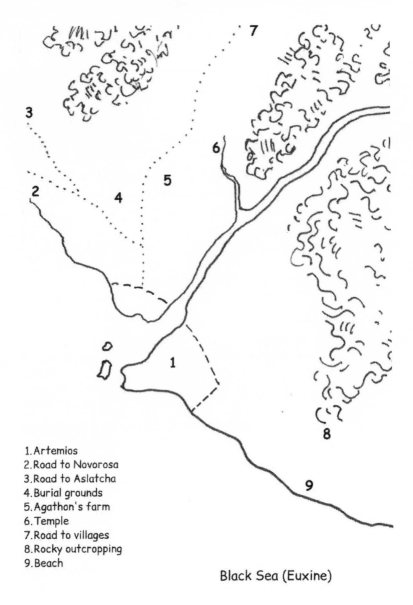

1. Artemios
2. Road to Novorosa
3. Road to Aslatcha
4. Burial grounds
5. Agathon's farm
6. Temple
7. Road to villages
8. Rocky outcropping
9. Beach

Black Sea (Euxine)

Chapter 36 | Battle for Artemios

THE young Persian man looked at her and smiled, a warm and welcoming smile. He was good looking with smooth brown skin and a trim black beard. Then blood poured from his nose and mouth and eyes. Tilkya woke with a start. Fuck, she thought. I killed that man.

It was still dark. Kaplea was putting on her trousers. Tilkya began to push herself up, muscles stiff.

"Go back to sleep, little oiropata," Kaplea said. "Preparations will take time. I will get you before we go."

Tilkya gladly laid back on her pillow. She welcomed more sleep but didn't want to see that man's face again in her dreams. It would be another long day of walking though the pace would be slower than yesterday's scout. She thought about the battle plan.

At Tilkya's suggestion, Kaplea would lead the Wolf army through the forest to emerge at the coast south of the city. The Wolves would then ride fast and hard in the hopes of taking the enemy's south encampment by surprise.

Kydoime would attack from the east and try to force the trench or find a way around it. Uratan would take 800 warriors out onto the plain and move on Artemios from the north. Tilkya thought Uratan's end-around was too risky and unlikely to achieve surprise but her objection was overruled.

Much would depend on what Agathon or Pantheras did with the troops inside Artemios. They would need to march out to aid the attack for any chance of victory. As Tilkya drifted off to sleep, images of how the battle might go swirled in her mind. No time at all seemed to pass before Kaplea pulled her to her feet.

"Get up, Pakshakiz. You have been lazy long enough."

~

The Wolves camped that evening along a stream, the column stretching at least a quarter mile. There was little grazing for the horses but plenty of water. They doled out what oats they had brought. Flies were a nuisance but settled down with the setting of the sun. Mosquitoes, however, picked up the slack. Tilkya brushed her horses, Hurlov and Polly. The Wolves had brought only a few hundred remounts so not everyone had two horses. She camped with her Storm Rats and the Billy Goats.

Satisfied Hurlov and Polly were in good shape, she went to the fire and sat by Kellvan, the Billy Goat leader. Thoeke sat behind her and re-braided her frayed ponytail. Tilkya's hair had grown and now reached the middle of her back.

"If things do not go well tomorrow, we will be in a tight spot," she said.

"Aye," Kellvan said through the side of his scarred face. "But our enemies will know they have been in a fight."

Tilkya rubbed the man's thickly muscled back. "Tomorrow we will show what the Billy Goats can do."

"I look forward to seeing our enemies' eyes when we bear down upon them," he said.

"We should armor up as soon as we hit the coast. The hunter says there will be an open area where we can assemble."

"Yes, Tilkya."

"I am going to get some sleep," she said. "May the gods be with us in the morning."

"You are with us so the gods are with us," Kellvan said.

~

The sun was not yet at its height when the Wolf army emerged from the forest into a narrow valley that stretched to the sea. Tilkya thanked the gods there was no rain to dampen bow strings. In a village near the shore, she could see a handful of men ready with spears. The men soon lowered them when the full number of the emerging army became clear. Fishermen, she figured, probably wondering what kind of horror they now faced. Kaplea ignored them and so did the rest of the Wolves. The villagers seemed content to be ignored and just looked on at the multitude of horses and warriors assembling before them.

Kaplea ordered everyone to ready for battle and for the arim leaders to report head counts. Tilkya donned her armor and fastened the saddle to Hurlov. He did not have Polly's speed and agility but he was tested in battle. She trusted him. Kaplea called Tilkya to the head of the column.

"I want you by my side when we approach," Kaplea said. "If the hoplite camp is unprepared, we will storm it immediately. If a phalanx is ready to receive us, we will make our plan of attack then."

Kaplea was radiant under the blaze of the high sun, her mane waving in the sea breeze. The scales of her armor glittered over her black tunic and tiger-striped trousers, stripes that Chunya had worked hard to perfect. Kaplea rode Skolov, Taval's muscular chestnut stallion whose mane was braided with gold rings. The horse was Tilkya's by right when Taval died but there had been no question about who he really belonged to.

The column assembled along the track that served as the coast road. Several villagers gathered to the side near Kaplea, many in the surf, men and women. They prostrated themselves, muttering prayers and stretching their hands toward the red-haired goddess. She continued to ignore them. She raised her hand and a signaler blew a whistle. The column began its ride to Artemios.

~

Kaplea started at a walk then, when everyone was moving, picked up speed to a trot. Mahalea and two other scouts galloped ahead. The track coursed through rough ground, winding around rocks and skirting cliff sides. A small force of hoplites positioned here might stymie their advance, Tilkya thought, but no such force was present. They ascended a ridge then descended toward a flat area. They could see a small camp and dead men pierced with arrows. Mahalea rode back to Kaplea and Tilkya and fell in beside them.

"Lookouts were here," Mahalea said. "One was riding away as we came, too far gone to catch. Someone probably watches in the hills. They will have news of our coming."

"We should give them as little time as possible to prepare," Tilkya said.

Kaplea nodded, barked an order, and the army picked up its pace to a gallop. After perhaps twenty minutes, they rounded a bend and came to the narrow Artemios plain, made wider over the years by the felling of trees for lumber and charcoal. Tilkya could see the walls of the town and the oikist's house at the end of the peninsula. She wondered if Nancy was looking out the window.

The Wolf army fanned out onto the plain. Tilkya saw the beached trireme. Men scrambled around it, preparing to shove it out to sea. Beyond the trireme she saw hoplites forming into files and ranks. Their camp was positioned between the trireme and Artemios, probably to prevent any attempt to raid the ship from the city.

"Kaplea!" Tilkya shouted above the thunder of hooves. "The ship -- we do not want it to launch."

"Go tell Halaba to take care of it," Kaplea shouted back.

Tilkya kicked Hurlov to a sprint, veered over to Halaba, who was leading the left flank nearest the shore. She gave him instructions and his arim raced toward the ship. Tilkya veered back over to Kaplea. She could see four battalions of hoplites forming into a battle line. Each battalion, she knew, would have 128 men, sixteen files across and eight ranks deep. They moved with discipline and arranged themselves in a line spanning the shore on one side and a rocky outcropping of a ridge on the other.

"We did not catch them napping," Tilkya said to Kaplea.

"Good. It will be a real fight."

Kaplea slowed the pace and the Wolf army came to a halt about 500 paces away from the phalanxes. The hoplites looked formidable with their long spears, painted shields and full-faced helmets. Kaplea signaled for trumpets to sound. This was to let Kydoime know the Wolves had arrived. What was Kydoime doing now, Tilkya wondered. Was she attacking?

Halaba's warriors, about 200 paces ahead, rained arrows down on the sailors who took cover behind the trireme. Halaba pressed his attack and soon the sailors were fleeing back to the phalanxes or taking to the water to swim away. Halaba stopped at the trireme and gathered his warriors into formation. Tilkya wondered if the phalanxes would advance in an effort to retake the ship. Halaba would be forced to retreat. She hoped they would. It might create an opportunity to outflank them. But the phalanxes did not move.

A few groups of light infantry were behind the enemy line, Persians most likely. Tilkya saw a large group heading toward the slope on the other side of the rocky promontory. Probably to guard that flank, she thought, but they also could be a threat to the Wolves' flank.

Kaplea ordered Gugama to organize four arims of archers to make passes at the phalanxes in succession. Tilkya signaled to the Storm Rats and the Billy Goats to be ready to make a charge on her order. Kaplea shouted at Tilkya.

"Come with me."

Tilkya followed Kaplea up the slope on their side of the ridge. The lower portion of the slope was mostly barren of trees. Tilkya signaled for one of the arims, made up of mostly javelineers, to follow them. About 100 paces up, they had a broader view of the situation. They went out a ways on the promontory and Tilkya looked through her binoculars.

In the distance, beyond the river that flowed into the city, she could see a column of hoplites marching along the village road toward where the trench line was. Another, larger column, marched in a wide arc around the city, heading for the river, a group of cavalry with them.

"I would say 500 hoplites head toward where Kydoime should be," Tilkya said. "She must be over there. I see no sign of Uratan. A thousand hoplites come our way with about 500 cavalry."

In less than an hour, the Wolf army would be outnumbered and the phalanxes would be able to push them off the plain. She handed the binoculars to Kaplea. With 500 hoplites reinforcing the trench, Kydoime might well be stymied.

Closer to hand she could see about twenty foot-archers behind the hoplites facing the Wolves, not that many but worrisome enough. Two arims of Wolves rode at the phalanxes to within 50 paces, pivoted right and loosed arrows as they passed along the battle line. The hoplites closed ranks and the foot-archers shot back. Two more Wolf arims performed the same sweep. The volleys of arrows were having little effect against the hoplites' wall of heavy shields. The Wolves wouldn't carry the day this way.

The enemy warriors pounded their shields and shouted taunts. They were undaunted and ready to fight.

"Where is your Agathon or your pretty boy, Pantheras?" Kaplea asked.

"Neither would just sit behind the walls and watch," Tilkya said.

Sweat trickled down her helmet's cheek guards. Kaplea ordered the warriors attending them to dismount and enter the woods to keep any enemy infantry in there busy.

"Tilkya, we have to act," Kaplea said. "We cannot wait. I think it is time to see what your Billy Goats can do."

As the pair rode back down the slope, Tilkya thought she could hear trumpets sounding from inside the city walls but couldn't be sure. Trumpets were sounding everywhere. Kaplea and Tilkya huddled with Gugama and other arim leaders. Tilkya laid out her plan and they all nodded.

"Get ready," Kaplea said. "On my mark we go."

Tilkya went back to the Storm Rats. "Shields up, javelins ready!" She shouted.

Behind her arim were the Billy Goats. The husky men looked terrifying in their full-faced helmets, many with horns attached, and shields painted with grim, monstrous faces. Their long spears pointed up at the sky. Tilkya shouted to Kellvan.

"Stay about a hundred paces behind. Go to full gallop when we are out of the way."

Tilkya wanted to give the enemy hoplites time to see what was coming at them.

Kaplea positioned herself and her large arim behind the Billy Goats. She reared Skolov up and screamed her war cry. The Wolf army began its attack.

~

Gugama sent his four arims out to make archery passes as they had done before which had about the same effect, invoking more taunts -- "Barbarian scum!" "Filthy cunts!" "Come meet our spears!"

When the last of the archer arims was making its pass, Tilkya moved out with her Storm Rats, 40 strong and in two ranks. She aimed her warriors at the center of the line toward the gap separating two phalanxes. Arrows from the Persian foot-archers whistled passed. The hoplites closed ranks again. When the Storm Rats closed to within 30 paces, she shouted, "Hurl!" Forty javelins arced into the enemy formation and the Storm Rats wheeled abruptly to the right, managing to stay just out of reach of the spears. She heard the thuds and clinks of javelins hitting shields and armor. The Storm Rats paralleled the battle line for a ways then turned away.

The Billy Goats were now bearing down at full gallop. She looked back and could see the phalanx still intact. The javelins appeared to have caused some disruption but the enemy spears remained ready. Dread lodged in her chest. The Billy Goats were riding to their deaths.

They charged on, nevertheless, in two tight, staggered ranks, lowering their spears and crouching low in their saddles behind their shields. Then, when the Billy Goats were within 30 paces and it became clear that the horse warriors would not veer off, that the full weight of horses, men, armor and spears would crash into them at speed, the hoplites panicked. Some tried to move aside, others backwards. Many dropped their spears and tried to flee.

The sound of the collision of flesh and metal and wood was unearthly. Screams of men and horses followed. The momentum of the charge plunged the Billy Goats deep into the seam between the battalions. The phalanxes started to lose cohesion and a wedge-like gap appeared in their line.

And that is where Kaplea and her horse warriors -- archers paired with spear wielders -- entered the fray. Kaplea rode tall on Skolov, shooting arrows into the now exposed flanks of the hoplites. Others shot arrows, too, in a constant murderous onslaught, but Kaplea's every shot was meting out death. Panicked hoplites tried to get away from the red-headed terror that was upon them.

Gugama, meanwhile, had pushed most of the remaining arims up to the battle line to engage the other enemy battalions with arrows and javelins. Tilkya wanted to get the Storm Rats back into the fight. When she stopped to signal them to rally around her, she noticed an arrow had pierced Hurlov's neck. Blood dripped from his nostrils and mouth.

"Oh no, goddammit," she said.

Hurlov started to waiver on his feet. She dismounted. Donya rode up beside her.

"He is dead, Tilkya." Donya ordered a warrior to fetch another horse from the remuda. "Quickly, get Polly if you can."

Tilkya unstrapped her saddle and set it on the ground. She drew her sagaris and cocked it back.

"I'm sorry Hurlov, my good friend," she said then spiked the horse in the head.

"Fuck it all to hell!" she shouted in English.

~

From her vantage point, she couldn't tell what was going on. The chaos of battle reigned. The Storm Rats waited for her instructions.

"Pull me up," she ordered Donya, who helped Tilkya onto her horse. "Go up there. I want to see what is happening."

Donya's horse trotted up the slope toward the ledge of the outcropping and the Storm Rats followed. They could hear the sounds of fighting coming from the woods.

Below, the enemy hoplites were split into two masses. They had lost any sense of being an organized formation but many still fought fiercely. Nevertheless, the Wolves were prevailing. Looking northward she saw that the other, larger hoplite force was crossing the river and starting to form up into phalanxes on the other side. The cavalry force had split itself up and many of the Scyth horsemen were recrossing the river and riding around the hill toward the trench line. Kydoime's attack must be having some effect. Mazdak was reinforcing that sector.

Yet the 250 or so Scyth on this side of the river were forming up. If they attacked the Wolves while they were still engaged, that could spell trouble. Where was Pantheras? Or Uratan? She looked at the field below and saw several Wolf warriors, unhorsed, and coming back to find new mounts.

"Thoeke," Tilkya shouted. "Take two warriors and get mounts for those stragglers. Bring them up here."

"You have a plan?" Donya asked.

"See those Scyth over there? We cannot let them attack Kaplea and Gugama unmolested," Tilkya said.

"How do we stop them?"

"We go through the woods and come out behind them."

"Can we get through?"

"Of course, Samvi will guide us. I am Niava," Tilkya said.

"You are no niava, just a stray little bitch Taval dragged out of the forest," Donya said.

Tilkya slapped Donya on the back. "True enough, you fat whore, but are you with me?"

"To the death, little bitch, to the death."

~

A warrior brought Polly to Tilkya and helped saddle the energetic sorrel mare. Tilkya mounted and patted Polly on the neck. "Your turn, little lady."

She looked around. All the Storm Rats were present with about 20 other warriors. She looked north and saw the Scyth cavalry moving out. She pulled a javelin from its quiver and raised it in the air.

"Form three lines, single file," she ordered. "We ride into the woods. Kill anyone who looks like a Persian but do not stop. Rally around me, Donya or Thoeke when we emerge from the other side."

Tikya headed up one of the columns and they plunged into the woods at a brisk trot. The trees were dense but there was little ground clutter. Her column was slowed when they had to pick their way around a deadfall. A hundred paces on, she saw the backs of Wolf warriors crouched behind trees.

"Wolves!" She shouted. "Coming through!"

Their faces showed astonishment as she and her Storm Rats trotted past. She saw a Persian warrior just ahead. She threw her javelin. It imbedded itself in his shield and he ducked aside. Pakeus was behind her and finished the man off with a thrust from his spear. They kept going. From the shouts behind her, she surmised she was through the skirmish line.

"Pakeus. Blow your whistle and keep blowing," she ordered.

The sound, she hoped, would help the other Storm Rats gauge her direction. All the traveling they had done lately in the forest had accustomed the horses to the trees and Polly was handling it well. Yet she couldn't go too fast or she might break a leg on a root or rock. They worked their way down the far slope and soon she could see where the trees ended. She ordered Pakeus to stop whistling. She emerged onto the plain and saw to her left, not more than 50 paces away, the Scyth cavalry riding toward the main battle. She had come out behind them.

Damn, I'm a lucky little bitch, she thought.

~

Donya's and Thoeke's columns soon emerged and they formed around Tilkya, though not all had made it through. She heard yelling and fighting coming from the woods. She had to hope that situation would take care of itself.

"Form two ranks! Quickly!" She shouted.

She looked toward the river and saw the enemy hoplites had formed into twelve battalions. What were they going to do about them? She didn't know. She raised a javelin.

"Full sprint! Go!"

The Storm Rats chased the rear of the Scyth cavalry formation. Tilkya had no plan but to plunge into them and disrupt their attack. It was quite likely the last thing she would ever do. She had to check Polly's speed to stay in line with the others.

As they gained on the Scyth, she saw that the south gate of the city was open and a troop of cavalry was riding out led by a man with a red-plumed helmet. Callias and his Thracian riders. Thank the gods, she thought. Behind them followed a mass of Thracian footmen who ran toward the main battle. Callias was aiming his troop, perhaps 100 strong, toward the Scyth riders. The Scyth turned to meet the attack. As they did so, the Storm Rats were upon them.

"Hurl!" Tilkya shouted and 50 javelins plunged into the surprised enemy with devastating effect. Horses and men screamed. Many fell. Tilkya suddenly found herself in their midst and the world became a swirling melee.

Just as she readied another javelin, Polly slammed into the side of a Scyth horse which went sprawling to the ground, its rider with it. Tilkya lurched forward and Polly stumbled. Somehow Polly kept her feet and Tilkya stayed mounted. She wanted to wheel around but the momentum of the battle kept her going forward. A Scyth appeared beside her and threw a javelin which she deflected with her shield. She threw her javelin and missed but someone else's hit and the Scyth tumbled off his horse.

Javelins gone, Tilkya grabbed her spear and looked for targets to jab. The Scyth were retreating now back toward the river.

"Hold up! Do not pursue!" She shouted.

Pakeus was somehow still beside her and blew his whistle to rally the Storm Rats. There was carnage all around. As she tried to get a head count, she saw a long column of hoplites marching briskly from the city onto the field. They were led by a man on a white horse who wore a gleaming bronze cuirass, a blue cape and a red crest on his full-faced helmet.

Pantheras, Tilkya thought, it must be.

~

The presence of six battalions of Artemios hoplites and the retreat of the Scyth cavalry took the fight out of the enemy hoplites the Wolves had engaged. They surrendered, but there was little time to enjoy the victory. The other twelve enemy battalions had begun their advance. The man on the white horse aligned his battalions to meet them while the Wolves hustled to assemble themselves in some kind of order.

Tilkya instructed the Storm Rats to look for javelins and arrows to replenish their quivers. Then she rode toward Kaplea and found her shouting orders to people dealing with the wounded. She was splattered with blood but apparently unhurt. Tilkya wondered if she could be hurt.

"There you are, Tilkya. I hope you are having fun saving your city," Kaplea said.

"Looks like the easy part is over," Tilkya said.

"Yes, where is that bitch, Kydoime, and her useless husband?"

"They have problems of their own, I wager," Tilkya said. "We should go to the Greek commander and figure out a plan."

Kaplea found Gugama and the three of them rode toward the man on the white horse. Tilkya trailed behind a few paces. The man turned to them. He had his helmet pulled back and she could see it was indeed Pantheras.

"Hail! Well met. Do you command these Scythians?" Pantheras asked Gugama.

"Kaplea is war leader," Gugama replied in stilted Greek.

"My apologies, honored Kaplea," Pantheras said, turning to her. "Thank you for coming to our aid. I am Pantheras, oikist and, for the moment, polemarch of Artemios. Are you with Kydoime? Where is she?"

Kaplea squinted, apparently unsure what to make of this smooth-faced man. Tilkya nudged Polly forward.

"Kydoime, we believe, is trying to break through the trench line that guards the village road," she said.

"Emily! By the gods, you have come back to us. And in a warrior's garb."

"Yes, Pantheras, I am here. I am glad to see you are well," Tilkya said. "Kaplea, this is the friend I told you about who was wounded by the tiger."

"A most unpleasant experience," Pantheras said. "But worth it, I think, for this if nothing else."

On a cord around his neck hung a huge claw. Kaplea leaned forward and took it in her hand.

"This is the tiger's claw?" She asked.

"None other," Pantheras said.

"I have seen your tiger," Kaplea said. "I ask you, Pantheras, does your heart match the token? Are you ready to fight?"

Pantheras appeared taken aback but regained himself and became serious.

"I am ready to fight, Kaplea," he said. "I fully expect to die out here."

"Good," Kaplea said and let go of the claw.

"Regarding the battle," Tilkya said. "We do not have much time."

"Yes, things will get prickly very soon," Pantheras said.

They discussed plans. The Artemios phalanxes would hold the center while the Wolves massed on the flanks. Some Wolves would line up behind the phalanxes and offer archery support. Tilkya suggested the woods might offer an opportunity to get around the enemy if the Persians had not reinforced their pickets. Pantheras suggested the left flank might offer an opening as well.

"If they get too close to the walls, Alex's catapults will make things uncomfortable for them," he said.

"I do not know if it will be enough," Tilkya said. "We are outnumbered. If only we could help Kydoime break through."

"There is no way to reach her. She will have to break through on her own," Kaplea said.

Tilkya visualized the situation on a map in her imagination. An idea occurred to her.

"Pantheras, what enemy forces are stationed beyond the north gate?"

"A couple of hoplite battalions and some light infantry, I think. They are positioned well back. The catapults have seen to that."

"Mazdak has over committed himself, I think. Here's what I have in mind. The Storm Wolves will ride through the city, up the village road and attack the trench from behind."

"That is lunacy," Pantheras said. "But it might work."

~

Tilkya gathered up her Storm Rats. Pakeus handed her four javelins to stuff into her quiver. She also rounded up the remaining Billy Goats. Twenty-one of 30 were still in fighting condition. Five had died, including Kellvan, two were wounded and two had lost their mounts. Shavaris, the stout Lion warrior, would lead them now.

Tilkya dismounted to adjust the straps of her saddle. Just as she finished, someone grabbed her from behind and lifted her up.

"Nyfitsa! You are here. Artemis has answered my prayers."

"Put me down, Coystus," Tilkya said. The barrel-chested Thracian did so. She turned to him.

"It is good to see you," she said. "I am glad you live. I must go now. Fight well for me."

Tilkya gave him a kiss on the cheek then mounted Polly. Coystus howled and ran back to his band of Thracian peltasts. As Tilkya joined Kaplea at the front of their newly formed column, the Thracians started chanting, "Nyfitsa! Nyfitsa! Nyfitsa!" Soon the hoplites were chanting it, too, as they prepared to meet the oncoming enemy.

"Your stupid Greeks do not know the difference between a weasel and squirrel," Kaplea said.

~

Led by Kaplea and Tilkya, the Wolf detachment entered Artemios, riding at a trot so as not to stress the unshod hooves of their horses on the cobbled avenue. The column consisted of Kaplea and Halaba's arims, the Rats and the Billy Goats, representing the whole of the Storm Wolves, about 180 strong. City residents brave enough to stay outside looked on with bewilderment at the gaudy-colored barbarians. Were they conquerors or saviors? Tilkya looked up at the oikist's house. She waved in case Nancy was looking on.

The column passed through the deserted market. Tilkya could see part of the harbor and many people massed at the docks. Did they hope to escape on merchant ships, taking their chances against the remaining enemy trireme?

The Storm Wolves crossed the bridge and when they hit the dirt of the marshaling yard, they picked up the pace to a gallop. Pantheras had sent a rider ahead to have the north gate opened. She saw guards lifting the bars. They pushed the doors wide and the Storm Wolves raced through.

Tilkya saw surprised hoplites and Persian infantry scrambling to get into formation. The enemy force was positioned at the intersection of the coast and village roads and numbered about 300. Mazdak had spread himself thin here. If Uratan had come down the coast road as planned, this battle would be all but over, Tilkya thought. What had happened to him?

The Storm Wolves, however, had other business than to fight this blocking force. Instead of proceeding down the road, they cut through a field, trampling summer wheat as they raced eastward toward the trench line. Without supporting cavalry, the enemy hoplites could do little but watch them ride away.

They picked up the village road and passed Agathon's farm, its yard filled with dozens of supply wagons. Panicked slaves and attendants scrambled to get out of their way. Soon Tilkya could see the trench and the backsides of its guarding infantry.

~

In the field behind the trench, many riderless horses stamped around while slaves scurried to keep them in order. There were many wounded men pulled back from the line, some crying out for attention. Tilkya could hear fighting coming from the woods of the temple hill. Kydoime must be trying to outflank the trench that way.

A line of hoplites, two ranks deep, stood just behind the trench, their spears protruding over the gap. Behind them an arim of Scyth cavalry waited. Tilkya figured this must be the Persians' last reserve, maybe 50 of them. The Storm Wolves' approach had not gone unnoticed. A small group of commanders barked orders and some of the hoplites withdrew from the line, hurrying to form another line to oppose the threat from their rear. Kaplea slowed the column to a trot.

"Halaba, engage the Scyth with your arim," Kaplea ordered. "Tilkya, lead your Rats ahead of the Goats like before. Form up!"

Halaba's arim broke off and charged the Scyth. Tilkya brought the Storm Rats to the front while Kaplea's arim lined up behind the Billy Goats.

"Kydoime!" Kaplea shouted.

"Kydoime!" The rest of the Storm Wolves shouted and kicked their horses to a gallop. Tilkya headed for the new line of hoplite spears, aiming toward the right flank closest to the base of the wooded hill. Like before, the Storm Rats hurled their javelins and turned to the right. The Billy Goats were just behind them. This time Tilkya didn't look back but she heard the collisions of horses, men, shields and spears.

"Rats! Into the woods," Tilkya shouted as she readied another javelin.

Polly pulled her way up the slope, dodging trees. Tilkya hadn't ridden very far in when she encountered a line of crouching Persian infantry. A man stood up, turned, looking bewildered. Tilkya threw her javelin and struck his chest. She turned Polly to the right again, dodging more trees, riding along the enemy line. The Perisans were surprised and apparently unsure if the Rats were friend or foe. Tilkya let them know by hurling another javelin which sunk into a man's thigh. Then the forest erupted in shouts. Lion warriors fighting on foot on the other side of the line surged forward.

Tilkya threw her last javelin but couldn't tell if she hit anyone. She looked back and saw Donya still riding behind her. She wheeled Polly around and shouted, "Back to the field! Back to the field!"

She stopped a few yards from the line and kept shouting to make sure all the Rats heard her. Then something struck her helmet and all went dark.

Chapter 37 | Alexander

ALEX finished his lunch in the courtyard of the oikist's house. Nikanor sat across from him, not eating much but drinking plenty of wine. He had been drinking more than usual since the siege began. Alex knew he worried about Kallisto who chose to stay at the temple rather than seek safety behind the walls. After the battle of the harbor, emissaries met with the Persian commander, Mazdak, who said the priestess and the temple would not be molested. Nikanor worried anyway. Alex worried.

There was much to be worried about. Pantheras had sent Byon to seek the Scythian queen's help, five or six days ago, it must be, but no help had come. Some hoped the cities of Ionia would send ships but knowledgeable folks didn't think it likely. The Ionian cities were in rebellion against the Persians and probably had trouble enough at home.

"Well, Nikanor, my friend, I believe I will go inspect the catapults," Alex said.

"Do you think their condition has changed since yesterday?" Nikanor asked.

"Probably not. I should check the still, too."

Alex walked out of the gate and was accompanied by two slaves and his bodyguard, a Thracian warrior with a gimpy leg and a taciturn nature. Alex was an important man, they told him, and a hero. His catapults had saved the day when four triremes tried to force the harbor. Alex remembered almost having a breakdown when it was happening. His "Molotov cocktails" had engulfed two of the ships in flames but it had taken all that they had. If the other two ships had continued instead of retreating, Artemios would have been lost. Thinking about the men burned on those ships made him feel nauseous.

It was a sunny day but not too hot, a good day for a walk. He turned on an avenue toward the east wall where the two mobile catapults were positioned. The other catapults were in fixed positions at the harbor or on the islands and one in the backyard of the oikist's house. There was no real need to inspect them. Their crews knew more about them now than he did.

He thought about Emily. He missed her and envied her. She had escaped and now roamed free on the plains with a band of Scythians, like the Sioux or Comanches. He felt like a prisoner here, especially now, though he had friends, wanted for nothing and enjoyed considerable prestige. Bereneke was even trying to line him up with a Greek wife. His wife, his son, from that other life, seemed so far away. Perhaps it was time to try again.

But what if Artemios falls to the Persians, which every day became more likely? What happens to him then? If he survives, it probably means a gilded captivity with the Persians. God, Emily, come and take me away from here.

~

He approached the walls and saw the mobile catapults mounted on wheels. They were positioned on either side of a guard tower. In addition to the crews, several officers milled about at the base of the tower. They were Pantheras' retinue. Pantheras was up in the tower. Something must be going on, Alex thought.

Pantheras climbed down the ladder and leapt off near the bottom. He never failed to display his athleticism.

"Muster the troops, all of them," Pantheras told his officers. "Today may be the day we have been hoping for."

"Queen Kydoime? Has she come?" Alex asked.

"Possibly. One of the guards thought he heard battle cries. Persian infantry are marching around the temple hill and the Scyth mercenaries are mounting their horses."

Alex felt elation and hope but also dread. Battle was such a contingent thing, the outcome so unpredictable. He liked things that behaved predictably. He had made his living from them.

A messenger, a teenage boy, ran up to Pantheras.

"Oikist, the south camp of the enemy is assembling. Their hoplites are preparing for battle," the boy said.

"Are they moving out?" Pantheras asked.

"No. They are pointing their spears to the south."

"To the south? What in Ares' name could that be?" One of the officers asked.

"I do not know," Pantheras said. "But I think the game is on. If you will excuse me, Alex, I had better go to the south gate to see what is happening."

Pantheras and his officers mounted their chariots and drove off. Alex decided to hurry back to the house. From there he should be able to see what was happening, at least to the south. "Please God, or gods, let us live through the day," he muttered.

~

Alex found Nancy in one of the bedrooms on the north side of the house where she had been for most of the past several days, ever since Agathon was wounded. She was at his side, a papyrus scroll in her hand. She liked to read poetry though she was not very good at reading Greek. Agathon probably just enjoyed hearing her voice.

"We heard trumpets," Nancy said. "Is something happening? Has Kydoime come?"

"We do not know. Nobody has seen anything yet but the Persians appear to be readying for an attack," Alex said.

"We will need to help her. Muster the hoplites," Agathon croaked, his voice a horse whisper. An arrow had pierced his right side at the Battle of the Cliffs, puncturing a lung. The physicians had patched him up as best they could. Nancy had been giving him antibiotics and pain pills, the last of the supply. Few thought he would live but he seemed better these last couple of days.

"Hush, honey," Nancy said. "You really should not speak."

"Pantheras has ordered all the troops to assemble," Alex said. "He thinks there may be some action on the other side of the temple hill. The Persians also appear to be preparing for an attack from the south."

Agathon nodded but Nancy shushed him to silence before he could speak.

"I am going to one of the south rooms to have a look," Alex said. "I will let you know if I see anything."

~

Alex walked along the inner balcony that served as a hallway. He passed Phoibe who was sweeping the planks.

"Phoibe, tell Gaina I am going to her room to look out the windows. It has the best view."

Phoibe nodded without saying a word as was her habit. She never talked much but she had lost her spriteliness since Emily left. It always saddened Alex to look at her.

Alex felt like an intruder in Gaina's room. He avoided even looking at what was in it for fear of making a breach of privacy. He opened the shutter and looked out.

Beyond the ramparts, he saw the Phanagorian phalanxes occupying the ground between a rocky promontory and the beach. In the distance beyond, he saw a column of riders galloping along the coast road onto the plain. Scythians, he thought, by the look of their colorful outfits. How the hell did they get over there, he wondered.

He saw sailors and oarsman running to their beached ships, most going for the trireme. The Scythian column fanned out as it entered the plain, forming itself into distinct groups. One peeled off from the main body and raced toward the trireme. The sailors were just starting to shove the ship when the Scythians were upon them, shooting arrows and sending them fleeing, those not struck down.

Nancy walked into the room.

"Agathon dozed off," she said in English. "Why do people have to do this? Go to war? It seems so senseless."

"I don't know, but we're here and we have to hope the battle goes our way," Alex said. "Come look, the Scythians have surrounded the warship. That's good news, I think."

Nancy looked out the window, seemed lost in thought at the wonder and horror of it. The Scythian army was a mosaic of color, liquid-like in how it moved. The enemy phalanxes were symmetrical, orderly and rigid. The wall of spears looked impregnable.

"How can they get through that?" Nancy asked.

"I don't know. Shoot them with arrows, I suppose," Alex said.

"They look different somehow from Kydoime's soldiers," Nancy said.

"What do you mean?"

"The Lion Tribe wears red caps or red plumes on their helmets. These wear blue and orange."

"You're right. I'm not sure who they are."

"Agathon told me Kydoime was trying to convince the Wolf Tribe to fight for her."

"The Wild Scythians. That's the group Emily joined," Alex said. "Maybe it is the Wolf Tribe. I don't know what colors they wear."

A group of Scythians, perhaps sixty or so, galloped toward the phalanxes, followed by another group. They turned some yards away, riding parallel to the line of spears, shooting arrows. It was like a giant circus display of synchronized horsemanship but it did not appear to have much effect on the well-armored hoplites. Alex could hear their taunts and shouts. Many knocked the rims of their shields against their spears.

"Look, there's a group headed up the slope over there," Nancy said.

On the slope on the other side of the promontory, Alex saw a pair of riders followed by a larger group. One of the pair wore a polished bronze helmet with a blue and orange crest, a long braid dangled from under it. The other woman wore no headgear on her flowing mass of red hair.

"Woman warriors," Nancy said. "The one looks kind of small."

There was something different in the way the small one rode her horse, Alex thought. He noticed she used a different kind of saddle, a little like an English riding saddle. Alex felt the blood drain from his face.

"Ah, Jesus," he said.

"What?"

"I can't believe it."

"What?"

"The small one. That's her."

"Who?"

"Emily. It's Emily, Nancy. She's here."

"I don't know," Nancy said. "How can you tell? It's so far away."

"Stirrups. She's got stirrups."

Nancy just stared out the window, shaking her head. The pair of riders had ventured out onto the promontory and appeared to survey the situation below them. The small one pulled something out of a shoulder bag, a black object that she put to her eyes.

"Oh my fucking God," Nancy said, clutching Alex's hand. "Emily, you stupid girl! What are you doing out there?"

Alex laughed, a grainy, strained, high-pitched laugh. "She's here to rescue us and she brought a fucking army."

It was then he noticed Phoibe standing behind them, hands clasped and pressed to her chest, hopping up and down, tears streaming down her cheeks.

~

A tiger sprinted across the starry sky bearing a red-cloaked woman with night-black skin. She carried a spear tipped with a gleaming white tooth of a great shark. The woman raised her spear and the tiger stopped. The woman turned and her head became that of a youthful man with curly blond hair and a golden crown of leaves. The man-woman waived in a gesture that suggested she should be followed. She lowered her spear and the tiger resumed its sprint across the heavens. Soon the beast and the man-woman were gone and the night sky retreated from the sun's emerging rays.

~

She felt something wet and rough rubbing her face. She turned her head and the light of the world returned. And smell, the smell of horse. And sound, the sound of a man's voice.

"She lives, get a stretcher," the voice said.

Tilkya's shield was still on her arm and her spear beside her. She looked up to see Polly and Byon. She shook her head. It throbbed. Byon dismounted and knelt beside her.

"You picked a strange time to take a nap," he said.

Tilkya sat up.

"I was not napping. Just resting my eyes."

Byon picked up her helmet which was lying on the ground and ran his finger over a crease in its crown. A spear or javelin must have deflected off of it. Tilkya pushed herself up, using her spear as a prop. She felt nauseous. Byon put a hand on her head and felt the lump. She grimaced.

"Tough girl," he said.

"How is the battle going?" Tilkya asked. "I should get back to my arim."

"The battle goes well," Byon said. "We routed the defenders of the trench. Kydoime came over with many warriors. She and Kaplea crossed the river to attack the enemy from the rear. It will be a slaughter, I think, if they do not surrender. Your warriors and mine are handling the prisoners here and seeing to the wounded."

"The hoplites by the north gate, they could be trouble," Tilkya said.

"They could be but they must not have liked their chances. They fled up the coast road."

"How did you find me?"

"Your people were worried and shouted your name," Byon said. "I saw your horse and mounted it. She took me right to you. How do you ride with this crazy saddle?"

Tilkya felt wobbly. She put a foot in a stirrup and, with Byon's help, mounted Polly. He handed the helmet to her. She brushed leaves off the crest and put it in the saddle bag.

"Hop up," she said. "We will go for a ride."

Byon smiled and mounted behind her. The feel of his arms around her waist buoyed her and her head began to clear. She walked Polly slowly down the wooded slope.

Thoeke and another warrior were running up with a stretcher. They were surprised to see Tilkya in the saddle.

"I am fine. Just a little ding to the head. Save that stretcher for someone who needs it."

They emerged from the trees onto a field strewn with bodies of men and horses. A mass of prisoners sat on the ground -- Persians, Scyth and Greek hoplites from Novorosa or Phanagoria. Their faces told the story, seemed to say, how could this have happened. Victory was assured.

"Tilkya! Tilkya lives!" Pakeus shouted.

The remaining Storm Rats, Billy Goats and Thracian peltasts cheered. Tilkya saw planks spanning the trench.

"When we came out of the woods, the defenders of the trench were forced to turn toward us," Byon said. "It was a chaos of fighting. Some of Kydoime's warriors carried planks to the trench. They were guarded by archers, Aella among them. She started shooting and men started dropping. It terrified even me. Kaplea was out of arrows but felled many with her hammer. Then, all at once, it seemed, our enemies dropped their weapons and went to the ground, begging for mercy. The trench was ours."

Distant sounds of battle came from the other side of the river. Tilkya felt an urge to rush to the fight but knew the Storm Rats were tasked with guard duty. Donya rode over to her.

"Not only do you live, Tilkya Niava, but you found yourself a man in the forest," she said.

"Yes, he looked like he needed a ride," Tilkya said. "What is the toll on the Storm Rats?"

"Seven dead. Four wounded," Donya said and recited their names. "All fought well."

"We should gather javelins and arrows and reassemble," Tilkya said. "If the main battle goes badly we may need to cover a retreat. Byon, your men should do the same and make sure the planks are clear for crossing. Donya, find Byon a horse."

~

Thirty-one Storm Rats, sixteen Billy Goats and 25 peltasts were ready for action if needed. But the distant sound of battle subsided and, before long, trumpets sounded. Tilkya took it as a good sign. She rode over to Shavaris.

"The Billy Goats did well today, better than I could have hoped," she said. "I think we owe our victory to you and your men. I am sorry so many died."

"We owe our victory to you," Shavaris said. "I know we would all do it again without second thoughts. I do have ideas about how we could perform better."

"Excellent," Tilkya said. "I suppose you will want to return to the Lion Tribe when this is over."

"I want to stay with you and Kaplea," Shavaris said. "We could build an army of Billy Goats and descend on Persia like the griffins of old. Who could stop us with you as our general?"

Tilkya patted the young warrior's face. He beamed at the gesture.

She rode over to view the prisoners. Most stared at her with sunken expressions. Some were tending to their many wounded. A Greek officer directed the effort. He looked at Tilkya as she rode by. She recognized him -- Euneus, the man who tried to rape her. She wasn't sure if he recognized her but she was sure he was afraid. She rode on.

Looking south, Tilkya saw a rider fording the river, headed their way. She, Donya and Byon rode out to greet him, a Lion warrior on a spotted gelding.

"Good news. The battle is won. Mazdak has surrendered," the warrior said. "Kydoime asks if there is news of Tilkya."

"She lives. She is right here," Donya said.

"Noble Tilkya," the warrior said. "Kydoime would like to speak with you."

"Shall we go," Tilkya said to Donya and Byon.

"You should go alone," Byon said. "It will be better that way."

Tilkya didn't understand what he meant. Donya reached over and pulled Tilkya's helmet out of the saddle bag and wiped smudges off with a cloth.

"Wear this so they will know who you are," Donya said.

~

Tilkya put on her helmet, rode to the river and splashed across. She held herself high in the saddle, spear in hand, as she trotted toward the mass of warriors south of the city. Polly strutted as if she were the queen of horses. A troop of Artemios hoplites marching a group of prisoners toward the river halted and faced Tilkya as she went by.

Lion and Wolf warriors cleared a way for her and she saw Kaplea, Kydoime, Pantheras and others conferring. They all turned and watched her approach. She halted Polly and dismounted. She expected a wisecrack from Kaplea or Pantheras but none came. Perhaps because of the Persian man standing with them wearing golden armor and an empty scabbard on his belt.

"Noble Tilkya," Kydoime said. "I am pleased to see you are well. We all were very worried."

Tilkya caught Kaplea's eyes, that fierce squint, and knew she was happy.

"Ah, Emily, you are a sight," Pantheras said. "I should introduce you to our new friend, General Mazdak, agent of Great King Darius."

The thick-bearded Persian man smiled a weary smile and bowed before Tilkya. Smallish and rotund, he was not the menacing figure of her imagination.

"Honored Tilkya," Mazdak said. "You have been on my mind for some time. The priests said you were a danger. I tried to catch you but you slipped through my grasp more than once. I suspect you are the true architect of my defeat. A well-played match. My congratulations."

"Pleased to meet you, noble Mazdak," Tilkya said. "Though I am glad it is on these terms."

"Terms have a way of changing," Mazdak said. "Perhaps someday we will match wits again."

Tilkya grinned. "I look forward to it."

~

The sun was setting when Uratan and his warriors finally arrived. They had been delayed by a column of Persian infantry and Scyth cavalry, apparently headed to reinforce Mazdak's attack on Artemios. Uratan scattered them after a pitched battle on the rocky hills between Artemios and Aslatsha.

The Lovta leaders as well as Pantheras and Callias met in war council under Alex's pavilion at Agathon's farm. They decided to spend a few days here to rest and feed hungry horses before making their attack on Aslatsha. Pantheras pledged 1,000 hoplites to the expedition, saying he would lead them himself.

Uratan reported that Lion herdspeople were angry with Takahal for allowing Persian soldiers to occupy their lands. The herders were ready to take up arms against him. Takahal's reign would be a short one, Tilkya thought. With Mazdak captured, what was left of the Persian infantry and Scyth cavalry would have little motive to fight.

"Ah, what a thrill this has been, Emily," Pantheras said. "Artemios, I now believe, is here to stay. I have a mind to march on Novorosa and Phanagoria and teach those rats a lesson."

"Mazdak employed a mercenary captain named Bolinthos," Tilkya said. "Do we know if he was killed or captured? He is clever and dangerous. He almost trapped a Wolf arim during our raid last year."

"Mazdak sent Bolinthos north a few days ago," Kydoime said, "to deal with a large party of bandits."

"Not bandits," Tilkya said. "Warriors of the Eagle Tribe from the deep steppe. I suggested to them that they might find easy plunder along the shores of Maeota Lake."

"Then Bolinthos has all he can handle and may already be dead," Kydoime said, clearly amused.

"What will happen to the prisoners?" Tilkya asked.

"They will be ransomed or sold as slaves," Pantheras said. "We will keep Mazdak and his commanders here as hostages. You will, of course, receive your share of the proceeds."

"I would not shortchange us if I were you," Tilkya said.

"I would not dream of it. Who do you think I am, a scoundrel?"

"Yes."

Kaplea slapped Pantheras on the back. "You did well today for a scoundrel and a Greek man. Remember, you are bound to us by that token around your neck."

Pantheras fingered the tiger's massive claw. "Yes, I do believe I have become a barbarian."

~

Tilkya slept in the open with her Storm Rats. The morning brought a stiff breeze from the sea that blew the smell of death inland. Every muscle in her body, it seemed, ached. It would be a day of rest for the Wolf warriors except for a few who rode to the villages to retrieve the rest of the remuda and baggage. She drank spring water instead of wine. She figured she'd better limit the alcohol she consumed. She patted her belly which was beginning to swell.

"Hang in there, little one," she said.

A small army of slaves arrived in the fields to clean up the mess and take care of the bodies. The enemy dead would be interred in the trench they had conveniently dug for themselves. Tilkya found Donya splashing water on her face.

"Can you take care of things for a while?" Tilkya asked. "I want to go into the city."

"Yes. Go find your friends," Donya said.

Tilkya mounted Polly, rode to where Kaplea's arim was camped and found her and Mahalea brushing their horses and talking.

"I am going to the city," Tilkya said. "You should come, Kaplea, and you too, Mahalea."

Kaplea muttered something about things that needed doing.

"Come," Tilkya said. "The Wolves can get by without their tiger for a bit."

Mahalea mounted her horse and looked eager to go. Kaplea reluctantly mounted Skolov. They trotted down the road and had not gone far when they saw a wagon pulled by mules coming toward them. Tilkya could see it was driven by Cleon, the foreman of Agathon's farm. A young, skinny woman hopped out and ran toward Tilkya. Without a word the woman hugged Tilkya's thigh. Polly snorted and stamped.

"Hello, Phoibe," Tilkya said. "It is good to see you, too."

She grasped Phoibe's arms. "Come on, hop up," she said and helped Phoibe onto the back of the horse. Phoibe wrapped her arms around Tilkya and buried her face in her back.

"Now there is a pair of squirrelly girls," Kaplea said.

Mahalea laughed her gravelly laugh.

When they got to the wagon, Cleon halted it and Nancy stepped out. Tilkya dismounted and helped Phoibe off.

"Oh, Emily," Nancy said and the two embraced.

Nancy, as beautiful as ever, looked splendid in her fine blue chiton, braided hair and sparkling jewelry.

"I told you I'd come back," Tilkya said in English.

"It only took you a fucking year," Nancy said. "Phew, you stink."

"It's been a rough couple of days," Tilkya said then switched to Greek. "I should introduce you to my good friends, Mahalea, and my war leader, Kaplea."

Nancy shook hands with Mahalea then with Kaplea who seemed taken aback by Nancy's good looks.

"So you are the terror of the steppe," Nancy said. "You do not look so terrible to me. You are beautiful, actually. And your hair. By the gods, what a woman would give for hair like that. A little work and men would crumble at your feet and you would not need bows and arrows."

Kaplea stammered and looked perplexed. She had finally met her match, Tilkya thought.

"We are headed for the city," Tilkya said. "I would like to see Alex, and Agathon if he is well enough."

"Agathon is in good spirits today. I know he would love to see you," Nancy said. "Alex was going to come with us but something broke on one of his precious catapults. You'll find him sooner or later. We are going to the farm house to get things back into shape. You can stay there tonight. You too, Kaplea and Mahalea. It will be like old times."

"I would like that," Tilkya said.

"Come, Phoibe, we should go," Nancy said. "We will see Emily later."

Phoibe shook her head and hugged Tilkya's arm.

"Well, Emily, I do not think Heracles himself could pry her away from you right now."

"That's okay. She can come with us."

Kaplea instructed Mahalea to go back to the farm with Nancy and to tell the Wolves they should help out in any way needed. Nancy would be quite a sight to the warriors of the steppe, Tilkya thought. They would need little encouragement to lend a hand.

~

Phoibe hugged Tilkya tight on the back of Polly as they continued toward Artemios.

"Phoibe," Tilkya said. "I am pregnant. I am going to need someone to help me care for the baby. Would you like to do that?"

Tilkya could feel Phoibe's head nodding against her back.

"Are you sure? Life with the Scythians will not be easy and I will not always be around."

Phoibe continued to nod.

"Okay. I will talk with Agathon and arrange your freedom. Do you understand that? You will be a free woman and will need to learn to live your own life. It is the way of the Scythians."

"That man of yours," Kaplea said "Are you going to take him on, too?"

"Byon? I think he wants to go back to Thrace."

"He is a fine warrior. I saw him fight while you were napping in the woods. He is a demon with a spear and a sword."

"If he is willing. And you. You are my war leader."

"You say I am your war leader but I think it is the other way around, Pakshakiz. You see more clearly than me and your instincts for battle are better than even Taval's were. When it comes to strategy, I follow you."

"To the fortress of the Great King himself?"

"I can think of nothing I would rather do."

~

Tilkya and Kaplea passed the caduceus and approached the now open north gate. The hoplite guards stood at attention when they went through. The marshaling yard was busy. Many of the soldiers recognized them and stopped what they were doing to watch them go by.

They crossed the bridge to see that the market was open and alive with activity. Yesterday's victory changed the prospects for the local merchants. The flourishing trade would resume. But people weren't too busy to stop what they were doing and gawk at the two warrior women of the steppe riding by on muscular steeds. Soon the road was lined with onlookers.

As they were leaving the market area, a man pushed through the crowd and ran toward them. He wore a white tunic trimmed with blue. He had a beard and hair cropped Greek style.

"There you are," Alex said. "I was wondering what was causing the commotion. By God, Emily, you are a sight for sore eyes."

Alex and Tilkya shook hands.

"Meet Kaplea, war leader of the Wolf Tribe."

Alex shook her hand. "Honored to meet you, Kaplea."

Kaplea nodded and said nothing.

"She seems formidable," Alex said in English.

"I doubt you'll ever meet anyone more formidable." Tilkya said. "I think she likes you, though."

"Um, yes, well, likewise ..."

"You don't want to cross her, however,"

"The furthest thing from my mind."

"We're going to visit Agathon. Come with us."

Alex walked beside the horses. His bodyguard and slaves walked behind them.

"I hear the catapults worked out well," Tilkya said.

"Yes, but it took some doing. Like everything, it's easier in theory than practice," Alex said. "I built a still and was able to use the alcohol to create Molotov cocktails with clay pots. That was challenging, too. The ignition sources kept blowing out when we launched them. We finally had to attach a kind of cage to the pots to hold hot coals."

"We're all glad you had success," Tilkya said. "By the way, I'm hoping to enlist your aid in a little project I've been thinking about."

"I'm at your service."

"Good."

People were coming out of their houses, lining the streets. Tilkya was surprised to see many women among them. A growing train of children followed, boys and girls. Kaplea frowned and appeared wary of the strange people around her in this strange place. They headed up the peninsula toward the oikist's house. As they approached, they could see Pantheras and his mother, Bereneke, waiting on the front steps. Bereneke seemed a little alarmed. Pantheras grinned widely.

"Okay, you've piqued my curiosity," Alex said. "What's this little project you have in mind?"

"I'm thinking about conquering the world," Tilkya said.

Just then Kaplea reared Skolov up and let go her piercing war cry. The children scattered, screaming. Bereneke looked like she was going to faint.

Mark Murphy Harms

thepeltast.net

markmurphyharms@gmail.com